A Book of
Short Stories 1

PERSPECTIVES IN LITERATURE
SECOND EDITION

A Book of Short Stories 1
A Book of Poetry 1
A Book of Drama 1
A Book of Nonfiction 1

A Book of Short Stories 2
A Book of Poetry 2
A Book of Drama 2
A Book of Nonfiction 2

SECOND EDITION **A BOOK OF SHORT STORIES 1**

Secondary English Editorial Staff
Harcourt Brace Jovanovich, Publishers

HARCOURT BRACE JOVANOVICH, PUBLISHERS **HBJ**

Orlando   New York   Chicago   San Diego   Atlanta   Dallas

For permission to reprint copyrighted material, grateful acknowledgment is made to the following sources:

Atheneum Publishers: "Conquistador" (copyright 1952, 1980 by Prudencia de Pereda) in *Windmills in Brooklyn.* Copyright © 1960 by Prudencio de Pereda (New York: Atheneum 1960).

Curtis Brown, Ltd.: "The Storm" by McKnight Malmar. Copyright © 1944 by McKnight Malmar. Published in *Good Housekeeping,* February 1944.

The Borden Deal Family Trust (Borden Deal, Trustee): "Antaeus" by Borden Deal in *Southwest Review,* Spring 1961. Copyright © 1961 by Southern Methodist University Press.

Doubleday & Company, Inc.: "The Silver Mine" from *The Girl From the Marsh Croft* by Selma Lagerlof. Copyright 1910 by Selma Lagerlof. "The Ransom of Red Chief" from *Whirligigs* by O. Henry.

Harcourt Brace Jovanovich, Inc.: "Twelve-Winter" under the original title "Then He Goes Free" by Jessamyn West reprinted from her volume *Cress Delahanty.* Copyright 1948, 1976 by Jessamyn West. First published in *The New Yorker* Magazine. "A Worn Path" by Eudora Welty reprinted from her volume *A Curtain of Green and Other Stories.* Copyright 1941, 1969 by Eudora Welty.

Harper & Row Publishers, Inc.: "An Encounter with an Interviewer" from *Tom Sawyer Abroad* by Mark Twain, Harper & Row.

Daniel Keyes: "Flowers for Algernon" by Daniel Keyes in *Magazine of Fantasy and Science Fiction,* 1959. © 1959 by Mercury Press, Inc.

Harold Matson Company, Inc.: "The Pedestrian" by Ray Bradbury. Copyright © 1951 by Ray Bradbury, © renewed 1979 by Ray Bradbury. "Top Man" by James Ramsey Ullman. Copyright © 1940 by James Ramsey Ullman, © renewed 1968 by James Ramsey Ullman.

The New Yorker: "A Game of Catch" by Richard Wilbur. © 1953 The New Yorker Magazine, Inc.

Harold Ober Associates Incorporated: "Thank You M'am" from *The Langston Hughes Reader* by Langston Hughes. Copyright © 1958 by Langston Hughes.

Critical Reader: L. Harlan Ford, Ed.D.
President of American Technological University, Killeen, Texas
Former Deputy Commissioner of Education for the State of Texas

Cover Photo: © H. Abernathy/H. Armstrong Roberts

Production: LMD Service for Publishers

CONTENTS

A Book of
Short Stories 1

INTRODUCTION

The collection *The Arabian Nights' Entertainments*[1] contains the tales of clever Scheherazade, who saved her life by telling her husband, the king, a new story each night. By the time her stories numbered a thousand and one, the king loved her so much he could not kill her. What an enviable skill—to invent such a multitude of interesting tales. The modern short story writer might well wish for a small share of Scheherazade's talent.

The history of short prose fiction is almost as old as language itself. Through the centuries, tales, legends, myths, and fables have been enjoyed everywhere in the world. The short story was not regarded as a distinct literary form, however, until the nineteenth century, when authors in Germany, Russia, France, and the United States began to compose and define different types of fiction. The American critic, poet, and short story writer Edgar Allan Poe made an outstanding contribution to the development of the short story when he wrote that all of the details in a story should contribute to a "unique or single effect."

Today, a short story may be as brief as 500 words or as long as several thousand words. The difference between a short story and other fictional forms, such as the novel, lies in its unity: the conversation, the action, and the idea on which a short story is based will all deliberately focus on one predominant effect.

Short stories are written to be enjoyed. Of course, you don't need to understand how a story is written in order to enjoy it. Understanding the elements of a short story, however, will

1. **The Arabian Nights' Entertainments:** a group of Oriental stories (also called *The Thousand and One Nights*) dating from the tenth century, narrated by Queen Scheherazade (shə·hĕr′ə·zäd′). The king postponed her death (the usual fate of his wives) from day to day so he could hear another of her interesting stories. Aladdin, Ali Baba, and Sinbad the Sailor are among the characters in these tales.

heighten your enjoyment because it will help you to read *critically;* that is, it will help you to evaluate and compare different stories so that you will understand why a story affects you in a certain way and why you like some stories more than others.

Elements of the Short Story

Not all short stories contain all of the following elements. Depending on the author's purpose, some factors may receive more emphasis than others; some may not be used at all.

Conflict

The reason a story grows in tension and suspense as it moves is that the pressure of conflict, the struggle between two opposing forces, is increased by each event. Conflict in a story may be (1) person against person, (2) human against nature, (3) one against oneself, (4) the individual against society, or (5) a combination of one or more of these types.

An example of person against person would be two people fighting for the same goal. A human against nature might involve a person caught in a storm at sea. An athlete debating the morality of accepting a bribe would illustrate one against oneself. And a doctor who meets opposition to a new medicine or vaccination would be an example of an individual against society. It is possible, obviously, to have more than one conflict within a story.

Conflict can be *external* or *internal*. Physical or external conflict is easy to recognize, especially in an adventure story which emphasizes a vivid physical struggle. Internal conflict may be represented by a character's struggle with conscience, or between what is and what should be. The character might be struggling against an impulse to commit a crime, or a tendency to be cowardly, or a fear that something disastrous is going to happen. The best stories combine external and internal conflict.

The forces opposing each other in a conflict are labeled the *protagonist* and the *antagonist*. The protagonist is the hero or heroine who is faced with a basic problem or struggle. The antagonist is the person, place, idea, or physical force opposing the protagonist. To succeed, the protagonist must overcome the antagonist.

Plot

This is the plan of the story—the sequence of actions and events that tells what happened. In many short stories, the plot has a well-defined *beginning, middle,* and *end.*

The story begins with a situation or problem that is real and important to the hero or heroine. Many authors try to arouse the reader's curiosity in the first sentence. The author keeps the reader in *suspense,* wondering what will happen next. Suspense is increased by withholding information that would satisfy the reader's curiosity.

The beginning of the story often introduces a *conflict* that will be important to the story. The opposing forces must seem to be so evenly matched that the reader is kept in suspense about who or what will win out. Usually the opposing forces are people, but some excellent stories have been written about internal conflict. The hero or heroine, who is also called the *protagonist,* might be struggling against an impulse to commit a crime, or a fear that something disastrous is going to happen. The opposing force, person, place, or idea in the conflict is called the *antagonist.*

In the middle of the story, the tension created in the opening situation must be increased. To maintain the reader's interest, *complications* are introduced. The goal that the hero or heroine wishes to attain does not appear as easy to reach as it first did, or the opponent may become more formidable. Barriers and detours are presented, creating a need for new plans and decisions.

As the main character struggles with these conflicts, the reader begins to recognize a growing or rising action in the plot toward a particular high point of interest called the *climax.* This is the point of highest dramatic intensity. All action builds toward it.

Following the climax comes the *dénouement,* which is the final unraveling or solution of the plot. At the end of the story, it should be clear that one side or the other triumphs, a main character meets success or failure, a mystery is solved, or some misunderstanding is cleared up. Some stories end, as conflicts in life often do, with no clear-cut answers or solutions.

Foreshadowing

This means exactly what the name implies—a hint of things to come. A word, a phrase, or a sentence can contain an important clue that has been inserted by the author to prepare the reader for a later event. Alert readers store such a clue in their mind and recall it when the unexpected takes place or when a character reacts in a manner that at first appears strange or unreasonable.

Character Portrayal

There are a number of techniques an author can use to help characters come alive. These include:

1. A physical description of a character and/or a description of the kind of person he or she is: the writer may tell you that a person is stingy and mean, or kind and considerate.
2. A description by another character.
3. Dialogue or presentation of a character's conversations.
4. An explanation of a character's inner thoughts.
5. The actions of a character.
6. The characters' responses and reactions to each other or to situations.
7. A combination of several of these methods.

Character and plot are closely related. A well-conceived plot involves meaningful human action, which means that characters act consciously and deliberately. A plot is believable only if the characters in a story act in a reasonable, consistent, and natural way. To believe in the characters, you must believe in the plot.

Everything you are told about a character should be significant. The good short story writer is selective and includes only details that are essential to the effect of the story.

Point of View

There are basically two points of view from which a writer can tell a story:

1. First-Person Narrator (author participant). Here the writer usually has a major or a minor character tell the story in his or her own words ("I said"; "I did"; "I remember"). The author, through this first-person narrator, can reveal only what the narrator might reasonably be expected to know. If a ten-year-old girl tells the story, her powers of observation and expression would naturally be limited. The use of the first-person narrator gives an illusion of immediacy and authority.

2. Third-Person Narrator (author omniscient). If an author feels that the reader should know more than any one person can tell, the story may be written from an all-knowing point of view. Any character's actions or thoughts may be commented upon.

Tone

Tone is a writer's attitude toward his or her subject and characters. It may be sorrowful, sentimental, angry, ironic, sympathetic, or objective and impersonal. The writer chooses and selects details that will help to set the desired tone, thus setting up how readers will react to each character.

Setting and Atmosphere

The setting of a story—the time and place of a story's action—is most often stressed in a story of *local color,* which emphasizes the particular characteristics of a region and its inhabitants. It is also important in *science-fiction* stories, where the author has to create an impression of reality to make imagined scientific changes of the future real to present-day readers. When evaluating the role of setting in a short story, ask yourself what the setting contributes to the story and if it could possibly be eliminated as an essential element in the story.

As a rule, setting is not a dominant element, but it does serve to establish or heighten atmosphere. This is especially evident in stories where the author wants to create a special feeling or mood.

Atmosphere, an integral part of plot, theme, and character, is something you sense or feel. Descriptive details give an emotional coloring to a story, but there are many other ways of obtaining atmosphere. For example, style—the author's choice of words, the kind and quantity of verbs, adjectives, and adverbs, and the length and rhythmical pattern of sentences—helps to create atmosphere.

Symbol

A symbol is something which represents or suggests a relationship or association. For example, a flag symbolizes patriotism; a lamp represents knowledge; a cross stands for the Church.

In fiction, symbols are often concrete objects used to represent abstract ideas. A stack of gold coins might, during the course of a story, come to stand for greed, or a lovely rose, for beauty.

Characters' names may also be symbolic. "Red," for example, could be a name associated with a hotheaded person. A "Mrs. Oakwood" might manifest both physical and moral strength.

Theme

Another important element is the theme, the central insight or intuition on which the story is based. A theme is rarely stated; usually it is implied. Generally, a theme is a significant insight about human life.

The central insight—not a summary, not the plot—of a story can often be stated in one or two sentences. For example, the theme might be "Honesty is the best policy." Or the theme might be that all persons are responsible beings who must someday answer for their acts. Not every story has a theme, but in some stories, the theme is more important than the plot. In general, the most memorable stories have a serious idea or comment about life underlying the plot.

Commercial or Quality Stories

The word *commercial* refers to a story written for the mass market or the general public. Commercial short stories usually have stock characters and conventional themes that are generally accepted by a mass readership. Their plots have strong suspense, and the tone is often romantic.

You are probably familiar with such *stock characters* of television and the movies as the difficult mother-in-law, the bumbling but lovable father, the mad scientist. Stock characters are not lifelike. They require little or no imagination or insight from the writer, reader, or viewer because they act in a predictable way and sometimes even have a particular way of talking.

Like stock characters, conventional themes conform to approved and established practices and customs. One of the most common movie themes is the cliché "love conquers all." The story will usually deal with the love of a handsome young man and a beautiful girl. Various complications that prevent their being married are one by one eliminated, and they live "happily ever after."

A *quality* story, on the other hand, usually emphasizes character and theme rather than plot. The characters are individualized and true to life; the theme is an idea that unifies the entire story and has universal meaning.

Analysis of a Short Story

In order to discover the underlying meaning of a story, you need to learn to read more than just the printed words. Much of the pleasure of reading comes from being able to supply what the author does not say but only suggests. For example, when you read "The Secret Life of Walter Mitty," notice that Walter Mitty never says he is deathly tired of being nagged and henpecked, but listen as Mrs. Mitty talks at him. Every word is a pin in a balloon, a pop in his soap-bubble world.

The key to a story will most often be found by asking the question "Why?" Of each story, ask two *why's*. The first *why* is directed toward the characters' motivations. Why do the characters act and speak as they do? What motives do they have for their choices and decisions? These decisions are what bring the action or plot to its climax. The dénouement should be determined by the nature of the characters. You should be able to believe that certain characters would make the kinds of choices they do. Through their characters, authors are able to tell their readers something about human beings—what pressures they face and how they react, or what they will live or die for.

The second *why* will help relate the different parts or elements of the story. Short stories are limited. They do not include extras. Ask then, why did the author use this type of setting, this kind of dialogue, these events, these characters, this particular point of view? Asking these questions will help you to understand how the story's meaning is conveyed through the relationship of all the parts of the story: that is, the method of this particular writer in this particular story. In every well-written story, there will be good reasons for the author's selection and arrangement of material. Be sure to check details in particular.

PRUDENCIO DE PEREDA
(born 1912)

Prudencio de Pereda was born in Brooklyn, New York. He is of Spanish parentage. This Spanish background, he has used frequently in his novels and short stories.

He received an A.B. from City College of New York, did graduate work at New York University and received a Masters of Library Science degree from Pratt Institute, in Brooklyn in 1955.

When he was six years old, de Pereda decided to become a writer. A year later he wrote his first short story. During his junior year in high school he wrote another story, "The Spaniard," which was published in the prestigious *Story* magazine and was included in two collections of best short stories.

While in college, de Pereda first read the work of Ernest Hemingway and seriously began his career as a writer. During the Spanish Civil War, from 1936 to 1939, he worked with Hemingway on the commentary for two Spanish films. His work has subsequently been compared favorably with Hemingway's.

His first novel, *All the Girls We Love,* was published in 1948. His novel *Fiesta* (1953) was called "the best novel available in English on modern Spain." The story is laid in a small provincial town in which five young men contend for the coveted role of the Christ in a presentation of the local Passion play. *Fiesta* has been published in the United States, Canada, England, France and Finland. His 1960 novel, *Windmills in Brooklyn,* introduce the same characters that appear in the story reprinted here. The first part of the novel is called "Agapito" after the narrator's uncle. Part Two is called "Good Pair," which is how the grandfather describes himself and the narrator, his grandson. It was said of the grandfather that he was a man of ideals, like Don Quixote, the fictional Spanish hero who went on knightly quests and titled with windmills as though they were dragons. Except, as the grandmother character in the novel observes, there "are no windmills in Brooklyn."

De Pereda's many short stories have been published in *Nation, Story, Twice a Year, Gentry,* and *New Republic.*

CONQUISTADOR

I thought, when I was young, that you worked according to your nationality. We were Spanish, and my father, grandfather, and uncles were all in the cigar business. There was a definite rule about this, I believed—a *law*. I thought so particularly during those times when I listened to my father and the other men of our family talk business, and heard them complain bitterly about the cigar business and about what a dishonorable trade it was, and how they were cursed the moment they took it up.

This used to surprise me—especially in regard to my father, because on the rare visits to his store it had seemed like a wonderful place. It had a broad, rich-looking, nickel-plated counter, neatly stacked with bright-colored boxes of cigars, and with shining hookahs[1] and lighters along its top. The floor was white tile, and the inside wall of the store was a great mirror. The customers I'd seen had been well-dressed men with booming voices, rich gold chains around their full stomachs, and canes and gloves in their hands. There had been an air of wealth and strength in that store as I remembered it.

Still, my father was one of the most vehement[2] in his denunciations[3] of the cigar business. "Let them raise the blood to my face in shame," he once said, in his correct, intense Spanish, "if I permit any of my sons to go into this business. Yes. Let them do that!" I admired my father for his feelings, but felt that he was just talking, that my three brothers and I were all fated for the

First-person narrator.

Foreshadowing of conflict.

Contrast. Characterization by store.

---

1. **hookahs:** an Eastern pipe for smoking tobacco. The smoke is drawn by a long tube through an urn of water which cools it.
2. **vehement:** emphatic; characterized by forcefulness of expression and intensity of emotion.
3. **denunciation:** an open condemnation or censure.

cigar business, just as my father and uncles had
been. Indeed, even at this time, my older
brother, who was only ten but figured himself a
wise American, had already begun to do some
special errands for my father. He would not
only deliver boxes of cigars to the hotels in the
neighborhood of my father's store in the Borough Hall[4] section of Brooklyn, but would even
take the elevated[5] and go over the river and into
the city to make deliveries.

When I begged him to tell me about this,
he acted very casual and unafraid, and when,
out of my genuine concern for him, I asked,
"Aren't you going to be an aviator any more?"
he said, "Sure! What's the matter with you?
What'd you think I'm saving my money for?" I
pitied him all the more, and worried myself inside for him. He was doomed—just as my father

and uncles had been doomed. He would never
be an aviator; nor would I ever be a bullfighter—and poor Justo would never have his
big shoeshine parlor, or have his twin, Bifanio,
as a sweeper. Bifanio hadn't made up his mind,
yet, as to what he wanted to be, but the twins
always did things together.

My older brother would never take me
with him when he went on his errands. I was
too young—though I was only two years
younger than he. After he came home from
school, he would put on his Sunday suit and
new shoes and go down to my father's store on
the trolley.[6] I often wept as I pleaded with him
to take me—just once, just this once! I didn't
want to get into the cigar business, and was

---

4. Borough Hall section: The principal commercial district of the borough (or
township) of Brooklyn, where administrative offices and courthouses for that
part of New York City are housed.
5. elevated: the city railroad raised above the streets (in Chicago and New
York, for example) which allowed for vehicle and pedestrian traffic at the street
level.
6. trolley: here, an electric streetcar.

afraid of the city, but I would have risked anything to be allowed to ride on an elevated train.

My brother never relented, and my first experience in the cigar business came through an accident and without his help. It was something bigger than he'd ever done, and I should have felt boastful; instead, it filled me with terror and shame, and, at once, I understood the feelings of my father and the other men of our family.

Foreshadowing.

How it happened was natural enough. Mother was making another try to have a girl, "a little sister," as she explained formally to us, and we three younger boys were farmed out. My older brother, Joe, stayed at home because he could do errands, make phone calls, and generally help around the house, and besides, as he explained to me, he was old enough to understand things. I didn't feel too bad, because I was going to Grandmother's and not to an aunt's, as the twins had. Going to Grandmother's had some responsibility, for there were always errands to be done and I would often have to act as translator. My grandmother spoke only about ten words of English, and my grandfather just a few more.

Beginning of major plot.

Ages established.

Central characters introduced.

On the third day of my stay there—it was the Fourth of July—Grandfather had announced early that he wouldn't "go out" today. "Going out" meant going to work. My grandfather was in the most stigmatized form of the cigar business—he was a *teveriano* or "junk dealer," one of those itinerant salemen who were scorned by the rest of the trade because they dealt completely in lies: in false representation, and false merchandise—very cheap cigars for which they secured exorbitant prices—and so brought still more disgrace to the Spaniards who had enough as it was by merely being in the legitimate cigar business.

I had heard all this at home—listening ea-

Time established.

Characterization by occupation and contrast.

gerly because the *teveriano* was certainly the most interesting of all the cigar men—but I'd never been able to connect the fabulous stories of *teverianos* with my mild, sad grandfather. For one thing, he was always very poor.

Grandmother didn't turn to look at him as she answered: "Do you observe American holidays now?" She had a great dislike for everything American. she had been a great lady in Spain.

"One has to dance to the song they play," Grandfather said, shrugging his shoulders.

"And one has to pay the rent they ask!" Grandmother said this very sharply. I knew I should have left the room then, but I felt too sorry for my grandfather. He was growing very red. "We're at the fourth, now," Grandmother said. "That's five days late."

"I know that."

"Well?" Grandmother said, turning.

"I know that. I'm in accord with you. But not in front of the boy, please! Not in front of the boy, woman!"

The boy knows it!"

"But not from me!" Grandfather stood up suddenly and came over to me. His hands were trembling. He took my arm and led me into the front parlor. He stood me by the window and sat down in the big chair. "Watch the celebrations!" he said. "Watch the celebrations!" I stared fixedly out the open window, knowing there weren't going to be any celebrations around here, but not wanting to tell my grandfather.

We stayed there only a short time, because the bell rang in a few moments—I couldn't see who it was—and quick, happy steps came up the stairs and we heard Agapito's voice greeting my grandmother. He called her "Dona," the most respectful title in Spanish, but he was laughing and warm as he talked.

Just as Grandfather was not, Agapito was the perfect example of the *teveriano*. He was still a very young man and had only been in America a short time, but he was easily the most famous—as well as the most criticized—of the salesmen. He was dressed that day as I imagined a *teveriano* would dress: a fine white linen suit, brown patent-leather shoes with button tops, a bright polka-dot bow tie, and a panama straw[7] with a multicolored band. When he came smiling into the front room, I thought he looked like the perfect man of the world, and he seemed to fill the room with brightness. He was very respectful to my grandfather, as he'd been to Grandmother, and when he suggested that they go out for a little bit, he said it in a quiet, serious voice. "We'll take the boy with us, yes?" he said, patting my shoulder and smiling at me. Agapito had neat white teeth and a small black mustache. He had a dark Spanish skin, and I though he was very handsome. I'd always liked him, in spite of the stories I'd heard about him.

Narrator's opinion of Agapito given.

Grandfather answered Agapito's suggestion to go out by quietly shrugging his shoulders, but when Agapito suggested that they take me, his face took on the dark, stubborn look again.

Reader's curiosity aroused by grandfather's reaction to Agapito.

"Yes, take the boy!" my grandmother called from the kitchen. "He hasn't been out. He may see some things. Holiday things." My grandfather shrugged his shoulders again.

We took a trolley—an open summer trolley—and we stayed on till the end of the line, and I saw that we'd come to the dock secion.[8]

Use of local color.

7. **Panama straw:** a hat made of natural straw hand-plaited; the product of Central and South America.
8. **dock-section:** the port of Brooklyn, near the Brooklyn Navy Yards; the Northern most part of Brooklyn.

Suspense
building.

Gradual
movement
forward in time.

Atmosphere
established.
Contrast with
father's store.

We could see the colored stacks of the big liners tied up at the piers. The big street was empty and quiet and that made the wonderful ships seem more intimate in the sun. Agapito kept pointing out things to me, but Grandfather walked along very quietly. He was dressed in his best black suit, with a black derby hat, and his face looked very worried. His black, drooping mustache made his face look very sad.

When we'd gone a few blocks, we turned into a side street and went into a small cigar store. I saw that this was Miguelin's. I knew Miguelin from seeing him at home and at the Spanish dances. He was a little, gray old man, and his store was dusty and old. He wrapped up seven new boxes of cigars for us, not wrapping them in brown paper but just with a heavy string so that you could see it was cigars and all the beautiful labels showed. Agapito gave him fourteen dollars. I counted them—and figured out that meant two dollars per box. Grandfather wanted to pay, but Agapito stopped him and made him put his wallet away. Agapito seemed to have charge of everything—he'd paid our fares on the trolley, too—and he would bend over and talk to Grandfather in a low voice while he patted him on the shoulder. I felt happy about this. I wanted my grandfather to lose his worry.

When we left Miguelin's, we turned to the big street again, and walked back the way we'd come. We walked very slowly, and Agapito kept talking to Grandfather and looking into each saloon that we passed. The saloons were the only places that were open today and there weren't many men in any of them. We were coming to a big one on the opposite corner, when Agapito said to my grandfather: "This one! This one seems good." The saloon had a big, bright shiny front and had a big hotel upstairs. I read the name "Monaghan" on the big

Description of
saloon as a
pleasant place.

sign over the swinging doors. As we crossed, Agapito took my hand firmly, and as we went in, I saw that the saloon was big and shiny and clean. It reminded me of my father's store. There was a big counter on one side with a great mirror on the wall and another counter on the other side with trays of food filling it all along. The tile floor was very clean and had no sawdust on it, and there was a big back room with tables that had white tablecloths.

Agapito stood inside the doorway, smiling and looking around as if he liked the place. Then, he led us over to the big counter with the mirror. We found a place easily because there were only a few men standing there, and Agapito placed the cigar boxes on the counter and nodded and smiled to the man behind the counter. He pointed to my grandfather and then to himself and said "Whiskey!" very plainly. He pronounced it "vhiskey." He patted me on the head, and smiled at the man again, and said, "Ginger ale!" He pronounced this well, except that he said "al" instead of "ale."

Importance of cigars growing.

There was another man behind the counter, standing farther back. He had his jacket off and his sleeves rolled up, but he didn't have an apron on. He was a big man with a red face and he was smoking a big cigar. He had a gold chain across his vest and two big rings on his right hand, and he looked like one of my father's rich customers. When I stared at him, he winked at me and laughed. He'd been watching Agapito and my grandfather who were leaning on the big counter with their feet on the brass rail. Agapito had been talking in Spanish and laughing as he and my grandfather drank their whiskey.

New character introduced.

Narrator's reaction to new character given.

The big man walked up to them slowly and patted the cigar boxes. Agapito turned his head up suddenly, in surprise, and then smiled at the big man and bowed to him.

Beginning of Agapito's swindle.

"Havanas?" the big man said. He had a strong deep voice.

Agapito nodded quickly. "Yes! I am from Havana. I am from Havana."

"I mean the cigars," the big man said, laughing. He had brown teeth, but a nice face.

"Oh! Also, also!" Agapito said. He laughed and kept nodding his head. "From Havana, also. For my friend! I bring them." He pointed outside. "The ship! You understand? From Havana to Spain. I bring them to friend here. I stop off." He spoke in short spurts, but he pronounced very clearly. He stopped smiling and became very serious as he pulled one of the boxes out of the bundle, opened it with his little gold knife and picked out two cigars carefully. He handed them over to the big man and nodded vigorously when the big man seemed to hesitate.

Dialogue used for characterization.

"For Fourth of July!" Agapito said. He smiled again. "Happy Fourth of July!" He nodded and pressed the cigars into the man's hand.

The big man smelled the cigars and nodded to him. "Good flavor," he said. He turned and said something to the man in the apron and this man took the bottle and poured more whiskey into Agapito's and my grandfather's glasses. Agapito raised his glass to him, and then my grandfather did.

The big man kept smelling the cigars and then he patted the boxes again. "What would they cost?—How much?" he said, when Agapito looked puzzled. Agapito spread his hand. "For a friend," he said. "You understand. No. . . ." He made the motion with his hands again.

"Customs?" the big man said.

"Customs!" Agapito nodded quickly and smiled. He rubbed his hands. "No customs! Customs."

"Well, how much? How much, anyway?" The big man patted the boxes.

Agapito held a finger up, and turned to my

grandfather. "This one seems to have money," he said in Spanish. "This one can pay."

"Take care, hombre,"[9] my grandfather said.

"No, don't disquiet yourself, Don Jose. I know what I'm doing." Agapito patted Grandfather's arm, turned to the big man and smiled. "My friend, here. He remember. He remember everything." He ran his finger up and down the boxes. "All the boxes. Seven! Sixty dollars. Cost for my friend."

Sixty dollars! This was a shock to me—if a man buys seven boxes of cigars for fourteen dollars, two dollars per box, and sells them for— sixty dollars! I understood why the big man made such a face and then laughed. I hadn't minded all the lies that Agapito had told because I knew that *teverianos* worked like that, but when he asked this high, high figure, I got shocked and embarrassed—and then, very frightened for us. The glass felt heavy in my hand, and I held my head down because I knew that I was blushing. *Building tension.*

I'd heard that *teverianos* asked robber prices, but I never thought that Agapito would take the chance today, when he had my grandfather and me with him. He was going to get us into trouble. He was making us take a chance—because he wanted to. And we were all going to get into trouble. *Narrator worried and in trouble.*

The big man said something to Agapito and Agapito said, "Well—you know, sir, Havanas!"

I didn't hear the big man answer but then Agapito said very brightly, "You interested? You interested in cigars?" I hated his accent, now. His lying. *Change in narrator's attitude towards Agapito.*

"I was looking for ten boxes. I could use ten boxes," the big man said slowly.

9. **hombre:** Spanish for man.

Agapito was talking in Spanish, then. He must have been talking to my grandfather. "You stay here," he said, still speaking respectfully. "I will run to Miguelin's and get three more boxes. I will run fast. You stay here. This is a good thing."

"Yes, hombre, it is," I heard my grandfather say. "Let him take these seven boxes and let us be through here. Let it stay a good thing.

"There is no danger," Agapito said quickly.

"If there is, entrust it to me," my grandfather said sternly and I looked up suddenly to see that his face had taken on the stubborn look again. "I wasn't thinking of that. I was thinking that we have a good thing. Let us take it, and be gone."

"I don't work like that," Agapito said. "You know that, Don Jose," he said more softly.

"Then, as you wish."

"You will stay?"

"As you wish!"

I watched, in rage but fascinated, as Agapito turned back to smile at the big man who was leaning on the counter with his old cigar in his mouth. Agapito brought his hands together. "We fix it," he said, and nodded. "Three more boxes, I will bring from the boat. For ten boxes"—he ran his fingers up and down the seven on the counter and held up three fingers—"ten boxes—for eighty dollars—for you!" He pointed at the big man.

The big man stared at Agapito for a moment, and then nodded and said, "Okay. Eighty dollars." What a fool this one is, too, I thought. His face looked stupid to me, now.

"You give me fifty dollars, now," Agapito said. He smiled. "I give money to guard—small money. You understand? My friend wait here, I come back. With three more."

Did Grandfather understand that? Did Grandfather know what Agapito was saying? I

Building conflict between grandfather and Agapito.

Narrator has ambiguous feelings about Agapito and saloonkeeper.

stared at his face, but couldn't see anything. I was weak with fright and fear, but I didn't dare say a word. The big man had taken out his wallet without hesitation and given Agapito five new bills—tens they must have been. Agapito smiled and nodded as he put them in his wallet quickly. He patted Grandfather on the arm, saying, "Don't worry yourself. I'll be back immediately," and then patted me on the head—I couldn't duck fast enough—and went out into the street.

Beginning of the climax.

I stared at the floor. I wouldn't look at my grandfather. I'd finished the ginger ale, but I wouldn't go over to put the glass on the counter. I heard the big man say something to Grandfather that Grandfather didn't answer. "No speak English, eh?" the big man said, and laughed. He took up the bundle of cigars and moved down to the end of the counter—where I could see him by just lifting my eyes a little—and he began to open every box.

I had to look at my grandfather, then. Did he see what danger we were in? He was staring at the mirror. His hands were steady, but he was sweating. I glared at him, at first, but then wanted to cry. I went up and put the glass by his side and he looked down at me and then turned to stare up at the big man as he was opening each box. Then, he turned back, finished his drink in one slug and turned to me. His back was to the big man and he put his hand on my shoulder. I could smell the whiskey on his breath as he bent down. "Get thee out of here," he said. "Act as if thou art going out calmly." My grandfather always used the familiar "thee"[10] with us, and his

Sustained suspense. Reader senses danger.

10. **the familiar "thee":** the intimate form of the second person singular pronoun in many romance languages such as French, Spanish and Italian. The more formal second person plural pronoun "You" (which is usual in English) would be used in these languages except for most intimate friends and for children.

voice was calm and easy now but I could see that he was sweating badly. His hand felt very tight on my shoulder. "Get thyself to the trolley station. Stand by the trees there and wait for me. No matter how long, I will come. Do nothing but wait for me. I will escape this in some way. I well get out, and get to thee. I will escape this and get to thee. In whatever way, I will.

"Without crying, thee!" he said. "Without crying!" I hadn't started to cry yet, but my lip had begun to tremble. I bit my lip and started to shake my head even before he'd finished. "And think well of me," he was saying. "Think well of me. I did not want this situation for thee. Thou wilt not? Thou wilt not do it?"

"No. I stay. I stay here with you." His face had the stubborn look again and he pushed my shoulder but held his grip tightly on it. He glared at me, but I kept shaking my head. "Stay, then!" he said. "Stay!" He dropped his hand from my shoulder but reached to take my hand and then turned to lean on the bar again, holding my hand. A moment later, when he poured more whiskey into his glass, he did it with his left hand, but poured it very neatly. He lifted the glass in his left hand, and began to sip the whiskey slowly.

Flashback.   Grandfather had been a waiter in Spain. He was very proud of that. He'd been a waiter at the best hotel in Tangier[11] just before he'd come to the United States, and a prince, a duke, and two princesses had been among his patrons. My mother was born in Tangier, and, though she couldn't remember anything of her part in the life there, she told us many stories about it. The three years spent in Tangier had been the happiest time in the life of her family.

My grandmother's brother had come to

---

11. **Tangier:** a seaport in Morocco in Northern Africa near the coast of Spain.

the United States some years before and made an immediate success as a *teveriano*. He wrote glowing letters to my grandmother, telling her of the wonderful opportunities in the trade and urging her to make Jose, my grandfather, see reason and come to America. Does he want to be a waiter all his life? the brother would ask. He'd felt very bad when she'd married a waiter. He was her only brother and they were very close.

Foreshadowing of later conflict.

Grandfather was content. He didn't want to leave. The letter got more boastful, and then pleading. Finally, my granduncle sent enough money to pay first-class passage for all three and the pressure was too much for my grandfather. He consented, and he came to the United States with his family—to a tenement district in Hoboken, New Jersey. They moved to Brooklyn shortly after, when my aunt was born, but to a tenement district again, and they had never lived better than that. Grandfather—as Mother would say, in ending these stories—was just not a good salesman.

I was thinking these things as I gripped Grandfather's hand and stared up at him, and the anger that I'd felt before turned to pity. I love you, I thought. Once, I pulled his arm and said, "We could go to the bathroom—first me, then you—sneak out that way." He glared down at me with a stubborn look. "No. In no such manner. When we go, we go through the front door. We are men." He turned to stare at the mirror, but then turned quickly back to me. "Dost thou have to go to the toilet? Truly?"

Narrator's change of feeling towards his grandfather.

I shook my head.

"Good!" he said, and turned to the mirror.

I though we stood like that for a long time—it seemed like a long, long time to me—but Agapito said later that he'd only been gone sixteen minutes, that he'd counted them. Agapito's face was sweating when he came back, and his Panama was pushed back on his head, but he was smiling and looked very happy, and his clothes were still very neat. "I run! I run!" he said to the big man. "To ship. To ship and back!" He'd put the new boxes on the counter and was opening each one with his penknife and holding the open box up to the big man. The boxes looked very new and I thought that one of the labels looked wet. Surely, the big man would see, now. He would see the truth, now, I thought. And it would serve Agapito right. He'd be in it, now. Grandfather and I could run. We'd get away. Agapito was the one they'd hold.

The big man smelled every box and even touched the wet wrapper, but he nodded seriously and then stupidly took out his wallet and gave Agapito three more ten dollar bills. The man with the apron had filled Agapito's glass again and Agapito held out one of the bills to him, but he shook his head. Then, Agapito put the bills in his wallet and picked out a one-dollar bill that he folded and handed to the man in the apron. "For you," he said. "For you." He smiled and nodded. Then, he held up the whiskey, smiled and nodded again, and drank it in one gulp.

I had been tugging at Grandfather's hand, wanting to start, wanting us to go, but Grandfather held his tight grip and waited until Agapito had shaken hands with both men, and then he himself nodded to them, and we all turned towards the door.

We walked very slowly as we went outside and crossed the street. Grandfather wanted to walk fast, but Agapito was holding his arm and walking very slowly. "Don't worry yourself," he said, after a moment. "We'll turn down the first street. For now, we walk slowly—very slowly, and with dignity."

We turned down the first street, walked

down that block, and then turned in the direction of the trolleys. As soon as we'd made this last turn, Agapito stopped and took out his wallet. He handed Grandfather three ten-dollar bills. Grandfather pushed them back. "Hombre!" he said, "don't embarrass me."

Dénouement.
Agapito defends
his deception.

"Please!" Agapito said. "This is your share."

"It's too much."

"It's half. We were equally involved." Agapito pressed the bills into Grandfather's hand. "Equally!" he said, letting go.

Grandfather put the bills in his little black purse. "I'm very appreciative. Very!" he said.

"For nothing!" Agapito said. "For nothing!" As we walked, now, he was smiling and happy again. He took off his hat and rubbed his face with a big silk handkerchief. "One has to see these things, Don Jose. One has to see them. To believe them, one has to see them. Havanas!" he shook his head and laughed. "And you mustn't feel that we cheat them!" he said, when Grandfather didn't answer. "This one buys them as Havanas. he gives them out as Havanas—probably at some festival—and those who take them, take them as Havanas, and smoke them. No matter how bad the cigars, for them they are Havanas. Yes, Don Jose. We sell Havanas—they buy Havanas!"

On the trolley, after he'd paid our fares, Agapito slipped a half dollar into the conductor's pocket. "For Fourth of July!" he said. The conductor blushed, and nodded. Later, Agapito stood up and took off his hat. "Life for the United States of America!" he called out. "Happy Fourth of July to everybody!" The two people who were sitting up at the front end of the trolley smiled and shook their heads. They thought he was drunk.

Implied contrast
of reactions to
America.

Agapito left, soon after we got home.

Then, Grandmother went out. "I'll get some ham," she said. "We'll eat well, tonight." Grandfather and I were in the front room, and she'd come to the door. "The delicatessen has good ham."

Grandfather nodded. "We're most fortunate," he said, without looking up. "Most fortunate."

Grandmother turned back and stared at him with a cold face. She was dressed in her black skirt and black silk waist,[12] and she looked like the pictures of the Queen Mother in the Spanish magazines we had, except that Grandmother was much more beautiful. "Yes," she said, in a calm voice. "Most fortunate. You, in particular! You needn't go out for some days, now. Perhaps grow a beard, here."

Grandfather got very red, but didn't look up. He shrugged his shoulders as Grandmother turned and went out. After a moment, he reached over to me and pulled me to the side of the chair. He kept his arm around me and patted my head. "Thou!" he said. He looked straight at me. "Thou must forget what thou heardst today, what thou sawst. All of it! Forget especially what thy grandmother said. She is a fine woman. Nothing of today was like her. It is I who am weak. The fault is mine. Thou wilt understand this some day. Thou wilt, yes. What thou must remember is this"—he pressed my shoulder—"that thou must be strong. Remember that! Let no woman—whether she be thy mother who is my own flesh, or the woman thou wilt marry—let none of them press thee or influence thee in choosing thy profession. Thou, thou alone, must move through the world to make thy money, thou alone must suffer—so thou must choose. And hold to that!

Grandfather reveals his own sense of his character.

---

12. **waist:** a term used for a woman's blouse during the period about which this story is written.

"Thou art the bullfighter, no?"

"Or one who guides an elevated train," I said. "One of those."

"Good. Thou might change, but whatever thou shouldst choose—hold to it. Grip it well."

I nodded.

"Dost thou know what she referred to in that of the beard?" he said, in a softer voice.

"No, Grandfather," I lied.

"Well, it was this: I had a fine beard when I was a waiter in Tangier. It was a full, well-cut beard and I was a fine figure with it. One afternoon, the major-domo[13]—he who was chief of all our waiters—the major-domo, Don Felix, came to me and said, 'Jose, you must shave that beard. Too many patrons are coming in and talking to you and treating you as the major-domo. I regret this, but you must shave it, because there is only one major-domo here, and it is me. No one else can look like a major-domo. No one else will.'

Flashback.

"I went home to thy grandmother and told her this, and she said, 'Yes. The man has reason. You must shave your beard.' I had thought that she would have objections, that she would show anger. I had thought that she loved the beard as I did—it was a fine beard. But she did not—or, if she did, she would not let it stand before Don Felix's objection.

"So, I cut it off!" my grandfather said. He brushed his hand under his chin. "That was a mistake. I should have held to my first thought. I should have defended myself. I should have left my place and sought another job in Tangier—or Gibraltar or La Linea[14] where there are fine hotels. *I* was doing the waiting, and *I* should have thought of *myself*." He stopped and stared at me.

Beard presented as a symbol of grandfather's integrity and independence.

---

13. major-domo: latin, literally "the head of the house" used for the head waiter or steward of a restaurant.

14. La Linea: a Spanish seaport across the Strait of Gibraltar from Morocco.

"Thou seest?" he said. "Stop thou at the first mistake. Stop there."

I nodded, and he pressed my shoulder again and then reached over and lifted me on to his lap. He cradled my head on his shoulder and rocked slowly back and forth. "We must gladden ourselves," he said, "before she comes. We must gladden ourselves and be smiling. This is difficult for her, too. Difficult. We must gladden ourselves, now. Yes! We must gladden ourselves for her."

I was nodding my head to say, Yes, when my forehead felt something wet, and I looked up and saw that the tears were falling down his cheeks.

Story Analysis

To understand a story and really get the most from it you should probably read it twice. The first time you meet the characters, notice the setting and atmosphere, and watch the action build, peak and fall. However, on your second reading you will notice details that you missed the first time. On your second reading the importance of various conflicts and the way they influence and parallel each other will be clearer to you. The understanding of the central theme will deepen. See how Prudencio de Pereda used some of the elements of the short story.

Plot

The plot or sequence of events and incidents in "Conquistador" begins when the narrator goes to stay, with his grandparents. A good deal of background material has been filled in. The narrator's father has been introduced and a speech characteristic of him has been reported. The boy's brothers are also introduced and a few brief scenes between him and his older brother having to do with the cigar business are presented.

The central episode of the story centers around the Fourth of

July. And the main incident is a visit from the boy's uncle and the subsequent outing the boy and his grandfather take with him.

You have read that plot and conflict are closely related and that it is conflict that sets in motion a sequence of events. In "Conquistador" there are three major conflicts in each of which the boy's grandfather is the protagonist, or the character around whom the action centers. In the first conflict the antagonist is his wife, the boy's grandmother. This conflict has to do with American ways and the grandfather's independence and integrity. In the second conflict the antagonist is the boy's uncle Agapito. This conflict also has to do with independence, but it is a more overt kind of conflict and it involves some suspense and danger when the uncle involves the grandfather and the boy in a swindle and leaves them for awhile during which time they might be discovered in their fraud and would be liable for arrest and conviction.

The tension that is created in the opening situation is reflected in the second conflict. What grandmother expects of grandfather is the exact opposite of what uncle Agapito expects of him. What uncle Agapito expects is that grandfather will be his accomplice in his crime. The expectation is open and obvious. What grandmother expects is more subtle, less obvious. It is more often implied than expressed. It is implied through irony, both in what she says and what she leaves unsaid.

The scene in the saloon with the cigars and the easily dooped saloonkeeper is the most suspenseful—it is like observing a crime and wondering if the crime will be discovered, wondering if the criminals will be suspected. Much of the suspense is built up through the dialogue between the grandfather and the boy as they discuss what they should do about the predicament uncle Agapito has gotten them into. Much of the action also goes on in the boy's head as he realizes more and more of the truth of the situation.

Perhaps the major conflict in the story however is between grandfather and himself; between what he would like to have been and what he has become; between honor, dignity and independence and what he considers his own weakness, dependence and venialness. In this third conflict the antagonist you could say is grandfather's own inner self. As he observes, people must make up their own minds about what they will do, who they will become.

You have heard that a plot is a sequence of events or incidents. Yet these events and incidents do not have to be told in the same sequence in which they occurred. Writers may use the technique called *flashback*. They may interrupt the logical sequence of time and relate an episode or a scene that occurred prior to the present situation. There are two flashbacks in "Conquistador." Both of them have to do with grandfather's conflict with his wife and his conflict with himself. The first flashback has to do with grandfather's life as a waiter in Spain and in Spanish Morocco. This flashback accounts for the facts that brought grandfather and his bride from Morocco to the United States. The first flashback sets up a contrast: in Morocco "Grandfather was content. He didn't want to leave." In America (after he had been bullied by his wife's brother to come to the United States and accept a less honorable profession than waiter, as a *teveriano,* a junk dealer, his daughter would say grandfather "was just not a good salesman." Life in the old country was good for grandfather. Life in the new country—forced on him by his wife's brother, who resented her marrying a mere waiter—was hateful and unsuccessful for him. The second flashback also involves grandfather's life in Tangier, his life as a waiter. It involves his beard which becomes a symbol of his independence and his integrity. In this flashback, grandfather is forced to remove his beard because it gives him too much a look of authority and his immediate superior is jealous of the attention the customers of the restaurant give to him. Grandmother, whom grandfather expects to support him ("I had thought that she loved the beard as I did—it was a fine beard," he says) does not in the matter of the beard. So grandfather is forced to remove his beard and later to move to the United States and take up a new profession. These two flashbacks provide clues to grandfather's conflicts with grandmother and also for the inner conflict that he is having about his own integrity and independence.

Yet, despite the mistakes grandfather thinks he has made because of his wife and her family, the story ends with his assertion of love for her and his tears of both regret and love.

Character Portrayal

Characterization is one of the most important elements in "Conquistador." None of the characters are simply good or bad. All of them are complex. Even the narrator's father who is only briefly introduced has some complexity of feeling. While he continues in the cigar trade and is employing his oldest son to run errands, his feelings are mixed about the cigar business.

One of the major characters in the story is Agapito. When he is first introduced the narrator gives us some descriptive details. He is warm and laughing in his conversation with grandmother and he is respectful of her. We are told that he is very young and has only recently come to the United States and yet that he is already famous—and criticized—in the community. We are told how he is dressed and how his appearance strikes the narrator: "I thought he looked like the perfect man of the world." Agapito is described physically: he had "neat white teeth and a small black moustache"; "He had dark Spanish skin, and I thought he was very handsome." But he is also characterized by what he does and what he says. We see his self assurance in Miguelin's shop and his bravado with the saloonkeeper, filling the narrator with "rage, but fascination." Agapito is a scoundrel and a swindler but he is not an uncomplicated villain. The reader's feelings towards him will probably be as mixed as the boy's are. The complexity of his character is also indicated by his ingenious defense for his deception.

A much more interesting and sympathetic character, of course, is the grandfather. For characterizing grandfather, the author uses several techniques:

1. He tells us how grandfather looks and what his background is.
2. He presents grandfather's conversation both inside his family circle and in public at Monaghan's.
3. He shows the reactions of grandmother, Agapito and the narrator to grandfather's behavior, and in some instances gives their remarks and conversations with him.
4. He reveals grandfather's attitudes towards others, particularly towards the boy.
5. He contrasts grandfather's attitude towards the cigar business, particularly with Agapito's.
6. He describes grandfather's reactions at key moments in the story.

What the narrator says about grandfather tells us a lot about grandfather's character. We are told that he is "mild and sad." "I felt too sorry for my grandfather," the boy says. The interaction between them which is the final outcome of the story also illustrates a great deal about grandfather and his feelings about himself.

His conflict with himself which is symbolized by his lost beard is explained to the boy in the advice grandfather gives him.

Setting and Atmosphere

Physical setting is a very important ingredient in the total meaning of "Conquistador." It is treated with some detail. The tenement districts of Hoboken and Brooklyn are mentioned. They are contrasted with the Borough Hall district where the boy's father has a store. The store plays a role in establishing both setting and atmosphere and two other settings in the store may be compared or contrasted with it.

Miguelin's shop is small, old and dusty. Miguelin himself "was a little, gray old man." The narrator himself compares Monaghan's saloon, where a central episode takes place, with his father's shop.

Setting and atmosphere are further enhanced by mention of elevated railways and open summer trolleys and the dock section of Brooklyn, which suggest far away times.

In addition, these factors should be considered in noting how atmosphere contributes to the total effect of the story:

1. The story takes place on the Fourth of July. Why is this holiday an appropriate background for the major conflicts in the story?
2. The boy's father says, "Let them raise the blood to my face in shame. . . ."; his grandfather says, "Yes, hombre" to Agapito, and to the boy, "Thou must forget that thou heardst today, what thou sawst. . . . Thou wilt understand this some day." Why are these expressions appropriate to the story? How do they help to establish setting and atmosphere?

Point of View

As indicated in the marginal notes, the author has used a first-person narrator. Interestingly, you never find out the narrator's name. He is always referred to as "the boy" and is addressed as thou or you. The story is obviously written by an adult, yet he chooses to relate events as they would be observed by an alert eight-year-old. In a controversy between grandmother and grandfather, he is aware of the tension and says "I knew I should have left the room then. . . ." Grandfather realizes that the boy is not entirely ignorant of what has been going on. The boy also shows some sophistication when grandmother mentions grandfather's former beard. Grandfather asks, "Dost thou know what she referred to in that of the beard?" "'No, Grandfather,' I lied" the boy reports. What effect is the author trying to create by limiting the narrator's scope of knowledge?

Levels of Interpretation

Most stories can be interpreted on more than one level. The first or basic level is simply the plot itself, the chain of events in the story. Other levels of meaning in "Conquistador" lead the reader to an understanding of what the story is really about.

The central episode of "Conquistador" is interesting and suspenseful enough to satisfy most readers. The setting and the characters are exotic enough to hold our interest. It is always interesting to observe a con-man at work, and Agapito is a flamboyant enough character to capture our attention.

But the central episode is no more than that. It is an illustration of the characters, actions and themes of several other parts of the story.

Because of the framework the author presents, we are interested in the Spanish in America—the foreigners, the displaced, the emigrants. This is an important element in the whole meaning of the story. "Grandmother had a great dislike for everything American," the narrator tells us, "She had been a great lady in Spain."

There is also the framework of the cigar business which is related to the nationality of the characters. Within that strand of the story there is also the tension between the honest cigar dealers and the *teveriano,* the dishonest one. A further tension is between Agapito, a successful *teveriano* and grandfather, an unsuccessful one. All of these themes and subplots add to the resonance of the central figure, grandfather.

In grandfather and his regard for his dignity and independence, we have a universal character and a universal theme in which all people can see themselves. The universal character and theme transcend the local circumstances of Brooklyn and the cigar business whether honest or dishonest and strikes the reader as something that must concern us all.

JAMES RAMSEY ULLMAN
(1907–1971)

James Ramsey Ullman was born in New York and died in Boston, but much of his life was spent in exotic places mountain climbing or beach combing. He was a freelance writer and journalist who wrote about what he knew firsthand. During the 1930s he wrote and produced plays; after that period he became increasingly interested in mountain climbing and exploring, and his books reflected those interests. In 1963, he was a member of the American Mount Everest expedition. His life appears to have been as exciting as his stories. Among his many books are: *The Other Side of the Mountain, High Conquest, The White Tower, Island of the Blue Macaws, Banner in the Sky, The Age of Mountaineering, Down the Colorado with Major Powell,* and *Americans on Everest.*

TOP MAN

The gorge bent. The walls fell suddenly away, and we came out on the edge of a bleak, boulder-strewn valley. . . . *And there it was.*

Osborn saw it first. He had been leading the column, threading his way slowly among the huge rock masses of the gorge's mouth. Then he came to the first flat bare place and stopped. He neither pointed nor cried out, but every man behind him knew instantly what it was. The long file sprang taut, like a jerked rope. As swiftly as we could, but in complete silence, we came out one by one into the open space where Osborn stood, and we raised our eyes with his.

In the records of the Indian Topographical Survey it says: "Kalpurtha: altitude 27,930 feet. The highest peak in the Garhwal Himalayas and probably fourth highest in the world. Also known as K3. A Tertiary formation of sedimentary limestone. . . ."

There were men among us who had spent months of their lives—in some cases years—reading, thinking, planning about what now lay before us; but at that moment statistics and geology, knowledge, thought, and plans, were as remote and forgotten as the faraway western cities from which we had come. We were men bereft of everything but eyes, everything but the single electric perception: *there it was!*

Before us the valley stretched into miles of rocky desolation. To right and left it was bounded by low ridges, which, as the eye followed them, slowly mounted and drew closer together, until the valley was no longer a valley at all, but a narrowing, rising corridor between the cliffs. What happened then I can describe only as a stupendous crash of music. At the end of the corridor and above it—so far above it that it shut out half the sky—hung the blinding white mass of K3.

It was like the many pictures I had seen, and at the same time utterly unlike them. The shape was there, and the familiar distinguishing features: the sweeping skirt of glaciers; the monstrous vertical precipices of the face and the jagged ice-line of the east ridge; finally, the symmetrical summit pyramid that transfixed the sky. But whereas in the pictures the mountain had always seemed unreal—a dream-image of cloud, snow, and crystal—it was now no longer an image at all. It was a mass: solid, immanent, appalling. We were still too far away to see the windy whipping of its snow plumes or to hear the cannonading of its avalanches, but in that sudden silent moment every man of us was for the first time aware of it not as a picture in his mind, but as a thing, an antagonist. For all its twenty-eight thousand feet of lofty grandeur it seemed, somehow, less to tower than to crouch—a white-hooded giant, secret and remote, but living. Living and on guard.

I turned my eyes from the dazzling glare and looked at my companions. Osborn still stood a little in front of the others. He was absolutely motionless, his young face tense and shining, his eyes devouring the mountain as a lover's might devour the form of his beloved. One could feel in the very set of his body the overwhelming desire that swelled in him to act, to come to grips, to conquer. A little behind him were ranged the other white men of the expedition: Randolph, our leader, Wittmer and Johns, Dr. Schlapp and Bixler. All were still, their eyes cast upward. Off to one side a little stood Nace, the Englishman, the only one among us who was not staring at K3 for the first time. He had been the last to come up out of the gorge and stood now with arms folded on his chest, squinting at the great peak he had known so long and fought so tirelessly and fiercely. His lean British face, under its mask of stubble and windburn, was expressionless. His lips were a thin line, and his eyes seemed almost shut. Behind the sahibs[1] ranged the porters, bent forward over their staffs, their brown seamed faces straining upward from beneath their loads.

For a long while no one spoke or moved. The only sounds between earth and sky were the soft hiss of our breathing and the pounding of our hearts.

Through the long afternoon we wound slowly between the great boulders of the valley and at sundown pitched camp in the bed of a dried-up stream. The porters ate their rations in silence, wrapped themselves in their blankets, and fell asleep under the stars. The rest of us, as was our custom, sat close about the fire that blazed in the circle of tents, discussing the events of the day and the plans for the next. It was a flawlessly clear Himalayan night, and K3 tiered[2] up into the blackness like a monstrous beacon lighted from within. There was no wind, but a great tide of cold air crept down the valley from the ice fields above, penetrating our clothing, pressing gently against the canvas of the tents.

"Another night or two and we'll be needing the sleeping bags," commented Randolph.

Osborn nodded. "We could use them tonight would be my guess."

Randolph turned to Nace. "What do you say, Martin?"

The Englishman puffed at his pipe a moment. "Rather think it might be better to wait," he said at last.

"Wait? Why?" Osborn jerked his head up.

"Well, it gets pretty nippy high up, you know. I've seen it thirty below at twenty-five thousand on the east ridge. Longer we wait for the bags, better acclimated we'll get."

Osborn snorted. "A lot of good being acclimated will do, if we have frozen feet."

"Easy, Paul, easy," cautioned Randolph. "It seems to me Martin's right."

Osborn bit his lip, but said nothing. The other men entered the conversation, and soon it had veered to other matters: the weather, the porters and pack animals, routes, camps, and strategy, the inevitable, inexhaustible topics of the climber's world.

There were all kinds of men among the eight of us, men with a great diversity of background and interest. Sayre Randolph,

---

1. **sahibs** (sä'ĭbs): a word used in India to refer to people of high rank.
2. **tiered** (tērd) **up:** rose upward in rows or *tiers*.

whom the Alpine Club had named leader of our expedition, had for years been a well-known explorer and lecturer. Now in his middle fifties, he was no longer equal to the grueling physical demands of high climbing, but served as planner and organizer of the enterprise. Wittmer was a Seattle lawyer, who had recently made a name for himself by a series of difficult ascents in the Coast Range of British Columbia. Johns was an Alaskan, a fantastically strong, able sourdough,[3] who had been a ranger in the U.S. Forestry Service and had accompanied many famous Alaskan expeditions. Schlapp was a practicing physician from Milwaukee, Bixler a government meteorologist with a talent for photography. I, at the time, was an assistant professor of geology at an eastern university.

Finally, and preeminently, there were Osborn and Nace. I say "preeminently" because, even at this time, when we had been together as a party for little more than a month, I believe all of us realized that these were the two key men of our venture. None, to my knowledge, ever expressed it in words, but the conviction was none the less there that if any of us were eventually to stand on the summit of K3, it would be one of them, or both. They were utterly dissimilar men. Osborn was twenty-three and a year out of college, a compact, buoyant mass of energy and high spirits. He seemed to be wholly unaffected by either the physical or mental hazards of mountaineering and had already, by virtue of many spectacular ascents in the Alps and Rockies, won a reputation as the most skilled and audacious of younger American climbers. Nace was in his forties—lean, taciturn,[4] introspective. An official in the Indian Civil Service, he had explored and climbed in the Himalayas for twenty years. He had been a member of all five of the unsuccessful British expeditions to K3, and in his last attempt had attained to within five hundred feet of the summit, the highest point which any man had reached on the unconquered giant. This had been the famous, tragic attempt in which his fellow climber and lifelong friend, Captain Furness, had slipped and fallen ten thousand feet to his death. Nace rarely mentioned his name, but on the steel head of his ice ax were engraved the words: TO MARTIN FROM JOHN. If fate were to grant that the ax of any one of us should be planted upon the summit of K3, I hoped it would be this one.

3. **sourdough:** *slang,* pioneer or prospector.
4. **taciturn** (tas′ə·tûrn): reserved, quiet.

Such were the men who huddled about the fire in the deep, still cold of a Himalayan night. There were many differences among us, in temperament as well as in background. In one or two cases, notably that of Osborn and Nace, there had already been a certain amount of friction, and as the venture continued and the struggles and hardships of the actual ascent began, it would, I knew, increase. But differences were unimportant. What mattered—all that mattered—was that our purpose was one: to conquer the monster of rock and ice that now loomed above us in the night; to stand for a moment where no man, no living thing, had ever stood before. To that end we had come from half a world away, across oceans and continents to the fastnesses[5] of inner Asia. To that end we were prepared to endure cold, exhaustion, and danger, even to the very last extremity of human endurance. . . . Why? There is no answer, and at the same time every man among us knew the answer; every man who has ever looked upon a great mountain and felt the fever in his blood to climb and conquer knows the answer. George Leigh Mallory, greatest of mountaineers, expressed it once and for all when he was asked why he wanted to climb unconquered Everest.

"I want to climb it," said Mallory, "because it is there."

Day after day we crept on and upward. Sometimes the mountain was brilliant above us, as it had been when we first saw it; sometimes it was partially or wholly obscured by tiers of clouds. The naked desolation of the valley was unrelieved by any motion, color, or sound; and as we progressed, the great rock walls that enclosed it grew so high and steep that its floor received the sun for less than two hours each day. The rest of the time it lay in ashen half-light, its gloom intensified by the dazzling brilliance of the ice slopes above. As long as we remained there we had the sensation of imprisonment; it was like being trapped at the bottom of a deep well or in a sealed court between great skyscrapers. Soon we were thinking of the ascent of the shining mountain not only as an end in itself, but as an escape.

In our nightly discussions around the fire our conversation narrowed more and more to the immediate problems confronting us, and during them I began to realize that the tension between Osborn and Nace went deeper than I had at first surmised. There

5. **fastnesses:** fortresses or strongholds.

was rarely any outright argument between them—they were both far too able mountain men to disagree on fundamentals—but I saw that at almost every turn they were rubbing each other the wrong way. It was a matter of personalities, chiefly. Osborn was talkative, enthusiastic, optimistic, always chafing to be up and at it, always wanting to take the short straight line to the given point. Nace, on the other hand, was matter-of-fact, cautious, slow. He was the apostle of trial-and-error and watchful waiting. Because of his far greater experience and intimate knowledge of K3, Randolph almost invariably followed his advice, rather than Osborn's, when a difference of opinion arose. The younger man usually capitulated with good grace, but I could tell that he was irked.

During the days in the valley I had few occasions to talk privately with either of them, and only once did either mention the other in any but the most casual manner. Even then, the remarks they made seemed unimportant and I remember them only in view of what happened later.

My conversation with Osborn occurred first. It was while we were on the march, and Osborn, who was directly behind me, came up suddenly to my side. "You're a geologist, Frank," he began without preamble. "What do you think of Nace's theory about the ridge?"

"What theory?" I asked.

"He believes we should traverse[6] under it from the glacier up. Says the ridge itself is too exposed."

"It looks pretty mean through the telescope."

"But it's been done before. He's done it himself. All right, it's tough—I'll admit that. But a decent climber could make it in half the time the traverse will take."

"Nace knows the traverse is longer," I said. "But he seems certain it will be much easier for us."

"Easier for *him* is what he means." Osborn paused, looking moodily at the ground. "He was a great climber in his day. It's a shame a man can't be honest enough with himself to know when he's through." He fell silent and a moment later dropped back into his place in line.

It was that same night, I think, that I awoke to find Nace sitting up in his blanket and staring at the mountain.

"How clear it is!" I whispered.

---

6. **traverse** (trăv'ərs): In climbing, to crisscross instead of going straight up.

The Englishman pointed. "See the ridge?"

I nodded, my eyes fixed on the great, twisting spine of ice that climbed into the sky. I could see now, more clearly than in the blinding sunlight, its huge indentations and jagged, wind-swept pitches. "It looks impossible," I said.

"No, it can be done. Trouble is, when you've made it you're too done in for the summit."

"Osborn seems to think its shortness would make up for its difficulty."

Nace was silent a long moment before answering. Then for the first and only time I heard him speak the name of his dead companion. "That's what Furness thought," he said quietly. Then he lay down and wrapped himself in his blanket.

For the next two weeks the uppermost point of the valley was our home and workshop. We established our base camp as close to the mountain as we could, less than half a mile from the tongue of its lowest glacier, and plunged into the arduous tasks of preparation for the ascent. Our food and equipment were unpacked, inspected and sorted, and finally repacked in lighter loads for transportation to more advanced camps. Hours were spent poring over maps and charts and studying the monstrous heights above us through telescope and binoculars. Under Nace's supervision, a thorough reconnaissance of the glacier was made and the route across it laid out; then began the backbreaking labor of moving up supplies and establishing the chain of camps.

Camps I and II were set up on the glacier itself, in the most sheltered sites we could find. Camp III we built at its upper end, as near as possible to the point where the great rock spine of K3 thrust itself free of ice and began its precipitous ascent. According to our plans, this would be the advance base of operations during the climb. The camps to be established higher up, on the mountain proper, would be too small and too exposed to serve as anything more than one or two nights' shelter. The total distance between the base camp and Camp III was only fifteen miles, but the utmost daily progress of our porters was five miles, and it was essential that we should never be more than twelve hours' march from food and shelter. Hour after hour, day after day, the long file of men wound up and down among the hummocks[7] and crevasses of the

7. **hummocks:** here, mounds of ice.

glacier, and finally the time arrived when we were ready to advance.

Leaving Dr. Schlapp in charge of eight porters at the base camp, we proceeded easily and on schedule, reaching Camp I the first night, Camp II the second, and the advance base the third. No men were left at Camps I and II, inasmuch as they were designed simply as caches for food and equipment; and furthermore we knew we would need all the manpower available for the establishment of the higher camps on the mountain proper.

For more than three weeks now the weather had held perfectly, but on our first night at the advance base, as if by malignant prearrangement of nature, we had our first taste of the fury of a high Himalayan storm. It began with great streamers of lightning that flashed about the mountain like a halo; then heavily through the weird glare, snow began to fall. The wind rose. At first it was only sound—a remote, desolate moaning in the night high above us—but soon it descended, sucked down the deep valley as if into a gigantic funnel. Hour after hour it howled about the tents with hurricane frenzy, and the wild flapping of the canvas dinned in our ears like machine-gun fire.

There was no sleep for us that night or the next. For thirty-six hours the storm raged without lull, while we huddled in the icy gloom of the tents, exerting our last ounce of strength to keep from being buried alive or blown into eternity. At last, on the third morning, it was over, and we came out into a world transformed by a twelve-foot cloak of snow. No single landmark remained as it had been before, and our supplies and equipment were in the wildest confusion. Fortunately there had not been a single serious injury, but it was another three days before we had regained our strength and put the camp in order.

Then we waited. The storm did not return, and the sky beyond the ridges gleamed flawlessly clear; but night and day we could hear the roaring thunder of avalanches on the mountain above us. To have ventured so much as one step into that savage vertical wilderness before the new-fallen snow froze tight would have been suicidal. We chafed or waited patiently, according to our individual temperaments, while the days dragged by.

It was late one afternoon that Osborn returned from a short reconnaissance up on the ridge. His eyes were shining and his voice jubilant.

"It's tight!" he cried. "Tight as a drum. We can go!" All of us stopped whatever we were doing. His excitement leaped like an electric spark from one to another. "I went about a thousand feet, and it's sound all the way. What do you say, Sayre? Tomorrow?"

Randolph hesitated, then looked at Nace.

"Better give it another day or two," said the Englishman.

Osborn glared at him. "Why?" he challenged.

"It's usually safer to wait till—"

"Wait! Wait!" Osborn exploded. "Don't you ever think of anything but waiting? My God, man, the snow's firm, I tell you!"

"It's firm down here," Nace replied quietly, "because the sun hits it only two hours a day. Up above it gets the sun twelve hours. It may not have frozen yet."

"The avalanches have stopped."

"That doesn't necessarily mean it will hold a man's weight."

"It seems to me Martin's point—" Randolph began.

Osborn wheeled on him. "Sure," he snapped. "I know. Martin's right. The cautious bloody English are always right. Let him have his way, and we'll be sitting here chewing our nails until the mountain falls down on us." His eyes flashed to Nace. "Maybe with a little less of that bloody cautiousness you English wouldn't have made such a mess of Everest. Maybe your pals Mallory and Furness wouldn't be dead."

"Osborn!" commanded Randolph sharply.

The youngster stared at Nace for another moment, breathing heavily. Then abruptly he turned away.

The next two days were clear and windless, but we still waited, following Nace's advice. There were no further brushes between him and Osborn, but an unpleasant air of restlessness and tension hung over the camp. I found myself chafing almost as impatiently as Osborn himself for the moment when we would break out of that maddening inactivity and begin the assault.

At last the day came. With the first paling of the sky a roped file of men, bent almost double beneath heavy loads, began slowly to climb the ice slope, just beneath the jagged line of the great east ridge. In accordance with prearranged plan, we proceeded in relays, this first group consisting of Nace, Johns, myself, and eight porters. It was our job to ascend approximately two thousand feet in a day's climbing and establish Camp IV at the most level and sheltered site we could find. We would spend the night there and return to the advance base next day, while the second relay, consisting of Osborn, Wittmer, and eight more porters, went up with their loads. This process was to continue until all necessary supplies were at Camp IV, and then the whole thing would be repeated between Camps IV and V and V and VI. From VI, at an altitude of about twenty-six thousand feet, the ablest and fittest men—presumably Nace and Osborn—would make the direct assault on the summit. Randolph and Bixler were to remain at the advance base throughout the operations, acting as directors and co-ordinators. We were under the strictest orders that any man—sahib or porter—who suffered illness or injury should be brought down immediately.

How shall I describe those next two weeks beneath the great ice ridge of K3? In a sense there was no occurrence of importance, and at the same time everything happened that could possibly happen, short of actual disaster. We established Camp IV, came down again, went up again, came down again. Then we crept laboriously higher. With our axes we hacked uncountable thousands of steps in the gleaming walls of ice. Among the rocky outcroppings of the cliffs we clung to holds and strained at ropes until we thought our arms would spring from their sockets. Storms swooped down on us, battered us, and passed. The wind increased, and the air grew steadily colder and more difficult to breathe. One morning two of the porters awoke with their feet frozen black; they had to be sent down. A short while later Johns developed an uncontrollable nosebleed and was forced to descend to a lower camp. Wittmer was suffering from racking headaches and I from a continually dry throat. But providentially, the one enemy we feared the most in that icy gale-lashed hell did not again attack us. No snow fell. And day by day, foot by foot, we ascended.

It is during ordeals like this that the surface trappings of a man are shed and his secret mettle[8] laid bare. There were no shirkers or quitters among us—I had known that from the beginning—but now, with each passing day, it became more manifest which were the strongest and ablest among us. Beyond all argument, these were Osborn and Nace.

Osborn was magnificent. All the boyish impatience and

8. **mettle** (mĕt′l): courage, spirit.

moodiness which he had exhibited earlier were gone, and, now that he was at last at work in his natural element, he emerged as the peerless mountaineer he was. His energy was inexhaustible, his speed, both on rock and ice, almost twice that of any other man in the party. He was always discovering new routes and short cuts. Often he ascended by the ridge itself, instead of using the traverse beneath it, as had been officially prescribed; but his craftsmanship was so sure and his performance so brilliant that no one ever thought of taking him to task. Indeed, there was such vigor, buoyancy, and youth in everything he did that it gave heart to all the rest of us.

In contrast, Nace was slow, methodical, unspectacular. Since he and I worked in the same relay, I was with him almost constantly, and to this day I carry in my mind the clear image of the man: his tall body bent almost double against endless shimmering slopes of ice; his lean brown face bent in utter concentration on the problem in hand, then raised searchingly to the next; the bright prong of his ax rising, falling, rising, falling, with tireless rhythm, until the steps in the glassy incline were so wide and deep that the most clumsy of the porters could not have slipped from them had he tried. Osborn attacked the mountain head on. Nace studied it, sparred with it, wore it down. His spirit did not flap from his sleeve like a pennon;[9] it was deep inside him—patient, indomitable.

The day soon came when I learned from him what it is to be a great mountaineer. We were making the ascent from Camp IV to V, and an almost perpendicular ice wall had made it necessary for us to come out for a few yards on the exposed crest of the ridge. There were six of us in the party, roped together, with Nace leading, myself second, and four porters bringing up the rear. The ridge at this particular point was free of snow, but razor-thin, and the rocks were covered with a smooth glaze of ice. On either side the mountain dropped away in sheer precipices of five thousand feet.

Suddenly the last porter slipped. I heard the ominous scraping of boot nails behind me and, turning, saw a gesticulating figure plunge sideways into the abyss. There was a scream as the next porter was jerked off too. I remember trying frantically to dig into the ridge with my ax, realizing at the same time it would no more

9. **pennon** (pĕn′ən): flag.

hold against the weight of the falling men than a pin stuck in a wall. Then I heard Nace shout, "Jump!" As he said it, the rope went tight about my waist, and I went hurtling after him into space on the opposite side of the ridge. After me came the nearest porter. . . .

What happened then must have happened in five yards and a fifth of a second. I heard myself cry out, and the glacier, a mile below, rushed up at me, spinning. Then both were blotted out in a violent spasm, as the rope jerked taut. I hung for a moment, an inert mass, feeling that my body had been cut in two; then I swung in slowly to the side of the mountain. Above me the rope lay tight and motionless across the crest of the ridge, our weight exactly counterbalancing that of the men who had fallen on the far slope.

Nace's voice came up from below. "You chaps on the other side!" he shouted. "Start climbing slowly. We're climbing too."

In five minutes we had all regained the ridge. The porters and I crouched panting on the jagged rocks, our eyes closed, the sweat beading our faces in frozen drops. Nace carefully examined the rope that again hung loosely between us.

"All right, men," he said presently. "Let's get on to camp for a cup of tea."

Above Camp V the whole aspect of the ascent changed. The angle of the ridge eased off, and the ice, which lower down had covered the mountain like a sheath, lay only in scattered patches between the rocks. Fresh enemies, however, instantly appeared to take the place of the old. We were now laboring at an altitude of more than twenty-five thousand feet—well above the summits of the highest surrounding peaks—and day and night, without protection or respite, we were buffeted by the fury of the wind. Worse than this was that the atmosphere had become so rarefied it could scarcely support life. Breathing itself was a major physical effort, and our progress upward consisted of two or three painful steps followed by a long period of rest in which our hearts pounded wildly and our burning lungs gasped for air. Each of us carried a small cylinder of oxygen in his pack, but we used it only in emergencies and found that, while its immediate effect was salutary, it left us later even worse off than before. My throat dried and contracted until it felt as if it were lined with brass. The faces of all of us, under our beards and windburn, grew haggard and strained.

But the great struggle was now mental as much as physical. The lack of air induced a lethargy of mind and spirit; confidence and the powers of thought and decision waned, and dark foreboding crept out from the secret recesses of the subconscious. The wind seemed to carry strange sounds, and we kept imagining we saw things which we knew were not there. The mountain, to all of us, was no longer a mere giant of rock and ice; it had become a living thing, an enemy, watching us, waiting for us, hostile, relentless, and aware. Inch by inch we crept upward through that empty forgotten world above the world, and only one last thing remained to us of human consciousness and human will: to go on. To go on.

On the fifteenth day after we had first left the advance base we pitched Camp VI at an altitude of almost twenty-six thousand feet. It was located near the uppermost extremity of the great east ridge, directly beneath the so-called shoulder of the mountain. On the far side of the shoulder the monstrous north face of K3 fell sheer to the glaciers, two miles below. And above it and to the left rose the symmetrical bulk of the summit pyramid. The topmost rocks of its highest pinnacle were clearly visible from the shoulder, and the intervening two thousand feet seemed to offer no insuperable obstacles.

Camp VI, which was in reality no camp at all, but a single tent, was large enough to accommodate only three men. Osborn established it with the aid of Wittmer and one porter; then, the following morning, Wittmer and the porter descended to Camp V, and Nace and I went up. It was our plan that Osborn and Nace should launch the final assault—the next day, if the weather held—with myself in support, following their progress through binoculars and going to their aid or summoning help from below if anything went wrong. As the three of us lay in the tent that night, the summit seemed already within arm's reach, victory securely in our grasp.

And then the blow fell. With malignant timing, which no power on earth could have made us believe was a simple accident of nature, the mountain hurled at us its last line of defense. It snowed.

For a day and a night the great flakes drove down on us, swirling and swooping in the wind, blotting out the summit, the shoulder, everything beyond the tiny white-walled radius of our tents. Hour after hour we lay in our sleeping bags, stirring only to eat or to secure the straining rope and canvas. Our feet froze under their thick layers of wool and rawhide. Our heads and bodies throbbed with a dull nameless aching, and time crept over our numbed minds like a glacier. At last, during the morning of the following day, it cleared. The sun came out in a thin blue sky, and the summit pyramid again appeared above us, now whitely robed in fresh snow. But still we waited. Until the snow either froze or was blown away by the wind it would have been the rashest courting of destruction for us to have ascended a foot beyond the camp. Another day passed. And another.

By the third nightfall our nerves were at the breaking point. For hours on end we had scarcely moved or spoken, and the only sounds in all the world were the endless moaning of the wind outside and the harsh sucking noise of our breathing. I knew that, one way or another, the end had come. Our meager food supply was running out; even with careful rationing there was enough left for only two more days.

Presently Nace stirred in his sleeping bag and sat up. "We'll have to go down tomorrow," he said quietly.

For a moment there was silence in the tent. Then Osborn struggled to a sitting position and faced him.

"No," he said.

"There's still too much loose snow above. We can't make it."

"But it's clear. As long as we can see—"

Nace shook his head. "Too dangerous. We'll go down tomorrow and lay in a fresh supply. Then we'll try again."

"Once we go down we're licked. You know it."

Nace shrugged. "Better to be licked than . . ." The strain of speech was suddenly too much for him and he fell into a violent paroxysm of coughing. When it had passed there was a long silence.

Then suddenly Osborn spoke again. "Look, Nace," he said, "I'm going up tomorrow."

The Englishman shook his head.

"I'm going—understand?"

For the first time since I had known him I saw Nace's eyes flash in anger. "I'm the senior member of this group," he said. "I forbid you to go!"

Osborn jerked himself to his knees, almost upsetting the tiny tent. "You forbid me? This may be your sixth time on this mountain, and all that, but you don't *own* it! I know what you're up to.

You haven't got it in you to make the top yourself, so you don't want anyone else to make it. That's it, isn't it? Isn't it?" He sat down again suddenly, gasping for breath.

Nace looked at him with level eyes. "This mountain has beaten me five times," he said softly. "It killed my best friend. It means more to me to climb it than anything else in the world. Maybe I'll make it and maybe I won't. But if I do, it will be as a rational intelligent human being—not as a fool throwing my life away. . . ."

He collapsed into another fit of coughing and fell back in his sleeping bag. Osborn, too, was still. They lay there inert, panting, too exhausted for speech.

It was hours later that I awoke from dull, uneasy sleep. In the faint light I saw Nace fumbling with the flap of the tent.

"What is it?" I asked.

"Osborn. He's gone."

The words cut like a blade through my lethargy. I struggled to my feet and followed Nace from the tent.

Outside, the dawn was seeping up the eastern sky. It was very cold, but the wind had fallen and the mountain seemed to hang suspended in a vast stillness. Above us the summit pyramid climbed bleakly into space, like the last outpost of a spent and lifeless planet. Raising my binoculars, I swept them over the gray waste. At first I saw nothing but rock and ice; then, suddenly, something moved.

"I've got him," I whispered.

As I spoke, the figure of Osborn sprang into clear focus against a patch of ice. He took three or four slow upward steps, stopped, went on again. I handed the glasses to Nace.

The Englishman squinted through them, returned them to me, and reentered the tent. When I followed, he had already laced his boots and was pulling on his outer gloves.

"He's not far," he said. "Can't have been gone more than half an hour." He seized his ice ax and started out again.

"Wait," I said. "I'm going with you."

Nace shook his head. "Better stay here."

"I'm going with you," I said.

He said nothing further, but waited while I made ready. In a few moments we left the tent, roped up, and started off.

Almost immediately we were on the shoulder and confronted with the paralyzing two-mile drop of the north face; but we negotiated the short exposed stretch without mishap, and in ten minutes were working up the base of the summit pyramid. The going here was easier, in a purely climbing sense: the angle of ascent was not steep, and there was firm rock for hand- and footholds between the patches of snow and ice. Our progress, however, was creepingly slow. There seemed to be literally no air at all to breathe, and after almost every step we were forced to rest, panting and gasping as we leaned forward against our axes. My heart swelled and throbbed with every movement until I thought it would explode.

The minutes crawled into hours and still we climbed. Presently the sun came up. Its level rays streamed across the clouds, far below, and glinted from the summits of distant peaks. But, although the pinnacle of K3 soared a full three thousand feet above anything in the surrounding world, we had scarcely any sense of height. The wilderness of mountain valley and glacier that spread beneath us to the horizon was flattened and remote, an unreal, insubstantial landscape seen in a dream. We had no connection with it, or it with us. All living, all awareness, purpose, and will, was concentrated in the last step and the next: to put one foot before the other; to breathe; to ascend. We struggled on in silence.

I do not know how long it was since we had left the camp—it might have been two hours, it might have been six—when we suddenly sighted Osborn. We had not been able to find him again since our first glimpse through the binoculars; but now, unexpectedly and abruptly, as we came up over a jagged outcropping of rock, there he was. He was at a point, only a few yards above us, where the mountain steepened into an almost vertical wall. The smooth surface directly in front of him was obviously unclimbable, but two alternate routes were presented. To the left, a chimney[10] cut obliquely across the wall, forbiddingly steep, but seeming to offer adequate holds. To the right was a gentle slope of snow that curved upward and out of sight behind the rocks. As we watched, Osborn ascended to the edge of the snow, stopped, and probed it with his ax. Then, apparently satisfied that it would bear his weight he stepped out on the slope.

I felt Nace's body tense. "Paul!" he cried out.

His voice was too weak and hoarse to carry. Osborn continued his ascent.

---

10. **chimney:** formation of rock resembling a chimney.

Nace cupped his hands and called his name again, and this time Osborn turned. "Wait!" cried the Englishman.

Osborn stood still, watching us, as we struggled up the few yards to the edge of the snow slope. Nace's breath came in shuddering gasps, but he climbed faster than I had ever seen him climb before.

"Come back!" he called. "Come off the snow!"

"It's all right. The crust is firm," Osborn called back.

"But it's melting. There's . . ." Nace paused, fighting for air. "There's nothing underneath!"

In a sudden sickening flash I saw what he meant. Looked at from directly below, at the point where Osborn had come to it, the slope on which he stood appeared as a harmless covering of snow over the rocks. From where we were now, however, a little to one side, it could be seen that it was in reality no covering at all, but merely a cornice or unsupported platform clinging to the side of the mountain. Below it was not rock, but ten thousand feet of blue air.

"Come back!" I cried. "Come back!!"

Osborn hesitated, then took a downward step. But he never took the next. For in that same instant the snow directly in front of him disappeared. It did not seem to fall or to break away. It was just soundlessly and magically no longer there. In the spot where Osborn had been about to set his foot there was now revealed the abysmal drop of the north face of K3.

I shut my eyes, but only for a second, and when I reopened them Osborn was still, miraculously, there. Nace was shouting, "Don't move! Don't move an inch!"

"The rope—" I heard myself saying.

The Englishman shook his head. "We'd have to throw it, and the impact would be too much. Brace yourself and play it out." As he spoke, his eyes were traveling over the rocks that bordered the snow bridge. Then he moved forward.

I wedged myself into a cleft in the wall and let out the rope which extended between us. A few yards away Osborn stood in the snow, transfixed, one foot a little in front of the other. But my eyes now were on Nace. Cautiously, but with astonishing rapidity, he edged along the rocks beside the cornice. There was a moment when his only support was an inch-wide ledge beneath his feet, another where there was nothing under his feet at all, and he supported himself wholly by his elbows and hands. But he advanced steadily and at last reached a shelf wide enough for him to turn around on. At this point he was perhaps six feet away from Osborn.

"It's wide enough here to hold both of us," he said in a quiet voice. "I'm going to reach out my ax. Don't move until you're sure you have a grip on it. When I pull, jump."

He searched the wall behind him and found a hold for his left hand. Then he slowly extended his ice ax, head foremost, until it was within two feet of Osborn's shoulder. "Grip it!" he cried suddenly. Osborn's hands shot out and seized the ax. "Jump!"

There was a flash of steel in the sunlight and a hunched figure hurtled inward from the snow to the ledge. Simultaneously another figure hurtled out. The haft[11] of the ax jerked suddenly from Nace's hand, and he lurched forward and downward. A violent spasm convulsed his body as the rope went taut. Then it was gone. Nace did not seem to hit the snow; he simply disappeared through it, soundlessly. In the same instant the snow itself was gone. The frayed, yellow end of broken rope spun lazily in space. . . .

Somehow my eyes went to Osborn. He was crouched on the ledge where Nace had been a moment before, staring dully at the ax he held in his hands. Beyond his head, not two hundred feet above, the white untrodden pinnacle of K3 stabbed the sky.

Perhaps ten minutes passed, perhaps a half hour. I closed my eyes and leaned forward motionless against the rock, my face against my arm. I neither thought nor felt; my body and mind alike were enveloped in a suffocating numbness. Through it at last came the sound of Osborn moving. Looking up, I saw he was standing beside me.

"I'm going to try for the top," he said tonelessly.

I merely stared at him.

"Will you come?"

"No," I said.

Osborn hesitated; then turned and began slowly climbing the steep chimney above us. Halfway up he paused, struggling for breath. Then he resumed his laborious upward progress and presently disappeared beyond the crest.

I stayed where I was, and the hours passed. The sun reached its zenith above the peak and sloped away behind it. And at last I

11. **haft:** handle.

heard above me the sound of Osborn returning. As I looked up, his figure appeared at the top of the chimney and began the descent. His clothing was in tatters, and I could tell from his movements that only the thin flame of his will stood between him and collapse. In another few minutes he was standing beside me.

"Did you get there?" I asked dully.

He shook his head. "I couldn't make it," he answered. "I didn't have what it takes."

We roped together silently and began the descent to the camp.

There is nothing more to be told of the sixth assault on K3—at least not from the experiences of the men who made it. Osborn and I reached Camp V in safety, and three days later the entire expedition gathered at the advance base. It was decided, in view of the tragedy that had occurred, to make no further attempt on the summit, and by the end of the week we had begun the evacuation of the mountain.

It remained for another year and other men to reveal the epilogue.

The summer following our attempt a combined English-Swiss expedition stormed the peak successfully. After weeks of hardship and struggle they attained the topmost pinnacle of the giant, only to find that what should have been their great moment of triumph was, instead, a moment of the bitterest disappointment. For when they came out at last upon the summit they saw that they were *not* the first. An ax stood there. Its haft was embedded in rock and ice and on its steel head were the engraved words: TO MARTIN FROM JOHN.

They were sporting men. On their return to civilization they told their story, and the name of the conqueror of K3 was made known to the world.

Meaning

1. Most fiction tries to *show* rather than to describe. How does the author demonstrate the differences between Nace and Osborn before he describes them?

2. As has been said, *conflict* in a short story may be **a.** person against person, **b.** individual against society, **c.** human against nature, or **d.** persons against themselves. Which of these conflicts occur in this story? Justify your answer with specific textual references.
3. Moments of decision often reveal what a person is really like. In "Top Man" how do the two central characters act at times of decision? Cite examples. Which do you most admire?

Method

1. The *climax* is the highest point of interest or suspense in a story. It usually marks the turning point, at which the reader can foresee how the struggle will end. What point in this story would you consider the climax? How did the author build toward it?
2. How does the setting of this story become an integral part of the plot? What does it add to the story?
3. *Characterization* may be achieved by **a.** physical description of a character by the author, **b.** a description by another character, **c.** the use of dialogue or conversation, **d.** an explanation of a character's inner thoughts, **e.** the behavior or actions of a character, or **f.** the reactions of a character to another character or to a situation. Which of these methods does Ullman employ? Illustrate your choices with examples from the text.

Language: Meaning from Context

In your reading, you will come across words that are either completely new to you or that you have not noticed before. There are several ways to unlock the meanings of these words. You can consult a dictionary, ask another person, try to relate these words to words you already know, or attack the meaning through context.

Context comes from the Latin prefix *con* (together with) and the Latin verb *texere* (to weave). Applied here, context means the parts of a sentence, paragraph, or speech occurring just before and after a specified word. These words form a setting (a context) which can help to determine the meaning of a particular word when it is used in their company.

For example, look at the following sentences:
1. She flew into a *rage* when she saw her broken vase.
2. Hoop skirts were the *rage* in my grandmother's day.
In the first example, *rage* means violent anger; in the second, it means fashion or fad.

However, it is not unusual for an author to want to suggest ambiguity by using a word with more than one meaning. How might this be true of the title "Top Man"?

When you study a word in context, try to identify the place, time, situation, and speaker or writer associated with each problem word.

Try to define the italicized words in the following sentences, using contextual clues. Then check your definitions with a dictionary.

1. "Osborn was twenty-three and a year out of college, a compact, *buoyant* mass of energy and high spirits."
2. "Osborn was talkative, enthusiastic, optimistic, always *chafing* to be up and at it, always wanting to take the short straight line to a given point."
3. "There were no shirkers or quitters among us—I had known that from the beginning—but now, with each passing day, it became more *manifest* which were the strongest and ablest among us."
4. "The lack of air induced a lethargy of mind and spirit; confidence and the powers of thought and decision waned, and dark *foreboding* crept out from the secret recesses of the subconscious."

Composition

1. Good prose writers often use similes and metaphors to appeal to our senses and emotions. A simile is a comparison using *like* or *as*. For example: "The long file sprang taught, like a jerked rope." A metaphor is a comparison without *like* or *as*. For example: "For all its twenty-eight thousand feet of lofty grandeur it seemed, somehow, less to tower than to crouch—a white hooded giant, secret and remote, but living." Remember that a metaphor may be indicated by a verb or participle, as in "Beyond his head, not two hundred feet above, the white untrodden pinnacle of K3 *stabbed* the sky."

Write a composition in which you explain several of the similes and metaphors that Ullman uses in this story. Begin with the following topic sentence: "In 'Top Man' the author, James Ramsey Ullman, uses a number of imaginative comparisons to make scenes vivid to us." Develop this topic sentence by naming the similes and metaphors and explaining what each one means.

2. Write a character sketch of one of the two principal characters in "Top Man" so that the reader has a complete picture of the person. Try to catch the character's physical, mental, and moral qualities. Use as a guide the methods an author can use for characterization.

JACK LONDON
(1876–1916)

The life story of Jack London is as exciting as any of the novels and stories he wrote. He grew up on the waterfront of Oakland, California. He worked in a bowling alley, a mill, a cannery, and a laundry, led a boy's gang, ran away to sea, traveled over most of the United States as a tramp, prospected for gold in Alaska, and sailed home 1,900 miles in an open boat, all before he was twenty-two years old.

London educated himself primarily at public libraries. He attended high school for one year and the University of California for one year. In *Martin Eden* (1909), his autobiographical novel, he tells how he trained himself to be a professional author, daily studying and producing every kind of writing on a rigid schedule that he set for himself.

London's stories earned him a million dollars and great popularity at the height of his short career. Today he is not considered to be among the greatest of American authors, but his use of realistic detail influenced many other writers.

"To Build a Fire" is typical of London's best work. Here he depicts the splendor and terror of nature, and reveals his ideas about the superiority of animal instinct over human reason.

TO BUILD A FIRE

Day had broken cold and gray, exceedingly cold and gray, when the man turned aside from the main Yukon trail and climbed the high earth bank, where a dim and little-traveled trail led eastward through the fat spruce timberland. It was a steep bank, and he paused for breath at the top, excusing the act to himself by looking at his watch. It was nine o'clock. There was no sun or hint of sun, though there was not a cloud in the sky. It was a clear day, and yet there seemed an intangible pall[1] over the face

---

1. pall (pôl): a dark covering, usually a cloth draped over a coffin. Here it refers to the gloomy atmosphere.

of things, a subtle gloom that made the day dark, and that was due to the absence of sun. This fact did not worry the man. He was used to the lack of sun. It had been days since he had seen the sun, and he knew that a few more days must pass before that cheerful orb, due south, would just peep above the skyline and dip immediately from view.

The man flung a look back along the way he had come. The Yukon lay a mile wide and hidden under three feet of ice. On top of this ice were as many feet of snow. It was all pure white, rolling in gentle undulations[2] where the ice jams of the freeze-up had formed. North and south, as far as his eye could see, it was unbroken white, save for a dark hairline that curved and twisted from around the spruce-covered island to the south, and that curved and twisted away into the north, where it disappeared behind another spruce-covered island. This dark hairline was the trail— the main trail—that led south five hundred miles to the Chilkoot Pass, Dyea,[3] and salt water; and that led north seventy miles to Dawson, and still on to the north a thousand miles to Nulato, and finally to St. Michael on the Bering Sea, a thousand miles and half a thousand more.

But all this—the mysterious, far-reaching hairline trail, the absence of sun from the sky, the tremendous cold, and the strangeness and weirdness of it all—made no impression on the man. It was not because he was long used to it. He was a newcomer in the land, a cheechako,[4] and this was his first winter. The trouble with him was that he was without imagination. He was quick and alert in the things of life, but only in the things, and not in the significances. Fifty degrees below zero meant eighty-odd degrees of frost. Such fact impressed him as being cold and uncomfortable, and that was all. It did not lead him to meditate upon his frailty as a creature of temperature, and upon man's frailty in general, able only to live within certain narrow limits of heat and cold, and from there on it did not lead him to the conjectural[5] field of

2. **undulations** (ŭn′dyə·lā′shəns): waves. The snow had a rolling appearance.
3. **Dyea** (dī′ā): a former village in southeast Alaska. When gold was discovered in 1896 in the Klondike region, Dyea became the supply center and starting point for the trail over the Chilkoot Pass to the northern mining fields and towns such as Dawson and Nulato.
4. **cheechako** (chē·chä′kō): in Alaska, a newcomer; a tenderfoot.
5. **conjectural** (kən·jĕk′chər·əl): based on surmise or guesswork. To conjecture is to come to conclusions using incomplete or merely probable evidence.

immortality and man's place in the universe. Fifty degrees below zero stood for a bite of frost that hurt and that must be guarded against by the use of mittens, ear flaps, warm moccasins, and thick socks. Fifty degrees below zero was to him just precisely fifty degrees below zero. That there should be anything more to it than that was a thought that never entered his head.

As he turned to go on, he spat speculatively. There was a sharp, explosive crackle that startled him. He spat again. And again, in the air, before it could fall to the snow, the spittle crackled. He knew that at fifty below, spittle crackled on the snow, but this spittle had crackled in the air. Undoubtedly it was colder than fifty below—how much colder he did not know. But the temperature did not matter. He was bound for the old claim on the left fork of Henderson Creek, where the boys were already. They had come over across the divide from the Indian Creek country, while he had come the roundabout way to take a look at the possibilities of getting out logs in the spring from the islands in the Yukon. He would be into camp by six o'clock; a bit after dark, it was true, but the boys would be there, a fire would be going, and a hot supper would be ready. As for lunch, he pressed his hand against the protruding bundle under his jacket. It was also under his shirt, wrapped up in a handkerchief and lying against the naked skin. It was the only way to keep the biscuits from freezing. He smiled agreeably to himself as he thought of those biscuits, each cut open and sopped in bacon grease, and each enclosing a generous slice of fried bacon.

He plunged in among the big spruce trees. The trail was faint. A foot of snow had fallen since the last sled had passed over, and he was glad he was without a sled, traveling light. In fact, he carried nothing but the lunch wrapped in the handkerchief. He was surprised, however, at the cold. It certainly was cold, he concluded, as he rubbed his numb nose and cheekbones with his mittened hand. He was a warm-whiskered man, but the hair on his face did not protect the high cheekbones and the eager nose that thrust itself aggressively into the frosty air.

At the man's heels trotted a dog, a big native husky, the proper wolf dog, gray-coated and without any visible or temperamental difference from its brother, the wild wolf. The animal was depressed by the tremendous cold. It knew that it was no time for traveling. Its instinct told it a truer tale than was told to the man by the man's judgment. In reality, it was not merely colder than fifty below zero; it was colder than sixty below, than seventy below. It was seventy-five below zero. Since the freezing point is thirty-two above zero, it meant that one hundred and seven degrees of frost obtained. The dog did not know anything about thermometers. Possibly in its brain there was no sharp consciousness of a condition of very cold such as was in the man's brain. But the brute had its instinct. It experienced a vague but menacing apprehension that subdued it and made it slink along at the man's heels and that made it question eagerly every unwonted[6] movement of the man, as if expecting him to go into camp or to seek shelter somewhere and build a fire. The dog had learned fire, and it wanted fire, or else to burrow under the snow and cuddle its warmth away from the air.

The frozen moisture of its breathing had settled on its fur in a fine powder of frost, and especially were its jowls, muzzle, and eyelashes whitened by its crystaled breath. The man's red beard and mustache were likewise frosted, but more solidly, the deposit taking the form of ice and increasing with every warm, moist breath he exhaled. Also, the man was chewing tobacco, and the muzzle of ice held his lips so rigidly that he was unable to clear his chin when he expelled the juice. the result was that a crystal beard of the color and solidity of amber[7] was increasing its length on his chin. If he fell down it would shatter itself, like glass, into brittle fragments. But he did not mind the appendage. It was the penalty all tobacco chewers paid in that country, and he had been out before in two cold snaps. They had not been so cold as this, he knew, but by the spirit thermometer[8] at Sixty Mile he knew they had been registered at fifty below and at fifty-five.

He held on through the level stretch of woods for several miles, crossed a wide flat, and dropped down a bank to the frozen bed of a small stream. This was Henderson Creek, and he knew he was ten miles from the forks. He looked at his watch. It was ten o'clock. He was making four miles an hour, and he calculated that he would arrive at the forks at half-past twelve. He decided to celebrate that event by eating his lunch there.

The dog dropped in again at his heels, with a tail drooping discouragement, as the man swung along the creek bed. The fur-

6. **unwonted** (ŭn′·wun′tĭd): unusual, unfamiliar.
7. **amber:** a reddish- or brownish-yellow vegetable resin used in making beads.
8. **spirit thermometer:** an alcohol thermometer used particularly in severe cold.

To Build a Fire   57

row of the old sled trail was plainly visible, but a dozen inches of snow covered the marks of the last runners. In a month no man had come up or down that silent creek. The man held steadily on. He was not much given to thinking, and just then particularly he had nothing to think about save that he would eat lunch at the forks and that at six o'clock he would be in camp with the boys. There was nobody to talk to, and had there been, speech would have been impossible because of the ice muzzle on his mouth. So he continued monotonously to chew tobacco and to increase the length of his amber beard.

Once in a while the thought reiterated itself that it was very cold and that he had never experienced such cold. As he walked along he rubbed his cheekbones and nose with the back of his mittened hand. He did this automatically, now and again changing hands. But rub as he would, the instant he stopped his cheekbones went numb, and the following instant the end of his nose went numb. He was sure to frost his cheeks; he knew that, and experienced a pang of regret that he had not devised a nose strap of the sort Bud wore in cold snaps. Such a strap passed across the cheeks, as well, and saved them. But it didn't matter much, after all. What were frosted cheeks? A bit painful, that was all; they were never serious.

Empty as the man's mind was of thought, he was keenly observant, and he noticed the changes in the creek, the curves and bends and timber jams, and always he sharply noted where he placed his feet. Once, coming around a bend, he shied abruptly, like a startled horse, curved away from the place where he had been walking, and retreated several paces back along the trail. The creek, he knew, was frozen clear to the bottom—no creek could contain water in that arctic winter—but he knew also that there were springs that bubbled out from the hillsides and ran along under the snow and on top of the ice of the creek. He knew that the coldest snaps never froze these springs, and he knew likewise their danger. They were traps. They hid pools of water under the snow that might be three inches deep, or three feet. Sometimes a skin of ice half an inch thick covered them, and in turn was covered by the snow. Sometimes there were alternate layers of water and ice skin, so that when one broke through he kept on breaking through for a while, sometimes wetting himself to the waist.

That was why he had shied in such panic. He had felt the give under his feet and heard the crackle of a snow-hidden ice skin. And to get his feet wet in such a temperature meant trouble and danger. At the very least it meant delay, for he would be forced to stop and build a fire, and under its protection to bare his feet while he dried his socks and moccasins. He stood and studied the creek bed and its banks, and decided that the flow of water came from the right. He reflected a while, rubbing his nose and cheeks, then skirted to the left, stepping gingerly and testing the footing for each step. Once clear of the danger, he took a fresh chew of tobacco and swung along at his four-mile gait.

In the course of the next two hours he came upon several similar traps. Usually the snow above the hidden pools had a sunken, candied appearance that advertised the danger. Once again, however, he had a close call; and once, suspecting danger, he compelled the dog to go on in front. The dog did not want to go. It hung back until the man shoved it forward, and then it went quickly across the white, unbroken surface. Suddenly it broke through, floundered to one side, and got away to firmer footing. It had wet its forefeet and legs, and almost immediately the water that clung to it turned to ice. It made quick efforts to lick the ice off its legs, then dropped down in the snow and began to bite out the ice that had formed between the toes. This was a matter of instinct. To permit the ice to remain would mean sore feet. It did not know this. It merely obeyed the mysterious prompting that arose from the deep crypts[9] of its being. But the man knew, having achieved a judgment on the subject, and he removed the mitten from his right hand and helped tear out the ice particles. He did not expose his fingers more than a minute, and was astonished at the swift numbness that smote[10] them. It certainly was cold. He pulled on the mitten hastily, and beat the hand savagely across his chest.

At twelve o'clock the day was at its brightest. Yet the sun was too far south on its winter journey to clear the horizon. The bulge of the earth intervened between it and Henderson Creek, where

9. **crypts** (kripts): usually chambers or vaults wholly or partly underground, used for burial. As used here, the word refers to something deep and unknown in an animal's nature that causes it to act instinctively to protect itself.
10. **smote** (smōt): past tense of the verb *smite,* which means to strike, often suddenly and with great force.

the man walked under a clear sky at noon and cast no shadow. At half-past twelve, to the minute, he arrived at the forks of the creek. He was pleased at the speed he had made. If he kept it up, he would certainly be with the boys by six. He unbuttoned his jacket and shirt and drew forth his lunch. The action consumed no more than a quarter of a minute, yet in that brief moment the numbness laid hold of the exposed fingers. He did not put the mitten on, but instead struck the fingers a dozen sharp smashes against his leg. Then he sat down on a snow-covered log to eat. The sting that followed upon the striking of his fingers against his leg ceased so quickly that he was startled. He had had no chance to take a bite of biscuit. He struck the fingers repeatedly and returned them to the mitten, baring the other hand for the purpose of eating. He tried to take a mouthful, but the ice muzzle prevented. He had forgotten to build a fire and thaw out. He chuckled at his foolishness, and as he chuckled he noted the numbness creeping into the exposed fingers. Also, he noted that the stinging which had first come to his toes when he sat down was already passing away. He wondered whether the toes were warm or numb. He moved them inside the moccasins and decided that they were numb.

He pulled the mitten on hurriedly and stood up. He was a bit frightened. He stamped up and down until the stinging returned into the feet. It certainly was cold, was his thought. That man from Sulfur Creek had spoken the truth when telling how cold it sometimes got in the country. And he had laughed at him at the time! That showed one must not be too sure of things. There was no mistake about it, it *was* cold. He strode up and down, stamping his feet and threshing his arms, until reassured by the returning warmth. Then he got out matches and proceeded to make a fire. From the undergrowth, where high water of the previous spring had lodged a supply of seasoned twigs, he got his firewood. Working carefully from a small beginning, he soon had a roaring fire, over which he thawed the ice from his face and in the protection of which he ate his biscuits. For the moment the cold of space was outwitted. The dog took satisfaction in the fire, stretching out close enough for warmth and far enough away to escape being singed.

When the man had finished, he filled his pipe and took his comfortable time over a smoke. Then he pulled on his mittens, settled the ear flaps of his cap firmly about his ears, and took the creek trail up the left fork. The dog was disappointed and yearned back toward the fire. This man did not know cold. Possibly all the generations of his ancestry had been ignorant of cold, of real cold, of cold one hundred and seven degrees below freezing point. But the dog knew; all its ancestry knew, and it had inherited the knowledge. And it knew that it was not good to walk abroad in such fearful cold. It was the time to lie snug in a hole in the snow and wait for a curtain of cloud to be drawn across the face of outer space whence this cold came. On the other hand, there was no keen intimacy between the dog and the man. The one was the toil-slave of the other, and the only caresses it had ever received were the caresses of the whiplash and of harsh and menacing throat sounds that threatened the whiplash. So the dog made no effort to communicate its apprehension to the man. It was not concerned in the welfare of the man; it was for its own sake that it yearned back toward the fire. But the man whistled, and spoke to it with the sound of whiplashes, and the dog swung in at the man's heels and followed after.

The man took a chew of tobacco and proceeded to start a new amber beard. Also, his moist breath quickly powdered with white his mustache, eyebrows, and lashes. There did not seem to be so many springs on the left fork of the Henderson, and for half an hour the man saw no signs of any. And then it happened. At a place where there were no signs, where the soft, unbroken snow seemed to advertise solidity beneath, the man broke through. It was not deep. He wet himself halfway to the knees before he floundered out to the firm crust.

He was angry, and cursed his luck aloud. He had hoped to get into camp with the boys at six o'clock, and this would delay him an hour, for he would have to build a fire and dry out his footgear. This was imperative at that low temperature—he knew that much; and he turned aside to the bank, which he climbed. On top, tangled in the underbrush about the trunks of several small spruce trees, was a highwater deposit of dry firewood—sticks and twigs, principally, but also larger portions of seasoned branches and fine, dry, last year's grasses. He threw down several large pieces on top of the snow. This served for a foundation and prevented the young flame from drowning itself in the snow it otherwise would melt. The flame he got by touching a match to a small shred of birch bark that he took from his pocket. This burned even more readily than paper. Placing it on the foundation, he fed the young flame with wisps of dry grass and with the tiniest dry twigs.

He worked slowly and carefully, keenly aware of his danger. Gradually, as the flame grew stronger, he increased the size of the twigs with which he fed it. He squatted in the snow, pulling the twigs out from their entanglement in the brush and feeding directly to the flame. He knew there must be no failure. When it is seventy-five below zero, a man must not fail in his first attempt to build a fire—that is, if his feet are wet. If his feet are dry, and he fails, he can run along the trail for a half a mile and restore his circulation. But the circulation of wet and freezing feet cannot be restored by running when it is seventy-five below. No matter how fast he runs, the wet feet will freeze the harder.

All this the man knew. The old-timer on Sulfur Creek had told him about it the previous fall, and now he was appreciating the advice. Already all sensation had gone out of his feet. To build the fire, he had been forced to remove his mittens, and the fingers had quickly gone numb. His pace of four miles an hour had kept his heart pumping blood to the surface of his body and to all the extremities. But the instant he stopped, the action of the pump eased down. The cold of space smote the unprotected tip of the planet, and he, being on that unprotected tip, received the full force of the blow. The blood of his body recoiled before it. The blood was alive, like the dog, and like the dog it wanted to hide away and cover itself up from the fearful cold. So long as he walked four miles an hour, he pumped that blood, willy-nilly, to the surface; but now it ebbed away and sank down into the recesses of his body. The extremities were the first to feel its absence. His wet feet froze the faster, and his exposed fingers numbed the faster, though they had not yet begun to freeze. Nose and cheeks were already freezing, while the skin of all his body chilled as it lost its blood.

But he was safe. Toes and nose and cheeks would be only touched by the frost, for the fire was beginning to burn with strength. He was feeding it with twigs the size of his finger. In another minute he would be able to feed it with branches the size of his wrist, and then he could remove his wet footgear, and, while it dried, he could keep his naked feet warm by the fire, rubbing them at first, of course, with snow. The fire was a success. He was safe. He remembered the advice of the old-timer on Sulfur Creek, and smiled. The old-timer had been very serious in laying down the law that no man must travel alone in the Klondike after fifty below. Well, here he was; he had had the accident; he was alone;

and he had saved himself. Those old-timers were rather womanish, some of them, he thought. All a man had to do was to keep his head and he was all right. Any man who was a man could travel alone. But it was surprising, the rapidity with which his cheeks and nose were freezing. And he had not thought his fingers could go lifeless in so short a time. Lifeless they were, for he could scarcely make them move together to grip a twig, and they seemed remote from his body and from him. When he touched a twig he had to look and see whether or not he had hold of it. The wires were pretty well down between him and his finger ends.

All of which counted for little. There was the fire, snapping and crackling and promising life with every dancing flame. He started to untie his moccasins. They were coated with ice; the thick German socks were like sheaths of iron halfway to the knees; and the moccasin strings were like rods of steel all twisted and knotted as by some conflagration.[11] For a moment he tugged with his numb fingers, then, realizing the folly of it, he drew his sheath knife.

But before he could cut the strings it happened. It was his own fault, or, rather, his mistake. He should not have built the fire under the spruce tree. He should have built it in the open. But it had been easier to pull the twigs from the bush and drop them directly on the fire. Now the tree under which he had done this carried a weight of snow on its boughs. No wind had blown for weeks, and each bough was fully freighted. Each time he had pulled a twig he had communicated a slight agitation to the tree—an imperceptible agitation, so far as he was concerned, but an agitation sufficient to bring about the disaster. High up in the tree one bough capsized its load of snow. This fell on the boughs beneath, capsizing them. This process continued, spreading out and involving the whole tree. It grew like an avalanche, and it descended without warning upon the man and the fire, and the fire was blotted out! Where it had burned was a mantle of fresh and disordered snow.

The man was shocked. It was as though he had just heard his own sentence of death. For a moment he sat and stared at the spot where the fire had been. Then he grew very calm. Perhaps the old-timer on Sulfur Creek was right. If he had only had a trail-mate, he would have been in no danger now. The trailmate could

11. **conflagration** (kŏn′flə·grā′shən): a large, disastrous fire.

have built the fire. Well, it was up to him to build the fire over again, and this second time there must be no failure. Even if he succeeded, he would most likely lose some toes. His feet must be badly frozen by now, and there would be some time before the second fire was ready.

Such were his thoughts, but he did not sit and think them. He was busy all the time they were passing through his mind. He made a new foundation for a fire, this time in the open, where no treacherous tree could blot it out. Next he gathered dry grasses and tiny twigs from the high-water flotsam.[12] He could not bring his fingers together to pull them out, but he was able to gather them by the handful. In this way he got many rotten twigs and bits of green moss that were undesirable, but it was the best he could do. He worked methodically, even collecting an armful of the larger branches to be used later when the fire gathered strength. And all the while the dog sat and watched him, a certain yearning wistfulness in its eyes, for it looked upon him as the fire provider, and the fire was slow in coming.

When all was ready, the man reached in his pocket for a second piece of birch bark. He knew the bark was there, and, though he could not feel it with his fingers, he could hear its crisp rustling as he fumbled for it. Try as he would, he could not clutch hold of it. And all the time, in his consciousness, was the knowledge that each instant his feet were freezing. This thought tended to put him in a panic, but he fought against it and kept calm. He pulled on his mittens with his teeth, and threshed his arms back and forth, beating his hands with all his might against his sides. He did this sitting down, and he stood up to do it; and all the while the dog sat in the snow, its wolf brush of a tail curled around warmly over its forefeet, its sharp wolf ears pricked forward intently as it watched the man. And the man, as he beat and threshed with his arms and hands, felt a great surge of envy as he regarded the creature that was warm and secure in its natural covering.

After a time he was aware of the first faraway signals of sensation in his beaten fingers. The faint tingling grew stronger till it evolved into a stinging ache that was excruciating,[13] but which

---

12. flotsam (flŏt′səm): the floating wreckage of a ship or its cargo; hence, anything drifting about on a body of water. The word is derived from the Old English verb *flotian,* to float.
13. excruciating (ĭks·kroō′shē·ā′tĭng): causing great pain.

the man hailed with satisfaction. He stripped the mitten from his right hand and fetched forth the birch bark. The exposed fingers were quickly going numb again. Next he brought out his bunch of sulfur matches. But the tremendous cold had already driven the life out of his fingers. In his effort to separate one match from the others, the whole bunch fell in the snow. He tried to pick it out of the snow, but failed. The dead fingers could neither touch nor clutch. He was very careful. He drove the thought of his freezing feet, and nose, and cheeks, out of his mind, devoting his whole soul to the matches. He watched, using the sense of vision in place of that of touch, and when he saw his fingers on each side of the bunch, he closed them—that is, he willed to close them, for the wires were down, and the fingers did not obey. He pulled the mitten on the right hand, and beat it fiercely against his knee. Then, with both mittened hands, he scooped the bunch of matches, along with much snow, into his lap. Yet he was no better off.

After some manipulation he managed to get the bunch between the heels of his mittened hands. In this fashion he carried it to his mouth. The ice crackled and snapped when by a violent effort he opened his mouth. He drew the lower jaw in, curled the upper lip out of the way, and scraped the bunch with his upper teeth in order to separate a match. He succeeded in getting one, which he dropped on his lap. He was no better off. He could not pick it up. Then he devised a way. He picked it up in his teeth and scratched it on his leg. Twenty times he scratched before he succeeded in lighting it. As it flamed he held it with his teeth to the birch bark. But the burning brimstone[14] went up his nostrils and into his lungs, causing him to cough spasmodically.[15] The match fell into the snow and went out.

The old-timer on Sulfur Creek was right, he thought in the moment of controlled despair that ensued: after fifty below, a man should travel with a partner. He beat his hands, but failed in exciting any sensation. Suddenly he bared both hands, removing the mittens with his teeth. He caught the whole bunch between the heels of his hands. His arm muscles, not being frozen, enabled him to press the hand heels tightly against the matches. Then he scratched the bunch along his leg. It flared into flame, seventy

14. **brimstone:** sulfur.
15. **spasmodically** (spăz·mŏd′i·kǝ·lē): suddenly and violently.

sulfur matches at once! There was no wind to blow them out. He kept his head to one side to escape the strangling fumes, and held the blazing bunch to the birch bark. As he so held it, he became aware of sensation in his hand. His flesh was burning. He could smell it. Deep down below the surface he could feel it. The sensation developed into pain that grew acute. And still he endured it, holding the flame of the matches clumsily to the bark that would not light readily because his own burning hands were in the way, absorbing most of the flame.

At last, when he could endure no more, he jerked his hands apart. The blazing matches fell sizzling into the snow, but the birch bark was alight. He began laying dry grass and the tiniest twigs on the flame. He could not pick and choose, for he had to lift the fuel between the heels of his hands. Small pieces of rotten wood and green moss clung to the twigs, and he bit them off as well as he could with his teeth. He cherished the flame carefully and awkwardly. It meant life, and it must not perish. The withdrawal of blood from the surface of his body now made him begin to shiver, and he grew more awkward. A large piece of green moss fell squarely on the little fire. He tried to poke it out with his fingers, but his shivering frame made him poke too far, and he disrupted the nucleus of the little fire, the burning grasses and tiny twigs separating and scattering. He tried to poke them together again, but in spite of the tenseness of the effort, his shivering got away with him, and the twigs were hopelessly scattered. Each twig gushed a puff of smoke and went out. The fire provider had failed. As he looked apathetically[16] about him, his eyes chanced on the dog, sitting across the ruins of the fire from him, in the snow, making restless, hunching movements, slightly lifting one forefoot and then the other, shifting its weight back and forth on them with wistful eagerness.

The sight of the dog put a wild idea into his head. He remembered the tale of the man, caught in a blizzard, who killed a steer and crawled inside the carcass, and so was saved. He would kill the dog and bury his hands in the warm body until the numbness went out of them. Then he could build another fire. He spoke to the dog, calling it to him; but in his voice was a strange note of fear that frightened the animal, who had never known the man to speak in such a way before. Something was the matter, and its

16. **apathetically** (ăp′ə·thĕt′ĭ·kə·lē): without interest or emotion.

suspicious nature sensed danger—it knew not what danger, but somewhere, somehow, in its brain arose an apprehension of the man. It flattened its ears down at the sound of the man's voice, and its restless, hunching movements and the liftings and shiftings of its forefeet became more pronounced; but it would not come to the man. He got on his hands and knees and crawled toward the dog. This unusual posture again excited suspicion, and the animal sidled[17] mincingly[18] away.

The man sat up in the snow for a moment and struggled for calmness. Then he pulled on his mittens, by means of his teeth, and got up on his feet. He glanced down at first in order to assure himself that he was really standing up, for the absence of sensation in his feet left him unrelated to the earth. His erect position in itself started to drive the webs of suspicion from the dog's mind; and when he spoke peremptorily[19] with the sound of whiplashes in his voice, the dog rendered its customary allegiance and came to him. As it came within reaching distance, the man lost his control. His arms flashed out to the dog, and he experienced genuine surprise when he discovered that his hands could not clutch, that there was neither bend nor feeling in the fingers. He had forgotten for the moment that they were frozen and that they were freezing more and more. All this happened quickly, and before the animal could get away, he encircled its body with his arms. He sat down in the snow, and in this fashion held the dog, while it snarled and whined and struggled.

But it was all he could do, hold its body encircled in his arms and sit there. He realized that he could not kill the dog. There was no way to do it. With his helpless hands he could neither draw nor hold his sheath knife nor throttle[20] the animal. He released it, and it plunged wildly away, its tail between its legs and still snarling. It halted forty feet away and surveyed him curiously, with ears sharply pricked forward. The man looked down at his hands in order to locate them, and found them hanging on the ends of his arms. It struck him as curious that one should have to use his eyes in order to find out where his hands were. He began threshing his arms back and forth, beating the mittened hands against his sides.

17. **sidled** (sīd'əld): moved sideways in a cautious manner.
18. **mincingly** (mĭn'sĭng·lē): with short steps in a dainty, affected manner.
19. **peremptorily** (pə·rĕmp'tə·rə·lē): in a commanding manner.
20. **throttle** (thrŏt'l): choke or strangle. What is the mechanical meaning of this word?

He did this for five minutes, violently, and his heart pumped enough blood up to the surface to put a stop to his shivering. But no sensation was aroused in his hands. He had an impression that they hung like weights on the ends of his arms, but when he tried to run the impression down, he could not find it.

A certain fear of death, dull and oppressive, came to him. This fear quickly became poignant[21] as he realized that it was no longer a mere matter of freezing his fingers and toes, or of losing his hands and feet, but that it was a matter of life and death, with the chances against him. This threw him into a panic, and he turned and ran up the creek bed along the old, dim trail. The dog joined in behind and kept up with him. He ran blindly, without intention, in fear such as he had never known in his life. Slowly, as he plowed and floundered through the snow, he began to see things again—the banks of the creek, the old timber jams, the leafless aspens, and the sky. The running made him feel better. He did not shiver. Maybe, if he ran on, his feet would thaw out; and, anyway, if he ran far enough, he would reach the camp and the boys. Without doubt he would lose some fingers and toes and some of his face; but the boys would take care of him, and save the rest of him when he got there. And at the same time there was another thought in his mind that said he would never get to the camp and the boys; that it was too many miles away, that the freezing had too great a start on him, and that he would soon be stiff and dead. This thought he kept in the background and refused to consider. Sometimes it pushed itself forward and demanded to be heard, but he thrust it back and strove to think of other things.

It struck him as curious that he could run at all on feet so frozen that he could not feel them when they struck the earth and took the weight of his body. He seemed to himself to skim along above the surface, and to have no connection with the earth. Somewhere he had once seen a winged Mercury,[22] and he wondered if Mercury felt as he felt when skimming over the earth.

His theory of running until he reached camp and the boys had one flaw in it: he lacked the endurance. Several times he stumbled, and finally he tottered, crumpled up, and fell. When he tried to rise, he failed. He must sit and rest, he decided, and next

21. **poignant** (poin'yənt): painfully affecting the feelings; piercing.
22. **Mercury:** in Roman mythology, the herald and messenger of the gods. He is depicted as having winged feet.

time he would merely walk and keep on going. As he sat and regained his breath, he noted that he was feeling quite warm and comfortable. He was not shivering, and it even seemed that a warm glow had come to his chest and trunk. And yet, when he touched his nose or cheeks, there was no sensation. Running would not thaw them out. Nor would it thaw out his hands and feet. Then the thought came to him that the frozen portions of his body must be extending. He tried to keep this thought down, to forget it, to think of something else; he was aware of the panicky feeling that he caused, and he was afraid of the panic. But the thought asserted itself, and persisted, until it produced a vision of his body totally frozen. This was too much, and he made another wild run along the trail. Once he slowed down to a walk, but the thought of the freezing extending itself made him run again.

And all the time the dog ran with him, at his heels. When he fell down a second time, it curled its tail over its forefeet and sat in front of him, facing him, curiously eager and intent. The warmth and security of the animal angered him, and he cursed it till it flattened down its ears appeasingly.[23] This time the shivering came more quickly upon the man. He was losing in his battle with the frost. It was creeping into his body from all sides. The thought of it drove him on, but he ran no more than a hundred feet when he staggered and pitched headlong. It was his last panic. When he had recovered his breath and control, he sat up and entertained in his mind the conception of meeting death with dignity. However, the conception did not come to him in such terms. His idea of it was that he had been making a fool of himself, running around like a chicken with its head cut off—such was the simile that occurred to him. Well, he was bound to freeze anyway, and he might as well take it decently. With this new-found peace of mind came the first glimmerings of drowsiness. A good idea, he thought, to sleep off to death. It was like taking an anesthetic.[24] Freezing was not so bad as people thought. There were lots worse ways to die.

He pictured the boys finding his body next day. Suddenly he found himself with them, coming along the trail and looking for himself. And, still with them, he came around a turn in the trail and found himself lying in the snow. He did not belong with

---

23. appeasingly: trying to make peace.
24. anesthetic (ăn′ĭs·thĕt′ĭk): a drug or gas that causes loss of physical sensation or pain.

himself any more, for even then he was out of himself, standing with the boys and looking at himself in the snow. It certainly was cold, was his thought. When he got back to the States, he could tell the folks what real cold was. He drifted on from this to a vision of the old-timer on Sulfur Creek. He could see him quite clearly, warm and comfortable, and smoking a pipe.

"You were right, old hoss; you were right," the man mumbled to the old-timer of Sulfur Creek.

Then the man drowsed off into what seemed to him the most comfortable and satisfying sleep he had ever known. The dog sat facing him and waiting. The brief day drew to a close in a long, slow twilight. There were no signs of a fire to be made, and, besides, never in the dog's experience had it known a man to sit like that in the snow and make no fire. As the twilight drew on, its eager yearning for the fire mastered it, and with a great lifting and shifting of forefeet, it whined softly, then flattened its ears down in anticipation of being chidden[25] by the man. But the man remained silent. Later, the dog whined loudly. And still later it crept close to the man and caught the scent of death. This made the animal bristle[26] and back away. A little longer it delayed, howling under the stars that leaped and danced and shone brightly in the cold sky. Then it turned and trotted up the trail in the direction of the camp it knew, where were the other food providers and fire providers.

25. **chidden** (chĭd'n): scolded.
26. **bristle:** become agitated; take on an aggressive appearance.

Meaning

1. Cite incidents in the story that indicate the dog's instinct for survival to be more effective than the man's judgment. How does the man's judgment compare with Nace's in "Top Man"? with Osborn's?
2. What force defeats the man's attempts to build a fire? To what extent did the man defeat himself?
3. With the understanding you have gained from reading the entire story, list those things that could have made the man victorious in his struggle with the elements.

Method

1. The *protagonist* is the main character in a story. The *antagonist* is the person, place, idea, or force that opposes the protagonist. Identify the protagonist and the antagonist in this story. List some incidents that will support your answer.
2. What point in the story do you consider the climax? What descriptive details help to heighten the climax?
3. Why do you think the author did not name his main character?
4. What feeling or mood does London arouse by his repetition of the words *cold* and *gray* in his opening sentence? How is this mood sustained throughout the story?
5. Would the story have been less realistic and less interesting if London had chosen to have the man survive his ordeal in the Yukon? Why or why not?
6. Is there any foreshadowing of the final outcome of the story in the first paragraph? How does it contribute to suspense?

Language: Finding the Exact Meaning

You have learned that the *context* of an unfamiliar word will often give you its general meaning. You can read most stories and get a general understanding of what is happening without looking up a single word in the dictionary. However, to appreciate the author's choice of words, and to make a word part of your own vocabulary, you should look up the exact meaning of any unfamiliar word.

Use a dictionary to find the exact definition of the italicized words in the following sentences:

1. "As he turned to go on, he spat *speculatively*."
2. "It experienced a vague but menacing *apprehension* that subdued it . . ."
3. ". . . the thick German socks were like *sheaths* of iron halfway to the knees . . ."
4. ". . . there was no keen *intimacy* between the dog and the man."
5. ". . . he disrupted the *nucleus* of the little fire . . ."
6. "The faint tingling grew stronger till it evolved into a stinging ache that was *excruciating* . . ."

Discussion and Composition

1. *Comparing* means discussing things that are alike; *contrasting* means discussing things that are different. Write a composition in which you compare and contrast Nace, Osborn, and the man in "To Build a Fire." Discuss the problems they face and how they go about solving them.

2. When the implied meaning is quite different from the surface meaning, a statement is said to be ironic. For example, you might say "Nice going" or "Well done," after a friend has broken one of your prized possessions. Situations can also be ironic. For example, when something happens that is the opposite of what is expected. What ironies are there in the outcomes of "Top Man" and "To Build a Fire"?

3. Invent a plot in which the main character struggles against a natural force such as earthquake, tornado, fire, or water. Briefly describe the protagonist and antagonist. List the chain of events in your plot. Show how you would introduce suspense. Indicate what the climax and dénouement (outcome) of your story would be.

JAMES THURBER
(1894–1961)

Thurber was the man who left the world "a magnificent legacy of laughter" in his writings and cartoons. His drawings of flop-eared dogs, aggressive females, and their timid husbands had universal appeal. He drew rapidly but worked slowly and carefully in composing his stories and essays, for which he is primarily known. Because of a boyhood accident, he was almost completely blind by the time he was fifty. Yet he continued to write and rewrite, sometimes with heavy black pencil on long yellow sheets.

In 1926, Thurber joined the staff of *The New Yorker,* for which he wrote and drew throughout the rest of his life. His experiences on the magazine and with its editor and founder, Harold Ross, are recounted in *The Years with Ross* (1959).

Thurber's writing is almost never just amusing. Like most of his work, "The Secret Life of Walter Mitty" is funny, yet it makes a serious comment on modern life.

THE SECRET LIFE
OF WALTER MITTY

"We're going through!" The Commander's voice was like thin ice breaking. He wore his full-dress uniform, with the heavily braided white cap pulled down rakishly over one cold gray eye. "We can't make it, sir. It's spoiling for a hurricane, if you ask me." "I'm not asking you, Lieutenant Berg," said the Commander. "Throw on the power light! Rev her up to 8,500! We're going through!" The pounding of the cylinders increased: ta-pocketa-pocketa-pocketa-*pocketa-pocketa*. The Commander stared at the ice forming on the pilot window. He walked over and twisted a row of complicated dials. "Switch on No. 8 auxiliary!" he shouted. "Switch on No. 8 auxiliary!" repeated Lieutenant Berg. "Full strength in No. 3 turret!"[1] shouted the Commander. "Full

1. **turret:** the enclosure in an airplane for the gun and/or gunners.

strength in No. 3 turret!" The crew, bending to their various tasks in the huge, hurtling[2] eight-engined navy hydroplane,[3] looked at each other and grinned. "The Old Man'll get us through," they said to one another. "The Old Man ain't afraid of Hell! . . ."

"Not so fast! You're driving too fast!" said Mrs. Mitty. "What are you driving so fast for?"

"Hmm?" said Walter Mitty. He looked at his wife, in the seat beside him, with shocked astonishment. She seemed grossly unfamiliar, like a strange woman who had yelled at him in a crowd. "You were up to fifty-five," she said. "You know I don't like to go more than forty. You were up to fifty-five." Walter Mitty drove on toward Waterbury in silence, the roaring of the SN202 through the worst storm in twenty years of Navy flying fading in the remote, intimate airways of his mind. "You're tensed up again," said Mrs. Mitty. "It's one of your days. I wish you'd let Dr. Renshaw look you over."

Walter Mitty stopped the car in front of the building where his wife went to have her hair done. "Remember to get those overshoes while I'm having my hair done," she said. "I don't need overshoes," said Mitty. She put her mirror back into her bag. "We've been all through that," she said, getting out of the car. "You're not a young man any longer." He raced the engine a little. "Why don't you wear your gloves? Have you lost your gloves?" Walter Mitty reached into a pocket and brought out the gloves. He put them on, but after she had turned and gone into the building and he had driven on to a red light, he took them off again. "Pick it up, brother!" snapped a cop as the light changed, and Mitty hastily pulled on his gloves and lurched ahead. He drove around the streets aimlessly for a time, and then he drove past the hospital on his way to the parking lot.

. . . "It's the millionaire banker, Wellington McMillan," said the pretty nurse. "Yes?" said Walter Mitty, removing his gloves slowly. "Who has the case?" "Dr. Renshaw and Dr. Benbow, but there are two specialists here, Dr. Remington from New York and Dr. Pritchard-Mitford from London. He flew over." A door opened down a long, cool corridor and Dr. Renshaw came out. He looked distraught[4] and haggard.

---

2. **hurtling** (hûrt′ling): moving with a rushing or crashing sound.
3. **hydroplane** (hī′drə·plān′): an airplane that can land or take off from the water; it moves at great speed on the water.
4. **distraught** (dĭs·trôt′): worried and tense.

"Hello, Mitty," he said. "We're having the devil's own time with McMillan, the millionaire banker and close personal friend of Roosevelt. Obstreosis[5] of the ductal tract. Tertiary. Wish you'd take a look at him." "Glad to," said Mitty.

In the operating room there were whispered introductions: "Dr. Remington, Dr. Mitty. Dr. Pritchard-Mitford, Dr. Mitty." "I've read your book on streptothricosis," said Pritchard-Mitford, shaking hands. "A brilliant performance, sir." "Thank you," said Walter Mitty. "Didn't know you were in the States, Mitty," grumbled Remington. "Coals to Newcastle,[6] bringing Mitford and me up here for a tertiary." "You are very kind," said Mitty. A huge, complicated machine, connected to the operating table, with many tubes and wires, began at this moment to go pocketa-pocketa-pocketa. "The new anesthetizer[7] is giving away!" shouted an intern. "There is no one in the East who knows how to fix it!" "Quiet, man!" said Mitty, in a low, cool voice. He sprang to the machine, which now going pocketa-pocketa-queep-pocketa-queep. He began fingering delicately a row of glistening dials. "Give me a fountain pen!" he snapped. Someone handed him a fountain pen. He pulled a faulty piston out of the machine and inserted the pen in its place. "That will hold for ten minutes," he said. "Get on with the operation." A nurse hurried over and whispered to Renshaw, and Mitty saw the man turn pale. "Coreopsis has set in," said Renshaw nervously. "If you would take over, Mitty?" Mitty looked at him and at the craven[8] figure of Benbow, who drank, and at the grave, uncertain faces of the two great specialists. "If you wish," he said. They slipped a white gown on him; he adjusted a mask and drew on thin gloves; nurses handed him shining. . . .

"Back it up, Mac! Look out for that Buick!" Walter Mitty jammed on the brakes. "Wrong lane, Mac," said the parking-lot attendant, looking at Mitty closely. "Gee. Yeh," muttered Mitty.

---

5. obstreosis (əb·strē·ō′sĭs): Some of these medical terms are legitimate; others are not.

6. Coals to Newcastle: Newcastle is a city in England noted for its production of coal. "To carry coals to Newcastle" means to take things to a place where they are already in abundant supply; to waste labor.

7. anesthetizer (ə·nĕs′thə·tīz′ər): from the verb *anesthetize,* to make insensitive to pain, especially by the use of an **anesthetic** (ăn′ĭs·thĕt′ĭk), a drug or gas that deadens sensation.

8. craven (krā′vən): noticeably lacking in courage; afraid.

He began cautiously to back out of the lane marked "Exit Only." "Leave her sit there," said the attendant. "I'll put her away." Mitty got out of the car. "Hey, better leave the key." "Oh," said Mitty, handing the man the ignition key. The attendant vaulted into the car, backed it up with insolent skill, and put it where it belonged.

They're so darn cocky, thought Walter Mitty, walking along Main Street; they think they know everything. Once he had tried to take his chains off, outside New Milford, and he had got them wound around the axles. A man had had to come out in a wrecking car and unwind them, a young, grinning garageman. Since then Mrs. Mitty always made him drive to a garage to have the chains taken off. The next time, he thought, I'll wear my right arm in a sling; they won't grin at me then. I'll have my right arm in a sling and they'll see I couldn't possibly take the chains off myself. He kicked at the slush on the sidewalk. "Overshoes," he said to himself, and he began looking for a shoe store.

When he came out into the street again, with the overshoes in a box under his arm, Walter Mitty began to wonder what the other thing was his wife had told him to get. She had told him twice before they set out from their house for Waterbury. In a way he hated these weekly trips to town—he was always getting something wrong. Kleenex, he thought, Squibb's, razor blades? No. Toothpaste, toothbrush, bicarbonate, carborundum,[9] initiative,[10] and referendum?[11] He gave it up. But she would remember it. "Where's the what's-its-name?" she would ask. "Don't tell me you forgot the what's-its-name." A newsboy went by shouting something about the Waterbury trial.

. . . "Perhaps this will refresh your memory." The District Attorney suddenly thrust a heavy automatic at the quiet figure on the witness stand. "Have you ever seen this before?" Walter Mitty took the gun and examined it expertly. "This is my Webley-

---

9. carborundum (kär′bə·rŭn′dəm): a technical trade name for an abrasive used to wear or grind down something.
10. initiative (ĭn·ĭsh′ē·ə·tĭv): in government, the right of the voters to propose legislative matters by getting together a petition and submitting it to popular vote or to the legislature for approval.
11. referendum (rĕf′ə·rĕn′dəm): in government, the practice of submitting a measure passed upon by a legislative body or by popular initiative to a vote of the people for ratification or rejection.

Vickers 50.80,"[12] he said calmly. An excited buzz ran around the courtroom. The Judge rapped for order. "You are a crack shot with any sort of firearms, I believe?" said the District Attorney, insinuatingly.[13] "Objection!" shouted Mitty's attorney. "We have shown that the defendant could not have fired the shot. We have shown that he wore his right arm in a sling on the night of the fourteenth of July." Walter Mitty raised his hand briefly, and the bickering attorneys were stilled. "With any known make of gun," he said evenly, "I could have killed Gregory Fitzhurst at three hundred feet *with my left hand.*" Pandemonium broke loose in the courtroom. A woman's scream rose above the bedlam, and suddenly a lovely, dark-haired girl was in Walter Mitty's arms. The District Attorney struck at her savagely. Without rising from his chair, Mitty let the man have it on the point of the chin. "You miserable cur!"[14] . . .

"Puppy biscuit," said Walter Mitty. He stopped walking, and the buildings of Waterbury rose up out of the misty courtroom and surrounded him again. A woman who was passing laughed. "He said 'Puppy biscuit,'" she said to her companion. "That man said 'Puppy biscuit' to himself." Walter Mitty hurried on. He went into an A&P, not the first one he came to but a smaller one farther up the street. "I want some biscuit for small, young dogs," he said to the clerk. "Any special brand, sir?" The greatest pistol shot in the world thought a moment. "It says 'Puppies Bark for It' on the box," said Walter Mitty.

His wife would be through at the hairdresser's in fifteen minutes, Mitty saw in looking at his watch, unless they had trouble drying it; sometimes they had trouble drying it. She didn't like to get to the hotel first; she would want him to be there waiting for her as usual. He found a big leather chair in the lobby, facing the window, and he put the overshoes and the puppy biscuit on the floor beside it. He picked up an old copy of *Liberty* and sank down into the chair. "Can Germany Conquer the World Through the Air?" Walter Mitty looked at the pictures of bombing planes and of ruined streets.

. . . "The cannonading has got the wind up in young Ra-

12. **Webley–Vickers 50.80:** Mitty invents an impressive name and unlikely caliber for his obviously exceptional weapon.
13. **insinuatingly** (ĭn·sĭn′yoo·āt′ĭng·lē): in a sly or indirect manner.
14. **cur:** a mongrel dog; a contemptible person.

leigh, sir," said the sergeant. Captain Mitty looked at him through tousled hair. "Get him to bed," he said wearily, "with the others. I'll fly alone." "But you can't, sir," said the sergeant anxiously. "It takes two men to handle that bomber, and the Archies[15] are pounding hell out of the air. Von Richtman's circus is between here and Saulier." "Somebody's got to get that ammunition dump," said Mitty. "I'm going over. Spot of brandy?" He poured a drink for the sergeant and one for himself. War thundered and whined around the dugout and battered at the door. There was a rending of wood, and splinters flew through the room. "A bit of a near thing," said Captain Mitty carelessly. "The box barrage is closing in," said the sergeant. "We only live once, Sergeant," said Mitty, with his faint, fleeting smile. "Or do we?" He poured another brandy and tossed it off. "I never see a man could hold his brandy like you, sir," said the sergeant. "Begging your pardon, sir." Captain Mitty stood up and strapped on his huge Webley-Vickers automatic. "It's forty kilometers through hell, sir," said the sergeant. Mitty finished one last brandy. "After all," he said softly, "what isn't?" The pounding of the cannon increased; there was the rat-tat-tatting of machine guns, and from somewhere came the menacing pocketa–pocketa–pocketa of the new flame throwers. Walter Mitty walked to the door of the dugout humming "Auprès de ma Blonde."[16] He turned and waved to the sergeant. "Cheerio!" he said. . . .

Something struck his shoulder. "I've been looking all over this hotel for you," said Mrs. Mitty. "Why do you have to hide in this old chair? How did you expect me to find you?" "Things close in," said Walter Mitty vaguely. "What?" Mrs. Mitty said. "Did you get the what's–its–name? The puppy biscuit? What's in that box?" "Overshoes," said Mitty. "Couldn't you have put them on in the store?" "I was thinking," said Walter Mitty. "Does it ever occur to you that I am sometimes thinking?" She looked at him. "I'm going to take your temperature when I get you home," she said.

They went out through the revolving doors that made a faintly derisive[17] whistling sound when you pushed them. It was

15. Archies: a term used by the Allied troops in World War I for antiaircraft guns.
16. "Auprès de ma Blonde" (ŏ·prē·də·mə·blŏnde′): a French World War I song, "Close to My Blonde."
17. derisive (dĭ·rī′sĭv): expressing ridicule or scorn.

two blocks to the parking lot. At the drugstore on the corner she said, "Wait here for me. I forgot something. I won't be a minute." She was more than a minute. Walter Mitty lighted a cigarette. It began to rain, rain with sleet in it. He stood up against the wall of the drugstore, smoking. . . . He put his shoulders back and his heels together. "To hell with the handkerchief," said Walter Mitty scornfully. He took one last drag on his cigarette and snapped it away. Then, with that faint, fleeting smile playing about his lips, he faced the firing squad; erect and motionless, proud and disdainful, Walter Mitty the Undefeated, inscrutable[18] to the last.

18. **inscrutable** (ĭn·skrōō′tə·bəl): mysterious; not easily understood.

Meaning

1. Make a list of the settings Mitty sees himself in and the characters he becomes. In what general type of role does he see himself in his dreams?
2. This story is humorous, but it has its serious side too. Why does Mitty daydream so much? What serious comment about life is Thurber making?
3. Mitty's last daydream concerns a firing squad, which he faces "erect and motionless, proud and disdainful, Walter Mitty the Undefeated, inscrutable to the last."

   Are the words *undefeated* and *inscrutable* ironic, or could they really describe Mitty?

Method

1. Mitty's daydreams are the result of a process of association; they are related to the everyday world. For example, as he passes the hospital he imagines himself a surgeon. List some of the things and places in Mitty's life that start and end his daydreaming.
2. What is the author's purpose in beginning the story with a daydream rather than an actual event?
3. How would you describe Mrs. Mitty? In what ways is she a contrast to her husband? Give specific references in the text to substantiate your statements.

4. Second-rate movie and television stories often have stock characters who always have the same traits and whose actions are quite predictable; at a crucial moment, the beautiful young girl will be rescued by the dashing hero. By presenting Mitty's daydreams as stereotyped adventure situations, with hackneyed dialogue and stock characters, Thurber makes fun of such stories. What comment is Thurber making about Mitty's imagination?

5. There are various ways in which a writer can create humor. One is to present something that is incongruous, i.e., something that is not suitable, reasonable, or proper to the situation. Such an incongruity occurs in this story when the commander wears a full-dress uniform in the midst of battle.

Another way to create humor is to use names (such as Gregory Fitzhurst) that sound amusing, and to exaggerate descriptions (as in "huge, hurtling eight-engined navy hydroplane"). Still another method is to create nonsense words and expressions such as "obstreosis of the ductal tract."

Find two more examples of incongruity, amusing names, exaggeration, and nonsense words or expressions in the story.

Language: Onomatopoeia, a Word from a Sound

Several times in the story, Thurber uses the word *pocketa*. It is impossible to find this word in a dictionary, even a very large one, since it exists and has meaning only in the context of this story. Where did the author get the word? He made it up by writing an imitation of a sound, first a pounding cylinder in a hydroplane, and later the failing equipment in a hospital operating room. When spoken very rapidly, "pocketa-pocketa" sounds like the sputtering of a motor. What other machines can it be used to describe?

Words which sound like the things they describe are called onomatopoetic (ŏn'ə·măt'ə·pō·ĕt'ĭk) words. *Pop, zip, buzz, bow-wow,* and *splash* are examples of well known onomatopoeias (ŏn'ə·măt'ə·pē'əs). Name five other words that are onomatopoetic. Then make up five onomatopoetic words of your own and tell what they mean.

Discussion and Composition

1. Describe one of your favorite daydreams in one or two sentences. Then write dialogue and descriptive details that will show you playing the hero or heroine of your daydream.

2. Researchers into dreams claim that dreaming is essential to mental health. Why do you think this might be so? How are daydreams different from the dreams one has at night?

O. HENRY
(1862–1910)

William Sydney Porter first used the pen name O. Henry to hide his true identity when he wrote stories while serving a prison term. Born in Greensboro, North Carolina, Porter had left school at fifteen to work in his uncle's drugstore. When he was twenty, he went to Texas, where he worked on a ranch, and later in a bank.

The bank job resulted in the tragedy of Porter's life; yet out of his trouble came the warm sympathy for people down on their luck which underlies his best work. The bank was so poorly managed that it is not clear to this day exactly what happened. Some accounts were found short, and Porter was accused of embezzlement. Instead of waiting for a trial, he fled to Honduras. He returned to face trial when he learned that his wife was dying of tuberculosis.

During his three-year prison term, Porter worked as a night druggist in the prison hospital. During the day, he wrote adventure stories to earn the money that he needed to support his daughter.

After his release, Porter went to New York and worked for the *New York World,* for which he wrote a number of stories. He died of tuberculosis at the age of forty-eight.

O. Henry was influential in creating a pattern for a type of short story today called the commercial story, as opposed to the quality story. He wrote quickly, primarily for newspaper readers who wanted their stories exciting and easy to understand. His stories are often sentimental and filled with unlikely coincidences. At times, the surprise or trick ending (at which he excelled) seems a bit forced. Nevertheless, his popularity is deserved, for he was a master storyteller.

THE RANSOM
OF RED CHIEF

It looked like a good thing: but wait till I tell you. We were down South, in Alabama—Bill Driscoll and myself—when this kidnaping idea struck us. It was, as Bill afterward expressed it, "during a moment of temporary mental apparition";[1] but we didn't find that out till later.

There was a town down there, as flat as a flannel cake, and called Summit, of course. It contained inhabitants of as undeleterious[2] and self-satisfied a class of peasantry as ever clustered around a Maypole.

Bill and me had a joint capital of about six hundred dollars, and we needed just two thousand dollars more to pull off a fraudulent town-lot scheme in western Illinois with. We talked it over on the front steps of the hotel. Philoprogenitiveness,[3] says we, is strong in semirural communities; therefore, and for other reasons, a kidnaping project ought to do better there than in the radius of newspapers that send reporters out in plain clothes to stir up talk about such things. We knew that Summit couldn't get after us with anything stronger than constables and, maybe, some lackadaisical bloodhounds and a diatribe[4] or two in the *Weekly Farmers' Budget*. So, it looked good.

We selected for our victim the only child of a prominent citizen named Ebenezer Dorset. The father was respectable and tight, a mortgage fancier and a stern, upright collection-plate passer and forecloser. The kid was a boy of ten, with bas-relief[5] freckles, and hair the color of the cover of the magazine you buy at the newsstand when you want to catch a train. Bill and me figured

---

1. apparition (ăp′ə·rĭsh′ən): mispronunciation of *aberration* (ab′ə·rā′shən), disorder, or insanity.

2. undeleterious (ŭn·dĕl′ə·tîr′ē·əs): nondestructive, harmless.

3. philoprogenitiveness (fĭl′ō·prō·jĕn′ə·tĭv·nĭs): love of parents for their children.

4. diatribe (dī′ə·trīb): a bitter criticism or denunciation, as in an angry editorial.

5. bas-relief (bä′rĭ·lēf′): projecting slightly from the background; usually refers to a carving or sculpture.

that Ebenezer would melt down for a ransom of two thousand dollars to a cent. But wait till I tell you.

About two miles from Summit was a little mountain, covered with a dense cedar brake. On the rear elevation of this mountain was a cave. There we stored provisions.

One evening after sundown, we drove in a buggy past old Dorset's house. The kid was in the street, throwing rocks at a kitten on the opposite fence.

"Hey, little boy!" says Bill. "Would you like to have a bag of candy and a nice ride?"

The boy catches Bill neatly in the eye with a piece of brick.

"That will cost the old man an extra five hundred dollars," says Bill, climbing over the wheel.

That boy put up a fight like a welterweight cinnamon bear; but, at last, we got him down in the bottom of the buggy and drove away. We took him up to the cave, and I hitched the horse in the cedar brake. After dark I drove the buggy to the little village, three miles away, where we had hired it, and walked back to the mountain.

Bill was pasting court plaster[6] over the scratches and bruises on his features. There was a fire burning behind the big rock at the entrance of the cave, and the boy was watching a pot of boiling coffee, with two buzzard tail feathers stuck in his red hair. He points a stick at me when I come up, and says:

"Ha! cursèd paleface, do you dare to enter the camp of Red Chief, the terror of the plains?"

"He's all right now," says Bill, rolling up his trousers and examining some bruises on his shins. "We're playing Indian. We're making Buffalo Bill's show look like magic-lantern views of Palestine in the town hall. I'm Old Hank the Trapper, Red Chief's captive, and I'm to be scalped at daybreak. By Geronimo! That kid can kick hard!"

Yes, sir, that boy seemed to be having the time of his life. The fun of camping out in a cave had made him forget that he was a captive himself. He immediately christened me Snake-Eye the Spy, and announced that, when his braves returned from the war-path, I was to be broiled at the stake at the rising of the sun.

---

6. court plaster: cloth covered on one side with sticky material; formerly used to protect cuts in the skin. This was the forerunner of today's adhesive bandage.

Then we had supper; and he filled his mouth full of bacon and bread and gravy, and began to talk. He made a during-dinner speech something like this:

"I like this fine. I never camped out before; but I had a pet possum once, and I was nine last birthday. I hate to go to school. Rats ate up sixteen of Jimmy Talbot's aunt's speckled hen's eggs. Are there any real Indians in these woods? I want some more gravy. Does the trees moving make the wind blow? We had five puppies. What makes your nose so red, Hank? My father has lots of money. Are the stars hot? I whipped Ed Walker twice, Saturday. I don't like girls. You dassent catch toads unless with a string. Do oxen make any noise? Why are oranges round? Have you got beds to sleep on in this cave? Amos Murray has got six toes. A parrot can talk, but a monkey or a fish can't. How many does it take to make twelve?"

Every few minutes he would remember that he was a pesky redskin and pick up his stick rifle and tiptoe to the mouth of the cave to rubber[7] for the scouts of the hated paleface. Now and then he would let out a war whoop that made Old Hank the Trapper shiver. That boy had Bill terrorized from the start.

"Red Chief," says I to the kid, "would you like to go home?"

"Aw, what for?" says he. "I don't have any fun at home. I hate to go to school. I like to camp out. You won't take me back home again, Snake-Eye, will you?"

"Not right away," says I. "We'll stay here in the cave a while."

"All right!" says he. "That'll be fine. I never had such fun in all my life."

We went to bed about eleven o'clock. We spread down some wide blankets and quilts and put Red Chief between us. We weren't afraid he'd run away. He kept us awake for three hours, jumping up and reaching for his rifle and screeching: "Hist! pard," in mine and Bill's ears, as the fancied crackle of a twig or the rustle of a leaf revealed to his young imagination the stealthy approach of the outlaw band. At last, I fell into a troubled sleep and dreamed that I had been kidnaped and chained to a tree by a ferocious pirate with red hair.

---

7. **rubber:** short for *rubberneck,* to stretch one's neck while looking for something.

Just at daybreak, I was awakened by a series of awful screams from Bill. They weren't yells, or howls, or shouts, or whoops, or yawps, such as you'd expect from a manly set of vocal organs—they were simply indecent, terrifying, humiliating screams, such as women emit when they see ghosts or caterpillars. It's an awful thing to hear a strong, desperate, fat man scream incontinently[8] in a cave at daybreak.

I jumped up to see what the matter was. Red Chief was sitting on Bill's chest, with one hand twined in Bill's hair. In the other he had the sharp case knife we used for slicing bacon, and he was industriously and realistically trying to take Bill's scalp, according to the sentence that had been pronounced upon him the evening before.

I got the knife away from the kid and made him lie down again. But, from that moment, Bill's spirit was broken. He laid down on his side of the bed, but he never closed an eye again in sleep as long as that boy was with us. I dozed off for a while, but along toward sunup I remembered that Red Chief had said I was to be burned at the stake at the rising of the sun. I wasn't nervous or afraid; but I sat up and lit my pipe and leaned against a rock.

"What you getting up so soon for, Sam?" asked Bill.

"Me?" says I. "Oh, I got a kind of a pain in my shoulder. I thought sitting up would rest it."

"You're a liar!" says Bill. "You're afraid. You was to be burned at sunrise, and you was afraid he'd do it. And he would, too, if he could find a match. Ain't it awful, Sam? Do you think anybody will pay out money to get a little imp like that back home?"

"Sure," said I. "A rowdy kid like that is just the kind that parents dote on. Now, you and the Chief get up and cook breakfast, while I go up on the top of this mountain and reconnoiter."

I went up on the peak of the little mountain and ran my eye over the contiguous[9] vicinity. Over toward Summit I expected to see the sturdy yeomanry[10] of the village, armed with scythes and pitchforks, beating the countryside for the dastardly kidnapers. But what I saw was a peaceful landscape dotted with one man plowing with a dun mule. Nobody was dragging the creek; no couriers dashed hither and yon, bringing tidings of no news to the

---

8. **incontinently:** without self-restraint.
9. **contiguous** (kən·tĭg'yo͞o·əs): bordering.
10. **yeomanry** (yō'mən·rē): people who own a small amount of land.

distracted parents. There was a sylvan[11] attitude of somnolent[12] sleepiness pervading that section of the external outward surface of Alabama that lay exposed to my view. "Perhaps," says I to myself, "it has not yet been discovered that the wolves have borne away the tender lambkin from the fold. Heaven help the wolves!" says I, and I went down the mountain to breakfast.

When I got to the cave, I found Bill backed up against the side of it, breathing hard, and the boy threatening to smash him with a rock half as big as a coconut.

"He put a red-hot boiled potato down my back," explained Bill, "and then mashed it with his foot; and I boxed his ears. Have you got a gun about you, Sam?"

I took the rock away from the boy and kind of patched up the argument. "I'll fix you," says the kid to Bill. "No man ever yet struck the Red Chief but what he got paid for it. You better beware!"

After breakfast the kid takes a piece of leather with strings wrapped around it out of his pocket and goes outside the cave unwinding it.

"What's he up to now?" says Bill anxiously. "You don't think he'll run away, do you, Sam?"

"No fear of it," says I. "He don't seem to be much of a homebody. But we've got to fix up some plan about the ransom. There don't seem to be much excitement around Summit on account of his disappearance, but maybe they haven't realized yet that he's gone. His folks may think he's spending the night with Aunt Jane or one of the neighbors. Anyhow, he'll be missed today. Tonight we must get a message to his father demanding the two thousand dollars for his return."

Just then we heard a kind of war whoop, such as David might have emitted when he knocked out the champion Goliath. It was a sling that Red Chief had pulled out of his pocket, and he was whirling it around his head.

I dodged and heard a heavy thud and a kind of a sigh from Bill, like a horse gives out when you take his saddle off. A rock the size of an egg had caught Bill just behind his left ear. He loosened himself all over and fell in the fire across the frying pan of hot

---

11. **sylvan:** woodsy. Silvanus in Roman mythology was a god of forests, fields and herds; and represented a simple, uncomplicated life.
12. **somnolent** (sŏm'nə·lənt): drowsy.

water for washing the dishes. I dragged him out and poured cold water on his head for half an hour.

By and by, Bill sits up and feels behind his ear and says: "Sam, do you know who my favorite Biblical character is?"

"Take it easy," says I. "You'll come to your senses presently."

"King Herod,"[13] says he. "You won't go away and leave me here alone, will you, Sam?"

I went out and caught that boy and shook him until his freckles rattled.

"If you don't behave," says I, "I'll take you straight home. Now, are you going to be good or not?"

"I was only funning," says he sullenly. "I didn't mean to hurt Old Hank. But what did he hit me for? I'll behave, Snake-Eye, if you won't send me home, and if you'll let me play the Black Scout today."

"I don't know the game," says I. "That's for you and Mr. Bill to decide. He's your playmate for the day. I'm going away for a while, on business. Now, you come in and make friends with him and say you are sorry for hurting him, or home you go, at once."

I made him and Bill shake hands, and then I took Bill aside and told him I was going to Poplar Cove, a little village three miles from the cave, and find out what I could about how the kidnaping had been regarded in Summit. Also, I thought it best to send a peremptory[14] letter to old man Dorset that day, demanding the ransom and dictating how it should be paid.

"You know, Sam," says Bill, "I've stood by you without batting an eye in earthquakes, fire, and flood—in poker games, dynamite outrages, police raids, train robberies, and cyclones. I never lost my nerve yet till we kidnaped that two-legged sky-rocket of a kid. He's got me going. You won't leave me long with him, will you, Sam?"

"I'll be back some time this afternoon," says I. "You must keep the boy amused and quiet till I return. And now we'll write the letter to old Dorset."

Bill and I got paper and pencil and worked on the letter while Red Chief, with a blanket wrapped around him, strutted up

---

13. King Herod: King of Judea who tried to kill the infant Jesus by ordering the slaying of all male children under the age of two in Bethlehem.

14. peremptory (pə·rĕmp′tər·ē): sternly decisive.

and down, guarding the mouth of the cave. Bill begged me tearfully to make the ransom fifteen hundred dollars instead of two thousand. "I ain't attempting," says he, "to decry the celebrated moral aspect of parental affection, but we're dealing with humans, and it ain't human for anybody to give up two thousand dollars for that forty pound chunk of freckled wildcat. I'm willing to take a chance at fifteen hundred dollars. You can charge the difference up to me."

So, to relieve Bill, I acceded, and we collaborated a letter that ran this way:

Ebenezer Dorset, Esq.:
    We have your boy concealed in a place far from Summit. It is useless for you or the most skillful detectives to attempt to find him. Absolutely, the only terms on which you can have him restored to you are these: We demand fifteen hundred dollars in large bills for his return; the money to be left at midnight tonight at the same spot and in the same box as your reply—as hereinafter described. If you agree to these terms, send your answer in writing by a solitary messenger tonight at half-past eight o'clock. After crossing Owl Creek, on the road to Poplar Cove, there are three large trees about a hundred yards apart, close to the fence of the wheat field on the right-hand side. At the bottom of the fence post, opposite the third tree, will be found a small pasteboard box.
    The messenger will place the answer in this box and return immediately to Summit.
    If you attempt any treachery or fail to comply with our demand as stated, you will never see your boy again.
    If you pay the money as demanded, he will be returned to you safe and well within three hours. These terms are final, and if you do not accede to them, no further communication will be attempted.

Two Desperate Men

I addressed this letter to Dorset and put it in my pocket. As I was about to start, the kid comes up to me and says:

"Aw, Snake-Eye, you said I could play the Black Scout while you was gone."

"Play it, of course," says I. "Mr. Bill will play with you. What kind of a game is it?"

"I'm the Black Scout," says Red Chief, "and I have to ride to the stockade to warn the settlers that the Indians are coming. I'm tired of playing Indian myself. I want to be the Black Scout."

"All right," says I. "It sounds harmless to me. I guess Mr. Bill will help you foil the pesky savages."

"What am I to do?" asks Bill, looking at the kid suspiciously.

"You are the hoss," says Black Scout. "Get down on your hands and knees. How can I ride to the stockade without a hoss?"

"You'd better keep him interested," said I, "till we get the scheme going. Loosen up."

Bill gets down on his all fours, and a look comes in his eye like a rabbit's when you catch it in a trap.

"How far is it to the stockade, kid?" he asks, in a husky manner of voice.

"Ninety miles," says the Black Scout. "And you have to hump yourself to get there on time. Whoa, now!" The Black Scout jumps on Bill's back and digs his heels in his side.

"For heaven's sake," says Bill, "hurry back, Sam, as soon as you can. I wish we hadn't made the ransom more than a thousand. Say, you quit kicking me or I'll get up and warm you good."

I walked over to Poplar Cove and sat round the post office and store talking with the chaw-bacons that came in to trade. One whiskerando says that he hears Summit is all upset on account of Elder Ebenezer Dorset's boy having been lost or stolen. That was all I wanted to know. I bought some smoking tobacco, referred casually to the price of black-eyed peas, posted my letter surreptitiously,[15] and came away. The postmaster said the mail carrier would come by in an hour to take the mail on to Summit.

When I got back to the cave, Bill and the boy were not to be found. I explored the vicinity of the cave and risked a yodel or two, but there was no response.

So I lighted my pipe and sat down on a mossy bank to await developments.

In about half an hour I heard the bushes rustle, and Bill wabbled out into the little glade in front of the cave. Behind him was the kid, stepping softly like a scout, with a broad grin on his

---

15. surreptitiously (sûr′əp·tĭsh′əs·lē): secretly.

face. Bill stopped, took off his hat, and wiped his face with a red handkerchief. The kid stopped about eight feet behind him.

"Sam," says Bill, "I suppose you'll think I'm a renegade, but I couldn't help it. I'm a grown person with masculine proclivities[16] and habits of self-defense, but there is a time when all systems of egotism and predominances[17] fail. The boy is gone. I have sent him home. All is off. There was martyrs in old times," goes on Bill, "that suffered death rather than give up the particular graft they enjoyed. None of 'em ever was subjugated to such supernatural tortures as I have been. I tried to be faithful to our articles of depredation,[18] but there came a limit."

"What's the trouble, Bill?" I asks him.

"I was rode," says Bill, "the ninety miles to the stockade, not barring an inch. Then, when the settlers was rescued, I was given oats. Sand ain't a palatable substitute. And then, for an hour I had to try to explain to him why there was nothin' in holes, how a road can run both ways, and what makes the grass green. I tell you, Sam, a human can only stand so much. I takes him by the neck of his clothes and drags him down the mountain. On the way, he kicks my legs black-and-blue from the knees down; and I've got to have two or three bites on my thumb and hand cauterized.

"But he's gone"—continues Bill—"gone home. I showed him the road to Summit and kicked him about eight feet nearer there at one kick. I'm sorry we lose the ransom, but it was either that or Bill Driscoll to the madhouse."

Bill is puffing and blowing, but there is a look of ineffable peace and growing content on his rose-pink features.

"Bill," says I, "there isn't any heart disease in your family, is there?"

"No," says Bill, "nothing chronic except malaria and accidents. Why?"

"Then you might turn around," says I, "and have a look behind you."

Bill turns and sees the boy, and loses his complexion and sits down plump on the ground and begins to pluck aimlessly at grass

---

16. proclivities (prō·klĭv′ə·tēz): inclinations or traits.
17. systems of egotism and predominances: here, self-confidence and authority.
18. depredation (dĕp′rə·dā′shən): plundering, robbery.

and little sticks. For an hour I was afraid for his mind. And then I told him that my scheme was to put the whole job through immediately and that we would get the ransom and be off with it by midnight if old Dorset fell in with our proposition. So Bill braced up enough to give the kid a weak sort of a smile and a promise to play the Russian in a Japanese war with him as soon as he felt a little better.

I had a scheme for collecting that ransom without danger of being caught by counterplots that ought to commend itself to professional kidnapers. The tree under which the answer was to be left—and the money later on—was close to the road fence with big, bare fields on all sides. If a gang of constables should be watching for anyone to come for the note, they could see him a long way off crossing the fields or in the road. But no, siree! At half-past eight I was up in that tree, as well-hidden as a tree toad, waiting for the messenger to arrive.

Exactly on time, a half-grown boy rides up the road on a bicycle, locates the pasteboard box at the foot of the fence post, slips a folded piece of paper into it, and pedals away again back toward Summit.

I waited an hour and then concluded the thing was square. I slid down the tree, got the note, slipped along the fence till I struck the woods, and was back at the cave in another half an hour. I opened the note, got near the lantern, and read it to Bill. It was written with a pen in a crabbed hand, and the sum and substance of it was this:

Two Desperate Men:
Gentlemen, I received your letter today by post, in regard to the ransom you ask for the return of my son. I think you are a little high in your demands, and I hereby make you a counterproposition, which I am inclined to believe you will accept. You bring Johnny home and pay me two hundred and fifty dollars in cash, and I agree to take him off your hands. You had better come at night, for the neighbors believe he is lost, and I couldn't be responsible for what they would do to anybody they saw bringing him back.

Very respectfully,
Ebenezer Dorset

"Great pirates of Penzance!"[19] says I; "of all the impudent—"
But I glanced at Bill and hesitated. He had the most appealing
look in his eyes I ever saw on the face of a dumb or a talking brute.

"Sam," says he, "what's two hundred and fifty dollars, after
all? We've got the money. One more night of this kid will send me
to a bed in Bedlam.[20] Besides being a thorough gentleman, I think
Mr. Dorset is a spendthrift for making us such a liberal offer. You
ain't going to let the chance go, are you?"

"Tell you the truth, Bill," says I, "this little he ewe lamb has
somewhat got on my nerves, too. We'll take him home, pay the
ransom, and make our getaway."

We took him home that night. We got him to go by telling
him that his father had bought a silver-mounted rifle and a pair of
moccasins for him and that we were going to hunt bears the next
day.

It was just twelve o'clock when we knocked at Ebenezer's
front door. Just at the moment when I should have been abstract-
ing the fifteen hundred dollars from the box under the tree, according to the original proposition, Bill was counting out two
hundred and fifty dollars into Dorset's hand.

When the kid found out we were going to leave him at
home, he started up a howl like a calliope[21] and fastened himself as
tight as a leech to Bill's leg. His father peeled him away gradually,
like a porous plaster.

"How long can you hold him?" asks Bill.

"I'm not as strong as I used to be," says old Dorset, "but I
think I can promise you ten minutes."

"Enough," says Bill. "In ten minutes I shall cross the Central,
Southern, and Middle-Western states and be legging it trippingly
for the Canadian border."

And, as dark as it was, and as fat as Bill was, and as good a
runner as I am, he was a good mile and a half out of Summit
before I could catch up with him.

---

19. Penzance (pĕn·zăns′): seaport in England. *The Pirates of Penzance* (1879) is
a comic operetta by Gilbert and Sullivan.
20. Bedlam: slang for St. Mary of Bethlehem, a hospital for the insane in
London.
21. calliope (kə·lī′ə·pē): a mechanical organ consisting of a series of whistles.
In Greek mythology, Calliope was the Muse of eloquence and heroic poetry.

Meaning

1. A situation or event that turns out to be in strange contrast to what was intended or expected is said to be *ironic*. What is ironic about the actions of Sam and Bill in this story?
2. How much ransom was paid for Red Chief? Who paid it?
3. What are the conflicts in this story?

Method

1. To be effective, a surprise ending must be foreshadowed. How does O. Henry prepare the reader for the final turn of events?
2. What is the *climax* of this story, the point at which you could predict its outcome?
3. Which element of the story will you probably remember the longest: character, theme, or plot? Why?
4. Why do you think O. Henry chose to tell this story through the eyes of Sam? Do you think it would have been more or less amusing or effective if it had been told from Red Chief's point of view? Why?

Language: Formal and Colloquial Usage

O. Henry uses formal and colloquial language together for humorous effect. Formal English is used most often in serious, scholarly writing. It seems incongruous for "desperate kidnapers" such as Sam, and occasionally Bill, to use many-syllabled words (such as "philoprogenitiveness") which are rarely heard in conversation. Along with this highly formal language, however, Bill and Sam use colloquial words—informal slang expressions (such as "Wait till I tell you") that are typical of everyday speech. The kidnapers' errors in pronunciation and grammar make their attempts at fancy English even funnier.

Decide whether the following expressions from "The Ransom of Red Chief" are formal or colloquial. Note where errors have been made in pronunciation or grammar.

1. ". . . the fancied crackle of a twig or the rustle of a leaf revealed to his young imagination the stealthy approach of the outlaw band."

2. "We were down South, in Alabama—Bill Driscoll and myself—when this kidnaping idea struck us."
3. "There was a sylvan attitude of somnolent sleepiness pervading that section of the external outward surface of Alabama that lay exposed to my view."
4. "The kid was a boy of ten. . . ."
5. "Bill and me figured that Ebenezer would melt down for a ransom of two thousand dollars to a cent."

Discussion and Composition

1. Discuss the character of Red Chief and the attempts of Bill and Sam to get along with him. In Bill and Sam's place, what would you have done to change and improve Red Chief's behavior? Tell why.

2. Write a composition about children you have known. Use as your topic sentence any proverb about children. For example, your topic sentence might be, "Children should be seen but not heard," or "Little pitchers have big ears." Use examples and incidents to develop the topic sentence you have selected. You may want to concentrate on writing about one child, or you may prefer to tell about several different children you have known. Your composition may be serious or humorous.

DANIEL KEYES
(born 1927)

Novelist and short story writer Daniel Keyes was born in Brooklyn, New York. After graduating from high school, he enlisted in the United States Maritime Service. He was a merchant seaman and then a ship's purser before he entered Brooklyn College (now part of the City University of New York), where he received his bachelor's and master's degrees. He has worked as a fiction editor and a high school teacher, and is presently a professor of English at Ohio University in Athens, Ohio.

"Flowers for Algernon" (1959), which was originally published in a science fiction magazine, has appeared in more than twenty collections of short stories and has been translated into several languages. Mr. Keyes expanded the story into a novel which was published in 1966. It has also been a television play and a movie (retitled *Charly*).

FLOWERS FOR ALGERNON

PROGRIS RIPORT 1—MARTCH 5, 1965

Dr. Strauss says I shud rite down what I think and evrey thing that happins to me from now on. I dont know why but he says its importint so they will see if they will use me. I hope they use me. Miss Kinnian says maybe they can make me smart. I want to be smart. My name is Charlie Gordon. I am 37 years old. I have nuthing more to rite now so I will close for today.

PROGRIS RIPORT 2—MARTCH 6

I had a test today. I think I faled it. And I think maybe now they wont use me. What happind is a nice young man was in the room and he had some white cards and ink spillled all over them. He sed Charlie what do yo see on this card. I was very skared even tho I had my rabits foot in my pockit because when I was a kid I always faled tests in school and I spillled ink to.

I told him I saw a inkblot. He said yes and it made me feel good. I thot that was all but when I got up to go he said Charlie we are not thru yet. Then I dont remember so good but he wantid me to say what was in the ink. I dint see nuthing in the ink but he said there was picturs there other pepul saw some picturs. I couldnt see any picturs. I reely tryed. I held the card close up and then far away. Then I said if I had my glases I coud see better I usally only ware my glases in the movies or TV but I said they are in the closit in the hall. I got them. Then I said let me see that card agen I bet Ill find it now.

I tryed hard but I only saw the ink. I told him maybe I need new glases. He rote something down on a paper and I got skared of faling the test. I told him it was a very nice inkblot with littel points all around the edges. He looked very sad so that wasnt it. I said please let me try agen. Ill get it in a few minits becaus Im not so fast somtimes. Im a slow reeder too in Miss Kinnians class for slow adults but I'm trying very hard.

He gave me a chance with another card that had 2 kinds of ink spilled on it red and blue.

He was very nice and talked slow like Miss Kinnian does and he explaned it to me that it was a *raw shok*.[1] He said pepul see things in the ink. I said show me where. He said think. I told him I think a inkblot but that wasn't rite eather. He said what does it remind you—pretend something. I closed my eyes for a long time to pretend. I told him I pretend a fowtan pen with ink leeking all over a table cloth.

I dont think I passed the *raw shok* test

PROGRIS RIPORT 3—MARTCH 7
Dr Strauss and Dr Nemur say it dont matter about the ink-blots. They said that maybe they will still use me. I said Miss Kinnian never gave me tests like that one only spelling and reading. They said Miss Kinnian told that I was her bestist pupil in the adult nite school becaus I tryed the hardist and I reely wantid to lern. They said how come you went to the adult nite scool all by yourself Charlie. How did you find it. I said I asked pepul and sumbody told me where I shud go to lern to read and spell good. They said why did you want to. I told them becaus all my life I wantid to be smart and not dumb. But its very hard to be smart.

---

1. raw shok: Rorschach personality test, analyzes a subject's response to a series of inkblots. The test was devised by Hermann Rorschach (1884–1922), a Swiss psychiatrist.

They said you know it will probly be tempirery. I said yes. Miss Kinnian told me. I dont care if it herts.

Later I had more crazy tests today. The nice lady who gave it to me told me the name and I asked her how do you spellit so I can rite it my progris riport. THEMATIC APPERCEPTION TEST.[2] I dont know the frist 2 words but I know what *test* means. You got to pass it or you get bad marks. This test lookd easy becaus I coud see the picturs. Only this time she dint want me to tell her the picturs. That mixed me up. She said make up storys about the pepul in the picturs.

I told her how can you tell storys about pepul you never met. I said why shud I make up lies. I never tell lies any more becaus I always get caut.

She told her this test and the other one the raw-shok was for getting personality. I laffed so hard. I said how can you get that thing from inkblots and fotos. She got sore and put her picturs away. I don't care. It was sily. I gess I faled that test too.

Later some men in white coats took me to a difernt part of the hospitil and gave me a game to play. It was like a race with a white mouse. They called the mouse Algernon. Algernon was in a box with a lot of twists and turns like all kinds of walls and they gave me a pencil and a paper with lines and lots of boxes. On one side it said START and on the other end it said FINISH. They said it was *amazed* and that Algernon and me had the same *amazed* to do. I dint see how we could have the same *amazed* if Algernon had a box and I had a paper but I dint say nothing. Anyway there wasnt time because the race started.

One of the men had a watch he was trying to hide so I wouldnt see it so I tryed not to look and that made me nervus.

Anyway that test made me feel worser than all the others because they did it over 10 times with different *amazeds* and Algernon won every time. I dint know that mice were so smart. Maybe thats because Algernon is a white mouse. Maybe white mice are smarter than other mice.

PROGRIS RIPORT 4—MAR 8
Their going to use me! Im so exited I can hardly write. Dr Nemur and Dr Strauss had a argament about it first. Dr Nemur

2. Thematic Apperception Test: another popular test of personality. The subject is asked to make up stories about a series of pictures.

was in the office when Dr Strauss brot me in. Dr Nemur was worryed about using me but Dr Strauss told him Miss Kinnian rekemmended me the best from all the people who she was teaching. I like Miss Kinnian becaus shes a very smart teacher. And she said Charlie your going to have a second chance. If you volenteer for this experament you mite get smart. They dont know if it will be perminint but theirs a chance. Thats why I said ok even when I was scared because she said it was an operashun. She said dont be scared Charlie you done so much with so little I think you deserv it most of all.

So I got scaird when Dr. Nemur and Dr. Strauss argud about it. Dr. Strauss said I had something that was very good. He said I had a good *motorvation*. I never even knew I had that. I felt proud when he said that not every body with an eye-q[3] of 68 had that thing. I dont know what it is or where I got it but he said Algernon had it too. Algernons *motor-vation* is the cheese they put in his box. But it cant be that because I didn't eat any cheese this week.

Then he told Dr Nemur something I dint understand so while they were talking I wrote down some of the words.

He said Dr. Nemur I know Charlie is not what you had in mind as the first of your new brede of intelek* * (coudnt get the word) superman. But most people of his low ment* * are host* * and uncoop* * they are usually dull apath* * and hard to reach. He has a good natcher hes intristed and eager to please.

Dr Nemur said remember he will be the first human beeng ever to have his intellijence tripled by surgicle meens.

Dr. Strauss said exakly. Look at how well hes lerned to read and write for his low mentel age its as grate an acheve* * as you and I lerning einstines therey of * *vity[4] without help. That shows the inteness motor-vation. Its comparat* * a tremen* * achev* * I say we use Charlie.

I dint get all the words but it sounded like Dr Strauss was on my side and like the other one wasnt.

---

3. eye-q: I.Q. or intelligence quotient, a number arrived at by dividing a person's mental age (as determined by a standardized intelligence test) by his or her chronological age, and multiplying the result by 100. A score of 100 is considered average; 125–140 or above, gifted; below 70, mentally deficient (50–75 is considered educable). There is much controversy over how I.Q. tests are constructed and standardized.
4. einstines therey of * *vity: Einstein's theory of relativity. Albert Einstein (1879–1955). His theory of relativity revolutionized physics.

Then Dr Nemur nodded he said all right maybe your right. We will use Charlie. When he said that I got so exited I jumped up and shook his hand for being so good to me. I told him thank you doc you wont be sorry for giving me a second chance. And I mean it like I told him. After the operashun Im gonna try to be smart. Im gonna try awful hard.

PROGRIS RIPORT 5—MAR 10

Im skared. Lots of the nurses and the people who gave me the tests came to bring me candy and wish me luck. I hope I have luck. I got my rabits foot and my lucky penny. Only a black cat crossed me when I was comming to the hospitil. Dr Strauss says dont be supersitis Charlie this is science. Anyway Im keeping my rabits foot with me.

I asked Dr Strauss if Ill beat Algernon in the race after the operashun and he said maybe. If the operashun works Ill show that mouse I can be as smart as he is. Maybe smarter. Then Ill be abel to read better and spell the words good and know lots of things and be like other people. I want to be smart like other people. If it works perminint they will make everybody smart all over the wurld.

They dint give me anything to eat this morning. I dont know what that eating has to do with getting smart. Im very hungry and Dr. Nemur took away my box of candy. That Dr Nemur is a grouch. Dr Strauss says I can have it back after the operashun. You cant eat befor a operashun . . .

PROGRESS REPORT 6—MAR 15

The operashun dint hurt. He did it while I was sleeping. They took off the bandijis from my head today so I can make a PROGRESS REPORT. Dr. Nemur who looked at some of my other ones says I spell PROGRESS wrong and told me how to spell it and REPORT too. I got to try and remember that.

I have a very bad memary for spelling. Dr Strauss says its ok to tell about all the things that happin to me but he says I should tell more about what I feel and what I think. When I told him I dont know how to think he said try. All the time when the bandijis were on my eyes I tryed to think. Nothing happened. I dont know what to think about. Maybe if I ask him he will tell me how I can think now that Im suppose to get smart. What do smart people think about. Fancy things I suppose. I wish I knew some fancy things alredy.

PROGRESS REPORT 7—MAR 19

Nothing is happining. I had lots of tests and different kinds of races with Algernon. I hate that mouse. He always beats me. Dr. Strauss said I got to play those games. And he said some time I got to take those tests over again. Those inkblots are stupid. And those pictures are stupid too. I like to draw a picture of a man and a woman but I wont make up lies about people.

I got a headache from trying to think so much. I thot Dr Strauss was my frend but he dont help me. He dont tell me what to think or when Ill get smart. Miss Kinnian dint come to see me. I think writing these progress reports are stupid too.

PROGRESS REPORT 8—MAR 23

Im going back to work at the factory. They said it was better I shud go back to work but I cant tell anyone what the operashun was for and I have to come to the hospitil for an hour evry night after work. They are gonna pay me mony every month for learning to be smart.

Im glad Im going back to work because I miss my job and all my frends and all the fun we have there.

Dr Strauss says I shud keep writing things down but I dont have to do it every day just when I think of something or something speshul happins. He says dont get discoridged because it takes time and it happins slow. He says it took a long time with Algernon before he got 3 times smarter than he was before. Thats why Algernon beats me all the time because he had that operashun too. That makes me feel better. I coud probly do that *amazed* faster than a reglar mouse. Maybe some day Ill beat him. That would be something. So far Algernon looks smart perminent.

MAR 25 (I dont have to write PROGRESS REPORT on top any more just when I hand it in once a week for Dr Nemur. I just have to put the date on. That saves time)

We had a lot of fun at the factery today. Joe Carp said hey look where Charlie had his operashun what did they do Charlie put some brains in. I was going to tell him but I remembered Dr Strauss said no. Then Frank Reilly said what did you do Charlie forget your key and open your door the hard way. That made me laff. Their really my friends and they like me.

Sometimes somebody will say hey look at Joe or Frank or George he really pulled a Charlie Gordon. I dont know why they say that but they always laff. This morning Amos Borg who is the 4 man at Donnegans used my name when he shouted at Ernie the office boy. Ernie lost a packige. He said Ernie for godsake what are you trying to be a Charlie Gordon. I dont understand why he said that.

MAR 28   Dr Strauss came to my room tonight to see why I dint come in like I was suppose to. I told him I dont like to race with Algernon any more. He said I dont have to for a while but I shud come in. He had a present for me. I thot it was a little television but it wasnt. He said I got to turn it on when I go to sleep. I said your kidding why shud I turn it on when Im going to sleep. Who ever herd of a thing like that. But he said if I want to get smart I got to do what he says. I told him I dint think I was going to get smart and he puts his hand on my sholder and said Charlie you dont know it yet but your getting smarter all the time. You wont notice for a while. I think he was just being nice to make me feel good because I dont look any smarter.

Oh yes I almost forgot. I asked him when I can go back to the class at Miss Kinnians school. He said I wont go their. He said that soon Miss Kinnian will come to the hospitil to start and teach me speshul.

MAR 29   That crazy TV kept up all night. How can I sleep with something yelling crazy things all night in my ears. And the nutty pictures. Wow. I don't know what it says when Im up so how am I going to know when Im sleeping.

Dr Strauss says its ok. He says my brains are lerning when I sleep and that will help me when Miss Kinnian starts my lessons in the hospitl (only I found out it isn't a hospitil its a labatory.) I think its all crazy. If you can get smart when your sleeping why do people go to school. That thing I don't think will work. I use to watch the late show and the late late show on TV all the time and it never made me smart. Maybe you have to sleep while you watch it.

Dr Strauss showed me how to keep the TV turned low so now I can sleep. I don't hear a thing. And I still dont understand what it says. A few times I play it over in the morning to find out what I lerned when I was sleeping and I don't think so. Miss Kinnian says Maybe its another langwidge. But most times it sounds american. It talks faster than even Miss Gold who was my teacher in 6 grade.

I told Dr. Strauss what good is it to get smart in my sleep. I want to be smart when Im awake. He says its the same thing and I have two minds. Theres the *subconscious* and the *conscious* (thats how you spell it). And one dont tell the other one what its doing. They dont even talk to each other. Thats why I dream. And boy have I been having crazy dreams. Wow. Ever since that night TV. The late late late show.

I forgot to ask him if it was only me or if everybody had those two minds.

(I just looked up the word in the dictionary Dr Strauss gave me. The word is *subconscious. adj. Of the nature of mental operations yet not present in consciousness; as, subconscious conflict of desires.*) There's more but I still dont know what it means. This isnt a very good dictionary for dumb people like me.

Anyway the headache is from the party. My friends from the factery Joe Carp and Frank Reilly invited me to go to Muggsys Saloon for some drinks. I don't like to drink but they said we will have lots of fun. I had a good time.

Joe Carp said I shoud show the girls how I mop out the toilet in the factory and he got me a mop. I showed them and everyone laffed when I told that Mr. Donnegan said I was the best janiter he ever had because I like my job and do it good and never miss a day except for my operashun.

I said Miss Kinnian always said Charlie be proud of your job because you do it good.

Everybody laffed and we had a good time and they gave me lots of drinks and Joe said Charlie is a card when hes potted. I dont know what that means but everybody likes me and we have fun. I cant wait to be smart like my best friends Joe Carp and Frank Reilly.

I dont remember how the party was over but I think I went out to buy a newspaper and coffe for Joe and Frank and when I came back there was no one their. I looked for them all over till late. Then I dont remember so good but I think I got sleepy or sick. A nice cop brot me back home Thats what my landlady Mrs Flynn says.

But I got a headache and a big lump on my head. I think maybe I fell but Joe Carp says it was the cop they beat up drunks some times. I don't think so. Miss Kinnian says cops are to help people. Anyway I got a bad headache and Im sick and hurt all over. I dont think Ill drink anymore.

APRIL 6   I beat Algernon! I dint even know I beat him until Burt the tester told me. Then the second time I lost because I got so exited I fell off the chair before I finished. But after that I beat him 8 more times. I must be getting smart to beat a smart mouse like Algernon. But I don't *feel* smarter.

I wanted to race Algernon some more but Burt said thats enough for one day. They let me hold him for a minit. Hes not so bad. Hes soft like a ball of cotton. He blinks and when he opens his eyes their black and pink on the eges.

I said can I feed him because I felt bad to beat him and I wanted to be nice and make friends. Burt said no Algernon is a very specshul mouse with an operashun like mine, and he was the first of all the animals to stay smart so long. He told me Algernon is so smart that every day he has to solve a test to get his food. Its a thing like a lock on a door that changes every time Algernon goes in to eat so he has to lern something new to get his food. That made me sad because if he couldn't lern he woud be hungry.

I don't think its right to make you pass a test to eat. How would Dr Nemur like it to have to pass a test every time he wants to eat. I think Ill be friends with Algernon.

APRIL 9   Tonight after work Miss Kinnian was at the laboratory. She looked like she was glad to see me but scared. I told her dont worry Miss Kinnian Im not smart yet and she laffed. She said I have confidence in you Charlie the way you struggled so hard to read and right better than all the others. At werst you will have it for a littel wile and your doing somthing for science.

We are reading a very hard book. Its called *Robinson Crusoe* about a man who gets merooned on a dessert Iland. Hes smart and figers out all kinds of things so he can have a house and food and hes a good swimmer. Only I feel sorry because hes all alone and has no frends. But I think their must be somebody else on the iland because theres a picture with his funny umbrella looking at footprints. I hope he gets a frend and not be lonly.

APRIL 10   Miss Kinnian teaches me to spell better. She says look at a word and close your eyes and say it over and over until you remember. I have lots of truble with *through* that you say *threw* and *enough* and *tough* that you dont say *enew and tew*. You got to say *enuff* and *tuff*. Thats how I use to write it before I started to get smart. Im confused but Miss Kinnian says theres no reason in spelling.

APR 14   Finished *Robinson Crusoe*. I want to find out more about what happens to him but Miss Kinnian says thats all there is. *Why.*

APR 15   Miss Kinnian says Im lerning fast. She read some of the Progress Reports and she looked at me kind of funny. She says Im a fine person and Ill show them all. I asked her why. She said never mind but I shouldnt feel bad if I find out everybody isnt nice like I think. She said for a person who god gave so little to you done more then a lot of people with brains they never even used. I said all my friends are smart people but there good. They like me and they never did anything that wasnt nice. Then she got something in her eye and she had to run out to the ladys room.

APR 16   Today, I lerned, the *comma,* this is a comma (,) a period, with a tail, Miss Kinnian, says its important, because, it makes writing, better, she said, somebody, coud lose, a lot of money, if a comma, isnt, in the, right place, I dont have, any money, and I dont see, how a comma, keeps you, from losing it,

APR 17   I used the comma wrong. Its punctuation. Miss Kinnian told me to look up long words in the dictionary to lern to spell them. I said whats the difference if you can read it anyway. She said its part of your education so now on Ill look up all the words Im not sure how to spell. It takes a long time to write that way but I only have to look up once and after that I get it right.

You got to mix them up, she showed? me" how. to mix! them (and now; I can! mix up all kinds" of punctuation, in! my writing? There, are lots! of rules? to lern; but Im gettin'g them in my head.

One thing I like about, Dear Miss Kinnian: (thats the way it goes in a business letter if I ever go into business) is she, always gives me' a reason" when—I ask. She's a gen'ius! I wish I cou'd be smart" like, her;

(Punctuation, is; fun!)

APRIL 18   What a dope I am! I didn't even understand what she was talking about. I read the grammar book last night and it explanes the whole thing. Then I saw it was the same way as Miss Kinnian was trying to tell me, but I didn't get it.

Miss Kinnian said that the TV working in my sleep helped out. She and I reached a plateau. Thats a flat hill.

After I figured out how puncuation worked, I read over all my old Progress Reports from the beginning. Boy, did I have crazy spelling and punctuation! I told Miss Kinnian I ought to go over the pages and fix all the mistakes but she said, "No, Charlie, Dr. Nemur wants them just as they are. That's why he let you keep them after they were photostated, to see your own progress. You're coming along fast, Charlie."

That made me feel good. After the lesson I went down and played with Algernon. We don't race any more.

APRIL 20   I feel sick inside. Not sick like for a doctor, but inside my chest it feels empty like getting punched and a heartburn at the same time. I wasn't going to write about it, but I guess I got to, because its important. Today was the first time I ever stayed home from work.

Last night Joe Carp and Frank Reilly invited me to a party. There were lots of girls and some men from the factory. I remembered how sick I got last time I drank too much, so I told Joe I didn't want anything to drink. He gave me a plain coke instead.

We had a lot of fun for a while. Joe said I should dance with Ellen and she would teach me the steps. I fell a few times and I couldn't understand why because no one else was dancing besides Ellen and me. And all the time I was tripping because somebody's foot was always sticking out.

Then when I got up I saw the look on Joe's face and it gave me a funny feeling in my stomach. "He's a scream," one of the girls said. Everybody was laughing.

"Look at him. He's blushing. Charlie is blushing."

"Hey, Ellen, what'd you do to Charlie? I never saw him act like that before."

I didn't know what to do or where to turn. Everyone was looking at me and laughing and I felt naked. I wanted to hide. I ran outside and I threw up. Then I walked home. It's a funny thing I never knew that Joe and Frank and the others liked to have me around all the time to make fun of me.

Now I know what it means when they say "to pull a Charlie Gordon."

I'm ashamed.

PROGRESS REPORT 11

APRIL 21   Still didn't go into the factory. I told Mrs. Flynn my landlady to call and tell Mr. Donnegan I was sick. Mrs. Flynn looks at me very funny lately like she's scared.

I think it's a good thing about finding out how everybody laughs at me. I thought about it a lot. It's because I'm so dumb and I don't even know when I'm doing something dumb. People think it's funny when a dumb person can't do things the same way they can.

Anyway, now I know I'm getting smarter every day. I know punctuation and I can spell good. I like to look up all the hard words in the dictionary and I remember them. I'm reading a lot now, and Miss Kinnian says I read very fast. Sometimes I even understand what I'm reading about, and it stays in my mind. There are times when I can close my eyes and think of a page and it all comes back like a picture.

Besides history, geography and arithmetic, Miss Kinnian said I should start to learn foreign languages. Dr. Strauss gave me some more tapes to play while I sleep. I still don't understand how that conscious and unconscious mind works, but Dr. Strauss says not to worry yet. He asked me to promise that when I start learning college subjects next week I wouldn't read any books on psychology—that is, until he gives me permission.

I feel a lot better today, but I guess I'm still a little angry that all the time people were laughing and making fun of me because I wasn't so smart. When I become intelligent like Dr. Strauss says, with three times my I.Q. of 68, then maybe I'll be like everyone else and people will like me.

I'm not sure what an I.Q. is. Dr. Nemur said it was something that measured how intelligent you were—like a scale in the drugstore weighs pounds. But Dr. Strauss had a big argument with him and said an I.Q. didn't weigh intelligence at all. He said an I.Q. showed how much intelligence you could get, like the numbers on the outside of a measuring cup. You still had to fill the cup up with stuff.

Then when I asked Burt, who gives me my intelligence tests and works with Algernon, he said that both of them were wrong (only I had to promise not to tell them he said so). Burt says that the I.Q. measures a lot of different things including some of the things you learned already, and it really isn't any good at all.

So I still don't know what I.Q. is except that mine is going to be over 200 soon. I didn't want to say anything, but I don't see how if they don't know *what* it is, or *where* it is—I don't see how they know *how much* of it you've got.

Dr. Nemur says I have to take a *Rorshach Test* tomorrow. I wonder what *that* is.

APRIL 22   I found out what a Rorshach is. It's the test I took before the operation—the one with the inkblots on the pieces of cardboard.

I was scared to death of those inkblots. I knew the man was going to ask me to find the pictures and I knew I couldn't. I was thinking to myself, if only there was some way of knowing what kind of pictures were hidden there. Maybe there weren't any pictures at all. Maybe it was just a trick to see if I was dumb enough to look for something that wasn't there. Just thinking about that made me sore at him.

"All right, Charlie," he said, "you've seen these cards before, remember?"

"Of course I remember."

The way I said it, he knew I was angry, and he looked surprised. "Yes, of course. Now I want you to look at this. What might this be? What do you see on this card? People see all sorts of things in these inkblots. Tell me what it might be for you—what it makes you think of."

I was shocked. That wasn't what I had expected him to say. "You mean there are no pictures hidden in those inkblots?"

He frowned and took off his glasses. "What?"

"Pictures. Hidden in the inkblots. Last time you told me everyone could see them and you wanted me to find them too."

He explained to me that the last time he had used almost the exact same words he was using now. I didn't believe it, and I still have the suspicion that he misled me at the time just for the fun of it. Unless—I don't know any more—could I have been *that* feeble-minded?

We went through the cards slowly. One looked like a pair of bats tugging at something. Another one looked like two men fencing with swords. I imagined all sorts of things. I guess I got carried away. But I didn't trust him any more, and I kept turning them around, even looking on the back to see if there was anything there I was supposed to catch. While he was making notes, I peeked out of the corner of my eye to read it. But it was all in code that looked like this:

$$WF + A \qquad DdF\text{---}Ad \text{ orig.} \qquad WF\text{---}A$$
$$SF + obj$$

The test still doesn't make sense to me. It seems to me that anyone could make up lies about things that they didn't really imagine? Maybe I'll understand it when Dr. Strauss lets me read up on psychology.

APRIL 25   I figured out a new way to line up the machines in the factory, and Mr. Donnegan says it will save him ten thousand dollars a year in labor and increased production. He gave me a $25 bonus.

I wanted to take Joe Carp and Frank Reilly out to lunch to celebrate, but Joe said he had to buy some things for his wife, and Frank said he was meeting his cousin for lunch. I guess it'll take a little time for them to get used to the changes in me. Everybody seems to be frightened of me. When I went over to Amos Borg and tapped him, he jumped up in the air.

People don't talk to me much any more or kid around the way they used to. It makes the job kind of lonely.

APRIL 27   I got up the nerve today to ask Miss Kinnian to have dinner with me tomorrow night to celebrate my bonus.

At first she wasn't sure it was right, but I asked Dr. Strauss and he said it was okay. Dr. Strauss and Dr. Nemur don't seem to be getting along so well. They're arguing all the time. This evening I heard them shouting. Dr. Nemur was saying that it was *his* experiment and *his* research, and Dr. Strauss shouted back that he contributed just as much, because he found me through Miss Kinnian and he performed the operation. Dr. Strauss said that someday thousands of neuro-surgeons might be using his technique all over the world.

Dr. Nemur wanted to publish the results of the experiment at the end of this month. Dr. Strauss wanted to wait a while to be sure. Dr. Strauss said Dr. Nemur was more interested in the Chair of Psychology at Princeton than he was in the experiment. Dr. Nemur said Dr. Strauss was nothing but an opportunist trying to ride to glory on *his* coattails.

When I left afterwards, I found myself trembling. I don't know why for sure, but it was as if I'd seen both men clearly for the first time. I remember hearing Burt say Dr. Nemur had a shrew of a wife who was pushing him all the time to get things published so he could become famous. Burt said that the dream of her life was to have a big shot husband.

APRIL 28   I don't understand why I never noticed how beautiful Miss Kinnian really is. She has brown eyes and feathery brown hair that comes to the top of her neck. She's only thirty-four! I think from the beginning I had the feeling that she was an unreachable genius—and very, very old. Now, every time I see her she grows younger and more lovely.

We had dinner and a long talk. When she said I was coming along so fast I'd be leaving her behind, I laughed.

"It's true, Charlie. You're already a better reader than I am. You can read a whole page at a glance while I can take in only a few lines at a time. And you remember every single thing you read. I'm lucky if I can recall the main thoughts and the general meaning."

"I don't feel intelligent. There are so many things I don't understand."

She took out a cigarette and I lit it for her. "You've got to be a *little* patient. You're accomplishing in days and weeks what it takes normal people to do in a lifetime. That's what makes it so amazing. You're like a giant sponge now, soaking things in. Facts, figures, general knowledge. And soon you'll begin to connect them, too. You'll see how different branches of learning are related. There are many levels, Charlie, like steps on a giant ladder that take you up higher and higher to see more and more of the world around you.

"I can see only a little bit of that, Charlie, and I won't go much higher than I am now, but you'll keep climbing up and up, and see more and more, and each step will open new worlds that you never even knew existed." She frowned. "I hope . . . I just hope to God—"

"What?"

"Never mind, Charles. I just hope I wasn't wrong to advise you to go into this in the first place."

I laughed. "How could that be? It worked, didn't it? Even Algernon is still smart."

We sat there silently for a while and I knew what she was thinking about as she watched me toying with the chain of my rabbit's foot and my keys. I didn't want to think of that possibility any more than elderly people want to think of death. I *knew* that this was only the beginning. I knew what she meant about levels because I'd seen some of them already. The thought of leaving her behind made me sad.

I'm in love with Miss Kinnian.

PROGRESS REPORT 12

APRIL 30 I've quit my job with Donnegan's Plastic Box Company. Mr. Donnegan insisted it would be better for all concerned if I left. What did I do to make them hate me so?

The first I knew of it was when Mr. Donnegan showed me the petition. Eight hundred names, everyone in the factory, except Fanny Girden. Scanning the list quickly, I saw at once that hers was the only missing name. All the rest demanded that I be fired.

Joe Carp and Frank Reilly wouldn't talk to me about it. No one else would either, except Fanny. She was one of the few people I'd known who set her mind to something and believed it no matter what the rest of the world proved, said or did—and Fanny did not believe that I should have been fired. She had been against the petition on principle and despite the pressure and threats she'd held out.

"Which don't mean to say," she remarked, "that I don't think there's something mighty strange about you, Charlie. Them changes. I don't know. You used to be a good, dependable, ordinary man—not too bright maybe, but honest. Who knows what you done to yourself to get so smart all of a sudden. Like everybody around here's been saying, Charlie, it's not right."

"But how can you say that, Fanny? What's wrong with a

man becoming intelligent and wanting to acquire knowledge and understanding of the world around him?"

She stared down at her work and I turned to leave. Without looking at me, she said: "It was evil when Eve listened to the snake and ate from the tree of knowledge. It was evil when she saw that she was naked. If not for that none of us would ever have to grow old and sick, and die."

Once again, now, I have the feeling of shame burning inside me. This intelligence has driven a wedge between me and all the people I once knew and loved. Before, they laughed at me and despised me for my ignorance and dullness; now, they hate me for my knowledge and understanding. What in God's name do they want of me?

They've driven me out of the factory. Now I'm more alone than ever before. . . .

MAY 15   Dr. Strauss is very angry at me for not having written any progress reports in two weeks. He's justified because the lab is now paying me a regular salary. I told him I was too busy thinking and reading. When I pointed out that writing was such a slow process that it made me impatient with my poor handwriting, he suggested I learn to type. It's much easier to write now because I can type seventy-five words a minute. Dr. Strauss continually reminds me of the need to speak and write simply so people will be able to understand me.

I'll try to review all the things that happened to me during the last two weeks. Algernon and I were presented to the *American Psychological Association* sitting in convention with the *World Psychological Association*. We created quite a sensation. Dr. Nemur and Dr. Strauss were proud of us.

I suspect that Dr. Nemur, who is sixty—ten years older than Dr. Strauss—finds it necessary to see tangible results of his work. Undoubtedly the result of pressure by Mrs. Nemur.

Contrary to my earlier impressions of him, I realize that Dr. Nemur is not at all a genius. He has a very good mind, but it struggles under the spectre[5] of self-doubt. He wants people to take him for a genius. Therefore it is important for him to feel that his work is accepted by the world. I believe that Dr. Nemur was afraid of further delay because he worried that someone else might make a discovery along these lines and take the credit from him.

5. **spectre** (spĕk′tər): something that arouses fear or dread, such as a ghost.

Dr. Strauss on the other hand might be called a genius, although I feel his areas of knowledge are too limited. He was educated in the tradition of narrow specialization; the broader aspects of background were neglected far more than necessary—even for a neuro-surgeon.

I was shocked to learn the only ancient languages he could read were Latin, Greek and Hebrew, and that he knows almost nothing of mathematics beyond the elementary levels of the calculus of variations.[6] When he admitted this to me, I found myself almost annoyed. It was as if he'd hidden this part of himself in order to deceive me, pretending—as do many people I've discovered—to be what he is not. No one I've ever known is what he appears to be on the surface.

Dr. Nemur appears to be uncomfortable around me. Sometimes when I try to talk to him, he just looks at me strangely and turns away. I was angry at first when Dr. Strauss told me I was giving Dr. Nemur an inferiority complex. I thought he was mocking me and I'm oversensitive at being made fun of.

How was I to know that a highly respected psychoexperimentalist like Nemur was unacquainted with Hindustani and Chinese? It's absurd when you consider the work that is being done in India and China today in the very field of his study.

I asked Dr. Strauss how Nemur could refute Rahajamati's attack on his method if Nemur couldn't even read them in the first place. That strange look on Strauss' face can mean only one of two things. Either he doesn't want to tell Nemur what they're saying in India, or else—and this worries me—Dr. Strauss doesn't know either. I must be careful to speak and write clearly and simply so people won't laugh.

MAY 18 I am very disturbed. I saw Miss Kinnian last night for the first time in over a week. I tried to avoid all discussions of intellectual concepts and to keep the conversation on a simple, everyday level, but she just stared at me blankly and asked me what I meant about the mathematical variance equivalent in Dorbermann's *Fifth Concerto*.[7]

When I tried to explain she stopped me and laughed. I guess I

6. **calculus of variations:** a branch of higher mathematics developed by Jakob and Johann Bernoulli in the seventeenth century.
7. **Dorbermann's *Fifth Concerto*:** fictional music composer, and fictional composition.

got angry, but I suspect I'm approaching her on the wrong level. No matter what I try to discuss with her, I am unable to communicate. I must review Vrostadt's equations on *Levels of Semantic Progression*.[8] I find I don't communicate with people much any more. Thank God for books and music and things I can think about. I am alone at Mrs. Flynn's boarding house most of the time and seldom speak to anyone.

MAY 20   I would not have noticed the new dishwasher, a boy of about sixteen, at the corner diner where I take my evening meals if not for the incident of the broken dishes.

They crashed to the floor, sending bits of white china under the tables. The boy stood there, dazed and frightened, holding the empty tray in his hand. The catcalls from the customers (the cries of "hey, there go the profits!" . . . *"Mazeltov!"*[9] . . . and "well, *he* didn't work here very long . . ." which invariably seem to follow the breaking of glass or dishware in a public restaurant) all seemed to confuse him.

When the owner came to see what the excitement was about, the boy cowered as if he expected to be struck. "All right! All right, you dope," shouted the owner, "don't just stand there! Get the broom and sweep that mess up. A broom . . . a broom, you idiot! It's in the kitchen!"

The boy saw he was not going to be punished. His frightened expression disappeared and he smiled as he came back with the broom to sweep the floor. A few of the rowdier customers kept up the remarks, amusing themselves at his expense.

"Here, sonny, over here there's a nice piece behind you . . ."

"He's not so dumb. It's easier to break 'em than wash em!"

As his vacant eyes moved across the crowd of onlookers, he slowly mirrored their smiles and finally broke into an uncertain grin at the joke he obviously did not understand.

I felt sick inside as I looked at his dull, vacuous smile, the wide, bright eyes of a child, uncertain but eager to please. They were laughing at him because he was mentally retarded.

And I had been laughing at him too.

---

8. **Vrostadt's equations on *Levels of Semantic Progression*:** fictional semanticist. Semantics is the study of the development of speech forms, signs, and symbols.

9. **Mazeltov** (mäz′əl·tôv): expression of best wishes, used by Jews on fortunate occasions. It is a corruption of two Hebrew words, *Mazal tov.*

Suddenly I was furious at myself and all those who were smirking at him. I jumped up and shouted, "Shut up! Leave him alone! It's not his fault he can't understand! He can't help what he is! But he's still a human being!"

The room grew silent. I cursed myself for losing control. I tried not to look at the boy as I walked out without touching my food. I felt ashamed for both of us.

How strange that people of honest feelings and sensibility, who would not take advantage of a man born without arms or eyes—how such people think nothing of abusing a man born with low intelligence. It infuriated me to think that not too long ago I had foolishly played the clown.

And I had almost forgotten.

I'd hidden the picture of the old Charlie Gordon from myself because now that I was intelligent it was something that had to be pushed out of my mind. But today in looking at that boy, for the first time I saw what I had been. *I was just like him!*

Only a short time ago, I learned that people laughed at me. Now I can see that unknowingly I joined with them in laughing at myself. That hurts most of all.

I have often reread my progress reports and seen the illiteracy, the childish naiveté,[10] the mind of low intelligence peering from a dark room, through the keyhole at the dazzling light outside. I see that even in my dullness I knew I was inferior, and that other people had something I lacked—something denied me. In my mental blindness, I thought it was somehow connected with the ability to read and write, and I was sure that if I could get those skills I would automatically have intelligence too.

Even a feeble-minded man wants to be like other men.

A child may not know how to feed itself, or what to eat, yet it knows of hunger.

This then is what I was like. I never knew. Even with my gift of intellectual awareness, I never really knew.

This day was good for me. Seeing the past more clearly, I've decided to use my knowledge and skills to work in the field of increasing human intelligence levels. Who is better equipped for this work? Who else has lived in both worlds? These are my people. Let me use my gift to do something for them.

Tomorrow, I will discuss with Dr. Strauss how I can work in

---

10. naiveté (nä·ēv'tā'): innocence, simplicity.

this area. I may be able to help him work out the problems of widespread use of the technique which was used on me. I have several good ideas of my own.

There is so much that might be done with this technique. If I could be made into a genius, what about thousands of others like myself? What fantastic levels might be achieved by using this technique on normal people? On *geniuses?*

There are so many doors to open. I am impatient to begin.

PROGRESS REPORT 13
MAY 23   It happened today. Algernon bit me. I visited the lab to see him as I do occasionally, and when I took him out of his cage, he snapped at my hand. I put him back and watched him for a while. He was unusually disturbed and vicious.

MAY 24   Burt, who is in charge of the experimental animals, tells me that Algernon is changing. He is less co-operative; he refuses to run the maze any more; general motivation has decreased. And he hasn't been eating. Everyone is upset about what this may mean.

MAY 25   They've been feeding Algernon, who now refuses to work the shifting-lock problem. Everyone identifies me with Algernon. In a way we're both the first of our kind. They're all pretending that Algernon's behavior is not necessarily significant for me. But it's hard to hide the fact that some of the other animals who were used in this experiment are showing strange behavior.

Dr. Strauss and Dr. Nemur have asked me not to come to the lab any more. I know what they're thinking but I can't accept it. I am going ahead with my plans to carry their research forward. With all due respect to both these fine scientists, I am well aware of their limitations. If there is an answer, I'll have to find it out for myself. Suddenly, time has become very important to me.

MAY 29   I have been given a lab of my own and permission to go ahead with the research. I'm onto something. Working day and night. I've had a cot moved into the lab. Most of my writing time is spent on the notes which I keep in a separate folder, but from time to time I feel it necessary to put down my moods and thoughts from sheer habit.

I find the *calculus of intelligence* to be a fascinating study. Here is the place for the application of all the knowledge I have acquired.

MAY 31   Dr. Strauss thinks I'm working too hard. Dr. Nemur says I'm trying to cram a lifetime of research and thought into a few weeks. I know I should rest, but I'm driven on by something inside that won't let me stop. I've got to find the reason for the sharp regression in Algernon. I've got to know *if* and *when* it will happen to me.

June 4

LETTER TO DR. STRAUSS (*copy*)

Dear Dr. Strauss:

Under separate cover I am sending you a copy of my report entitled, "The Algernon-Gordon Effect: A Study of Structure and Function of Increased Intelligence," which I would like to have published.

As you see, my experiments are completed. I have included in my report all of my formulae, as well as mathematical analysis in the appendix. Of course, these should be verified.

Because of its importance to both you and Dr. Nemur (and need I say to myself, too?) I have checked and rechecked my results a dozen times in the hope of finding an error. I am sorry to say the results must stand. Yet for the sake of science, I am grateful for the little bit that I here add to the knowledge of the function of the human mind and of the laws governing the artificial increase of human intelligence.

I recall your once saying to me that an experimental *failure* or the *disproving* of a theory was as important to the advancement of learning as a success would be. I know now that this is true. I am sorry, however, that my own contribution to the field must rest upon the ashes of the work of two men I regard so highly.

Yours truly,
Charles Gordon

JUNE 5   I must not become emotional. The facts and the results of my experiments are clear, and the more sensational aspects of my own rapid climb cannot obscure the fact that the tripling of intelligence by the surgical technique developed by Drs. Strauss and Nemur must be viewed as having little or no practical applicability (at the present time) to the increase of human intelligence.

As I review the records and data on Algernon, I see that although he is still in his physical infancy, he has regressed mentally. Motor activity is impaired; there is a general reduction of glandular activity; there is an accelerated loss of coordination.

There are also strong indications of progressive amnesia.[11]

As will be seen in my report, these and other physical and mental deterioration[12] syndromes[13] can be predicted with significant results by the application of my formula.

The surgical stimulus to which we were both subjected has resulted in an intensification and acceleration of all mental processes. The unforeseen development, which I have taken the liberty of calling the *Algernon-Gordon Effect,* is the logical extension of the entire intelligence speed-up. The hypothesis here proven may be described simply in the following terms: Artificially increased intelligence deteriorates at a rate of time directly proportional to the quantity of the increase.

I feel that this, in itself, is an important discovery.

As long as I am able to write, I will continue to record my thoughts in these progress reports. It is one of my few pleasures. However, by all indications, my own mental deterioration will be very rapid.

I have already begun to notice signs of emotional instability and forgetfulness, the first symptoms of the burnout.

JUNE 10   Deterioration progressing. I have become absent-minded. Algernon died two days ago. Dissection[14] shows my predictions were right. His brain had decreased in weight and there

---

11. amnesia (ăm·nē′zhə): partial or total loss of memory, especially through shock, injury, psychological disturbance or illness.
12. deterioration (dĭ·tîr′ē·ə·rā′shən): loss or decay.
13. syndromes (sĭn′drōms′): combinations of signs indicating disease.
14. dissection (dĭ·sĕk′shən): dividing a dead animal into its parts in order to study structure or cause of death.

was a general smoothing out of cerebral convolutions,[15] as well as a deepening and broadening of brain fissures.[16]

I guess the same thing is or will soon be happening to me. Now that it's definite, I don't want it to happen.

I put Algernon's body in a cheese box and buried him in the back yard. I cried.

JUNE 15   Dr. Strauss came to see me again. I wouldn't open the door and I told him to go away. I want to be left to myself. I am touchy and irritable. I feel the darkness closing in. It's hard to throw off thoughts of suicide. I keep telling myself how important this journal will be.

It's a strange sensation to pick up a book you enjoyed just a few months ago and discover you don't remember it. I remembered how great I thought John Milton[17] was, but when I picked up *Paradise Lost* I couldn't understand it at all. I got so angry I threw the book across the room.

I've got to try to hold on to some of it. Some of the things I've learned. Oh, God, please don't take it all away.

JUNE 19   Sometimes, at night, I go out for a walk. Last night, I couldn't remember where I lived. A policeman took me home. I have the strange feeling that this has all happened to me before—a long time ago. I keep telling myself I'm the only person in the world who can describe what's happening to me.

JUNE 21   Why can't I remember? I've got to fight. I lie in bed for days and I don't know who or where I am. Then it all comes back to me in a flash. Fugues[18] amnesia. Symptoms of senility—second childhood. I can watch them coming on. It's so cruelly logical. I learned so much and so fast. Now my mind is deteriorating rapidly. I won't let it happen. I'll fight it. I can't help

15. **convolutions** (kŏn'və·loo'shəns): ridges or folds in the surface of the brain.
16. **fissures** (fĭsh'ərs): cracks.
17. **John Milton:** English poet and writer (1608–1674) in behalf of political and religious liberty. He wrote the long, richly allusive poem *Paradise Lost* (1665) after he had become blind.
18. **fugues** (fūgs): usually, music based on short themes which are repeated with slight variations; here, temporary flights from the real world.

thinking of the boy in the restaurant, the blank expression, the silly smile, the people laughing at him. No—please—not that again. . . .

JUNE 22   I'm forgetting things that I learned recently. It seems to be following the classic pattern—the last things learned are the first things forgotten. Or is that the pattern? I'd better look it up again. . . .

I re-read my paper on the *Algernon-Gordon Effect* and I get the strange feeling that it was written by someone else. There are parts I don't even understand.

Motor activity impaired. I keep tripping over things, and it becomes increasingly difficult to type.

JUNE 23   I've given up using the typewriter. My coordination is bad. I feel I'm moving slower and slower. Had a terrible shock today. I picked up a copy of an article I used in my research, Krueger's *Uber psychische Ganzheit,*[19] to see if it would help me understand what I had done. First I thought there was something wrong with my eyes. Then I realized I could no longer read German. I tested myself in other languages. All gone.

JUNE 30   A week since I dared to write again. It's slipping away like sand through my fingers. Most of the books I have are too hard for me now. I get angry with them because I know that I read and understood them just a few weeks ago.

I keep telling myself I must keep writing these reports so that somebody will know what is happening to me. But it gets harder to form the words and remember spellings. I have to look up even simple words in the dictionary now and it makes me impatient with myself.

Dr. Strauss comes around almost every day, but I told him I wouldn't see or speak to anybody. He feels guilty. They all do. But I don't blame anyone. I knew what might happen. But how it hurts.

JULY 7   I don't know where the week went. Todays Sunday I know because I can see through my window people going to church. I think I stayed in bed all week but I remember Mrs.

**19. Krueger's *Uber psychische Ganzheit:* ** fictional scientist's work in German (translation: *Concerning a Psychic Totality*).

Flynn bringing food to me a few times. I keep saying over and over I've got to do something but then I forget or maybe its just easier not to do what I say I'm going to do.

I think of my mother and father a lot these days. I found a picture of them with me taken at a beach. My father has a big ball under his arm and my mother is holding me by the hand. I dont remember them the way they are in the picture. All I remember is my father drunk most of the time and arguing with mom about money.

He never shaved much and he used to scratch my face when he hugged me. My Mother said he died but Cousin Miltie said he heard his dad say that my father ran away with another woman. When I asked my mother she slapped me and said my father was dead. I dont think I ever found out the truth but I dont care much. (He said he was going to take me to see cows on a farm once but he never did. He never kept his promises. . . .)

JULY 10 My landlady Mrs. Flynn is very worried about me. She says the way I lay around all day and dont do anything I remind her of her son before she threw him out of the house. She said she doesn't like loafers. If Im sick its one thing, but if Im a loafer thats another thing and she won't have it. I told her I think Im sick.

I try to read a little bit every day, mostly stories, but sometimes I have to read the same thing over and over again because I don't know what it means. And its hard to write. I know I should look up all the words in the dictionary but its so hard and Im so tired all the time.

Then I got the idea that I would only use the easy words instead of the long hard ones. That saves time. I put flowers on Algernons grave about once a week. Mrs. Flynn thinks Im crazy to put flowers on a mouses grave but I told her that Algernon was special.

JULY 14 Its sunday again. I dont have anything to do to keep me busy now because my television set is broke and I dont have any money to get it fixed. (I think I lost this months check from the lab. I dont remember)

I get awful headaches and asperin doesnt help me much. Mrs. Flynn knows Im really sick and she feels very sorry for me. Shes a wonderful woman whenever someone is sick.

JULY 22   Mrs. Flynn called a strange doctor to see me. She was afraid I was going to die. I told the doctor I wasnt too sick and I only forget sometimes. He asked me did I have any friends or relatives and I said no I dont have any. I told him I had a friend called Algernon once but he was a mouse and we used to run races together. He looked at me kind of funny like he thought I was crazy. He smiled when I told him I used to be a genius. He talked to me like I was a baby and he winked at Mrs. Flynn. I got mad and chased him out because he was making fun of me the way they all used to.

JULY 24   I have no more money and Mrs Flynn says I got to go to work somewhere and pay the rent because I havent paid for two months. I dont know any work but the job I used to have at Donnegans Box Company. I dont want to go back because they all knew me when I was smart and maybe they'll laugh at me. But I dont know what else to do to get money.

JULY 25   I was looking at some of my old progress reports and its very funny but I cant read what I wrote. I can make out some of the words but they dont make sense.

Miss Kinnian came to the door but I said go away I don't want to see you. She cried and I cried too but I wouldnt let her in because I didn't want her to laugh at me. I told her I didnt like her any more. I told her I didnt want to be smart any more. Thats not true. I still love her and I still want to be smart but I had to say that so shed go away. She gave Mrs. Flynn money to pay the rent. I dont want that. I got to get a job.

Please . . . please let me not forget how to read and write. . . .

JULY 27   Mr. Donnegan was very nice when I came back and asked him for my old job of janitor. First he was very suspicious but I told him what happened to me then he looked very sad and put his hand on my shoulder and said Charlie Gordon you got guts.

Everybody looked at me when I came downstairs and started working in the toilet sweeping it out like I used to. I told myself Charlie if they make fun of you dont get sore because you remember their not so smart as you once thot they were. And besides they were once your friends and if they laughted at you that doesnt meant anything because they liked you too.

One of the new men who came to work there after I went away made a nasty crack he said hey Charlie I hear your a very smart fella a real quiz kid. Say something intelligent. I felt bad but Joe Carp came over and grabbed him by the shirt and said leave him alone you lousy cracker or I'll break your neck. I didn't expect Joe to take my part so I guess hes really my friend.

Later Frank Reilly came over and said Charlie if anybody bothers you or trys to take advantage you call me or Joe and we will set em straight. I said thanks Frank and I got choked up so I had to turn around and go into the supply room so he wouldnt see me cry. Its good to have friends.

JULY 28   I did a dumb thing today I forgot I wasn't in Miss Kinnians class at the adult center any more like I use to be. I went in and sat down in my old seat in the back of the room and she looked at me funny and she said Charles. I dint remember she ever called me that before only Charlie so I said hello Miss Kinnian Im redy for my lesin today only I lost my reader that we was using. She startid to cry and run out of the room and everybody looked at me and I saw they wasnt the same pepul who use to be in my class.

Then all of a suddin I remembered some things about the operashun and me getting smart and I said holy smoke I reely pulled a Charlie Gordon that time. I went away before she come back to the room.

Thats why Im going away from New York for good. I dont want to do nothing like that agen. I dont want Miss Kinnian to feel sorry for me. Evry body feels sorry at the factery and I dont want that eather so Im going someplace where nobody knows that Charlie Gordon was once a genus and now he cant even reed a book or rite good.

Im taking a cuple of books along and even if I cant reed them Ill practise hard and maybe I wont forget every thing I lerned. If I try reel hard maybe Ill be a littel bit smarter then I was before the operashun. I got my rabits foot and my luky penny and maybe they will help me.

If you ever reed this Miss Kinnian dont be sorry for me Im glad I got a second chanse to be smart becaus I lerned a lot of things that I never even new were in this world and Im grateful that I saw it all for a littel bit. I dont know why Im dumb agen or what I did wrong maybe its because I dint try hard enuff. But if I try and practis very hard maybe Ill get a littl smarter and know what all the words are. I remember a littel bit how nice I had a feeling with the blue book that has the torn cover when I red it. Thats why Im gonna keep trying to get smart so I can have that feeling agen. Its a good feeling to know things and be smart. I wish I had it rite now if I did I would sit down and reed all the time. Anyway I bet Im the first dumb person in the world who ever found out something importent for science. I remember I did something but I dont remember what. So I gess its like I did it for all the dumb pepul like me.

Goodbye Miss Kinnian and Dr. Strauss and evreybody. And P.S. please tell Dr Nemur not to be such a grouch when pepul laff at him and he would have more frends. Its easy to make frends if you let pepul laff at you. Im going to have lots of frends where I go.

P.P.S. Please if you get a chanse put some flowrs on Algernons grave in the bak yard. . . .

Meaning

1. Why was Charlie chosen for the test?
2. How did Charlie's character and personality change as he grew more intelligent? How did his feelings about himself change?
3. Why did the factory workers demand that Charlie be fired?
4. What was the *Algernon-Gordon Effect*?
5. The *theme* of a story is the idea that underlies the plot. What is the theme of "Flowers for Algernon"? How does the ending contribute to the presentation of the theme?

Method

1. Why do you think Keyes chose the title "Flowers for Algernon"?
2. How does the author's use of progress reports to tell his story help to develop sympathy for Charlie?
3. A *motif* is an element (a character, idea, or phrase) that recurs several times in a story. How is the Algernon motif used to

foreshadow events as well as to unify the story and heighten the dramatic effect?

4. Which progress report provides the climax or turning point of the story?

5. What do you think of the *resolution* or dénouement of the story? Consider some alternative solutions. Would any of them fit the story better than the resolution that the author chose?

Language: Style

One of the best clues to the changes in Charlie's intelligence is the way his *style* in writing progress reports changes. Style is the way a writer uses language to express ideas. Consciously or unconsciously, a writer chooses and arranges words in sentences that can be simple or complicated. A sequence of several sentences can be varied or about the same in length and in structure.

Read the following sentences from "Flowers for Algernon." Identify the simple, monotonous style that was appropriate to Charlie's lower intelligence at the beginning and end of the story. Notice the simple vocabulary and the subject-followed-by-verb construction. How does Charlie's style change as he becomes more intelligent?

1. "I hope they use me. Miss Kinnian says maybe they can make me smart. I want to be smart."

2. "When I left afterwards, I found myself trembling. I don't know why for sure, but it was as if I'd seen both men clearly for the first time."

3. "Once again, now, I have the feeling of shame burning inside me. This intelligence has driven a wedge between me and all the people I once knew and loved."

4. "The surgical stimulus to which we were both subjected has resulted in an intensification and acceleration of all mental processes."

5. "I told him I saw a inkblot. He said yes and it made me feel good."

Discussion and Composition

1. Write a character sketch of Charlie as he was at the beginning and end of the story. Refer to specific details about what he said or did.

2. What are some attitudes toward handicapped people that you have observed or read about? What might be done to change people's attitudes?

3. Compare and contrast "Flowers for Algernon" with any other science fiction story that you have read or seen dramatized on television or in the movies. Be sure to include any similarities that you can see between the two stories. Tell which story you preferred and why.

4. Charlie's mental retardation was probably caused by brain damage at birth or by a disease early in his life. Scientists used to believe that intelligence was inherited. Now they think it is to some extent inherited, but also that it is greatly influenced by the environment that the young child grows up in. Do some research on how intelligence is acquired, and present the results of your research in a brief paper or in a talk to the class.

MARK TWAIN
(1835–1910)

The first great writer who caught the spirit of the West in his stories and novels was Samuel Clemens, whose pen name was Mark Twain. He grew up in Hannibal, Missouri, on the Mississippi River, the gateway to the frontier. When he was eleven, his father died, and Twain was apprenticed to a printer. In the 1850s, he realized his boyhood dream and became a river pilot. When the War between the States stopped river traffic, Twain served briefly in the Confederate Army. He later traveled to Nevada, where he prospected for silver and wrote for frontier newspapers.

In 1863, after he had tired out several other pen names, he began signing "Mark Twain" to humorous stories about his travels. The name comes from the cry of the steamboat leadsman at two fathoms, "by the mark, twain."

In 1866, Twain traveled to the Hawaiian Islands as a correspondent for a California newspaper. The humorous lectures and articles that he based on this trip made him famous. *The Innocents Abroad* (1869), his first book, was a collection of the letters he wrote about his trip to Europe and the Holy Land for California and New York newspapers.

Although Twain married and settled in the East, he always wrote as a Westerner. Instead of being awed by European customs, as many Americans up to his time had been, Twain poked fun at them. Although Twain's stories made millions laugh, he had a serious side that has given his work lasting significance. His finest book is considered to be *The Adventures of Huckleberry Finn*. Like most of his best work, it can be read on many levels.

Although he became increasingly pessimistic as he grew older, the majority of Mark Twain's work reflects the boisterous optimism of a young country, becoming confident of its destiny. Turning away from Europe, Americans looked to their own West and found a sense of national identity, strong, adventurous, irreverent—above all, democratic, belonging to the common people. They found in Mark Twain a spokesman.

AN ENCOUNTER WITH AN INTERVIEWER

The nervous, dapper, "peart"[1] young man took the chair I offered him and said he was connected with the *Daily Thunderstorm,* and added:

"Hoping it's no harm, I've come to interview you."

"Come to what?"

"*Interview* you."

"Ah, I see. Yes—yes. Um! Yes—yes."

I was not feeling bright that morning. Indeed, my powers seemed a bit under a cloud. However, I went to the bookcase, and when I had been looking six or seven minutes I found I was obliged to refer to the young man. I said:

"How do you spell it?"

"Spell what?"

"Interview."

"Oh, my goodness! What do you want to spell it for?"

"I don't want to spell it; I want to see what it means."

"Well, this is astonishing, I must say. *I* can tell you what it means, if you—if you—"

"Oh, all right! That will answer, and much obliged to you, too."

"In, *in,* ter, *ter, in*ter—"

"Then you spell it with an *I?*"

"Why, certainly!"

"Oh, that is what took me so long."

"Why, my *dear* sir, what did *you* propose to spell it with?"

"Well, I—I—hardly know. I had the Unabridged, and I was ciphering[2] around in the back end, hoping I might tree her among the pictures. But it's a very old edition."

"Why, my friend, they wouldn't have a *picture* of it in even the latest e—My dear sir, I beg your pardon, I mean no harm in the world, but you do not look as—as—intelligent as I had expected you would. No harm—I mean no harm at all."

---

1. **peart:** dialect form of *pert,* lively, clever.
2. **ciphering** (sī´fər·ən): writing in secret code.

"Oh, don't mention it! It has often been said, and by people who would not flatter and who could have no inducement to flatter, that I am quite remarkable in that way. Yes—yes; they always speak of it with rapture."

"I can easily imagine it. But about this interview. You know it is the custom, now, to interview any man who has become notorious."

"Indeed, I had not heard of it before. It must be very interesting. What do you do it with?"

"Ah, well—well—well—this is disheartening. It *ought* to be done with a club in some cases; but customarily it consists in the interviewer asking questions and the interviewed answering them. It is all the rage now. Will you let me ask you certain questions calculated to bring out the salient points of your public and private history?"

"Oh, with pleasure—with pleasure. I have a very bad memory, but I hope you will not mind that. That is to say, it is an irregular memory—singularly irregular. Sometimes it goes in a gallop, and then again it will be as much as a fortnight[3] passing a given point. This is a great grief to me."

"Oh, it is no matter, so you will try to do the best you can."

"I will. I will put my whole mind on it."

"Thanks. Are you ready to begin?"

"Ready."

Q. How old are you?

A. Nineteen, in June.

Q. Indeed. I would have taken you to be thirty-five or six. Where were you born?

A. In Missouri.

Q. When did you begin to write?

A. In 1836.

Q. Why, how could that be, if you are only nineteen now?

A. I don't know. It does seem curious, somehow.

Q. It does, indeed. Whom do you consider the most remarkable man you ever met?

A. Aaron Burr.[4]

---

3. fortnight: two weeks.
4. Aaron Burr: statesman and lawyer, the third vice-president of the United States. Burr (1756–1836) killed his political rival, Alexander Hamilton, in a duel.

Q. But you never could have met Aaron Burr, if you are only nineteen years—

A. Now, if you know more about me than I do, what do you ask me for?

Q. Well, it was only a suggestion; nothing more. How did you happen to meet Burr?

A. Well, I happened to be at his funeral, and he asked me to make less noise, and—

Q. But good heavens! If you were at his funeral, he must have been dead, and if he was dead how could he care whether you made a noise or not?

A. I don't know. He was always a particular kind of a man that way.

Q. Still, I don't understand it at all. You say he spoke to you, and that he was dead.

A. I didn't say he was dead.

Q. But wasn't he dead?

A. Well, some said he was, some said he wasn't.

Q. What did you think?

A. Oh, it was none of my business! It wasn't any of my funeral.

Q. Did you—However, we can never get this matter straight. Let me ask about something else. What was the date of your birth?

A. Monday, October 31, 1693.

Q. What! Impossible! That would make you a hundred and eighty years old. How do you account for that?

A. I don't account for it at all.

Q. But you said at first you were only nineteen, and now you make yourself out to be one hundred and eighty. It is an awful discrepancy.

A. Why, have you noticed that? (Shaking hands.) Many a time it has seemed to me like a discrepancy, but somehow I couldn't make up my mind. How quick you notice a thing!

Q. Thank you for the compliment, as far as it goes. Had you, or have you, any brothers or sisters?

A. Eh! I—I—I think so—yes—but I don't remember.

Q. Well, that is the most extraordinary statement I ever heard!

A. Why, what makes you think that?

Q. How could I think otherwise? Why, look here! Who is this a picture of on the wall? Isn't that a brother of yours?

A. Oh, yes, yes, yes! Now you remind me of it; that *was* a brother of mine. That's William—*Bill* we called him. Poor old Bill!

Q. Why? Is he dead, then?

A. Ah! Well, I suppose so. We never could tell. There was a great mystery about it.

Q. That is sad, very sad. He disappeared, then?

A. Well, yes, in a sort of general way. We buried him.

Q. *Buried* him! *Buried* him, without knowing whether he was dead or not?

A. Oh, no! Not that. He was dead enough.

Q. Well, I confess that I can't understand this. If you buried him, and you knew he was dead—

A. No! no! We only thought he was.

Q. Oh, I see! He came to life again?

A. I bet he didn't.

Q. Well, I never heard anything like this. *Somebody* was dead. *Somebody* was buried. Now, where was the mystery?

A. Ah! that's just it! That's it exactly. You see, we were twins—defunct and I—and we got mixed in the bathtub when we were only two weeks old, and one of us was drowned. But we didn't know which. Some think it was Bill. Some think it was me.

Q. Well, that *is* remarkable. What do *you* think?

A. Goodness knows! I would give whole worlds to know. This solemn, this awful mystery has cast a gloom over my whole life. But I will tell you a secret now, which I never have revealed to any creature before. One of us had a peculiar mark—a large mole on the back of his left hand; that was *me. That child was the one that was drowned!*

Q. Very well, then, I don't see that there is any mystery about it, after all.

A. You don't? Well, *I* do. Anyway, I don't see how they could ever have been such a blundering lot as to go and bury the wrong child. But, 'sh—don't mention it where the family can hear of it. Heaven knows they have heartbreaking troubles enough without adding this.

Q. Well, I believe I have got material enough for the present, and I am very much obliged to you for the pains you have taken.

But I was a good deal interested in that account of Aaron Burr's funeral. Would you mind telling me what particular circumstance it was that made you think Burr was such a remarkable man?

A. Oh! It was a mere trifle! Not one man in fifty would have noticed it at all. When the sermon was over, and the procession all ready to start for the cemetery, and the body all arranged nice in the hearse, he said he wanted to take a last look at the scenery, and so he *got up and rode with the driver.*

Then the young man reverently withdrew. He was very pleasant company, and I was sorry to see him go.

1875

Meaning

1. What meaning of the word *encounter* best fits the title of this story?
2. At what point in "Encounter with an Interviewer" did the interview begin to go badly for the nervous reporter? What do you think he might have said or done to make the interview go in the right direction again?
3. Did the interviewer ever realize that he was being "kidded"? When? Why do you think so?
4. How much is fact? How much is exaggeration? These are questions that readers of Mark Twain's works always have to keep in mind. As the Canadian humorist Stephen Leacock said, he gives the reader "what the traffic will bear." What are some of the more obvious "untruths" in "Encounter with an Interviewer"?

Method

1. The beginning and end of "Encounter with an Interviewer" are narrated from the first person point of view. Why do you think the author chose to begin and end with the first person point of view?
2. A *dialogue* is a conversation carried on by two or more characters. "Encounter with an Interviewer" is told almost completely through dialogue in the form of questions and answers. Describe the interviewer as he reveals himself through dialogue.

3. How does the narrator's difficulty about the meaning of the word *interview* set the tone of the story? What is the tone?

4. Mark Twain was a master at using exaggeration to create humor. Point out some examples of exaggeration in this story.

Language: Suffixes

Words can often be divided into parts that have their own meaning. When you know the meaning of each part, you can figure out the meaning of the whole word. The main or basic part of a word is called its *root*. A suffix is an element added after the root to make a different word which usually becomes a different part of speech. A verb, with a suffix added, for example, may become a noun. *Interview,* used as a verb by the reporter in this story, plus *-er* becomes *interviewer*.

Each of the following words from the story ends with a suffix.

Suffix	Meaning	Word
1. –ous	quality, full of, having	nervous
2. –ion	action, state, result	suggestion
3. –ment	result or action	inducement
4. –able	capable of	remarkable

What is the root of each word? Write another word of your own to illustrate each of the above suffixes. Use the word in a sentence you make up.

Discussion and Composition

1. The *lead* or first paragraph of a newspaper story on a particular topic usually contains the answers to a group of questions that have been called the *five W's and H: who, what, when, where, why,* and *how.* Write the first paragraph of the newspaper story that the interviewer might have written. Make up any of the facts that have been left to your imagination.

2. Choose any famous person whom you know about, and make up an interview using question–and–answer style that reveals the character and personality of the person you are interviewing.

3. The young man in the story was obviously poorly prepared to interview the narrator. How would you prepare to interview a famous person? Explain what you would do, step by step. Also tell what you would say first to the person you are interviewing, and describe briefly the line of questioning that you would pursue.

TONI CADE BAMBARA
(born 1939)

Drama, dance, and linguistics are some of the fields that Toni Cade Bambara has studied intensively. She was born in New York City and was graduated from Queens College in New York. She received her master's degree from the City University of New York, and has also studied in France and in Italy.

Her career has included work as a community organizer, health and youth worker, program director at settlement houses and hospitals, free-lance writer, editor, and college teacher. She has written and had published articles, book and film reviews, and three volumes of short stories. She has written one novel, *The Salt Eaters.*

BLUES AIN'T NO MOCKIN BIRD

The puddle had frozen over, and me and Cathy went stompin in it. The twins from next door, Tyrone and Terry, were swingin so high out of sight we forgot we were waitin our turn on the tire. Cathy jumped up and came down hard on her heels and started tap-dancin. And the frozen patch splinterin every which way underneath kinda spooky. "Looks like a plastic spider web," she said. "A sort of weird spider, I guess, with many mental problems." But really it looked like the crystal paperweight Granny kept in the parlor. She was on the back porch, Granny was, making the cakes drunk. The old ladle dripping rum into the Christmas tins, like it used to drip maple syrup into the pails when we lived in the Judson's woods, like it poured cider into the vats when we were on the Cooper place, like it used to scoop buttermilk and soft cheese when we lived at the dairy.

"Go tell that man we ain't a bunch of trees."

"Ma'am?"

"I said to tell that man to get away from here with that

camera." Me and Cathy look over toward the meadow where the men with the station wagon'd been roamin around all mornin. The tall man with a huge camera lassoed to his shoulder was buzzin our way.

"They're makin movie pictures," yelled Tyrone, stiffenin his legs and twistin so the tire'd come down slow so they could see.

"They're makin movie pictures," sang out Terry.

"That boy don't never have anything original to say," say Cathy grown-up.

By the time the man with the camera had cut across our neighbor's yard, the twins were out of the trees swingin low and Granny was onto the steps, the screen door bammin soft and scratchy against her palms. "We thought we'd get a shot or two of the house and everything and then—"

"Good mornin," Granny cut him off. And smiled that smile.

"Good mornin," he said, head all down the way Bingo does when you yell about the bones on the kitchen floor. "Nice place you got here, aunty. We thought we'd take a—"

"Did you?" said Granny with her eyebrows. Cathy pulled up her socks and giggled.

"Nice things here," said the man, buzzin his camera over the yard. The pecan barrels, the sled, me and Cathy, the flowers, the printed stones along the driveway, the trees, the twins, the toolshed.

"I don't know about the thing, the it, and the stuff," said Granny, still talkin with her eyebrows. "Just people here is what I tend to consider."

Camera man stopped buzzin. Cathy giggled into her collar.

"Mornin, ladies," a new man said. He had come up behind us when we weren't looking. "And gents," discovering the twins givin him a nasty look. "We're filmin for the county," he said with a smile. "Mind if we shoot a bit around here?"

"I do indeed," said Granny with no smile. Smilin man was smiling up a storm. So was Cathy. But he didn't seem to have another word to say, so he and the camera man backed on out the yard, but you could hear the camera buzzin still. "Suppose you just shut that machine off," said Granny real low through her teeth, and took a step down off the porch and then another.

"Now, aunty," Camera said, pointin the thing straight at her.

"Your mama and I are not related."

Smilin man got his notebook out and a chewed-up pencil.

"Listen," he said movin back into our yard, "we'd like to have a statement from you . . . for the film. We're filmin for the county, see. Part of the food stamp campaign. You know about the food stamps?"

Granny said nuthin.

"Maybe there's somethin you want to say for the film. I see you grow your own vegetables," he smiled real nice. "If more folks did that, see, there'd be no need—"

Granny wasn't sayin nuthin. So they backed on out, buzzin at our clothesline and the twins' bicycles, then back on down to the meadow. The twins were danglin in the tire, lookin at Granny. Me and Cathy were waitin, too, cause Granny always got somethin to say. She teaches steady with no let-up. "I was on this bridge one time," she started off. "Was a crowd cause this man was goin to jump, you understand. And a minister was there and the police and some other folks. His woman was there, too."

"What was they doin?" asked Tyrone.

"Trying to talk him out of it was what they was doin. The minister talkin about how it was a mortal sin, suicide. His woman takin bites out of her own hand and not even knowin it, so nervous and cryin and talkin fast."

"So what happened?" asked Tyrone.

"So here comes . . . this person . . . with a camera, takin pictures of the man and the minister and the woman. Takin pictures of the man in his misery about to jump, cause life so bad and people been messin with him so bad. This person takin up the whole roll of film practically. But savin a few, of course."

"Of course," said Cathy, hatin the person. Me standin there wonderin how Cathy knew it was "of course" when I didn't and it was *my* grandmother.

After a while Tyrone say, "Did he jump?"

"Yeh, did he jump?" say Terry all eager.

And Granny just stared at the twins till their faces swallow up the eager and they don't even care any more about the man jumpin. Then she goes back onto the porch and lets the screen door go for itself. I'm lookin to Cathy to finish the story cause she knows Granny's whole story before me even. Like she knew how come we move so much and Cathy ain't but a third cousin we picked up on the way last Thanksgivin visitin. But she knew it was on account of people drivin Granny crazy till she'd get up in the night and start packin. Mumblin and packin and wakin everybody

up sayin, "Let's get on away from here before I kill me somebody."
Like people wouldn't pay her for things like they said they would.
Or Mr. Judson bringin us boxes of old clothes and raggedy maga-
zines. Or Mrs. Cooper comin in our kitchen and touchin every-
thing and sayin how clean it all was. Granny goin crazy, and
Granddaddy Cain pullin her off the people, sayin, "Now, now,
Cora." But next day loadin up the truck, with rocks all in his jaw,
madder than Granny in the first place.

"I read a story once," said Cathy soundin like Granny
teacher. "About this lady Goldilocks who barged into a house that
wasn't even hers. And not invited, you understand. Messed over
the people's groceries and broke up the people's furniture. Had the
nerve to sleep in the folks' bed."

"Then what happened?" asked Tyrone. "What they do, the
folks, when they come in to all this mess?"

"Did they make her pay for it?" asked Terry, makin a first
"I'd've made her pay me."

I didn't even ask. I could see Cathy actress was very likely to
just walk away and leave us in mystery about this story which I
heard was about some bears.

"Did they throw her out?" asked Tyrone, like his father
sounds when he's bein extra nasty-plus to the washin-machine
man.

"Woulda," said Terry. "I woulda gone upside[1] her head with
my fist and—"

"You woulda done whatcha always do—go cry to Mama,
you big baby," said Tyrone. So naturally Terry starts hittin on
Tyrone, and next thing you know they tumblin out the tire and
rollin on the ground. But Granny didn't say a thing or send the
twins home or step out on the steps to tell us about how we can't
afford to be fightin amongst ourselves. She didn't say nuthin. So I
get into the tire to take my turn. And I could see her leanin up
against the pantry table, starin at the cakes she was puttin up for
the Christmas sale, mumblin real low and grumpy and holding her
forehead like it wanted to fall off and mess up the rum cakes.

Behind me I hear before I can see Granddaddy Cain comin
through the woods in his field boots. Then I twist around to see
the shiny black oilskin cuttin through what little left there was of
yellows, reds, and oranges. His great white head not quite round

---

1. **upside:** *dialect,* to hit on the side.

cause of this bloody thing high on his shoulder, like he was wearin a cap on sideways. He takes the shortcut through the pecan grove, and the sound of twigs snapping overhead and underfoot travels clear and cold all the way up to us. And here comes Smilin and Camera up behind him like they was goin to do somethin. Folks like to go for him sometimes. Cathy say it's because he's so tall and quiet and like a king. And people just can't stand it. But Smilin and Camera don't hit him in the head or nuthin. They just buzz on him as he stalks by with the chicken hawk slung over his shoulder, squawkin, drippin red down the back of the oilskin. He passes the porch and stops a second for Granny to see he's caught the hawk at last, but she's just starin and mumblin, and not at the hawk. So he nails the bird to the toolshed door, the hammerin crackin through the eardrums. And the bird flappin himself to death and droolin down the door to paint the gravel in the driveway red, then brown, then black. And the two men movin up on tiptoe like they was invisible or we were blind, one.

"Get them persons out of my flower bed, Mister Cain," say Granny moanin real low like at a funeral.

"How come your grandmother calls her husband 'Mister Cain' all the time?" Tyrone whispers all loud and noisy and from the city and don't know no better. Like his mama, Miss Myrtle, tell us never mind the formality as if we had no better breeding than to call her Myrtle, plain. And then this awful thing—a giant hawk—come wailin up over the meadow, flyin low and tilted and screamin, zigzaggin through the pecan grove, breakin branches and hollerin, snappin past the clothesline, flyin every which way, flying into things reckless with crazy.

"He's come to claim his mate," say Cathy fast, and ducks down. We all fall quick and flat into the gravel driveway, hawk on the door, tryin to fly up out of her death like it was just a sack flown into by mistake. Her body holdin her there on that nail, though. The mate beatin the air overhead and clutchin for hair, for heads, for landin space.

The camera man duckin and bendin and runnin and fallin, jigglin the camera and scared. And Smilin jumpin up and down swipin at the huge bird, tryin to bring the hawk down with just his raggedy ole cap. Granddaddy Cain straight up and silent, watchin the circles of the hawk, then aimin the hammer off his wrist. The giant bird fallin, silent and slow. Then here comes Camera and Smilin all big and bad now that the awful screechin thing is on its back and broken, here they come. And Granddaddy Cain looks up at them like it was the first time noticin, but not payin them too much mind cause he's listenin, we all listenin, to that low groanin music comin from the porch. And we figure any minute, somethin in my back tells me any minute now, Granny gonna bust through that screen with somethin in her hand and murder on her mind. So Granddaddy say above the buzzin, but quiet, "Good day, gentlemen." Just like that. Like he'd invited them in to play cards and they'd stayed too long and all the sand-wiches were gone and Reverend Webb was droppin by and it was time to go.

They didn't know what to do. But like Cathy say, folks can't stand Granddaddy tall and silent and like a king. They can't nei-ther. The smile the men smilin is pullin the mouth back and showin the teeth. Lookin like the wolf man, both of them. Then Grandaddy holds his hand out—this huge hand I used to sit in when I was a baby and he'd carry me through the house to my mother like I was a gift on a tray. Like he used to on the trains. They called the other men just waiters. But they spoke of Granddaddy separate and said, The Waiter. And said he had en-gines in his feet and motors in his hands and couldn't no train throw him off and couldn't nobody turn him round. They were big enough for motors, his hands were. He held that one hand out all still and it gettin to be not at all a hand but a person in itself.

"He wants you to hand him the camera," Smilin whispers to Camera, tiltin his head to talk secret like they was in the jungle or somethin and come upon a native that don't speak the language. The men start untyin the straps, and they put the camera into that great hand speckled with the hawk's blood all black and crackly now. And the hand don't even drop with the weight, just the fingers move, curl up around the machine. But Granddaddy lookin straight at the men. They lookin at each other and every-where but at Granddaddy's face.

"We filmin for the county, see," say Smilin. "We puttin together a movie for the food stamp program . . . filmin all around these parts. Uhh, filmin for the county.

"Can I have my camera back?" say the tall man with no machine on his shoulder, but still keepin it high like the camera was still there or needed to be. "Please, sir."

Then Grandaddy's other hand flies up like a sudden and

gentle bird, slaps down fast on top of the camera and lifts off half like it was a calabash cut for sharing.

"Hey," Camera jumps forward. He gathers up the parts into his chest and everything unrollin and fallin all over. "Whatcha tryin to do? You'll ruin the film." He looks down into his chest of metal reels and things like he's protectin a kitten from the cold.

"You standin in the misses' flower bed," say Grandaddy. "This is our own place."

The two men look at him, then at each other, then back at the mess in the camera man's chest, and they just back off. One sayin over and over all the way down to the meadow, "Watch it, Bruno. Keep ya fingers off the film" Then Grandaddy picks up the hammer and jams it into the oilskin pocket, scrapes his boots, and goes into the house. And you can hear the squish of his boots headin through the house. And you can see the funny shadow he throws from the parlor window onto the ground by the string-bean patch. The hammer draggin the pocket of the oilskin out so Granddaddy looked even wider. Granny was hummin now—high, not low and grumbly. And she was doin the cakes again, you could smell the molasses from the rum.

"There's this story I'm goin to write one day," say Cathy dreamer. "About the proper use of the hammer."

"Can I be in it?" Tyrone say with his hand up like it was a matter of first come, first served.

"Perhaps," say Cathy, climbin onto the tire to pump us up. "If you there and ready."

Meaning

1. Why was Granny angry at the cameraman? Do you think it was unfair of Granddaddy Cain to expose the film? Why or why not?

2. Explain the title, "Blues Ain't No Mockin Bird." What bird represents the "blues" in this story?

3. A *contrast* is a striking difference between two things. An author uses contrast for dramatic effect. How are Smilin and Camera a contrast to the Cains?

4. A *symbol* is an object, person, or place that suggests and stands for something else, usually an idea or an attitude. For example, the lion stands for courage, the lamb for meekness. What do the camera and the hammer symbolize in this story?

Method

1. This story is told from the first person point of view. What do you find out about the narrator? Why do you think the author chose this narrator and not any of the other characters in the story?

2. Are Smilin, Granny, and Cathy clearly drawn characters? Identify specific techniques of characterization in the story to support your answer.

3. What is the climax of the story? How does the author build towards this turning point?

4. How would you describe the *tone* of this story—the author's attitude toward her subject and her characters?

Language: Nonstandard English

Standard English is the kind of English that educated people consider to be correct and acceptable. It is the English you learn in school. Millions of Americans, however, speak *nonstandard* English in special situations if they are educated enough to make the choice between standard and nonstandard, or all the time.

Nonstandard English includes slang, the vernacular, and dialect. *Slang* is made up of words and expressions that have been given a new meaning, sometimes popular only for a short time (for example, "dig" for "understand," "laid back" for "relaxed.") The *vernacular* may include slang, but it refers specifically to the everyday, informal language that is commonly spoken by people in an area (for example, "I could have sunk through the floor," instead of "I was very embarrassed.") A *dialect* is the spoken language of a particular group whose pronunciation, grammar, vocabulary, and intonation may differ from the standard language.

The author's use of dialect in "Blues Ain't No Mockin Bird" makes her dialogue vivid and realistic. Reread the following sentences from "Blues Ain't No Mockin Bird." Decide how each one would be written in standard English. Notice how the use of standard English changes the flavor of the original and makes it less interesting.

1. "Then she goes back onto the porch and lets the screen door go for itself."
2. "'You woulda done whatcha always do—go cry to Mama, you big baby,' said Tyrone."
3. "Me and Cathy look over toward the meadow where the men with the station wagon'd been roamin around all mornin."
4. "'That boy don't never have anything original to say,' say Cathy grown-up."
5. "Like she knew how come we move so much and Cathy ain't but a third cousin we picked up on the way last Thanksgivin visitin."

Discussion and Composition

1. Using the information given in the story, write a character sketch of Granddaddy Cain. Try to give as complete a picture of the man as you can. Include a description of his outward appearance as well as a description of his personality.

2. The two elderly people in this story are strong, independent characters, quite unlike the old people usually represented on television and in the movies. Consider the elderly people that you know well. Write an essay on the subject of old age. Use examples from your reading and from your personal experience to develop one of these topic sentences or one of your own choice.

a. Growing old gracefully has become more difficult in today's world.

b. Elderly people play an important role in any society.

3. What makes you angry? Recall an experience you have witnessed or read about that has made you angry. Do not recount a personal injustice in your discussion or composition. Focus instead on situations that have happened to other people.

FRANK R. STOCKTON
(1834–1902)

Known primarily as an author of humorous fiction during his lifetime, Frank R. Stockton began writing only as a hobby. He was born in Philadelphia and was graduated from high school, but did not go to college. Instead, he began to earn his living as a wood-engraver and was quite successful; his work appeared in national magazines. In his spare time, Stockton began writing fairy tales for children. He enjoyed this pastime so much that he left his engraving business to begin a second career as a journalist, editor, and freelance writer.

For many years he was an editor of *St. Nicholas,* a magazine for children. In addition to fantasies, he wrote amusing, sometimes satirical stories and novels for adults. "The Lady or the Tiger," his most famous short story, was written to be read before a literary society. It stirred up so much discussion that Stockton published the story in a magazine. He was flooded with letters demanding a solution to the riddle, which he never gave.

THE LADY OR THE TIGER?

In the very olden time, there lived a semibarbaric king who was a man of exuberant fancy and of an authority so irresistible that, at his will, he turned his varied fancies into facts. He was greatly given to self-communing, and when he and himself agreed upon anything, the thing was done. When everything moved smoothly, his nature was bland and genial; but whenever there was a little hitch, he was blander and more genial still, for nothing pleased him so much as to make the crooked straight, and crush down uneven places.

Among his borrowed notions was that of the public arena, in which, by exhibitions of manly and beastly valor, the minds of his subjects were refined and cultured.

But even here the exuberant and barbaric fancy asserted itself. This vast amphitheater[1] with its encircling galleries, its mysterious vault, and its unseen passages, was an agent of poetic justice, in which crime was punished, or virtue rewarded, by the decrees of an impartial and incorruptible chance.

When a subject was accused of a crime of sufficient importance to interest the king, public notice was given that on an appointed day the fate of the accused person would be decided in the king's arena.

When all the people had assembled in the galleries, and the king, surrounded by his court, sat high up on his throne of royal state on one side of the arena, he gave a signal, a door beneath him opened, and the accused subject stepped out into the amphitheater. Directly opposite him, on the other side of the enclosed space, were two doors, exactly alike and side by side. It was the duty and the privilege of the person on trial to walk directly to these doors and open one of them. He could open either door he pleased. He was subject to no guidance or influence but that of the aforementioned impartial and incorruptible chance. If he opened the one, there came out of it a hungry tiger, the fiercest and most cruel that could be procured, which immediately sprang upon him and tore him to pieces as a punishment for his guilt. The moment that the case of the criminal was thus decided, doleful iron bells were clanged, great wails went up from the hired mourners posted on the outer rim of the arena, and the vast audience, with bowed heads and downcast hearts, wended slowly their homeward way, mourning greatly that one so young and fair, or so old and respected, should have merited so dire a fate.

But if the accused person opened the other door, there came forth from it a lady, the most suitable to his years and station that His Majesty could select among his fair subjects; and to this lady he was immediately married as a reward of his innocence. It mattered not that he might already possess a wife and family or that his affections might be engaged upon an object of his own selection. The king allowed no such arrangements to interfere with his great scheme of punishment and reward. The exercises, as in the other instance, took place immediately, and in the arena. Another door opened beneath the king, and a priest, followed by a band of choristers, and dancing maidens blowing joyous airs on golden

---

1. **amphitheater** (ăm′fə·thē′ə·tər): an oval or round area enclosed by rising tiers of seats.

horns, advanced to where the pair stood side by side, and the wedding was promptly and cheerily solemnized. Then the gay brass bells rang forth their merry peals, and the people shouted glad hurrahs, and the innocent man, preceded by children strewing flowers on his path, led his bride to his home.

This was the king's semibarbaric method of administering justice. Its perfect fairness is obvious. The criminal could not know out of which door would come the lady. He opened either he pleased, without having the slightest idea whether, in the next instant, he was to be devoured or married. On some occasions the tiger came out of one door, and on some, out of the other. The decisions were not only fair—they were positively decisive. The accused person was instantly punished if he found himself guilty, and if innocent, he was rewarded on the spot, whether he liked it or not. There was no escape from the judgments of the king's arena.

The institution was a very popular one. When the people gathered together on one of the great trial days, they never knew whether they were to witness a bloody slaughter or a hilarious wedding. This element of uncertainty lent an interest to the occasion which it could not otherwise have attained. Thus the masses were entertained and pleased, and the thinking part of the community could bring no charge of unfairness against this plan; for did not the accused person have the whole matter in his own hands?

This semibarbaric king had a daughter as blooming as his most rosy fancies, and with a soul as fervent and imperious[2] as his own. As is usual in such cases, she was the apple of his eye, and was loved by him above all humanity. Among his courtiers was a young man of that fineness of blood and lowness of station common to the heroes of romance who love royal maidens. This royal maiden was well satisfied with her lover, for he was handsome and brave to a degree unsurpassed in all this kingdom, and she loved him with an ardor that had enough of barbarism in it to make it exceedingly warm and strong. This love affair moved on happily for many months until, one day, the king happened to discover its existence. He did not hesitate nor waver in regard to his duty. The youth was immediately cast into prison, and a day was appointed for his trial in the king's arena. This, of course, was an especially

---

2. imperious (ĭm·pêr′ē·əs): arrogant, overbearing.

important occasion, and His Majesty, as well as all the people, was greatly interested in the workings and development of this trial. Never before had such a case occurred—never before had a subject dared to love the daughter of a king. In after years such things became commonplace enough, but then they were, in no slight degree, novel and startling.

The tiger cages of the kingdom were searched for the most savage and relentless beasts, from which the fiercest monster might be selected for the arena, and the ranks of maiden youth and beauty throughout the land were carefully surveyed by competent judges, in order that the young man might have a fitting bride in case fate did not determine for him a different destiny. Of course, everybody knew that the deed with which the accused was charged had been done. He had loved the princess, and neither he, she, nor anyone else thought of denying the fact. But the king would not think of allowing any fact of this kind to interfere with the workings of the court of judgment, in which he took such great delight and satisfaction. No matter how the affair turned out, the youth would be disposed of, and the king would take pleasure in watching the course of events which would determine whether or not the young man had done wrong in allowing himself to love the princess.

The appointed day arrived. From far and near the people gathered and thronged the great galleries of the arena, while crowds, unable to gain admittance, massed themselves against its outside walls. The king and his court were in their places, opposite the twin doors—those fateful portals, so terrible in their similarity!

All was ready. The signal was given. A door beneath the royal party opened, and the lover of the princess walked into the arena. Tall, beautiful, fair, his appearance was greeted with a low hum of admiration and anxiety. Half the audience had not known so grand a youth had lived among them. No wonder the princess loved him! What a terrible thing for him to be there!

As the youth advanced into the arena, he turned, as the custom was, to bow to the king. But he did not think at all of that royal personage; his eyes were fixed upon the princess, who sat to the right of her father. Had it not been for the barbarism in her nature, it is probable that lady would not have been there. But her intense and fervid soul would not allow her to be absent on an occasion in which she was so terribly interested. From the moment that the decree had gone forth that her lover should decide his fate in the king's arena, she had thought of nothing, night or day, but this great event and the various subjects connected with it. Possessed of more power, influence, and force of character than anyone who had ever before been interested in such a case, she had done what no other person had done—she had possessed herself of the secret of the doors. She knew in which of the two rooms behind those doors stood the cage of the tiger, with its open front, and in which waited the lady. Through these thick doors, heavily curtained with skins on the inside, it was impossible that any noise or suggestion should come from within to the person who should approach to raise the latch of one of them. But gold, and the power of a woman's will, had brought the secret to the princess.

Not only did she know in which room stood the lady, ready to emerge, all blushing and radiant, should her door be opened, but she knew who the lady was. It was one of the fairest and loveliest of the damsels of the court who had been selected as the reward of the accused youth, should he be proved innocent of the crime of aspiring to one so far above him; and the princess hated her. Often had she seen, or imagined that she had seen, this fair creature throwing glances of admiration upon the person of her lover, and sometimes she thought these glances were perceived and even returned. Now and then she had seen them talking together. It was but for a moment or two, but much can be said in a brief space. It may have been on most unimportant topics, but how could she know that? The girl was lovely, but she had dared to raise her eyes to the loved one of the princess, and, with all the intensity of the savage blood transmitted to her through long lines of wholly barbaric ancestors, she hated the woman who blushed and trembled behind that silent door.

When her lover turned and looked at her, and his eye met hers as she sat there paler and whiter than anyone in the vast ocean of anxious faces about her, he saw, by that power of quick perception which is given to those whose souls are one, that she knew behind which door crouched the tiger, and behind which stood the lady. He had expected her to know it. He understood her nature, and his soul was assured that she would never rest until she had made plain to herself this thing, hidden to all other lookers-on, even to the king. The only hope for the youth in which there was any element of certainty was based upon the success of the princess in discovering this mystery, and the moment he looked upon her, he saw she had succeeded.

Then it was that his quick and anxious glance asked the question, "Which?" It was as plain to her as if he shouted it from where he stood. There was not an instant to be lost. The question was asked in a flash; it must be answered in another.

Her right arm lay on the cushioned parapet before her. She raised her hand, and made a slight, quick movement toward the right. No one but her lover saw her. Every eye but his was fixed on the man in the arena.

He turned, and with a firm and rapid step he walked across the empty space. Every heart stopped beating, every breath was held, every eye was fixed immovably upon that man. Without the slightest hesitation, he went to the door on the right and opened it.

Now, the point of the story is this: Did the tiger come out of that door, or did the lady?

The more we reflect upon this question, the harder it is to answer. It involves a study of the human heart which leads us through roundabout pathways of passion, out of which it is difficult to find our way. Think of it, fair reader, not as if the decision of the question depended upon yourself, but upon that hot-blooded, semibarbaric princess, her soul at a white heat beneath the combined fires of despair and jealousy. She had lost him, but who should have him?

How often, in her waking hours and in her dreams, had she started in wild horror and covered her face with her hands as she thought of her lover opening the door on the other side of which waited the cruel fangs of the tiger!

But how much oftener had she seen him at the other door! How in her grievous reveries[3] had she gnashed her teeth and torn her hair when she saw his start of rapturous delight as he opened the door of the lady! How her soul had burned in agony when she had seen him rush to meet that woman, with her flushing cheek and sparkling eye of triumph; when she had seen him lead her forth, his whole frame kindled with the joy of recovered life; when she had heard the glad shouts from the multitude, and the wild ringing of the happy bells; when she had seen the priest, with his joyous followers, advance to the couple, and make them man and wife before her very eyes; and when she had seen them walk away together upon their path of flowers, followed by the tremen-

---

3. reveries (rĕv′ər·ēs): dreams.

dous shouts of the hilarious multitude, in which her one despairing shriek was lost and drowned!

Would it not be better for him to die at once, and go to wait for her in the blessed regions of semibarbaric futurity?

And yet, that awful tiger, those shrieks, that blood!

Her decision had been indicated in an instant, but it had been made after days and nights of anguished deliberation. She had known she would be asked, she had decided what she would answer, and without the slightest hesitation, she had moved her hand to the right.

The question of her decision is one not to be lightly considered, and it is not for me to presume to set up myself as the one person able to answer it. So I leave it with all of you: Which came out of the opened door—the lady or the tiger?

Meaning

1. How did the king determine his subjects' innocence or guilt? Why was his system of justice *ironic,* that is, quite the opposite of justice?
2. Why did the king want to dispose of the hero of this story?
3. What is the *theme* of "The Lady or the Tiger"? What double meaning do you read into the title of this story?
4. To what extent does the author attempt to arouse the reader's sympathy for his characters? Give evidence for your answer by citing examples from the story.

Method

1. Why do you think the author decided not to include dialogue in his story? Would you have liked some dialogue? Tell where you would have included it and why.
2. This story is told from the third person point of view. What is the author's attitude toward the king? How soon is his attitude evident?
3. Do you wish the author had *not* told you which door the hero opened? Give reasons for your answer.
4. Instead of using one adjective, noun, verb, or adverb, the author of "The Lady or the Tiger" often uses two to strengthen the dramatic effect. Here are some examples of this technique: ". . . his nature was bland and genial. . . ."

"It mattered not that he might already possess a wife and family. . . ."

". . . the wedding was promptly and cheerily solemnized."

"From far and near the people gathered and thronged. . . ."

Find other examples of this technique in the story.

Language: Latin Roots for English Words

Many English words are built on Latin roots. The words *opposite* and *disposed,* for example, use the Latin root *-pos* or *pon-* (to put or place). *Opposite* begins with the Latin prefix *op,* which means against, while *dispose* includes the Latin prefix *dis-,* which means opposite or away. How does knowing these Latin meanings help you understand the definitions of *opposite* and *dispose?*

The following words have been taken from "The Lady or the Tiger." Find the Latin root of each word and its meaning in your dictionary.

1. justice
2. virtue
3. audience
4. transmitted
5. barbaric
6. incorruptible
7. deliberation
8. imagined

Discussion and Composition

1. Which door do you think the princess chose? The one concealing the lady—or the tiger? Write your version of how the story might have ended. Begin immediately after the sentence, "Without the slightest hesitation, he went to the door on the right and opened it."

2. The author explains in clear and specific detail how the king's system of justice worked. Write an explanation of a procedure or process that you know well. Here are some points to keep in mind:

a. make sure you know exactly how to perform the procedure; **b.** begin by explaining the purpose of the procedure; tell how and by whom it is performed; **c.** divide the process into stages and present the steps in chronological order; **d.** use transitional words and expressions such as *first, on the average, next,* and *finally;* and **e.** conclude by stating the results that follow when the stages are followed carefully.

EUDORA WELTY
(born 1909)

The small towns of Mississippi have been the setting for Eudora Welty's fiction and for her life. Born in Jackson, Mississippi, she was the oldest child in a well-to-do family. As a young girl, she considered both writing and painting as future careers. She attended the Mississippi College for Women, and completed her education at the University of Wisconsin and Columbia University Graduate School of Business.

Because of the Depression, she was unable to get a job in advertising, her field at Columbia. Working instead for the Works Progress Administration, she traveled throughout Mississippi, combining her two interests of making visual and verbal pictures by photographing people and writing articles about them. In 1936, her first short story was published, and her photographs were exhibited in a New York gallery.

Clear but metaphorical language is typical of Miss Welty's style. In her use of first-person narration and dialogue she displays an excellent grasp of the rhythms of Southern speech. Much of her work focuses on such human problems as the conflicting needs for independence and for love. In 1973, her short novel *The Optimist's Daughter,* which contains some autobiographical information, was awarded the Pulitzer Prize.

A WORN PATH

It was December—a bright frozen day in the early morning. Far out in the country there was an old Negro woman with her head tied in a red rag, coming along a path through the pine-woods. Her name was Phoenix[1] Jackson. She was very old and small and she walked slowly in the dark pine shadows, moving a

---

1. Phoenix: in Egyptian mythology, a bird of great beauty said to live for 500 years in the desert, to burn and destroy itself by fire, to rise again from its ashes youthful and beautiful, and to live through another life cycle. The phoenix was supposedly the size of an eagle with partly red and partly golden plumage. It is often used as a symbol of immortality.

little from side to side in her steps, with the balanced heaviness and lightness of a pendulum in a grandfather clock. She carried a thin, small cane made from an umbrella, and with this she kept tapping the frozen earth in front of her. This made a grave and persistent noise in the still air, that seemed meditative like the chirping of a solitary little bird.

She wore a dark striped dress reaching down to her shoe tops, and an equally long apron of bleached sugar sacks, with a full pocket: all neat and tidy, but every time she took a step she might have fallen over her shoelaces, which dragged from her unlaced shoes. She looked straight ahead. Her eyes were blue with age. Her skin had a pattern all of its own of numberless branching wrinkles and as though a whole little tree stood in the middle of her forehead, but a golden color ran underneath, and the two knobs of her cheeks were illumined by a yellow burning under the dark. Under the red rag her hair came down on her neck in the frailest of ringlets, still black, and with an odor like copper.

Now and then there was a quivering in the thicket. Old Phoenix said, "Out of my way, all you foxes, owls, beetles, jack rabbits, coons, and wild animals! . . . Keep out from under these feet, little bobwhites. . . . Keep the big wild hogs out of my path. Don't let none of those come running my direction. I got a long way." Under her small black-freckled hand her cane, limber as a buggy whip, would switch at the brush as if to rouse up any hiding things.

On she went. The woods were deep and still. The sun made the pine needles almost too bright to look at, up where the wind rocked. The cones dropped as light as feathers. Down in the hollow was the mourning dove[2]—it was not too late for him.

The path ran up a hill. "Seem like there is chains about my feet, time I get this far," she said, in the voice of argument old people keep to use with themselves. "Something always take a hold of me on this hill—pleads I should stay."

After she got to the top, she turned and gave a full, severe look behind her where she had come. "Up through pines," she said at length. "Now down through oaks."

Her eyes opened their widest and she stared down gently. But before she got to the bottom of the hill a bush caught her dress.

---

2. **mourning dove:** the wild dove, which is known for its mournful cry.

Her fingers were busy and intent, but her skirts were full and long, so that before she could pull them free in one place they were caught in another. It was not possible to allow the dress to tear. "I in the thorny bush," she said. "Thorns, you doing your appointed work. Never want to let folks pass, no sir. Old eyes thought you was a pretty little *green* bush."

Finally, trembling all over, she stood free, and after a moment dared to stoop for her cane.

"Sun so high!" she cried, leaning back and looking, while the thick tears went over her eyes. "The time getting all gone here."

At the foot of this hill was a place where a log was laid across the creek.

"Now comes the trial," said Phoenix.

Putting her right foot out, she mounted the log and shut her eyes. Lifting her skirt, leveling her cane fiercely before her, like a festival figure in some parade, she began to march across. Then she opened her eyes and she was safe on the other side.

"I wasn't as old as I thought," she said.

But she sat down to rest. She spread her skirts on the bank around her and folded her hands over her knees. Up above her was a tree in a pearly cloud of mistletoe.[3] She did not dare to close her eyes, and when a little boy brought her a plate with a slice of marble cake on it she spoke to him. "That would be acceptable," she said. But when she went to take it there was just her own hand in the air.

So she left that tree, and had to go through a barbed-wire fence. There she had to creep and crawl, spreading her knees and stretching her fingers like a baby trying to climb the steps. But she talked loudly to herself: she could not let her dress be torn now, so late in the day, and she could not pay for having her arm or her leg sawed off if she got caught fast where she was.

At last she was safe through the fence and risen up out in the clearing. Big dead trees, like black men with one arm, were standing in the purple stalks of the withered cotton field. There sat a buzzard.

"Who you watching?"

In the furrow she made her way along.

---

3. mistletoe: semiparasitic green plant with yellow flowers and white berries. Druids, priests of the ancient Celtic religion, believed that mistletoe had magic powers, especially when it grew on an oak, which they considered a sacred tree.

"Glad this not the season for bulls," she said, looking sideways, "and the good Lord made his snakes to curl up and sleep in the winter. A pleasure I don't see no two-headed snake coming around that tree, where it come once. It took a while to get by him, back in the summer."

She passed through the old cotton and went into a field of dead corn. It whispered and shook and was taller than her head. "Through the maze now," she said, for there was no path.

Then there was something tall, black, and skinny there, moving before her.

At first she took it for a man. It could have been a man dancing in the field. But she stood still and listened, and it did not make a sound. It was as silent as a ghost.

"Ghost," she said sharply, "who be you the ghost of? For I have heard of nary[4] death close by."

But there was no answer, only the ragged dancing in the wind.

She shut her eyes, reached out her hand, and touched a sleeve. She found a coat and inside that an emptiness, cold as ice.

"You scarecrow," she said. Her face lighted. "I ought to be shut up for good," she said with laughter. "My senses is gone. I too old. I the oldest people I ever know. Dance, old scarecrow," she said, "while I dancing with you."

She kicked her foot over the furrow, and with mouth drawn down, shook her head once or twice in a little strutting way. Some husks blew down and whirled in streamers about her skirts.

Then she went on, parting her way from side to side with the cane, through the whispering field. At last she came to the end, to a wagon track where the silver grass blew between the red ruts. The quail were walking around like pullets,[5] seeming all dainty and unseen.

"Walk pretty," she said. "This the easy place. This the easy going."

She followed the track, swaying through the quiet bare fields, through the little strings of trees silver in their dead leaves, past cabins silver from weather, with the doors and windows boarded shut, all like old women under a spell sitting there. "I walking in their sleep," she said, nodding her head vigorously.

---

4. **nary:** *dialect,* not one.
5. **pullets:** young hens.

In a ravine she went where a spring was silently flowing through a hollow log. Old Phoenix bent and drank. "Sweet gum[6] makes the water sweet," she said, and drank more. "Nobody know who made this well, for it was here when I was born."

The track crossed a swampy part where the moss hung as white as lace from every limb. "Sleep on, alligators, and blow your bubbles." Then the track went into the road.

Deep, deep the road went down between the high green-colored banks. Overhead the live-oaks met, and it was as dark as a cave.

A black dog with a lolling[7] tongue came up out of the weeds by the ditch. She was meditating, and not ready, and when he came at her she only hit him a little with her cane. Over she went in the ditch, like a little puff of milkweed.

Down there, her senses drifted away. A dream visited her, and she reached her hand up, but nothing reached down and gave her a pull. So she lay there and presently went to talking. "Old woman," she said to herself, "that black dog come up out of the weeds to stall you off, and now there he sitting on his fine tail, smiling at you."

A white man finally came along and found her—a hunter, a young man, with his dog on a chain.

"Well Granny!" he laughed. "What are you doing there?"

"Lying on my back like a June bug waiting to be turned over, mister," she said, reaching up her hand.

He lifted her up, gave her a swing in the air, and set her down. "Anything broken, Granny?"

"No sir, them old dead weeds is springy enough," said Phoenix, when she had got her breath. "I thank you for your trouble."

"Where do you live, Granny?" he asked, while the two dogs were growling at each other.

"Away back yonder, sir, behind the ridge. You can't even see it from here."

"On your way home?"

"No sir, I going to town."

"Why, that's too far! That's as far as I walk when I come out myself, and I get something for my trouble." He patted the stuffed bag he carried, and there hung down a little closed claw. It was

6. **Sweet gum:** a tree that yields a sweet, gummy substance.
7. **lolling:** drooping.

one of the bobwhites, with its beak hooked bitterly to show it was dead. "Now you go on home, Granny!"

"I bound to go to town, mister," said Phoenix. "The time come around."

He gave another laugh, filling the whole landscape. "I know you old colored people! Wouldn't miss going to town to see Santa Claus!"

But something held old Phoenix very still. The deep lines in her face went into a fierce and different radiation. Without warning, she had seen with her own eyes a flashing nickel fall out of the man's pocket onto the ground.

"How old are you, Granny?" he was saying.

"There is no tellin, mister," she said, "no telling."

Then she gave a little cry and clapped her hands and said, "Git on away from here, dog! Look! Look at that dog!" She laughed as if in admiration. "He ain't scared of nobody. He a big black dog." She whispered, "Sic him!"

"Watch me get rid of that cur," said the man. "Sic him, Pete! Sic him!"

Phoenix heard the dogs fighting, and heard the man running and throwing sticks. She even heard a gunshot. But she was slowly bending forward by that time, further and further forward, the lids stretched down over her eyes, as if she were doing this in her sleep. Her chin was lowered almost to her knees. The yellow palm of her hand came out from the fold of her apron. Her fingers slid down and along the ground under the piece of money with the grace and care they would have in lifting an egg from under a setting hen. Then she slowly straightened up, she stood erect, and the nickel was in her apron pocket. A bird flew by. Her lips moved. "God watching me the whole time. I come to stealing."

The man came back, and his own dog panted about them. "Well, I scared him off that time," he said, and then he laughed and lifted his gun and pointed it at Phoenix.

She stood straight and faced him.

"Doesn't the gun scare you?" he said, still pointing it.

"No, sir, I seen plenty go off closer by, in my day, and for less than what I done," she said, holding utterly still.

He smiled, and shouldered the gun. "Well, Granny," he said, "you must be a hundred years old, and scared of nothing. I'd give you a dime if I had any money with me. But you take my advice and stay home, and nothing will happen to you."

"I bound to go on my way, mister," said Phoenix. She inclined her head in the red rag. Then they went in different directions, but she could hear the gun shooting again and again over the hill.

She walked on. The shadows hung from the oak trees to the road like curtains. Then she smelled wood smoke, and smelled the river, and she saw a steeple and the cabins on their steep steps. Dozens of little black children whirled around her. There ahead was Natchez[8] shining. Bells were ringing. She walked on.

In the paved city it was Christmas time. There were red and green electric lights strung and crisscrossed everywhere, and all turned on in the daytime. Old Phoenix would have been lost if she had not distrusted her eyesight and depended on her feet to know where to take her.

She paused quietly on the sidewalk where people were passing by. A lady came along in the crowd, carrying an armful of red-, green- and silver-wrapped presents; she gave off perfume like the red roses in hot summer, and Phoenix stopped her.

"Please, missy, will you lace up my shoe?" She held up her foot.

"What do you want, Grandma?"

"See my shoe," said Phoenix. "Do all right for out in the country, but wouldn't look right to go in a big building."

"Stand still then, Grandma," said the lady. She put her packages down on the sidewalk beside her and laced and tied both shoes tightly.

"Can't lace 'em with a cane," said Phoenix. "Thank you, missy. I doesn't mind asking a nice lady to tie up my shoe, when I gets out on the street."

Moving slowly and from side to side, she went into the big building, and into a tower of steps, where she walked up and around and around until her feet knew to stop.

She entered a door, and there she saw nailed up on the wall the document that had been stamped with the gold seal and framed in the gold frame, which matched the dream that was hung up in her head.

"Here I be," she said. There was a fixed and ceremonial stiffness over her body.

---

8. **Natchez** (năch'ĭz): a port city in southwest Mississippi located on the Mississippi River.

"A charity case, I suppose," said an attendant who sat at the desk before her.

But Phoenix only looked above her head. There was sweat on her face, the wrinkles in her skin shone like a bright net.

"Speak up, Grandma," the woman said. "What's your name? We must have your history, you know. Have you been here before? What seems to be the trouble with you?"

Old Phoenix only gave a twitch to her face as if a fly were bothering her.

"Are you deaf?" cried the attendant.

But then the nurse came in.

"Oh, that's just old Aunt Phoenix," she said. "She doesn't come for herself—she has a little grandson. She makes these trips just as regular as clockwork. She lives away back off the Old Natchez Trace."[9] She bent down. "Well, Aunt Phoenix, why don't you take a seat? We won't keep you standing after your long trip." She pointed.

The old woman sat down, bolt upright in the chair.

"Now, how is the boy?" asked the nurse.

Old Phoenix did not speak.

"I said, how is the boy?"

But Phoenix only waited and stared straight ahead, her face very solemn and withdrawn into rigidity.

"Is his throat any better?" asked the nurse. "Aunt Phoenix, don't you hear me? Is your grandson's throat any better since the last time you came for the medicine?"

With her hands on her knees, the old woman waited, silent, erect and motionless, just as if she were in armor.

"You mustn't take up our time this way, Aunt Phoenix," the nurse said. "Tell us quickly about your grandson, and get it over. He isn't dead, is he?"

At last there came a flicker and then a flame of comprehension across her face, and she spoke.

"My grandson. It was my memory had left me. There I sat and forgot why I made my long trip."

"Forgot?" The nurse frowned. "After you came so far?"

Then Phoenix was like an old woman begging a dignified

---

9. Old Natchez Trace: an old road, over 500 miles long, which runs from Nashville, Tennessee, to Natchez. *Trace* means a path or trail through the woods.

forgiveness for waking up frightened in the night. "I never did go to school, I was too old at the Surrender,"[10] she said in a soft voice. "I'm an old woman without an education. It was my memory fail me. My little grandson, he is just the same, and I forgot it in the coming."

"Throat never heals, does it?" said the nurse, speaking in a loud, sure voice to Old Phoenix. By now she had a card with something written on it, a little list. "Yes. Swallowed lye. When was it?—January—two-three years ago—"

Phoenix spoke unasked now. "No, missy, he not dead, he just the same. Every little while his throat begin to close up again, and he not able to swallow. He not get his breath. He not able to help himself. So the time come around, and I go on another trip for the soothing medicine."

"All right. The doctor said as long as you came to get it, you could have it," said the nurse. "But it's an obstinate case."

"My little grandson, he sit up there in the house all wrapped up, waiting by himself," Phoenix went on. "We is the only two left in the world. He suffer and it don't seem to put him back at all. He got a sweet look. He going to last. He wear a little patch quilt and peep out holding his mouth open like a little bird. I remembers so plain now. I not going to forget him again, no, the whole enduring time. I could tell him from all the other in creation."

"All right." The nurse was trying to hush her now. She brought her a bottle of medicine. "Charity," she said, making a check mark in a book.

Old Phoenix held the bottle close to her eyes, and then carefully put it into her pocket.

"I thank you," she said.

"It's Christmas time, Grandma," said the attendant. "Could I give you a few pennies out of my purse?"

"Five pennies is a nickel," said Phoenix stiffly.

"Here's a nickel," said the attendant.

Phoenix rose carefully and held out her hand. She received the nickel and then fished the other nickel out of her pocket and laid it beside the new one. She stared at her palm closely, with her head on one side.

---

10. Surrender: that is, of the Confederate forces under General Lee on April 9, 1865, at Appomattox Courthouse, which virtually ended the Civil War.

Then she gave a tap with her cane on the floor.

"This is what come to me to do," she said. "I going to the store and buy my child a little windmill they sells, made out of paper. He going to find it hard to believe there such a thing in the world. I'll march myself back where he waiting, holding it straight up in his hand."

She lifted her free hand, gave a little nod, turned around, and walked out of the doctor's office. Then her slow step began on the stairs, going down.

Meaning

1. Why was Phoenix Jackson going to Natchez? At what time of year was she making the trip?
2. Writers sometimes give their characters *symbolic* names, that is, names that suggest a deeper level of meaning. Find at least three places in the story that suggest that the name *Phoenix* was chosen to parallel the phoenix of Egyptian mythology.
3. The title of a story may also have symbolic meaning. What does the worn path into Natchez represent? What takes hold of Phoenix at one point and "pleads I should stay"?
4. The nurse noted that the medicine was given to Phoenix out of "charity." How charitable were the people Phoenix met in the city? Who in the story exemplifies the true spirit of charity?
5. Which of the following words do you think best describes Phoenix: pathetic, clever, enduring, suffering, worried? Cite examples from the story to prove your answer.

Method

1. What information does the author give you about Phoenix Jackson in the first paragraph? At what point in the story do you realize that she has difficulty in seeing?
2. What do we learn about Phoenix during her meeting with the hunter?
3. Find some examples of the use of dialect in the story. How does the dialect help to characterize Phoenix?
4. Why do you think the author does not tell the purpose of Phoenix's trip until the end of the story?

Language: Figures of Speech

Writers often use figurative rather than literal language. An expression is *literal* when it is factual. "Rain poured down as they walked to school," is an example of a literal language. Language is *figurative* when it appeals to your imagination by using figures of speech. "They walked to school under a curtain of rain," is an example of figurative language.

The two most common figures of speech are *simile* and *metaphor*. Both figures of speech compare two things that are essentially *unlike*. The writer's imagination sees one way in which the two things are strikingly *like* one another. When the writer tells the reader of the likeness that he or she sees, a vivid impression of the object is conveyed.

If the author says that the first thing compared is *like* the second, this direct comparison is called a *simile*. In describing Phoenix's hair, Eudora Welty says it had "an odor like copper."

If the writer does not use *like* or *as* in the comparison but still compares two objects, the implied comparison is called a *metaphor*. For example, Phoenix moved "with the balanced heaviness and lightness of a pendulum in a grandfather clock."

Identify which figure of speech is used in each of the following examples from "A Worn Path." Identify the two things that are compared in each figure of speech.

1. "This made a grave and persistent noise in the still air, that seemed meditative like the chirping of a solitary little bird."
2. ". . . her cane, limber as a buggy whip, would switch at the brush. . . ."
3. "The cones dropped as light as feathers."
4. "Over she went in the ditch, like a little puff of milk-weed."
5. "Moving slowly and from side to side, she went into the big building, and into a tower of steps. . . ."

Discussion and Composition

1. Is "A Worn Path" a quality story or a commercial story, written to please large numbers of people? Why do you think so?

2. What qualities did Phoenix have that caused her to survive, in spite of her infirmities? How important do you think these qualities are in today's world?

3. Many people cannot afford medical care. One solution that has been tried in other countries is socialized medicine. In a socialized system, the government employs doctors. Taxes pay doctors' salaries and other medical costs. Do some research on socialized medicine and other proposed solutions to the high cost of medical care. Present the information you find in an essay. Support with facts and examples one solution to the problem of the high cost of medical care.

JESSE STUART
(born 1907)

The writings of Jesse Stuart are strongly marked by his love for his native Kentucky, which provides both the subject matter and the language for his stories. Born in a one-room cabin, Stuart grew up on a mountain farm. He was the first member of his family to attend high school. By working at various times as a steel mill laborer, a quarryman, and a hired farm hand, he put himself through Lincoln Memorial University in Tennessee. He has had a noteworthy career as a teacher, a lecturer, and a writer. Stuart now lives with his family on a farm in eastern Kentucky.

His first literary success came in 1934 with the publication of *Man with a Bull-Tongue Plow,* a collection of more than seven hundred poems that reflect his love for the Kentucky hills. *The Thread That Runs So True* (1949) is an autobiographical account of his experiences as a schoolteacher, when he was younger than some of his pupils. *The Year of My Rebirth* (1956) deals with Stuart's recovery from a nearly fatal heart attack.

LOVE

Yesterday when the bright sun blazed down on the wilted corn my father and I walked around the edge of the new ground to plan a fence. The cows kept coming through the chestnut oaks on the cliff and running over the young corn. They bit off the tips of the corn and trampled down the stubble.

My father walked in the cornbalk.[1] Bob, our Collie, walked in front of my father. We heard a ground squirrel whistle down over the bluff among the dead treetops at the clearing's edge. "Whoop, take him, Bob," said my father. He lifted up a young stalk of corn, with wilted dried roots, where the ground squirrel had dug it up for the sweet grain of corn left on its tender roots. This has been a dry spring and the corn has kept well in the earth where the grain has sprouted. The ground squirrels love this corn.

---

1. **cornbalk:** unplowed land between each row of corn.

They dig up rows of it and eat the sweet grains. The young corn stalks are killed and we have to replant the corn.

I can see my father keep sicking Bob after the ground squirrel. He jumped over the corn rows. He started to run toward the ground squirrel. I, too, started running toward the clearing's edge where Bob was jumping and barking. The dust flew in tiny swirls behind our feet. There was a cloud of dust behind us.

"It's a big bull blacksnake," said my father. "Kill him, Bob! Kill him, Bob!"

Bob was jumping and snapping at the snake so as to make it strike and throw itself off guard. Bob had killed twenty-eight copperheads this spring. He knows how to kill a snake. He doesn't rush to do it. He takes his time and does the job well.

"Let's don't kill the snake," I said. "A blacksnake is a harmless snake. It kills poison snakes. It kills the copperhead. It catches more mice from the fields than a cat."

I could see the snake didn't want to fight the dog. The snake wanted to get away. Bob wouldn't let it. I wondered why it was crawling toward a heap of black loamy[2] earth at the bench[3] of the hill. I wondered why it had come from the chestnut oak sprouts and the matted greenbriars on the cliff. I looked as the snake lifted its pretty head in response to one of Bob's jumps. "It's not a bull blacksnake," I said. "It's a she-snake. Look at the white on her throat."

"A snake is an enemy to me," my father snapped. "I hate a snake. Kill it, Bob. Go in there and get that snake and quit playing with it!"

Bob obeyed my father. I hated to see him take this snake by the throat. She was so beautifully poised in the sunlight. Bob grabbed the white patch on her throat. He cracked her long body like an ox whip in the wind. He cracked it against the wind only. The blood spurted from her fine-curved throat. Something hit against my legs like pellets. Bob threw the snake down. I looked to see what had struck my legs. It was snake eggs. Bob had slung them from her body. She was going to the sand heap to lay her eggs, where the sun is the setting-hen that warms them and hatches them.

Bob grabbed her body there on the earth where the red

2. **loamy** (lōm′ē): fertile.
3. **bench:** narrow, level place.

blood was running down on the gray-piled loam. Her body was still writhing in pain. She acted like a greenweed held over a new-ground fire. Bob slung her viciously many times. He cracked her limp body against the wind. She was now limber as a shoe-string in the wind. Bob threw her riddled body back on the sand. She quivered like a leaf in the lazy wind, then her riddled body lay perfectly still. The blood colored the loamy earth around the snake.

"Look at the eggs, won't you?" said my father. We counted thirty-seven eggs. I picked an egg up and held it in my hand. Only a minute ago there was life in it. It was an immature seed. It would not hatch. Mother sun could not incubate it on the warm earth. The egg I held in my hand was almost the size of a quail's egg. The shell on it was thin and tough and the egg appeared under the suface to be a watery egg.

"Well, Bob, I guess you see now why this snake couldn't fight," I said. "It is life. Weaker devour the stronger even among human beings. Dog kills snake. Snake kills birds. Birds kill the butterflies. Man conquers all. Man, too, kills for sport."

Bob was panting. He walked ahead of us back to the house. His tongue was out of his mouth. He was tired. He was hot under his shaggy coat of hair. His tongue nearly touched the dry dirt and white flecks of foam dripped from it. We walked toward the house. Neither my father nor I spoke. I still thought about the dead snake. The sun was going down over the chestnut ridge. A lark was singing. It was late for a lark to sing. The red evening clouds floated above the pine trees on our pasture hill. My father stood beside the path. His black hair was moved by the wind. His face was red in the blue wind of day. His eyes looked toward the sinking sun.

"And my father hates a snake," I thought.

I thought about the agony women know of giving birth. I thought about how they will fight to save their children. Then, I thought of the snake I thought it was silly for me to think such thoughts.

This morning my father and I got up with the chickens. He says one has to get up with the chickens to do a day's work. We got the posthole digger, ax, spud,[4] measuring pole and the mat-

---

4. **spud:** sharp tool used to dig up weeds.

tock.[5] We started for the clearing's edge. Bob didn't go along.

The dew was on the corn. My father walked behind with the posthole digger across his shoulder. I walked in front. The wind was blowing. It was a good morning wind to breathe and a wind that makes one feel like he can get under the edge of a hill and heave the whole hill upside down.

I walked out the corn row where we had come yesterday afternoon. I looked in front of me. I saw something. I saw it move. It was moving like a huge black rope winds around a windlass.[6] "Steady," I says to my father. "Here is the bull blacksnake." He took one step up beside me and stood. His eyes grew wide apart.

"What do you know about this," he said.

"You have seen the bull blacksnake now," I said. "Take a good look at him! He is lying beside his dead mate. He has come to her. He, perhaps, was on her trail yesterday."

The male snake had trailed her to her doom. He had come in the night, under the roof of stars, as the moon shed rays of light on the quivering clouds of green. He had found his lover dead. He was coiled beside her and she was dead.

The bullsnake lifted his head and followed us as we walked around the dead snake. He would have fought us to his death. He would have fought Bob to his death. "Take a stick," said my father, "and throw him over the hill so Bob won't find him. Did you ever see anything to beat that? I've heard they'd do that. But this is my first time to see it." I took a stick and threw him over the bank into the dewy sprouts on the cliff.

5. **mattock** (măt′ɔk): flat-bladed tool used to dig up and cut roots.
6. **windlass:** cylinder with a rope or cable wrapped around it, used for pulling or lifting.

Meaning

1. At the beginning of "Love," how did the narrator and his father differ in their attitudes toward snakes?
2. How do the father's attitudes change? What brings about the change?
3. What is the theme of "Love"?

4. *Sentimental* means having an excess of sentiment or emotion. Commercial stories are often sentimental. Would you consider this story commercial? Is it sentimental? Why or why not?

Method

1. The author uses simple sentence construction, usually subject followed by verb. How is this style suited to the setting and subject of the story? How does he keep his style from becoming monotonous?
2. During the fight between the dog and the snake, how does the narrator show his sympathy for the snake?
3. Point out some places where beautiful and violent images occur close to one another in this story. For example, when the dog takes the snake by the throat, she is described as "beautifully poised in the sunlight." What effect does this contrast have on the reader?
4. What is the narrator's attitude toward country life? How does he make you aware of his attitude?
5. Compare this story to "A Worn Path." How are they alike and yet different in theme? Which story is more moving to you? Tell why you prefer one over the other.

Language: Denotation and Connotation

The *denotation* of a word is its actual meaning, its precise dictionary definition. The *connotation* of a word includes the meanings it suggests in addition to its literal definition.

Both *home* and *house* denote the place or dwelling where a person lives. However, the word *home* stirs up or connotes additional meanings and associations (usually favorable ones) such as comfort, shelter, coziness, friendliness, privacy, peace, and rest.

Connotative meanings may be suggested by individual words (such as *house* versus *home*), or by the context of the words. What connotations does the word *snake* have when the father in the story says, "A snake is an enemy to me. . ."?

Decide whether each of the words on the following page has favorable or unfavorable connotations. List two or three of the connotations after each word.

1. pretty
2. blood
3. setting-hen
4. writhing
5. quivered

6. mother
7. kill
8. lark
9. agony
10. dew

Discussion and Composition

1. The narrator describes what he sees and how he feels in the morning when he first goes outside. Describe what you see and how you feel when you first leave your house or apartment in the morning.

2. The killing of the female snake is described in vivid detail. Consider some action that you have witnessed which impressed you. Describe what happened and how you felt about it.

3. This story implies, if not states, that animals have feelings—and that they are even capable of such human emotions as love. Do you agree with this idea? Tell why or why not.

4. In literature, the country is often identified with simplicity, beauty, life, innocence, goodness, idealism, fertility. The city, on the other hand, is typically identified with sophistication, disease, death, evil, sterility, confusion. To what extent does "Love" contain elements that are associated with the country as an ideal world? In your opinion, are the country and city of literature true to the real world as you know it? Tell why or why not.

EDGAR ALLAN POE
(1809–1849)

No other American up to his time had excelled in the three major writing fields of poetry, short stories, and criticism. No other American up to his time so profoundly influenced European writers. Edgar Allan Poe's short life was filled with personal failure. Yet he set the pattern for modern mystery and detective fiction, created masterpieces of supernatural horror, and set down original theories on how to write poetry and short stories.

Poe was born in Boston of a Southern family of traveling actors. His mother died when he was two, and he was taken in by the Allans of Richmond, Virginia, a wealthy family. They gave him their name as his middle name and supported him through school in Virginia and in England, where they lived for five years.

After short periods of time at the University of Virginia, where he ran up heavy gambling debts, in the Army, where he rose in two years to the rank of sergeant-major, and at West Point, where he forced his own dismissal, Poe decided to earn his living by writing. Over the next eighteen years, he wrote and edited for several different magazines and newspapers, but he was unable to hold a job for long. Even a small amount of alcohol affected him greatly, and he could not control his need for it. He suffered extreme poverty and could not support his young wife, who died of tuberculosis when she was twenty-five. Two years later, after a party where he had drunk heavily, he died.

Many of Poe's tales of the supernatural were written originally for newspapers and magazines. His first detective story, "The Murders in the Rue Morgue," was published in 1841. His creative genius was recognized in Europe long before he was famous in America. It was not until publication of his poem "The Raven" in 1845 that he became nationally known.

Poe's stories and poems usually deal with love, beauty, and death. He felt that a story or poem should produce a single emotional effect, and that every word, even every sound, should contribute to that effect. His work shows clearly that he followed his own rules.

THE MASQUE* OF
THE RED DEATH

The "Red Death" had long devastated the country. No pestilence had ever been so fatal, or so hideous. Blood was its Avatar[1] and its seal—the redness and the horror of blood. There were sharp pains, and sudden dizziness, and then profuse bleeding at the pores, with dissolution.[2] The scarlet stains upon the body and especially upon the face of the victim were the pest ban[3] which shut him out from the aid and from the sympathy of his fellow men. And the whole seizure, progress, and termination of the disease were the incidents of half an hour.

But the Prince Prospero was happy and dauntless and sagacious. When his dominions were half depopulated, he summoned to his presence a thousand hale and light-hearted friends from among the knights and dames of his court, and with these retired to the deep seclusion of one of his castellated abbeys.[4] This was an extensive and magnificent structure, the creation of the prince's own eccentric yet august taste. A strong and lofty wall girdled it in. This wall had gates of iron. The courtiers, having entered, brought furnaces and massy hammers, and welded the bolts. They resolved to leave means neither of ingress nor egress[5] to the sudden impulses of despair or frenzy from within. The abbey was amply provisioned. With such precautions the courtiers might bid defiance to contagion. The external world could take care of itself. In the meantime, it was folly to grieve or to think. The prince had provided all the appliances of pleasure. There were buffoons, there

---

* **masque:** an elaborately staged dramatic performance popular in the sixteenth and seventeenth centuries. The actors wore masks and usually represented mythological or symbolic figures. The acting consisted mostly of dancing and pantomime. Masque also means a masquerade, or a mask.

1. Avatar (ăv′ə·tär′)**:** in Hindu theology, the bodily form taken by a god; the visible sign or indication of something; here, blood is the sign of the "Red Death."

2. dissolution: disintegration; decay; hence, death.

3. pest ban: the sign by which the disease (*pest*) was recognized and which resulted in the *banning* of the afflicted person.

4. castellated (kăs′tə·lā′tĭd) **abbeys:** castle-like monasteries.

5. ingress (ĭn′grĕs) **nor egress** (ē′grĕs)**:** entrance or exit.

were improvisatori,[6] there were ballet dancers, there were musicians, there was Beauty, there was wine. All these and security were within. Without was the Red Death.

It was toward the close of the fifth or sixth month of his seclusion, and while the pestilence raged most furiously abroad, that the Prince Prospero entertained his thousand friends at a masked ball of the most unusual magnificence.

It was a voluptuous[7] scene, that masquerade. But first let me tell of the rooms in which it was held. There were seven—an imperial suite. In many palaces, however, such suites form a long and straight vista, while the folding doors slide back nearly to the walls on either hand, so that the view of the whole extent is scarcely impeded. Here the case was very different, as might have been expected from the prince's love of the bizarre. The apartments were so irregularly disposed that the vision embraced but little more than one at a time. There was a sharp turn at every twenty or thirty yards, and at each turn a novel effect. To the right and left, in the middle of each wall, a tall and narrow Gothic window looked out upon a closed corridor which pursued the windings of the suite. These windows were of stained glass, whose color varied in accordance with the prevailing hue of the decorations of the chamber into which it opened. That at the eastern extremity was hung, for example, in blue—and vividly blue were its windows. The second chamber was purple in its ornaments and tapestries, and here the panes were purple. The third was green throughout, and so were the casements.[8] The fourth was furnished and lighted with orange, the fifth was white, the sixth with violet. The seventh apartment was closely shrouded in black velvet tapestries that hung all over the ceiling and down the walls, falling in heavy folds upon a carpet of the same material and hue. But, in this chamber only, the color of the windows failed to correspond with the decorations. The panes here were scarlet a—deep bloodcolor. Now in no one of the seven apartments was there any lamp or candelabrum,[9] amid the profusion of golden ornaments that lay

---

6. improvisatori (ĕm′prôv·ē·za·tō′rē): *Italian,* entertainers who improvise or make up songs, poems, or drama as they perform.
7. voluptuous (və·lŭp′choo·əs): delightful to the senses; yielding enjoyment through pleasures or luxuries.
8. casements: windows having sashes which open on hinges at the side.
9. candelabrum (kăn′də·lä′brəm): a large, ornamental, branched holder for candles.

scattered to and fro or depended[10] from the roof. There was no light of any kind emanating from lamp or candle within the suite of chambers. But in the corridors that followed the suite there stood, opposite each window, a heavy tripod, bearing a brazier[11] of fire, that projected its rays through the tinted glass and so glaringly illumined the room. And thus were produced a multitude of gaudy and fantastic appearances. But in the western or black chamber the effect of the firelight that streamed upon the dark hangings through the blood-tinted panes was ghastly in the extreme, and produced so wild a look upon the countenances of those who entered that there were few of the company bold enough to set foot within its precincts at all.

It was in this apartment, also, that there stood against the western wall a gigantic clock of ebony.[12] Its pendulum swung to and fro with a dull, heavy, monotonous clang; and when the minute hand made the circuit of the face, and the hour was to be stricken, there came from the brazen lungs of the clock a sound which was clear and loud and deep and exceedingly musical, but of so peculiar a note and emphasis that, at each lapse of an hour, the musicians of the orchestra were constrained to pause, momentarily, in their performance, to hearken to the sound; and thus the waltzers perforce[13] ceased their evolutions; and there was a brief disconcert[14] of the whole gay company; and, while the chimes of the clock yet rang, it was observed that the giddiest grew pale, and the more aged and sedate passed their hands over their brows as if in confused revery or meditation. But when the echoes had fully ceased, a light laughter at once pervaded the assembly; the musicians looked at each other and smiled as if at their own nervousness and folly, and made whispering vows, each to the other, that the next chiming of the clock should produce in them no similar emotion; and then, after the lapse of sixty minutes (which embrace three thousand and six hundred seconds of the Time that flies), there came yet another chiming of the clock, and then were the same disconcert and tremulousness and meditation as before.

But, in spite of these things, it was a gay and magnificent

10. **depended:** hung.
11. **brazier** (brā′zhər): a metal pan for holding burning coals.
12. **ebony** (ĕb′ə·nē): a rare black wood.
13. **perforce** (pər·fôrs′): by force of circumstances; of necessity.
14. **disconcert** (dĭs′kən·sûrt′): confusion. Explain this word by checking the meaning of its prefix and root.

revel. The tastes of the prince were peculiar. He had a fine eye for colors and effects. He disregarded the *decora*[15] of mere fashion. His plans were bold and fiery, and his conceptions glowed with barbaric luster. There are some who would have thought him mad. His followers felt that he was not. It was necessary to hear and see and touch him to be *sure* that he was not.

He had directed, in great part, the movable embellishments of the seven chambers, upon occasion of this great fete;[16] and it was his own guiding taste which had given character to the masqueraders. Be sure they were grotesque. There were much glare and glitter and piquancy and phantasm[17]—much of what has been seen in *Hernani*.[18] There were arabesque[19] figures with unsuited[20] limbs and appointments. There were delirious fancies such as the madman fashions. There were much of the beautiful, much of the wanton,[21] much of the bizarre, something of the terrible, and not a little of that which might have excited disgust. To and fro in the seven chambers there stalked, in fact, a multitude of dreams. And these—the dreams—writhed in and about, taking hue from the rooms, and causing the wild music of the orchestra to seem as the echo of their steps. And, anon, there strikes the ebony clock which stands in the hall of the velvet. And then, for a moment, all is still, and all is silent save the voice of the clock. The dreams are stiff-frozen as they stand. But the echoes of the chime die away—they have endured but an instant—and a light, half-subdued laughter floats after them as they depart. And now again the music swells, and the dreams live, and writhe to and fro more merrily than ever, taking hue from the many-tinted windows through which stream the rays from the tripods. But to the chamber which lies most westwardly of the seven, there are now none of the maskers who venture; for the night is waning away, and there flows a ruddier light through the blood-colored panes, and the blackness of the sable drapery appalls; and to him whose foot falls upon the sable carpet, there comes from the near clock of

---

15. *decora:* *Latin,* plural of *decorum;* that is, observances; proprieties.
16. **fete** (fāt): a lavish entertainment or festival.
17. **piquancy** (pē'kən·sē) **and phantasm** (făn'tăz·əm): liveliness and fantasy.
18. *Hernani:* a play by the French author Victor Hugo (1802–85).
19. **arabesque** (ăr'ə·bĕsk'): a design with an intricate pattern of angular and curved lines. Check your dictionary to find what position this refers to in ballet.
20. **unsuited:** unmatched.
21. **wanton** (wŏn'tən): unrestrained; unchaste.

ebony a muffled peal more solemnly emphatic than any which reaches *their* ears who indulge in the more remote gaieties of the other apartments.

But these other apartments were densely crowded, and in them beat feverishly the heart of life. And the revel went whirlingly on, until at length there commenced the sounding of midnight upon the clock. And then the music ceased; as I have told, and the evolutions of the waltzers were quieted, and there was an uneasy cessation of all things as before. But now there were twelve strokes to be sounded by the bell of the clock; and thus it happened, perhaps, that more of thought crept, with more of time, into the meditations of the thoughtful among those who reveled. And thus, too, it happened, perhaps, that before the last echoes of the last chime had utterly sunk into silence, there were many individuals in the crowd who had found leisure to become aware of the presence of a masked figure which had arrested the attention of no single individual before. And the rumor of this new presence having spread itself whisperingly around, there arose at length from the whole company a buzz, or murmur, expressive of disapprobation[22] and surprise—then, finally, of terror, of horror, and of disgust.

In an assembly of phantasms such as I have painted, it may well be supposed that no ordinary appearance could have excited such sensation. In truth the masquerade license[23] of the night was nearly unlimited; but the figure in question had out-Heroded Herod,[24] and gone beyond the bounds of even the prince's indefinite decorum. There are chords in the hearts of the most reckless which no jest can be made. The whole company, indeed seemed now deeply to feel that in the costume and bearing of the stranger neither wit nor propriety existed. The figure was tall and gaunt, and shrouded from head to foot in the habiliments of the grave. The mask which concealed the visage was made so nearly to resemble the countenance of a stiffened corpse that the closest scrutiny must have had difficulty in detecting the cheat. And yet all

---

22. disapprobation (dĭs'ăp·rə·bā'shən): disapproval.

23. masquerade license: freedom to act irresponsibly without fear of being recognized.

24. out-Heroded Herod: had outdone Herod in violence, outrage, or extravagance. Herod was the king of Judea who is reported to have ordered the slaughter of all the male infants under two years of age in Bethlehem in an attempt to kill the newly born Jesus.

this might have been endured, if not approved, by the mad revelers around. But the mummer[25] had gone so far as to assume the type of the Red Death. His vesture was dabbled in *blood*—and his broad brow, with all the features of the face, was besprinkled with the scarlet horror.

When the eyes of Prince Prospero fell upon this spectral image (which with a slow and solemn movement, as if more fully to sustain its role, stalked to and fro among the waltzers) he was seen to be convulsed, in the first moment, with a strong shudder either of terror or distaste; but, in the next, his brow reddened with rage.

"Who dares?" he demanded hoarsely of the courtiers who stood near him—"who dares insult us with this blasphemous mockery? Seize him and unmask him—that we may know whom we have to hang at sunrise, from the battlements!"

It was in the eastern or blue chamber in which stood the Prince Prospero as he uttered these words. They rang throughout the seven rooms loudly and clearly—for the prince was a bold and robust man, and the music had become hushed at the waving of his hand.

It was in the blue room where stood the prince, with a group of pale courtiers by his side. At first, as he spoke, there was a slight rushing movement of this group in the direction of the intruder, who at the moment was also near at hand, and now, with deliberate and stately step, made closer approach to the speaker. But from a certain nameless awe with which the mad assumptions of the mummer had inspired the whole party, there were found none who put forth hand to seize him, so that unimpeded, he passed within a yard of the prince's person; and while the vast assembly, as if with one impulse, shrank from the centers of the rooms to the walls, he made his way uninterruptedly, but with the same solemn and measured step which had distinguished him from the first, through the blue chamber to the purple—through the purple to the green—through the green to the orange—through this again to the white—and even thence to the violet, ere a decided movement had been made to arrest him. It was then, however, that the Prince Prospero, maddening with rage and the shame of his own momentary cowardice, rushed hurriedly through the six chambers, while none followed him on account of a deadly terror

25. **mummer:** one who acts in a disguise or mask, expecially during festivals.

that had seized upon all. He bore aloft a drawn dagger, and had approached, in rapid impetuosity, to within three or four feet of the retreating figure, when the latter, having attained the extremity of the velvet apartment, turned suddenly and confronted his pursuer. There was a sharp cry—and the dagger dropped gleaming upon the sable carpet, upon which, instantly afterward, fell prostrate in death the Prince Prospero. Then, summoning the wild courage of despair, a throng of the revelers at once threw themselves into the black apartment, and seizing the mummer, whose tall figure stood erect and motionless within the shadow of the ebony clock, gasped in unutterable horror at finding the grave-cerements[26] and corpse-like mask which they handled with so violent a rudeness, untenanted[27] by any tangible form.

And now was acknowledged the presence of the Red Death. He had come like a thief in the night.[28] And one by one dropped the revelers in the blood-bedewed halls of their revel, and died each in the despairing posture of his fall. And the life of the ebony clock went out with that of the last of the gay. And the flames of the tripods expired. And Darkness and Decay and the Red Death held illimitable dominion over all.

26. **cerements** (sîr′məntz): cloth which is treated with wax and used as wrappings for the dead.
27. **untenanted:** Figure out the meaning by breaking this word into its prefix and root.
28. **thief in the night:** a biblical reference (1 Thessalonians 5:2), ". . . the day of the Lord so cometh as a thief in the night."

Meaning

1. Why do you think Poe chose the name Prospero for the prince?
2. Why do all the guests fear the strange "mummer"? What happens when they seize him?
3. What are the conflicts in the story? Explain your answer.
4. What would you say is the theme of "The Masque of the Red Death"? What does Poe emphasize: plot character, atmosphere, or theme?

Method

1. The setting of the story, a masked ball, appears in paragraph three. What purposes, then, are served by paragraphs one and two?
2. To sustain the mood or atmosphere of horror, Poe makes a strong appeal to the senses, especially to sight and hearing. Find three passages that are visual images of horror. List three of the sounds that contribute to the same effect.
3. Notice that Poe sometimes uses very long sentences. Compare some of the sentences that go on for several lines. What do they seem to have in common? Why do you think Poe used such long, complicated sentences?
4. Poe's prose style has many of the characteristics of his poetry. Notice, for example, Poe's use of *alliteration,* that is, the repetition of the same sound at the beginning of words close together in a sentence. For example, "There were much glare and glitter and piquancy and phantasm. . . ."

   Notice also the *repetition* of words and phrases, as in "There were much of the beautiful, much of the wanton, much of the bizarre. . . ." List other examples of Poe's uses of alliteration and repetition.

Language: The Use of Adjectives

Notice, in the following sentences, the use of adjectives, sometimes three, even four, to achieve a *cumulative,* that is, a steadily increasing or mounting, effect.

1. "Its pendulum swung to and fro with a dull, heavy, monotonous clang. . . ."
2. ". . . a sound which was clear and loud and deep and exceedingly musical. . . ."
3. "His plans were bold and fiery, and his conceptions glowed with barbaric luster."

Notice that the *rhythm* of each sentence suits the idea that Poe wants to express. In the first sentence, Poe wants the reader to *hear* the clang of the pendulum, so he chooses to have adjectives in a series, with the number of syllables increasing with each word.

In the second sentence, what is the effect of Poe's use of *and* to separate the adjectives?

In the third sentence, Poe repeats the same idea twice, but *plans* and *conceptions* have quite different connotations. How does the second part of the sentence differ from the first part?

Discussion and Composition

1. Think of an event, real or imagined, that would produce a feeling of fear, joy, horror, suspense, pity, or calm. Write a paragraph in which you set the mood and atmosphere for the telling of such an event. Try to choose words that are rich in their power of suggestion. Construct every sentence with care. Remember that everything must relate to the single effect you wish to create.

2. Poe believed that a short story approached perfection only when every word, even every sound contributed to a single emotional effect. Of the short story writers other than Poe that you have read so far, who best follows Poe's ideas about writing? Which writer would you say Poe would like least? Support your answers with specific examples.

McKNIGHT MALMAR
(born 1903)

McKnight Malmar was born in Albany, New York, and grew up in suburban New York. While attending Mary Baldwin Seminary in Staunton, Virginia, she began writing and trying to get her stories published. "The Storm" was published in *Good Housekeeping* magazine in 1944 and has been dramatized several times, most recently for television nearly thirty years after publication under the title "The Victim." Another of her stories is "A Fair Stranger."

She has also written several mystery novels: *Never Say Die, The Past Won't Die,* and *Fog Is a Shroud.* Mrs. Malmar lives near Richmond, Virginia.

THE STORM

She inserted her key in the lock and turned the knob. The March wind snatched the door out of her hand and slammed it against the wall. It took strength to close it against the pressure of the gale, and she had no sooner closed it than the rain came in a pounding downpour, beating noisily against the windows as if trying to follow her in. She could not hear the taxi as it started up and went back down the road.

She breathed a sigh of thankfulness at being home again and in time. In rain like this, the crossroads always were flooded. Half an hour later her cab could not have got through the rising water, and there was no alternative route.

There was no light anywhere in the house. Ben was not home, then. As she turned on the lamp by the sofa she had a sense of anticlimax.[1] All the way home—she had been visiting her sister—she had seen herself going into a lighted house, to Ben, who would be sitting by the fire with his paper. She had taken delight in picturing his happy surprise at seeing her, home a week earlier than he had expected her. She had known just how his round face would light up, how his eyes would twinkle behind his glasses, how he would catch her by the shoulders and look down into her

---

1. **anticlimax:** drop in interest from the important to the commonplace.

face to see the changes a month had made in her, and then kiss her resoundingly on both cheeks, like a French general bestowing a decoration. Then she would make coffee and find a piece of cake, and they would sit together by the fire and talk.

But Ben wasn't here. She looked at the clock on the mantel and saw it was nearly ten. Perhaps he had not planned to come home tonight, as he was not expecting her; even before she had left he frequently was in the city all night because business kept him too late to catch the last train. If he did not come soon, he would not be able to make it at all.

She did not like the thought. The storm was growing worse. She could hear the wild lash of the trees, the whistle of the wind around the corners of the little house. For the first time she regretted this move to the far suburbs. There had been neighbors at first, a quarter-mile down the road; but they moved away several months ago, and now their house stood empty.

She had thought nothing of the lonesomeness. It was perfect here—for two. She had taken such pleasure in fixing up her house—her very own house—and caring for it that she had not missed company other than Ben. But now, alone and with the storm trying to batter its way in, she found it frightening to be so far away from other people. There was no one this side of the crossroads; the road that passed the house wandered past farmland into nothingness in the thick woods a mile farther on.

She hung her hat and her coat in the closet and went to stand before the hall mirror to pin up the soft strands of hair that the wind had loosened. She did not really see the pale face with its blunt little nose, the slender, almost childish figure in its grown-up black dress, or the big brown eyes that looked back at her.

She fastened the last strands into the pompadour[2] and turned away from the mirror. Her shoulders drooped a little. There was something childlike about her, like a small girl craving protection, something immature and yet appealing, in spite of her plainness. She was thirty-one and had been married for fifteen months. The fact that she had married at all still seemed a miracle to her.

Now she began to walk through the house, turning on lights as she went. Ben had left it in fairly good order. There was very little trace of an untidy masculine presence; but then, he was a tidy

2. **pompadour** (pŏm′pə·dōr): hair style in which the hair is combed up high from the forehead, sometimes over a roll.

man. She began to realize that the house was cold. Of course, Ben would have lowered the thermostat. He was very careful about things like that. He would not tolerate waste.

No wonder it was cold; the thermostat was set at fifty-eight. She pushed the little needle up to seventy, and the motor in the cellar started so suddenly and noisily that it frightened her for a moment.

She went into the kitchen and made some coffee. While she waited for it to drip she began to prowl around the lower floor. She was curiously restless and could not relax. Yet it was good to be back again among her own things, in her own home. She studied the living-room with fresh eyes. Yes, it was a pleasant room even though it was small. The bright, flowered chintzes on the furniture and at the windows were cheerful and pretty, and the lowboy[3] she had bought three months ago was just right for the middle of the long wall. But her plants, set so bravely along the window sill, had died. Ben had forgotten to water them, in spite of all her admonitions, and now they drooped, shrunken and pale, in whitened, powdery soil. The sight of them added to the depression that was beginning to blot out all the pleasure of homecoming.

She returned to the kitchen and poured herself a cup of coffee, wishing that Ben would come home to share it with her. She carried her cup into the living-room and set it on the small, round table beside Ben's special big chair. The furnace was still mumbling busily, sending up heat, but she was colder than ever. She shivered and got an old jacket of Ben's from the closet and wrapped it around her before she sat down.

The wind hammered at the door and the windows, and the air was full of the sound of water, racing in the gutters, pouring from the leaders, thudding on the roof. Listening, she wished for Ben almost feverishly. She never had felt so alone. And he was such a comfort. He had been so good about her going for this long visit, made because her sister was ill. He had seen to everything and had put her on the train with her arms loaded with books and candy and fruit. She knew those farewell gifts had meant a lot to him—he didn't spend money easily. To be quite honest, he was a little close.

3. **lowboy:** a chest of drawers on short legs. It is about the height of a table.

But he was a good husband. She sighed unconsciously, not knowing it was because of youth and romance missed. She repeated it to herself, firmly, as she sipped her coffee. He was a good husband. Suppose he was ten years older than she, and a little set in his ways; a little—perhaps—dictatorial at times, and moody. He had given her what she thought she wanted, security and a home of her own; if security were not enough, she could not blame him for it.

Her eye caught a shred of white protruding under a magazine on the table beside her. She put out a hand toward it, yet her fingers were almost reluctant to grasp it. She pulled it out nevertheless and saw that it was, as she had known instinctively, another of the white envelopes. It was empty, and it bore, as usual, the neat, typewritten address: *Benj. T. Willsom, Esq., Wildwood Road, Fairport, Conn.* The postmark was *New York City*. It never varied.

She felt the familiar constriction about the heart as she held it in her hands. What these envelopes contained she never had known. What she did know was their effect on Ben. After receiving one—one came every month or two—he was irritable, at times almost ugly. Their peaceful life together fell apart. At first she had questioned him, had striven to soothe and comfort him; but she soon had learned that this only made him angry, and of late she had avoided any mention of them. For a week after one came they shared the same room and the same table like two strangers, in a silence that was morose[4] on his part and a little frightened on hers.

This one was postmarked three days before. If Ben got home tonight he would probably be cross, and the storm would not help his mood. Just the same she wished he would come.

She tore the envelope into tiny pieces and tossed them into the fireplace. The wind shook the house in its giant grip, and a branch crashed on the roof. As she straightened, a movement at the window caught her eye.

She froze there, not breathing, still half-bent toward the cold fireplace, her hand still extended. The glimmer of white at the window behind the sheeting blur of rain had been—she was sure of it—a human face. There had been eyes. She was certain there had been eyes staring in at her.

The wind's shout took on a personal, threatening note. She

4. morose (mə·rōs′): gloomy.

was rigid for a long time, never taking her eyes from the window. But nothing moved there now except the water on the window-pane; beyond it there was blackness, and that was all. The only sounds were the thrashing of the trees, the roar of water, and the ominous howl of the wind.

She began to breathe again, at last found courage to turn out the light and go to the window. The darkness was a wall, impenetrable and secret, and the blackness within the house made the storm close in, as if it were a pack of wolves besieging the house. She hastened to put on the light again.

She must have imagined those staring eyes. Nobody could be out on a night like this. Nobody. Yet she found herself terribly shaken.

If only Ben would come home. If only she were not so alone.

She shivered and pulled Ben's coat tighter about her and told herself she was becoming a morbid fool. Nevertheless, she found the aloneness intolerable. Her ears strained to hear prowling foot-steps outside the windows. She became convinced that she did hear them, slow and heavy.

Perhaps Ben could be reached at the hotel where he some-times stayed. She no longer cared whether her homecoming was a surprise to him. She wanted to hear his voice. She went to the telephone and lifted the receiver.

The line was quite dead.

The wires were down, of course.

She fought panic, The face at the window had been an illu-sion, a trick of the light reflected on the sluicing pane; and the sound of footsteps was an illusion, too. Actual ones would be in-audible in the noise made by the wild storm. Nobody would be out tonight. Nothing threatened her, really. The storm was held at bay beyond these walls, and in the morning the sun would shine again.

The thing to do was to make herself as comfortable as possible and settle down with a book. There was no use going to bed—she couldn't possibly sleep. She would only lie there wide awake and think of that face at the window, hear those footsteps.

She would get some wood for a fire in the fireplace. She hesitated at the top of the cellar stairs. The light, as she switched it on, seemed insufficient; the concrete wall at the foot of the stairs was dank with moisture and somehow gruesome. And wind was chilling her ankles. Rain was beating in through the outside door to the cellar, because that door was standing open.

The inner bolt sometimes did not hold, she knew very well. If it had not been carefully closed, the wind could have loosened it. Yet the open door increased her panic. It seemed to argue the presence of something less impersonal than the gale. It took her a long minute to nerve herself to go down the steps and reach out into the darkness for the doorknob.

In just that instant she was soaked; but her darting eyes could find nothing outdoors but the black, wavering shapes of the maples at the side of the house. The wind helped her and slammed the door resoundingly. She jammed the bolt home with all her strength and then tested it to make sure it would hold. She almost sobbed with the relief of knowing it to be firm against any intruder.

She stood with her wet clothes clinging to her while the thought came that turned her bones to water. Suppose—suppose the face at the window had been real, after all. Suppose its owner had found shelter in the only shelter to be had within a quarter-mile—this cellar.

She almost flew up the stairs again, but then she took herself firmly in hand. She must not let herself go. There had been many storms before; just because she was alone in this one, she must not let morbid fancy run away with her. But she could not throw off the reasonless fear that oppressed her, although she forced it back a little. She began to hear again the tread of the prowler outside the house. Although she knew it to be imagination, it was fearfully real—the crunch of feet on gravel, slow, persistent, heavy, like the patrol of a sentinel.

She had only to get an armful of wood. Then she could have a fire, she would have light and warmth and comfort. She would forget these terrors.

The cellar smelled of dust and old moisture. The beams were fuzzed with cobwebs. There was only one light, a dim one in the corner. A little rivulet was running darkly down the wall and already had formed a foot-square pool on the floor.

The woodpile was in the far corner away from the light. She stopped and peered around. Nobody could hide here. The cellar was too open, the supporting stanchions too slender to hide a man.

The oil burner went off with a sharp click. Its mutter, she

suddenly realized, had had something human and companionable about it. Nothing was down here with her now but the snarl of the storm.

She almost ran to the woodpile. Then something made her pause and turn before she bent to gather the logs.

What was it? Not a noise. Something she had seen as she hurried across that dusty floor. Something odd.

She searched with her eyes. It was a spark of light she had seen, where no spark should be.

An inexplicable dread clutched at her heart. Her eyes widened, round and dark as a frightened deer's. Her old trunk that stood against the wall was open just a crack; from the crack came this tiny pinpoint of reflected light to prick the cellar's gloom.

She went toward it like a woman hypnotized. It was only one more insignificant thing, like the envelope on the table, the vision of the face at the window, the open door. There was no reason for her to feel smothered in terror.

Yet she was sure she had not only closed, but clamped the lid on the trunk; she was sure because she kept two or three old coats in it, wrapped in newspapers and tightly shut away from moths.

Now the lid was raised perhaps an inch. And the twinkle of light was still there.

She threw back the lid.

For a long moment she stood looking down into the trunk, while each detail of its contents imprinted itself on her brain like an image on a film. Each tiny detail was indelibly clear and never to be forgotten.

She could not have stirred a muscle in that moment. Horror was a black cloak thrown around her, stopping her breath, hobbling her limbs.

Then her face dissolved into formlessness. She slammed down the lid and ran up the stairs like a mad thing. She was breathing again, in deep, sobbing breaths that tore at her lungs. She shut the door at the top of the stairs with a crash that shook the house; then she turned the key. Gasping, she clutched one of the sturdy maple chairs by the kitchen table and wedged it under the knob with hands she could barely control.

The wind took the house in its teeth and shook it as a dog shakes a rat.

Her first impulse was to get out of the house. But in the time it took her to get to the front door she remembered the face at the window.

Perhaps she had not imagined it. Perhaps it was the face of a murderer—a murderer waiting for her out there in the storm; ready to spring on her out of the dark.

She fell into the big chair, her huddled body shaken by great tremors. She could not stay here—not with that thing in her trunk. Yet she dared not leave. Her whole being cried out for Ben. He would know what to do. She closed her eyes, opened them again, rubbed them hard. The picture still burned into her brain as if it had been etched with acid. Her hair, loosened, fell in soft, straight wisps about her forehead, and her mouth was slack with terror.

Her old trunk had held the curled-up body of a woman.

She had not seen the face; the head had been tucked down into the hollow of the shoulder and a shower of fair hair had fallen over it. The woman had worn a red dress. One hand had rested near the edge of the trunk, and on its third finger there had been a man's ring, a signet bearing the raised figure of a rampant[5] lion with a small diamond between its paws. It had been the diamond that caught the light. The little bulb in the corner of the cellar had picked out this ring from the semidarkness and made it stand out like a beacon.

She never would be able to forget it. Never forget how the woman looked, the pale, luminous flesh of her arms; her doubled-up knees against the side of the trunk, with their silken covering shining softly in the gloom; the strands of hair that covered her face. . . .

Shudders continued to shake her. She bit her tongue and pressed her hand against her jaw to stop the chattering of her teeth. The salty taste of blood in her mouth steadied her. She tried to force herself to be rational, to plan; yet all the time the knowledge that she was imprisoned with the body of a murdered woman kept beating at her nerves like a flail.

She drew the coat closer about her, trying to dispel the mortal cold that held her. Slowly something beyond the mere fact of murder, of death, began to penetrate her mind. Slowly she realized that beyond this fact there would be consequences. That body in

---

5. rampant: standing on its hind legs.

the cellar was not an isolated phenomenon; some train of events had led to its being there and would follow its discovery there.

There would be policemen.

At first the thought of policemen was a comforting one; big, brawny men in blue, who would take the thing out of her cellar, take it away so she never need think of it again.

Then she realized it was *her* cellar—hers and Ben's; and policemen are suspicious and prying. Would they think *she* had killed the woman? Could they be made to believe she never had seen her before?

Or would they think Ben had done it? Would they take the letters in the white envelopes, and Ben's absences on business, and her own visit to her sister, about which Ben had been so helpful, and out of them build a double life for him? Would they insist that the woman had been a discarded mistress, who had hounded him with letters until out of desperation he had killed her? That was a fantastic theory, really; but the police might do that.

They might.

Now a sudden panic invaded her. The dead woman must be taken out of the cellar, must be hidden. The police must never connect her with this house.

Yet the dead woman was bigger than she herself was; she could never move her.

Her craving for Ben became a frantic need. If only he would come home! Come home and take that body away, hide it somewhere so the police could not connect it with this house. He was strong enough to do it.

Even with the strength to move the body by herself she would not dare do it, because there was the prowler—real or imaginary—outside the house. Perhaps the cellar door had not been open by chance. Or perhaps it had been, and the murderer, seeing it so welcoming, had seized the opportunity to plant the evidence of his crime upon the Willsoms' innocent shoulders.

She crouched there, shaking. It was as if the jaws of a great trap had closed on her: on one side the storm and the silence of the telephone, on the other the presence of the prowler and of that still, cramped figure in her trunk. She was caught between them, helpless.

As if to accent her helplessness, the wind stepped up its shriek and a tree crashed thunderously out in the road. She heard glass shatter.

Her quivering body stiffened like a drawn bow. Was it the prowler attempting to get in? She forced herself to her feet and made a round of the windows on the first floor and the one above. All the glass was intact, staunchly resisting the pounding of the rain.

Nothing could have made her go into the cellar to see if anything had happened there.

The voice of the storm drowned out all other sounds, yet she could not rid herself of the fancy that she heard footsteps going round and round the house, that eyes sought an opening and spied upon her.

She pulled the shades down over the shiny black windows. It helped a little to make her feel more secure, more sheltered; but only a very little. She told herself sternly that the crash of glass had been nothing more than a branch blown through a cellar window.

The thought brought her no comfort—just the knowledge that it would not disturb that other woman. Nothing could comfort her now but Ben's plump shoulder and his arms around her and his neat, capable mind planning to remove the dead woman from this house.

A kind of numbness began to come over her, as if her capacity for fear were exhausted. She went back to the chair and curled up in it. She prayed mutely for Ben and for daylight.

The clock said half-past twelve.

She huddled there, not moving and not thinking, not even afraid, only numb, for another hour. Then the storm held its breath for a moment, and in the brief space of silence she heard footsteps on the walk—actual footsteps, firm and quick and loud. A key turned in the lock. The door opened and Ben came in.

He was dripping, dirty, and white with exhaustion. But it was Ben. Once she was sure of it she flung herself on him, babbling incoherently of what she had found.

He kissed her lightly on the cheek and took her arms down from around his neck. "Here, here, my dear. You'll get soaked. I'm drenched to the skin." He removed his glasses and handed them to her, and she began to dry them for him. His eyes squinted at the light. "I had to walk in from the crossroads. What a night!" He began to strip off rubbers and coat and shoes. You'll never know what a difference it made, finding the place lighted. Lord, but it's good to be home."

She tried again to tell him of the past hours, but again he cut her short. "Now, wait a minute, my dear. I can see you're both-ered about something. Just wait until I get into some dry things; then I'll come down and we'll straighten it out. Suppose you rustle up some coffee and toast. I'm done up—the whole trip out was a nightmare, and I didn't know if I'd ever make it from the crossing. I've been hours."

He did look tired, she thought with concern. Now that he was back, she could wait. The past hours had taken on the quality of a nightmare, horrifying but curiously unreal. With Ben here, so solid and commonplace and cheerful, she began to wonder if the hours *were* nightmare. She even began to doubt the reality of the woman in the trunk, although she could see her as vividly as ever. Perhaps only the storm was real.

She went to the kitchen and began to make fresh coffee. The chair, still wedged against the kitchen door, was a reminder of her terror. Now that Ben was home it seemed silly, and she put it back in its place by the table.

He came down very soon, before the coffee was ready. How good it was to see him in that old gray bathrobe of his, his hands thrust into its pockets. How normal and wholesome he looked with his round face rubbed pink by a rough towel and his hair standing up in damp little spikes around his bald spot. She was almost shamefaced when she told him of the face at the window, the open door, and finally of the body in the trunk. None of it, she saw quite clearly now, could possibly have happened.

Ben said so, without hesitation. But he came to put an arm around her. "You poor child. The storm scared you to death, and I don't wonder. It's given you the horrors."

She smiled dubiously. "Yes, I'm almost beginning to think so. Now that you're back, it seems so safe. But—but you will *look* in the trunk, Ben? I've got to *know*. I can see her so plainly. How could I imagine a thing like that?"

He said indulgently, "Of course I'll look, if it will make you feel better. I'll do it now. Then I can have my coffee in peace."

He went to the cellar door and opened it and snapped on the light. Her heart began to pound once more, a deafening roar in her ears. The opening of the cellar door opened, again, the whole vista of fear: the body, the police, the suspicions that would cluster about her and Ben. The need to hide this evidence of somebody's crime.

She could not have imagined it; it was incredible that she

could have believed, for a minute, that her mind had played such tricks on her. In another moment Ben would know it, too.

She heard the thud as he drew back the lid of the trunk. She clutched at the back of a chair, waiting for his voice. It came in an instant.

She could not believe it. It was as cheerful and reassuring as before. He said, "There's nothing here but a couple of bundles. Come take a look."

Nothing!

Her knees were weak as she went down the stairs, down into the cellar again.

It was still musty and damp and draped with cobwebs. The rivulet was still running down the wall, but the pool was larger now. The light was still dim.

It was just as she remembered it except that the wind was whistling through a broken window and rain was splattering in on the bits of shattered glass on the floor. The branch lying across the sill had removed every scrap of glass from the frame and left not a single jagged edge.

Ben was standing by the open trunk, waiting for her. His stocky body was a bulwark. "See," he said, "there's nothing. Just some old clothes of yours, I guess."

She went to stand beside him. Was she losing her mind? Would she, now, see that crushed figure in there, see the red dress and the smooth, shining knees, when Ben could not? And the ring with the diamond between the lion's paws?

Her eyes looked, almost reluctantly, into the trunk. "It *is* empty!"

There were the neat, newspaper-wrapped packages she had put away so carefully, just as she had left them deep in the bottom of the trunk. And nothing else.

She must have imagined the body. She was light with the relief the knowledge brought her, and yet confused and frightened, too. If her mind could play such tricks, if she could imagine anything so gruesome in the complete detail with which she had seen the dead woman in the trunk, the thought of the future was terrifying. When might she not have another such hallucination?

The actual, physical danger did not exist, however, and never had existed. The threat of the law hanging over Ben had been based on a dream.

"I—dreamed it all. I must have," she admitted. "Yet it was so horribly clear and I wasn't asleep." Her voice broke. "I thought—oh, Ben, I thought—"

"What did you think, my dear?" His voice was odd, not like Ben's at all. It had a cold, cutting edge to it.

He stood looking down at her with an immobility that chilled her more than the cold wind that swept in through the broken window. She tried to read his face, but the light from the little bulb was too weak. It left his features shadowed in broad, dark planes that made him look like a stranger, and somehow sinister.

She said, "I—" and faltered.

He still did not move, but his voice hardened. "What was it you thought?"

She backed away from him.

He moved then. It was only to take his hands from his pockets, to stretch his arms toward her; but she stood for an instant staring at the thing that left her stricken, with a voiceless scream forming in her throat.

She was never to know whether his arms had been outstretched to take her within their shelter or to clutch at her white neck. For she turned and fled, stumbling up the stairs in a mad panic of escape.

He shouted, "Janet! Janet!" His steps were heavy behind her. He tripped on the bottom step and fell on one knee and cursed.

Terror lent her strength and speed. She could not be mistaken. Although she had seen it only once, she knew that on the little finger of his left hand there had been the same, the unmistakable ring the dead woman had worn.

The blessed wind snatched the front door from her and flung it wide, and she was out in the safe, dark shelter of the storm.

Meaning

1. How and why does Mrs. Willsom's attitude toward the storm change?
2. What do you think happened after Mrs. Willsom ran out into the storm? Why do you think so?
3. What theme, if any, does this story contain?
4. If Mrs. Willsom had come home a week later, the murderer would have had time to dispose of the body. What other coincidences are important to the plot?

Method

1. "The Storm" is told from the author omniscient (third-person) point of view. Throughout the story you are told what Mrs. Willsom thinks and how she feels. Suppose that Mrs. Willsom had narrated the story. Do you think it would have been more or less effective?
2. What are the important features of Mrs. Willsom's characterization? How is her characterization important to the plot?
3. "The Storm" is a story of suspense and mood rather than of character or theme. How does the author create and sustain the mood of suspense and fear? What words and expressions especially contribute to the overall effect?
4. How is the surprise ending of this story effectively foreshadowed? What unanswered questions are left at the end of the story?

Language: Prefixes

A *prefix* is an element that is placed before the root of a word to change its use or meaning. Three of the most common prefixes are *un-*, *in-*, and *im-*, all of which mean "not." The prefixes *in-*, and *im-* can also mean "in, on, or without." The following words are from "The Storm." Write a new sentence for each word. Be sure you understand the meaning of each root word before you write your sentence.

1. immature	5. intolerable	9. inexplicable
2. imprisoned	6. inaudible	10. insignificant
3. unconsciously	7. immobility	11. incoherently
4. impenetrable	8. insufficient	12. incredible

Discussion and Composition

1. Hundreds of thousands of mysteries are written every year. Why do you think so few mysteries qualify as great literature?

2. What kind of story do you like best: fantasy, mystery, science fiction, romance, realistic? Do you like stories that have strong themes, or do you prefer a story that might be short on theme but long on action and suspense? Write an essay about the kind of story you like best to read. Give reasons and examples.

LANGSTON HUGHES
(1902–1967)

One of the first to portray realistically the black experience in America was Langston Hughes, who wrote poetry, short stories, songs, movies, plays, and nonfiction. His parents separated shortly after his birth, and he was raised by his mother and grandmother.

Hughes began writing poetry early. He was selected as class poet of his grammar school. A year after he was graduated from high school in Cleveland, he wrote perhaps his most famous poem, "The Negro Speaks of Rivers." He taught at a school in Mexico for a year, and then he spent a year at Columbia University. He left Columbia to live in Harlem, where black artists, writers, and musicians were beginning to gather, providing the mutual encouragement and inspiration that would culminate in the Harlem Renaissance of the late 1920s.

Although Hughes was writing steadily at this time, he received little payment for his work. After several bare-subsistence jobs in New York, he shipped aboard a freighter bound for Africa. He continued to write poetry while working as a seaman and a cook; later, working as a busboy and a waiter in European nightclubs, he became familiar with blues and jazz played by the great musicians of his time.

Returning to the United States, Hughes found work as a busboy in a Washington, D.C., hotel. In 1925, when the poet Vachel Lindsay visited the hotel, Hughes left three of his poems beside Lindsay's plate. Lindsay immediately recognized Hughes' abilities; the favorable publicity resulting from this incident helped Hughes get a scholarship to Lincoln University. Before he was graduated in 1929, two books of his poetry had been published to critical acclaim.

Although Hughes traveled to many countries lecturing and writing, his works traveled further. He is one of the most frequently translated twentieth century American writers. He edited several collections of writing by black authors, especially young unknown poets in the United States and in Africa. Although he is best known for his poems, which capture the essence of gospel and jazz rhythms, he produced every form of writing with one central purpose, in his words, "to explain and illuminate the Negro condition in America."

THANK YOU, M'AM

She was a large woman with a large purse that had everything in it but hammer and nails. It had a long strap and she carried it slung across her shoulder. It was about eleven o'clock at night, and she was walking alone, when a boy ran up behind her and tried to snatch her purse. The strap broke with the single tug the boy gave it from behind. But the boy's weight, and the weight of the purse combined caused him to lose his balance so, instead of taking off full blast as he had hoped, the boy fell on his back on the sidewalk, and his legs flew up. The large woman simply turned around and kicked him right square in his blue jeaned sitter. Then she reached down, picked the boy up by his shirt front, and shook him until his teeth rattled.

After that the woman said, "Pick up my pocketbook, boy, and give it here."

She still held him. But she bent down enough to permit him to stoop and pick up her purse. Then she said, "Now ain't you ashamed of yourself?"

Firmly gripped by his shirt front, the boy said, "Yes'm."

The woman said, "What did you want to do it for?"

The boy said, "I didn't aim to."

She said, "You a lie!"

By that time two or three people passed, stopped, turned to look, and some stood watching.

"If I turn you loose, will you run?" asked the woman.

"Yes'm," said the boy.

"Then I won't turn you loose," said the woman. She did not release him.

"I'm very sorry lady, I'm sorry," whispered the boy.

"Um-hum! And your face is dirty. I got a great mind to wash your face for you. Ain't you got nobody home to tell you to wash your face?"

"No'm," said the boy.

"Then it will get washed this evening," said the large woman starting up the street, dragging the frightened boy behind her.

He looked as if he were fourteen or fifteen, frail and willow-wild, in tennis shoes and blue jeans.

The woman said, "You ought to be my son. I would teach

you right from wrong. Least I can do right now is to wash your face. Are you hungry?"

"No'm," said the being-dragged boy. "I just want you to turn me loose."

"Was I bothering *you* when I turned that corner?" asked the woman.

"No'm."

"But you put yourself in contact with *me*," said the woman. "If you think that that contact is not going to last awhile, you got another thought coming. When I get through with you, sir, you are going to remember Mrs. Luella Bates Washington Jones."

Sweat popped out on the boy's face and he began to struggle. Mrs. Jones stopped, jerked him around in front of her, put a half-nelson[1] about his neck, and continued to drag him up the street. When she got to her door, she dragged the boy inside, down a hall, and into a large kitchenette-furnished room at the rear of the house. She switched on the light and left the door open. The boy could hear other roomers laughing and talking in the large house. Some of their doors were open, too, so he knew he and the woman were not alone. The woman still had him by the neck in the middle of her room.

She said, "What is your name?"

"Roger," answered the boy.

"Then, Roger, you go to that sink and wash your face," said the woman, whereupon she turned him loose—at last. Roger looked at the door—looked at the woman—looked at the door—*and went to the sink*.

"Let the water run until it gets warm," she said. "Here's a clean towel."

"You gonna take me to jail?" asked the boy, bending over the sink.

"Not with that face, I would not take you nowhere," said the woman. "Here I am trying to get home to cook me a bite to eat and you snatch my pocketbook! Maybe you ain't been to your supper either, late as it be. Have you?"

"There's nobody home at my house," said the boy.

"Then we'll eat," said the woman. "I believe you're hungry—or been hungry—to try to snatch my pocketbook."

---

1. half-nelson: wrestling hold; from behind, one arm is placed under the opponent's corresponding arm, with the hand placed against the back of the neck.

"I wanted a pair of blue suede shoes," said the boy.

"Well, you didn't have to snatch *my* pocketbook to get some suede shoes," said Mrs. Luella Bates Washington Jones. "You could of asked me."

"M'am?"

The water dripping from his face, the boy looked at her. There was a long pause. A very long pause. After he had dried his face and not knowing what else to do dried it again, the boy turned around, wondering what next. The door was open. He could make a dash for it down the hall. He could run, run, run, run, *run!*

The woman was sitting on the day-bed. After awhile she said, "I were young once and I wanted things I could not get."

There was another long pause. The boy's mouth opened. Then he frowned, but not knowing he frowned.

The woman said, "Um-hum! You thought I was going to say *but,* didn't you? You thought I was going to say, *but I didn't snatch people's pocketbooks.* Well, I wasn't going to say that." Pause. Silence. "I have done things, too, which I would not tell you, son— neither tell God, if he didn't already know. So you set down while I fix us something to eat. You might run that comb through your hair so you will look presentable."

In another corner of the room behind a screen was a gas plate and an icebox. Mrs. Jones got up and went behind the screen. The woman did not watch the boy to see if he was going to run now, nor did she watch her purse which she left behind her on the day-bed. But the boy took care to sit on the far side of the room where he thought she could easily see him out of the corner of her eye, if she wanted to. He did not trust the woman *not* to trust him. And he did not want to be mistrusted now.

"Do you need somebody to go the store," asked the boy, "maybe to get some milk or something?"

"Don't believe I do," said the woman, "unless you just want sweet milk yourself. I was going to make cocoa out of this canned milk I got here."

"That will be fine," said the boy.

She heated some lima beans and ham she had in the icebox, made the cocoa, and set the table. The woman did not ask the boy anything about where he lived, or his folks, or anything else that would embarrass him. Instead, as they ate, she told him about her job in a hotel beauty-shop that stayed open late, what the work was like, and how all kinds of women came in and out, blondes, red-heads, and Spanish. Then she cut him a half of her ten-cent cake.

"Eat some more, son," she said.

When they were finished eating she got up and said, "Now, here, take this ten dollars and buy yourself some blue suede shoes. And next time, do not make the mistake of latching onto *my* pocketbook *nor nobody else's*—because shoes come by devilish like that will burn your feet. I got to get my rest now. But I wish you would behave yourself, son, from here on in."

She led him down the hall to the front door and opened it. "Goodnight! Behave yourself, boy!" she said, looking out into the street.

The boy wanted to say something else other than, "Thank you, m'am," to Mrs. Luella Bates Washington Jones, but he couldn't do so as he turned at the barren stoop and looked back at the large woman in the door. He barely managed to say "Thank you," before she shut the door. And he never saw her again.

Meaning

1. Do you think that Roger was used to stealing? Why or why not?
2. How did Roger's attitude toward Mrs. Jones change? How did he feel about her at the end of the story?
3. What word does the author use several times to describe Mrs. Jones' physical appearance? Describe Mrs. Jones' character and personality.

Method

1. This story begins with a physical conflict in the first paragraph. What more important conflicts are there later on in the story?
2. Instead of telling what Roger is thinking, Langston Hughes writes, "There was a long pause." Why do you think he chose not to reveal the boy's thoughts?
3. "Thank You, Ma'am" is told primarily in dialogue. What effect does this use of dialogue have on the reader?
4. What is the writer's attitude toward his subject and his characters? How do you know?

Language: Dialogue

Well-written dialogue reproduces the way the characters in a story would actually talk. Good dialogue makes a story lively and interesting. It reveals character as well as advancing the plot. Reread the following dialogue between Roger and Mrs. Jones. Notice how the language differs from standard English. Try rewriting the conversation in standard English. What advantage does the original language have over standard English?

1. "The woman said, 'What did you want to do it for?' The boy said, 'I didn't aim to.' She said, 'You a lie!'"
2. " 'You gonna take me to jail?' asked the boy. . . . 'Not with that face, I would not take you nowhere,' said the woman. 'Here I am trying to get home to cook me a bite to eat and you snatch my pocketbook! Maybe you ain't been to your supper either, late as it be. Have you?'"

Discussion and Composition

1. Write a dialogue between two people. Show some aspect of the personality and character of at least one of the people in the dialogue. Here are some ideas:

A storeclerk and a teenager
A young person and a grandparent
A student and a teacher
A highway patrol officer and a driver

2. Imagine that you are Roger, about ten years later, at twenty-five. Write a letter to Mrs. Jones telling her where you are and what you are doing.

3. Suppose that Mrs. Jones had taken Roger to the police station instead of to her apartment. How do you think this action would have affected him? At first, he seemed to be afraid that she would beat him. How do you think a beating would have affected him?

4. Each person's life has many turning points. Often these turning points involve personal choices. Sometimes they involve, as in Roger's case, another person's action. Write a narrative about a turning point in someone's life. Your story may be true or imaginary. Include some dialogue in your story. Try to tell as little as possible about the characters. Instead, let them reveal themselves through their speech and actions.

SAKI (H. H. MUNRO)
(1870–1916)

The British humorist and satirist, Hector Hugh Munro, took the pen name Saki early in his writing career. Saki, the "bringer of drink," was a character in *The Rubáiyát,*[1] a book of Persian poetry that Munro greatly admired.

Munro was born in Burma, where his English father was a police officer. After the death of his mother when he was two, he was brought up in England by two tyrannical aunts. He later avenged himself on their strictness by portraying them in his writing.

At the age of twenty-five, Munro began his writing career as a political satirist for a newspaper. He then worked and traveled for six years as a foreign correspondent. In 1908, Munro settled near London and began to earn his living as a professional writer of often whimsical, sometimes bitterly satirical short stories. At the outbreak of World War I, he enlisted in the British army and was killed in action in 1916.

Like O. Henry, with whom he is often compared, Munro is considered a master of the well-contrived plot and the surprise ending.

THE STORY-TELLER

It was a hot afternoon, and the railway carriage was correspondingly sultry, and the next stop was at Templecomb, nearly an hour ahead. The occupants of the carriage were a small girl, and a smaller girl, and a small boy. An aunt belonging to the children

---

[1] **The Rubáiyát** (r͞oo'bī·yät) **of Omar Khayyám** (kī·äm'): a book of verses written in the eleventh century by Omar Khayyám, a Persian poet and astronomer. It contains the poet's meditations on life and his counsel to eat, drink, and be merry while life lasts. A translation by Edward FitzGerald (1809–1883) appeared in England in 1859. *Rubáiyát* is the Arabic word for quatrains, or four-lined stanzas.

occupied one corner seat, and the further corner seat on the opposite side was occupied by a bachelor who was a stranger to their
party, but the small girls and the small boy emphatically occupied
the compartment. Both the aunt and the children were conversa-
tional in a limited, persistent way, reminding one of the attentions
of a housefly that refused to be discouraged. Most of the aunt's
remarks seemed to begin with "Don't," and nearly all of the children's remarks began with "Why?" The bachelor said nothing out
loud.

"Don't, Cyril, don't," exlaimed the aunt, as the small boy
began smacking the cushions of the seat, producing a cloud of dust
at each blow.

"Come and look out of the window," she added.

The child moved reluctantly to the window. "Why are those
sheep being driven out of that field?" he asked.

"I expect they are being driven to another field where there is
more grass," said the aunt weakly.

"But there is lots of grass in that field," protested the boy;
"there's nothing else but grass there. Aunt, there's lots of grass in
that field."

"Perhaps the grass in the other field is better," suggested the
aunt fatuously.[2]

"Why is it better?" came the swift, inevitable question.

"Oh, look at those cows!" exclaimed the aunt. Nearly every
field along the line had contained cows or bullocks, but she spoke
as though she were drawing attention to a rarity.

"Why is the grass in the other field better?" persisted Cyril.

The frown on the bachelor's face was deepening to a scowl.
He was a hard, unsympathetic man, the aunt decided in her mind.
She was utterly unable to come to any satisfactory decision about
the grass in the other field.

The smaller girl created a diversion by beginning to recite
"On the Road to Mandalay."[3] She only knew the first line, but
she put her limited knowledge to the fullest possible use. She repeated the line over and over again in a dreamy but resolute and
very audible voice; it seemed to the bachelor as though someone

2. **fatuously:** foolishly, stupidly.
3. **"On the Road to Mandalay":** a poem by the English author and poet,
Rudyard Kipling (1865–1936).

had had a bet with her that she could not repeat the line aloud two thousand times without stopping. Whoever it was who had made the wager was likely to lose his bet.

"Come over here and listen to a story," said the aunt, when the bachelor had looked twice at her and once at the communication cord.[4]

The children moved listlessly toward the aunt's end of the carriage. Evidently her reputation as a storyteller did not rank high in their estimation.

In a low, confidential voice, interrupted at frequent intervals by loud, petulant questions from her listeners, she began an unenterprising and deplorably uninteresting story about a little girl who was good, and made friends with every one on account of her goodness, and was finally saved from a mad bull by a number of rescuers who admired her moral character.

"Wouldn't they have saved her if she hadn't been good?" demanded the bigger of the small girls. It was exactly the question that the bachelor had wanted to ask.

"Well, yes," admitted the aunt lamely, "but I don't think they would have run quite so fast to her help if they had not liked her so much."

"It's the stupidest story I've ever heard," said the bigger of the small girls, with immense conviction.

"I didn't listen after the first bit, it was so stupid," said Cyril.

The smaller girl made no actual comment on the story, but she had long ago recommenced a murmured repetition of her favorite line.

"You don't seem to be a success as a storyteller," said the bachelor suddenly from his corner.

The aunt bristled in instant defense at this unexpected attack.

"It's a very difficult thing to tell stories that children can both understand and appreciate," she said stiffly.

"I don't agree with you," said the bachelor.

"Perhaps *you* would like to tell them a story," was the aunt's retort.

"Tell us a story," demanded the bigger of the small girls.

"Once upon a time," began the bachelor, "there was a little girl called Bertha, who was extraordinarily good."

The children's momentarily aroused interest began at once to

---

4. **communication cord:** emergency cord.

flicker; all stories seemed dreadfully alike, no matter who told them.

"She did all that was told, she was always truthful, she kept her clothes clean, ate milk puddings as though they were jam tarts, learned her lessons perfectly, and was polite in her manners."

"Was she pretty?" asked the bigger of the small girls.

"Not as pretty as any of you," said the bachelor, "but she was horribly good."

There was a wave of reaction in favor of the story; the word *horrible* in connection with goodness was a novelty that commended itself. It seemed to introduce a ring of truth that was absent from the aunt's tales of infant life.

"She was so good," continued the bachelor, "that she won several medals for goodness, which she always wore, pinned on to her dress. There was a medal for obedience, another medal for punctuality, and a third for good behavior. They were large metal medals and they clinked against one another as she walked. No other child in the town where she lived had as many as three medals, so everybody knew that she must be an extra good child."

"Horribly good," quoted Cyril.

"Everybody talked about her goodness, and the Prince of the country got to hear about it, and he said that as she was so very good she might be allowed once a week to walk in his park, which was just outside the town. It was a beautiful park, and no children were ever allowed in it, so it was a great honor for Bertha to be allowed to go there."

"Were there any sheep in the park?" demanded Cyril.

"No," said the bachelor, "there were no sheep."

"Why weren't there any sheep?" came the inevitable question arising out of that answer.

The aunt permitted herself a smile, which might almost have been described as a grin.

"There were no sheep in the park," said the bachelor, "because the Prince's mother had once had a dream that her son would either be killed by a sheep or else by a clock falling on him. For that reason the Prince never kept a sheep in his park or a clock in his palace."

The aunt suppressed a gasp of admiration.

"Was the Prince killed by a sheep or by a clock?" asked Cyril.

"He is still alive so we can't tell whether the dream will come true," said the bachelor unconcernedly; "anyway, there were no sheep in the park, but there were lots of little pigs running all over the place."

"What color were they?"

"Black with white faces, white with black spots, black all over, gray with white patches, and some were white all over."

The storyteller paused to let a full idea of the park's treasures sink into the children's imaginations; then he resumed:

"Bertha was rather sorry to find that there were no flowers in the park. She had promised her aunts, with tears in her eyes, that she would not pick any of the kind Prince's flowers, and she had meant to keep her promise, so of course it made her feel silly to find that there were no flowers to pick."

"Why weren't there any flowers?"

"Because the pigs had eaten them all," said the bachelor promptly. "The gardeners had told the Prince that you couldn't have pigs and flowers, so he decided to have pigs and no flowers."

There was a murmur of approval at the excellence of the Prince's decision; so many people would have decided the other way.

"There were lots of other delightful things in the park. There were ponds with gold and blue and green fish in them, and trees with beautiful parrots that said clever things at a moment's notice, and humming birds that hummed all the popular tunes of the day. Bertha walked up and down and enjoyed herself immensely, and thought to herself: "If I were not so extraordinarily good I should not have been allowed to come into this beautiful park and enjoy all that there is to be seen in it,' and her three medals clinked against one another as she walked and helped to remind her how very good she really was. Just then an enormous wolf came prowling into the park to see if it could catch a fat little pig for its supper."

"What color was it?" asked the children, amid an immediate quickening of interest.

"Mud-color all over, with a black tongue and pale gray eyes that gleamed with unspeakable ferocity. The first thing that it saw in the park was Bertha; her pinafore was so spotlessly white and clean that it could be seen from a great distance. Bertha saw the wolf and saw that it was stealing toward her, and she began to wish that she had never been allowed to come into the park. She ran as hard as she could, and the wolf came after her with huge leaps and bounds. She managed to reach a shrubbery of myrtle bushes and she hid herself in one of the thickest of the bushes. The wolf came sniffing among the branches, its black tongue lolling out of its mouth and its pale gray eyes glaring with rage. Bertha was terribly frightened, and thought to herself: 'If I had not been so extraordinarily good, I should have been safe in the town at this moment.' However, the scent of the myrtle was so strong that the wolf could not sniff out where Bertha was hiding, and the bushes were so thick that he might have hunted about in them for a long time without catching sight of her, so he thought he might as well go off and catch a little pig instead. Bertha was trembling very much at having the wolf prowling and sniffing so near her, and as she trembled the medal for obedience clinked against the medals for good conduct and punctuality. The wolf was just moving away when he heard the sound of the medals clinking and stopped to listen; they clinked again in a bush quite near him. He dashed into the bush, his pale gray eyes gleaming with ferocity and triumph, and dragged Bertha out and devoured her to the last morsel. All that was left of her were her shoes, bits of clothing, and the three medals for goodness.''

"Were any of the little pigs killed?"

"No, they all escaped."

"The story began badly," said the smaller of the small girls, "but it had a beautiful ending."

"It is the most beautiful story that I ever heard," said the bigger of the small girls, with immense decision.

"It is the *only* beautiful story I have ever heard," said Cyril.

A dissentient[5] opinion came from the aunt.

"A most improper story to tell to young children! You have undermined the effect of years of careful teaching."

"At any rate," said the bachelor, collecting his belongings preparatory to leaving the carriage, "I kept them quiet for ten minutes, which was more than you were able to do."

"Unhappy woman!" he observed to himself as he walked down the platform of Templecombe station; "for the next six months or so those children will assail her in public with demands for an improper story!"

5. **dissentient** (dĭ·sĕn′shənt): dissenting; expressing disagreement.

Meaning

1. What makes the theme of the bachelor's story unconventional?
2. Which do you think is more annoying to the bachelor—the children's behavior or the aunt's? Give reasons for your answer.
3. What is ironic about the way the "horribly good girl" met her end?
4. Compare and contrast the aunt's story and the bachelor's story. How are they alike? How do they differ?

Method

1. How does the bachelor's story appeal to the children's senses of sight and sound?
2. Why is the railway car setting essential to the plot of this story? What is the function of setting in the bachelor's story?
3. Sometimes to create a humorous or dramatic effect a writer will deliberately exaggerate or overstate a fact. An extravagantly exaggerated statement is called *hyberbole* (hī·pûr′bə·lē). Saki uses hyberbole in "The Story-Teller" when he writes, "She was so good that she won several medals for goodness."

   Saki also achieves humorous effects by the use of *irony.* Irony is typical of Saki's style. In *verbal irony* or irony of statement, the author or speaker says the opposite of what he really means, or the opposite of what the listener or reader expects. In *irony of situation,* what happens is the opposite of what is expected.

   Another way Saki creates humor is by using words that are *ambiguous,* that is, words that have double meanings.

   Explain which of the above methods each of the following quotations from "The Story-Teller" involves:

   a. "The gardeners had told the Prince that you couldn't have pigs and flowers, so he decided to have pigs and no flowers."
   b. "She had promised her aunts, with tears in her eyes, that she would not pick any of the kind Prince's flowers, . . . so of course it made her feel silly to find that there were no flowers to pick."
   c. ". . . and humming birds that hummed all the popular tunes of the day."

d. "The wolf was just moving away when he heard the sound of the medals clinking and stopped to listen; they clinked again in a bush quite near him."

e. ". . . for the next six months or so those children will assail her in public with demands for an improper story!"

Language: Repetition for Effect

In "The Story-Teller," there is a great deal of repetition for humorous effect. Throughout the story, the bachelor links the word *horribly* with *good girl*. The boy Cyril even echoes the phrase *horribly good* for emphasis. The bachelor's constant repetition of the phrase *medals for goodness,* or some variation of it, eventually makes the entire idea of the "metal medals" sound ludicrous.

What other words or phrases are repeated in his story until they reach the point where they sound absurd?

Discussion and Composition

1. *Satire* is the use of exaggeration, wit, or irony to expose or discredit an idea or custom. Along with exaggeration, Saki's ironic praise of the horribly good child is typical of the satirist's weapons. Write a satire attacking something that seems foolish to you. Use exaggeration and ironic praise to convey your ideas.

2. Write a composition in which you tell how Saki, through the storyteller, is satirizing the stories adults usually tell to children. Give examples of the techniques that he uses to ridicule his subject.

3. A *moral* is a lesson which sums up the theme of a fable in adage form. Writel a moral for the storyteller's fable.

GUY DE MAUPASSANT*
(1850–1893)

France's most famous short story writer was Guy de Maupassant. He lived the greater part of his short life in Paris, and was one of the first fiction writers to be financially successful; it is estimated that for several years before his death, his earnings amounted to more than $70,000 a year.

Maupassant's parents were unhappily married and separated when he was eleven. At seventeen, he met Gustave Flaubert, the great French novelist, who became his friend, foster father, and writing teacher. Maupassant began law studies in Paris, but enlisted in the French army when war broke out. After the war, he became a government clerk and began writing under Flaubert's guidance. In 1880, a month before Flaubert's death, Maupassant became famous with the publication of his story *"Boule de Suif"* ("Ball of Fat").

Despite a serious nervous disorder, which ended in insanity and death in his early forties, Maupassant wrote more than three hundred short stories and six novels.

A shrewd observer of people, Maupassant fashioned his characters with sharp, clean lines—like photographs taken with a well-focused camera. He used a minimum of details and wrote with unusual objectivity. His style has served as a model for many writers.

THE NECKLACE

She was one of those pretty and charming girls, born, as if by an accident of fate, into a family of clerks. With no dowry,[1] no prospects, no way of any kind of being met, understood, loved, and married by a man both prosperous and famous, she was finally married to a minor clerk in the Ministry of Education.

---

* **Guy de Maupassant** (gē də mō·pȧ·sän').
1. dowry (dour′ē): money or property that a woman brings to her husband at marriage.

She dressed plainly because she could not afford fine clothes, but was as unhappy as a woman who has come down in the world; for women have no family rank or social class. With them, beauty, grace, and charm take the place of birth and breeding. Their natural poise, their instinctive good taste, and their mental cleverness are the sole guiding principles which make daughters of the common people the equals of ladies in high society.

She grieved incessantly, feeling that she had been born for all the little niceties and luxuries of living. She grieved over the shabbiness of her apartment, the dinginess of the walls, the worn-out appearance of the chairs, the ugliness of the draperies. All these things, which another woman of her class would not even have noticed, gnawed at her and made her furious. The sight of the little Breton[2] girl who did her humble housework roused in her disconsolate[3] regrets and wild daydreams. She would dream of silent chambers, draped with Oriental tapestries and lighted by tall bronze floor lamps, and of two handsome butlers in knee breeches, who, drowsy from the heavy warmth cast by the central stove,[4] dozed in large overstuffed armchairs.

She would dream of great reception halls hung with old silks, of fine furniture filled with priceless curios, and of small, stylish, scented sitting rooms just right for the four o'clock chat with intimate friends, with distinguished and sought-after men whose attention every woman envies and longs to attract.

When dining at the round table, covered for the third day with the same cloth, opposite her husband who would raise the cover of the soup tureen, declaring delightedly, "Ah! a good stew! There's nothing I like better. . . ." she would dream of fashionable dinner parties, of gleaming silverware, of tapestries making the walls alive with characters out of history and strange birds in a fairyland forest; she would dream of delicious dishes served on wonderful china, of gallant compliments whispered and listened to with a sphinxlike smile as one eats the rosy flesh of a trout or nibbles at the wings of a grouse.

She had no evening clothes, no jewels, nothing. But those were the things she wanted; she felt that was the kind of life for

---

2. Brĕton (brĕt'n): a native of Brittany, a province in northwestern France; servants were frequently recruited from outlying districts for service in Paris.

3. disconsolate (dĭs·kŏn'sə·lĭt): inconsolable; hopelessly depressing.

4. central stove: a large stove for heating placed in the center of a room, used in France at the time this story takes place.

her. She so much longed to please, be envied, be fascinating and sought after.

She had a well-to-do friend, a classmate of convent school days, whom she would no longer go to see, simply because she would feel so distressed on returning home. And she would weep for days on end from vexation, regret, despair, and anguish.

Then one evening, her husband came home proudly holding out a large envelope.

"Look," he said, "I've got something for you."

She excitedly tore open the envelope and pulled out a printed card bearing these words:

"The Minister of Education and Mme Georges Ramponneau[5] beg M. and Mme Loisel[6] to do them the honor of attending an evening reception at the ministerial mansion on Friday, January 18."

Instead of being delighted, as her husband had hoped, she scornfully tossed the invitation on the table, murmuring, "What good is that to me?"

"But, my dear, I thought you'd be thrilled to death. You never get a chance to go out, and this is a real affair, a wonderful one! I had an awful time getting a card. Everybody wants one; it's much sought after, and not many clerks have a chance at one. You'll see all the most important people there."

She gave him an irritated glance, and burst out impatiently, "What do you think I have to go in?"

He hadn't given that a thought. He stammered, "Why, the dress you wear when we go to the theater. That looks quite nice, I think."

He stopped talking, dazed and distracted to see his wife burst out weeping. Two large tears slowly rolled from the corners of her eyes to the corners of her mouth. He gasped, "Why, what's the matter? What's the trouble?"

By sheer will power she overcame her outburst and answered in a calm voice while wiping the tears from her wet cheeks:

"Oh, nothing. Only I don't have an evening dress and therefore I can't go to that affair. Give the card to some friend at the office whose wife can dress better than I can."

---

5. **Mme Georges Ramponneau** (må·dåm′zhôrzh råm′pə·nō).
6. **M. . . . Loisel** (mə·syûr′ . . . lwå·zĕl′).

He was stunned. He resumed, "Let's see, Mathilde.[7] How much would a suitable outfit cost—one you could wear for other affairs too—something very simple?"

She thought it over for several seconds, going over her allowance and thinking also of the amount she could ask for without bringing an immediate refusal and an exclamation of dismay from the thrifty clerk.

Finally, she answered hesitatingly, "I'm not sure exactly, but I think with four hundred francs[8] I could manage it."

He turned a bit pale, for he had set aside just that amount to buy a rifle so that, the following summer, he could join some friends who were getting up a group to shoot larks on the plain near Nanterre.[9]

However, he said, "All right. I'll give you four hundred francs. But try to get a nice dress."

As the day of the party approached, Mme Loisel seemed sad, moody, and ill at ease. Her outfit was ready, however. Her husband said to her one evening, "What's the matter? You've been all out of sorts for three days."

And she answered, "It's embarrassing not to have a jewel or a gem—nothing to wear on my dress. I'll look like a pauper: I'd almost rather not go to that party."

He answered, "Why not wear some flowers? They're very fashionable this season. For ten francs you can get two or three gorgeous roses."

She wasn't at all convinced. "No . . . There's nothing more humiliating than to look poor among a lot of rich women."

But her husband exclaimed, "My, but you're silly! Go see you friend Mme Forestier[10] and ask her to lend you some jewelry. You and she know each other well enough for you to do that."

She gave a cry of joy, "Why, that's so! I hadn't thought of it."

The next day she paid her friend a visit and told her of her predicament.

Mme Forestier went toward a large closet with mirrored

7. **Mathilde** (mȧ·tēld′).
8. **four hundred francs:** at that time, about eighty dollars.
9. **Nanterre** (nän·târ′): a French town near Paris.
10. **Forestier** (fô·rə·styā′).

doors, took out a large jewel box, brought it over, opened it, and said to Mme Loisel: "Pick something out, my dear."

At first her eyes noted some bracelets, then a pearl necklace, then a Venetian cross, gold and gems, of marvelous workmanship. She tried on these adornments in front of the mirror, but hesitated, unable to decide which to part with and put back. She kept on asking, "Haven't you something else?"

"Oh, yes, keep on looking. I don't know just what you'd like."

All at once she found, in a black satin box, a superb diamond necklace: and her pulse beat faster with longing. Her hands trembled as she took it up. Clasping it around her throat, outside her high-necked dress, she stood in ecstasy looking at her reflection.

Then she asked, hesitatingly, pleading, "Could I borrow that, just that and nothing else?"

"Why, of course."

She threw her arms around her friend, kissed her warmly, and fled with her treasure.

The day of the party arrived. Mme Loisel was a sensation. She was the prettiest one there, fashionable, gracious, smiling, and wild with joy. All the men turned to look at her, asked who she was, begged to be introduced. All the cabinet officials wanted to waltz with her. The minister took notice of her.

She danced madly, wildly, drunk with pleasure, giving no thought to anything in the triumph of her beauty, the pride of her success, in a kind of happy cloud composed of all the adulation,[11] of all the admiring glances, of all the awakened longings, of a sense of complete victory that is so sweet to a woman's heart.

She left around four o'clock in the morning. Her husband, since midnight, had been dozing in a small empty sitting room with three other gentlemen whose wives were having too good a time.

He threw over her shoulders the wraps he had brought for going home, modest garments of everyday life whose shabbiness clashed with the stylishness of her evening clothes. She felt this and longed to escape, unseen by the other women who were draped in expensive furs.

Loisel held her back.

"Hold on! You'll catch cold outside. I'll call a cab."

---

11. adulation (ăj′o͞o·lā′shən): excessive flattery or admiration.

But she wouldn't listen to him and went rapidly down the stairs. When they were on the street, they didn't find a carriage; and they set out to hunt for one, hailing drivers whom they saw going by at a distance.

They walked toward the Seine,[12] disconsolate and shivering. Finally on the docks they found one of those carriages that one sees in Paris only after nightfall, as if they were ashamed to show their drabness during daylight hours.

It dropped them at their door in the Rue des Martyrs,[13] and they climbed wearily up to their apartment. For her, it was all over. For him, there was the thought that he would have to be at the ministry at ten o'clock.

Before the mirror, she let the wraps fall from her shoulders to see herself once again in all her glory. Suddenly she gave a cry. The necklace was gone.

Her husband, already half-undressed, said, "What's the trouble?"

She turned toward him despairingly, "I . . . I . . . I don't have Mme Forestier's necklace."

"What! You can't mean it! It's impossible!"

They hunted everywhere, through the folds of the dress, through the folds of the coat, in the pockets. They found nothing.

He asked, "Are you sure you had it when leaving the dance?"

"Yes, I felt it when I was in the hall of the ministry."

"But, if you had lost it on the street we'd have heard it drop. It must be in the cab."

"Yes. Quite likely. Did you get its number?"

"No. Didn't you notice it either?"

"No."

They looked at each other aghast. Finally Loisel got dressed again.

"I'll retrace our steps on foot," he said, "to see if I can find it."

And he went out. She remained in her evening clothes, without the strength to go to bed, slumped in a chair in the unheated room, her mind a blank.

---

12. **Seine** (sān): a river which runs through Paris.
13. **Rue des Martyrs:** Street of the Martyrs in Montmartre, a working class section near Place Pigalle, named for St. Dennis and companions.

Her husband came in about seven o'clock. He had had no luck.

He went to the police station, to the newspapers to post a reward, to the cab companies, everywhere the slightest hope drove him.

That evening Loisel returned, pale, his face lined; still he had learned nothing.

"We'll have to write your friend," he said, "to tell her you have broken the catch and are having it repaired. That will give us a little time to turn around."

She wrote to his dictation.

At the end of a week, they had given up all hope.

And Loisel, looking five years older, declared, "We must take steps to replace that piece of jewelry."

The next day they took the case to the jeweler whose name they found inside. He consulted his records. "I didn't sell that necklace, madame," he said. "I only supplied the case."

Then they went from one jeweler to another hunting for a similar necklace, going over their recollections, both sick with despair and anxiety.

They found, in a shop in Palais Royal,[14] a string of diamonds which seemed exactly like the one they were seeking. It was priced at forty thousand francs. They could get it for thirty-six.[15]

They asked the jeweler to hold it for them for three days. And they reached an agreement that he would take it back for thirty-four thousand if the lost one was found before the end of February.

Loisel had eighteen thousand francs he had inherited from his father. He would borrow the rest.

He went about raising the money, asking a thousand francs from one, four hundred from another, a hundred here, sixty there. He signed notes, made ruinous deals, did business with loan sharks, ran the whole gamut[16] of moneylenders. He compromised the rest of his life, risked his signature without knowing if he'd be able to honor it, and then, terrified by the outlook for the future, by the blackness of despair about to close around him, by the

14. **Palais Royal** (pà·lā′ rwà·yàl′): or Royal Palace. A very fashionable set of buildings and gardens in Paris well known for its exclusive shops.
15. **thirty-six [thousand francs]:** in 1884, the year of "The Necklace," about seven thousand two hundred dollars.
16. **gàmut** (găm′ət): the whole range of something.

prospect of all the privations[17] of the body and tortures of the spirit, he went to claim the new necklace with the thirty-six thousand francs which he placed on the counter of the shopkeeper.

When Mme Loisel took the necklace back, Mme Forestier said to her frostily, "You should have brought it back sooner; I might have needed it."

She didn't open the case, an action her friend was afraid of. If she had noticed the substitution, what would she have thought? What would she have said? Would she have thought her a thief?

Mme Loisel experienced the horrible life the needy live. She played her part, however, with sudden heroism. That frightful debt had to be paid. She would pay it. She dismissed her maid; they rented a garret under the eaves.

She learned to do the heavy housework, to perform the hateful duties of cooking. She washed dishes, wearing down her shell-pink nails scouring the grease from pots and pans; she scrubbed dirty linen, shirts, and cleaning rags, which she hung on a line to dry; she took the garbage down to the street each morning and brought up water, stopping on each landing to get her breath. And, clad like a peasant woman, basket on arm, guarding sou[18] by sou her scanty allowance, she bargained with the fruit dealers, the grocer, the butcher, and was insulted by them.

Each month notes had to be paid, and others renewed to give more time.

Her husband labored evenings to balance a tradesman's accounts, and at night, often, he copied documents at five sous a page.

And this went on for ten years.

Finally, all was paid back, everything including the exorbitant[19] rates of the loan sharks and accumulated compound interest.

Mme Loisel appeared an old woman, now. She became heavy, rough, harsh, like one of the poor. Her hair untended, her skirts askew, her hands red, her voice shrill, she even slopped water on her floors and scrubbed them herself. But, sometimes, while her husband was at work, she would sit near the window and think of that long-ago evening when, at the dance, she had been so beautiful and admired.

17. **privations** (prī·vā′shəns): the lack of what is essential for existence.
18. **sou** (soo): a coin at that time worth about a penny.
19. **exorbitant** (ĭg·zôr′bə·tənt): excessive.

What would have happened if she had not lost that necklace? Who knows? Who can say? How strange and unpredictable life is! How little there is between happiness and misery!

Then one Sunday when she had gone for a walk on the Champs Élysées[20] to relax a bit from the week's labors, she suddenly noticed a woman strolling with a child. It was Mme Forestier, still young-looking, still beautiful, still charming.

Mme Loisel felt a rush of emotion. Should she speak to her? Of course. And now that everything was paid off, she would tell her the whole story. Why not?

She went toward her. "Hello, Jeanne."

The other, not recognizing her, showed astonishment at being spoken to so familiarly by this common person. She stammered, "But . . . madame . . . I don't recognize . . . You must be mistaken."

"No, I'm Mathilde Loisel."

Her friend gave a cry, "Oh, my poor Mathilde, how you've changed!"

"Yes, I've had a hard time since last seeing you. And plenty of misfortunes—and all on account of you!"

"Of me . . . How do you mean?"

"Do you remember that diamond necklace you lent me to wear to the dance at the ministry?"

"Yes, but what about it?"

"Well, I lost it."

"You lost it! But you returned it."

"I brought you another just like it. And we've been paying for it for ten years now. You can imagine that wasn't easy for us who had nothing. Well, it's over now, and I am glad of it."

Mme Forestier stopped short. "You mean to say you bought a diamond necklace to replace mine?"

"Yes. You never noticed, then? They were quite alike."

And she smiled with proud and simple joy.

Mme Forestier, quite overcome, clasped her by the hands, "Oh, my poor Mathilde. But mine was only paste.[21] Why, at most it was worth only five hundred francs!"[22]

---

20. **Champs Élysées** (shän zā·lē·zā'): a fashionable avenue in Paris.
21. **paste:** a brilliant glass used in making imitation diamonds.
22. **five hundred francs:** about one hundred dollars then.

Meaning

1. What kind of persons are Mathilde and her husband at the beginning of the story? How do they change after the necklace is lost? Are their actions consistent with their characteristics and values? Why or why not?
2. Why did it never occur to the Loisels that the necklace might be paste?
3. The things we value are the things by which we set our goals and make our decisions. What comment on values does this story make?
4. What is the theme of the story?

Method

1. A *symbol* is something that has meaning in itself but also suggests a further meaning. How is the necklace used as a symbol in this story?
2. Do you think that "The Necklace" has a *trick* ending—a conclusion that comes as a surprise to the reader? Or has the reader been prepared for the ironic ending? Give reasons for your answer.
3. Maupassant and O. Henry have often been compared as story-tellers. They both usually take the author omniscient (third-person narrator) point of view. Compared with O. Henry in "The Ransom of Red Chief," does Maupassant write more or less *objectively*? An author is said to write objectively when he or she does not give opinions about the characters. Give some examples from both of these authors' stories in this book to support your answer.
4. Why didn't Maupassant end the story by telling how Mathilde felt when she learned the necklace was false? How would this have changed the story?

Language: Forming Adjectives and Adverbs

A suffix added to a word can change the word to an adjective or adverb. The sample adjectives and adverbs on the following page are taken from "The Necklace":

Adjectives

Suffix	Meaning	Adjective
1. *-able, ible*	able, fit, likely	suitable
2. *-ful*	full of, marked by	wonderful
3. *-like*	like, similar	sphinxlike
4. *-ous*	marked by, given to	prosperous
5. *-y*	showing, suggesting, apt to	drowsy, moody

Adverbs

Suffix	Meaning	Adverb
-ly	like, of nature of, in the manner of	finally, plainly

Add a suffix to each of the following words to form an adjective or an adverb. Write a sentence for each new word you form.

1. marvel		6. soul	
2. simple		7. courage	
3. play		8. war	
4. joy		9. hope	
5. peace		10. prosper	

Discussion and Composition

1. Continue the story by telling what might have happened next. Write new dialogue to extend the conversation between Mathilde and Mme Forestier, or develop the scene when Mathilde tells her husband that the necklace was paste.

2. The author writes, "What would have happened if she had not lost that necklace? Who knows? Who can say? How strange and unpredictable life is! How little there is between happiness and misery!"

Write a paragraph in which you tell what you think were Mathilde's chances for happiness had she *not* lost the necklace. Be sure to give reasons.

3. Write a composition, pro or con, on one of the following topics: "Fine feathers make (or don't make) fine birds." "It's not what you know, it's whom you know." Give reasons for your choice, and support your argument with facts, examples, and incidents.

SELMA LAGERLÖF*
(1858–1940)

In 1909, Selma Lagerlöf, a Swedish writer, became the first woman ever to receive the Nobel Prize for literature. She was born in southern Sweden, a region noted for its beautiful lakes and its folk culture of song, dance, and colorful costumes. At three, she was afflicted by polio, which left her in frail health but did not prohibit a long, creative life. Besides being an author of books and stories for both children and adults, she was a distinguished worker in the cause of world peace.

The author's favorite subjects were her family, folklore, fantasy, and Swedish traditions. Her stories have the simple, dignified, and idealistic qualities of folk tales. Her birthplace, Värmland, and Dalecarlia, where she taught school, are the backgrounds for most of her stories. Dalecarlia, the setting for "The Silver Mine," is a region rich in mineral resources.

THE SILVER MINE

King Gustaf III[1] was traveling through Dalecarlia.[2] He was pressed for time, and all the way he wanted to drive like lightning. Although they drove with such speed that the horses were extended like stretched rubber bands and the coach cleared the turns on two wheels, the King poked his head out of the window and shouted to the postilion,[3] "Why don't you go ahead? Do you think you are driving over eggs?"

Since they had to drive over poor country roads at such a mad pace, it would have been almost a miracle had the harness and wagon held together! And they didn't, either; for at the foot of a steep hill the pole broke—and there the King sat! The courtiers

---

* **Lagerlöf** (lä′yər·lœf).
1. **Gustaf III** (go͞os′täf).
2. **Dalecarlia** (dal′ə·kär′li·ä): a region in west central Sweden.
3. **postilion** (pōs·tĭl′yən): a rider or guide on one of the leading horses in a team attached to a coach.

sprang from the coach and scolded the driver, but this did not lessen the damage done. There was no possibility of continuing the journey until the coach was mended.

When the courtiers looked around to try to find something with which the King could amuse himself while he waited, they noticed a church spire looming high above the trees in a grove a short distance ahead. They intimated to the King that he might step into one of the coaches in which the attendants were riding and drive up to the church. It was a Sunday, and the King might attend services to pass the time until the royal coach was ready.

The King accepted the proposal and drove toward the church. He had been traveling for hours through dark forest regions, but here it looked more cheerful, with fairly large meadows and villages, and with the Dal River gliding on light and pretty, between thick rows of alder bushes.

But the King had ill luck to this extent: the bell ringer took up the recessional chant just as the King was stepping from the coach on the church knoll[4] and the people were coming out from the service. But when they came walking past him, the King remained standing, with one foot in the wagon and the other on the footstep. He did not move from the spot—only stared at them. They were the finest lot of folk he had ever seen. All the men were above the average height, with intelligent and earnest faces, and the women were dignified and stately, with an air of Sabbath peace about them.

The whole of the preceding day the King had talked only of the desolate tracts he was passing through, and had said to his courtiers again and again, "Now I am certainly driving through the very poorest part of my kingdom!" But now, when he saw the people, garbed in the picturesque dress of this section of the country, he forgot to think of their poverty; instead his heart warmed, and he remarked to himself, "The King of Sweden is not so badly off as his enemies think. So long as my subjects look like this, I shall probably be able to defend both my faith and my country."

He commanded the courtiers to make known to the people that the stranger who was standing among them was their King and that they should gather around him, so he could talk to them.

And then the King made a speech to the people. He spoke

4. **knoll** (nōl): a small round hill; mound.

from the high steps outside the vestry,[5] and the narrow step upon which he stood is there even today.

The King gave an account of the sad plight in which the kingdom was placed. He said that the Swedes were threatened with war by both Russians and Danes. Under ordinary circumstances it would not be such a serious matter, but now the army was filled with traitors, and he did not dare depend upon it. Therefore there was no other course for him to take than to go himself into the country settlements and ask his subjects if they would be loyal to their King and help him with men and money, so he could save the Fatherland.

The peasants stood quietly while the King was speaking, and when he had finished they gave no sign either of approval or disapproval.

The King himself thought that he had spoken well. The tears had sprung to his eyes several times while he was speaking. But when the peasants stood there all the while, troubled and undecided, and could not make up their minds to answer him, the King frowned and looked displeased.

The peasants understood that it was becoming monotonous for the King to wait, and finally one of them stepped out from the crowd.

"Now, you must know, King Gustaf, that we were not expecting a royal visit in the parish today," said the peasant, "and therefore we are not prepared to answer you at once. I advise you to go into the vestry and speak with our pastor, while we discuss among ourselves this matter which you have laid before us."

The king apprehended[6] that a more satisfactory response was not to be had immediately, so he felt that it would be best for him to follow the peasant's advice.

When he came into the vestry, he found no one there but a man who looked like a peasant. He was tall and rugged, with big hands, toughened by labor, and he wore neither cassock nor collar, but leather breeches and a long white homespun coat, like all the other men.

He rose and bowed to the King when the latter entered.

5. **vestry** (věs′trē): a room in a church where altar linens, sacred vessels, and the vestments of the clergy are kept.
6. **apprehended** (ăp′rə·hĕnd·əd): understood. To *apprehend* can also mean *arrest,* and to *dread.*

"I thought I should find the parson in here," said the King.

The man grew somewhat red in the face. He thought it annoying to mention the fact that he was the parson of this parish, when he saw that the King had mistaken him for a peasant. "Yes," said he, "the parson is usually on hand in here."

The King dropped into a large armchair which stood in the vestry at that time and which stands there today, looking exactly like itself, with this difference: the congregation has had a gilded crown attached to the back of it.

"Have you a good parson in this parish?" asked the King, who wanted to appear interested in the welfare of the peasants.

When the King questioned him in this manner, the parson felt that he couldn't possibly tell who he was. "It's better to let him go on believing that I'm only a peasant," thought he, and replied that the parson was good enough. He preached a pure and clear gospel and tried to live as he taught.

The King thought that this was a good commendation but he had a sharp ear and marked a certain doubt in the tone. "You sound as if you were not quite satisfied with the parson," said the King.

"He's a bit arbitrary," said the man, thinking that if the King should find out later who he was, he would not think that the parson had been standing here and blowing his own horn. Therefore he wished to come out with a little faultfinding also. "There are some, no doubt, who say the parson wants to be the only one to counsel and rule in this parish," he continued.

"Then, at all events, he has led and managed in the best possible way," said the King. He didn't like it that the peasant complained of one who was placed above him. "To me it appears as though good habits and old-time simplicity were the rule here."

"The people are good enough," said the curate, "but then they live in poverty and isolation. Human beings here would certainly be no better than others if this world's temptations came closer to them."

"But there's no fear of anything of the sort happening," said the King, with a shrug.

He said nothing further, but began thrumming on the table with his fingers. He thought he had exchanged a sufficient number of gracious words with this peasant and wondered when the others would be ready with their answer.

"These peasants are not very eager to help their King,"

thought he. "If I only had my coach, I would drive away from them and their palaver!"[7]

The pastor sat there troubled, debating with himself as to how he should decide an important matter which he must settle. He was beginning to feel happy because he had not told the King who he was. Now he felt that he could speak with him about matters which otherwise he could not have placed before him.

After a while the parson broke the silence and asked the King if it was an actual fact that enemies were upon them and that the kingdom was in danger.

The King thought this man ought to have sense enough not to trouble him further. He simply glared at him and said nothing.

"I ask because I was standing in here and could not hear very well," said the parson. "But if this is really the case, I want to say to you that the pastor of this congregation might perhaps be able to procure for the King as much money as he will need."

"I thought that you said just now that everyone here was poor," said the King, thinking that the man did not know what he was talking about.

"Yes, that's true," replied the rector, "and the parson has no more than any of the others. But if the King would condescend to listen to me for a moment, I will explain how the pastor happens to have the power to help him."

"You may speak," said the King. "You seem to find it easier to get the words past your lips than your friends and neighbors out there who never will be ready with what they have to tell me."

"It is not so easy to reply to the King! I'm afraid that, in the end, it will be the parson who must undertake this on behalf of the others."

The King crossed his legs, folded his arms, and let his head sink down on his breast. "You may begin now," he said, in the tone of one already asleep.

"Once upon a time there were five men from this parish who were out on a moose hunt," began the clergyman. "One of them was the parson of whom we are speaking. Two of the others were soldiers, named Olaf and Eric Svärd; the fourth man was the innkeeper in this settlement, and the fifth was a peasant named Israel Per Persson."

---

7. palaver (pə·lăv′ər): public discussion, especially of an empty, lengthy nature; also idle chatter.

"Don't go to the trouble of mentioning so many names," muttered the King, letting his head droop to one side.

"Those men were good hunters," continued the parson, "who usually had luck with them, but that day they had wandered long and far without getting anything. Finally they gave up the hunt altogether and sat down on the ground to talk. They said there was not a spot in the whole forest fit for cultivation; all of it was only mountain and swampland. 'Our Lord has done right by us in giving us such a poor land to live in,' said one. 'In other localities people can get riches for themselves in abundance, but here, with all our toil and drudgery we can scarcely get our daily bread.'"

The pastor paused a moment, as if uncertain that the King heard him, but the latter moved his little finger to show that he was awake.

"Just as the hunters were discussing this matter, the parson saw something that glittered at the base of the mountain, where he had kicked away a moss tuft. 'This is a queer mountain,' he thought, as he kicked off another moss tuft. He picked up a sliver of stone that came with the moss and which shone exactly like the other. 'It can't be possible that this stuff is lead,' said he.

"Then the others sprang up and scraped away the turf with the butt ends of their rifles. When they did this, they saw plainly that a broad vein of ore followed the mountain.

"'What do you think this might be?' asked the parson.

"The men chipped off bits of stone and bit into them. 'It must be lead, or zinc at least,' said they.

"'And the whole mountain is full of it,' added the innkeeper."

When the parson had got thus far in his narrative, the King's head was seen to straighten up a little and one eye opened. "Do you know if any of these persons knew anything about ore and minerals?" he asked.

"They did not," replied the parson.

Then the King's head sank and both eyes closed.

"The clergyman and his companions were very happy," continued the speaker, without letting himself be disturbed by the King's indifference; "they fancied that now they had found that which would give them and their descendants wealth. 'I'll never have to do any more work,' said one. 'Now I can afford to do nothing at all the whole week through, and on Sundays I shall drive to church in a golden chariot!' They were otherwise sensible men, but the great find had gone to their heads, and they talked like children. Still they had enough presence of mind to put back the moss tufts and conceal the vein of ore. Then they carefully noted the place where it was, and went home. Before they parted company, they agreed that the parson should travel to Falun and ask the mining expert what kind of ore this was. He was to return as soon as possible, and until then they promised one another on oath not to reveal to a single soul where the ore was to be found."

The King's head was raised again a trifle, but he did not interrupt the speaker with a word. It appeared as though he was beginning to believe that the man actually had something of importance he wished to say to him, since he didn't allow himself to be disturbed by his indifference.

"Then the parson departed with a few samples of ore in his pocket. He was just as happy in the thought of becoming rich as the others were. He was thinking of rebuilding the parsonage, which at present was no better than a peasant's cottage, and then he would marry a dean's[8] daughter whom he liked. He had thought that he might have to wait for her many years. He was poor and obscure and knew that it would be a long while before he should get any post that would enable him to marry.

"The parson drove over to Falun in two days, and there he had to wait another whole day because the mining expert was away. Finally he ran across him and showed him the bits of ore. The mining expert took them in his hand. He looked at them first, then at the parson. The parson related how he had found them in a mountain at home in his parish, and wondered if it might not be lead.

" 'No, it's not lead,' said the mining expert.

" 'Perhaps it is zinc, then?' asked the parson.

" 'Nor is it zinc,' said the mineralogist.

"The parson thought that all the hope within him sank. He had not been so depressed in many a long day.

" 'Have you many stones like these in your parish?' asked the mineralogist.

" 'We have a whole mountainful,' said the parson.

"Then the mineralogist came up closer, slapped the parson on the shoulder, and said, 'Let us see that you make such good use of

8. **dean's:** A dean is the head of a cathedral or collegiate church.

this that it will prove a blessing both to yourselves and to the country, for this is silver.'

" 'Indeed?' said the parson, feeling his way. 'So it is silver!'

"The mineralogist began telling him how he should go to work to get legal rights to the mine and gave him many valuable suggestions; but the parson stood there dazed and did not listen to what the mineralogist was saying. He was thinking how wonderful it was that at home in his poor parish stood a whole mountain of silver ore, waiting for him."

The King raised his head so suddenly that the parson stopped short in his narrative. "It turned out, of course, that when he got home and began working the mine, he saw that the mineralogist had only been fooling him." said the King.

"Oh, no, the mineralogist had not fooled him," said the parson.

"You may continue," said the King as he settled himself more comfortably in the chair to listen.

"When the parson was at home again and was driving through the parish," continued the clergyman, "he thought that first of all he should inform his partners of the value of their find. And as he drove alongside the innkeeper Sten Stensson's place, he intended to drive up to the house to tell him they had found silver. But when he stopped outside the gate, he noticed that a broad path of evergreen was strewn all the way up to the doorstep.

" 'Who has died in this place?' asked the parson of a boy who stood leaning against the fence.

" 'The innkeeper himself,' answered the boy. Then he let the clergyman know that the innkeeper had drunk himself full every day for a week. 'Oh, so much brandy, so much brandy, has been drunk here!'

" 'How can that be?' asked the parson. 'The innkeeper used never to drink himself full.'

" 'Oh,' said the boy, 'he drank because he said he had found a mine. He was very rich. He should never have to do anything now but drink, he said. Last night he drove off, full as he was, and the wagon turned over and he was killed.'

"When the parson heard this, he drove homeward, distressed over what he had heard. He had come back so happy, rejoicing because he could tell the great news.

"When the parson had driven a few paces, he saw Israel Per Persson walking along. He looked about as usual, and the parson thought it was well that fortune had not gone to his head too. Him he would cheer at once with the news that he was a rich man.

"'Good day!' said Per Persson. 'Do you come from Falun now?'

"'I do,' said the parson. 'And now I must tell you that it has turned out even better than we had imagined. The mineralogist said it was silver ore that we had found.'

"That instant Per Persson looked as though the ground had opened under him. 'What are you saying, what are you saying? Is it silver?"

"'Yes,' answered the parson. 'We'll all be rich men now, all of us, and can live like gentlemen.'

"'Oh, is it silver?' said Per Persson once again, looking more and more mournful.

"'Why, of course it is silver,' replied the parson. 'You mustn't think that I want to deceive you. You mustn't be afraid to be happy.'

"'Happy!' said Per Persson. 'Should I be happy? I believed it was only glitter that we had found, so I thought it would be better to take the certain for the uncertain; I have sold my share in the mine to Olaf Svärd for a hundred dollars.'

"He was desperate, and when the parson drove away from him, he stood on the highway and wept.

"When the clergyman got back to his home, he sent a servant to Olaf Svärd and his brother to tell them that it was silver they had found. He thought that he had had quite enough of driving around and spreading the good news.

"But in the evening, when the parson sat alone, his joy asserted itself again. He went out in the darkness and stood on a hillock upon which he contemplated building the new parsonage. It should be imposing, of course, as fine as a bishop's palace. He stood there long that night; nor did he content himself with rebuilding the parsonage! It occurred to him that, since there were such riches to be found in the parish, throngs of people would pour in, and finally a whole city would be built around the mine. And then he would have to erect a new church in place of the old one. Toward this object a large portion of his wealth would probably go. And he was not content with this, either, but fancied that, when his church was ready, the King and many bishops would come to the dedication. Then the King would be pleased with the church, but he would remark that there was no place where a king might put up, and then he would have to erect a castle in the new city."

Just then one of the King's courtiers opened the door of the vestry and announced that the big royal coach was mended.

At the first moment the King was ready to withdraw, but on second thought he changed his mind. "You may tell your story to the end," he said to the parson. "But you can hurry it a bit. We know all about how the man thought and dreamed. We want to know how he acted."

"But while the parson was still lost in his dreams," continued the clergyman, "word came to him that Israel Per Persson had made away with himself. He had not been able to bear the disappointment of having sold his share in the mine. He had thought, no doubt, that he could not endure to go about every day seeing another enjoying the wealth that might have been his."

The King straightened up a little. He kept both eyes open. "Upon my word," he said, "if I had been that parson, I should have had enough of the mine!"

"The King is a rich man," said the parson. "He has quite enough, at all events. It is not the same thing with a poor curate who possesses nothing. The unhappy wretch thought instead, when he saw that God's blessing was not with his enterprise, 'I will dream no more of bringing glory and profit to myself with these riches, but I can't let the silver lie buried in the earth! I must take it out, for the benefit of the poor and needy. I will work the mine, to put the whole parish on its feet.'

"So one day the parson went out to see Olaf Svärd, to ask him and his brother what should be done immediately with the silver mountain. When he came in the vicinity of the barracks he met a cart surrounded by armed peasants, and in the cart sat a man with his hands tied behind him and a rope around his ankles.

"When the parson passed by, the cart stopped and he had time to regard the prisoner, whose head was tied up so it was not easy to see who he was. But the parson thought he recognized Olaf Svärd. He heard the prisoner beg those who guarded him to let him speak a few words with the parson.

"The parson drew nearer, and the prisoner turned toward him. 'You will soon be the only one who knows where the silver mine is,' said Olaf.

"'What are you saying, Olaf?' asked the parson.

"'Well, you see, parson, since we have learned that it was a silver mine we had found, my brother and I could no longer be as good friends as before. We were continually quarreling. Last night we got into a controversy over which one of us five it was who first discovered the mine. It ended in strife between us, and we came to blows. I have killed my brother and he has left me with a souvenir across the forehead to remember him by. I must hang now, and then you will be the only one who knows about the mine; therefore I wish to ask something of you.'

" 'Speak out!' said the parson. 'I'll do what I can for you.'

" 'You know that I am leaving several little children behind me,' began the soldier, but the parson interruped him.

" 'As regards this, you can rest easy. That which comes to your share in the mine they shall have, exactly as if you yourself were living.'

" 'No,' said Olaf Svärd, 'it was another thing I wanted to ask of you. Don't let them have any portion of that which comes from the mine!'

"The parson staggered back a step. He stood there dumb and could not answer.

" 'If you do not promise me this, I cannot die in peace,' said the prisoner.

" 'Yes,' said the parson slowly and painfully. 'I promise you what you ask of me.'

"Thereupon the murderer was taken away, and the parson stood on the highway thinking how he should keep the promise he had given him. On the way home he thought of the wealth which he had been so happy over. What if it really were true that the people in this community could not stand riches? Already four were ruined who hitherto had been dignified and excellent men. He seemed to see the whole community before him, and he pictured to himself how this silver mine would destroy one after another. Was it befitting that he, who had been appointed to watch over these poor human beings' souls, should let loose upon them that which would be their destruction?"

All of a sudden the King sat bolt upright in his chair. "I declare!" said he, "you'll make me understand that a parson in this isolated settlement must be every inch a man."

"Nor was what had already happened enough," continued the parson, "for as soon as the news about the mine spread among the parishioners, they stopped working and went about in idleness, waiting for the time when great riches should pour in on them. All the ne'er-do-wells there were in this section steamed in, and drunkenness and fighting were what the parson heard talked of continually. A lot of people did nothing but tramp around in the forest searching for the mine, and the parson marked that as soon as he left the house people followed him stealthily to find out if he wasn't going to the silver mountain and to steal the secret from him.

"When matters were come to this pass, the parson called the peasants together to vote. To start with, he reminded them of all the misfortunes which the discovery of the mountain had brought upon them, and he asked them if they were going to let themselves be ruined or if they would save themselves. Then he told them that they must not expect him, who was their spiritual adviser, to help on their destruction. Now he had decided not to reveal to anyone where the silver mine was, and never would he himself take riches from it. And then he asked the peasants how they would have it henceforth. If they wished to continue their search for the mine and wait upon riches, then he would go so far away that no word of their misery could reach him; but if they would give up thinking about the silver mine and be as heretofore, he would remain with them. 'Whichever way you may choose,' said the parson, 'remember this, that from me no one shall ever know anything about the silver mountain.'"

"Well," said the King, "how did they decide?"

"They did as their pastor wished," said the parson. "They understood that he meant well by them when he wanted to remain poor for their sakes. And they commissioned him to go to the forest and conceal the vein or ore with evergreen and stone, so that no one would be able to find it—neither they themselves nor their posterity."[9]

"And ever since the parson has been living here just as poor as the rest?"

"Yes," answered the curate, "he has lived here just as poor as the rest."

"He married, of course, and built a new parsonage?" said the King.

"No, he couldn't afford to marry, and he lives in the old cabin."

"It's a pretty story that you have told me," said the King.

---

9. **posterity** (pŏ·stĕr'ə·tē): descendants; all future generations.

After a few seconds he resumed, "Was it of the silver mountain that you were thinking when you said that the parson here would be able to procure for me as much money as I need?"

"Yes," said the other.

"But I can't put the thumbscrews[10] on him," said the King. "Or how would you advise that I get such a man to show me the mountain—a man who has renounced his sweetheart and all the allurements of life?"

"Oh, that's a different matter," said the parson. "But if it's the Fatherland that is in need of the fortune, he will probably give in."

"Will you answer for that?" asked the King.

"Yes, that I will answer for," said the clergyman.

"Doesn't he care, then, what becomes of his parishioners?"

"That can rest in God's hands."

The King rose from his chair and walked over to the window. he stood for a moment and looked upon the group of people outside. The longer he looked, the clearer his large eyes shone; and his figure seemed to grow. "You may greet the pastor of this congregation and say that for Sweden's King there is no sight more beautiful than to see a people such as this!"

Then the King turned from the window and looked at the clergyman. He began to smile. "Is it true that the pastor of this parish is so poor that he removes his black clothes as soon as the service is over and dresses himself like a peasant?" asked the King.

"Yes, so poor is he," said the curate, and a crimson flush leaped into his roughhewn face.

The King went back to the window. One could see that he was in his best mood. All that was noble and great within him had been quickened into life. "You must let that mine lie in peace," said the King. "Inasmuch as you have labored and starved a lifetime to make this people such as you would have it, you may keep it as it is."

"But if the kingdom is in danger?" said the parson.

"The kingdom is better served with men than with money," remarked the King. When he had said this, he bade the clergyman farewell and went out from the vestry.

Without stood the group of people, as quiet and taciturn[11] as

10. **thumbscrews:** instruments of torture for compressing the thumbs.
11. **taciturn** (tăs'ə·tûrn): not inclined to talk.

they were when he went in. As the King came down the steps, a peasant stepped up to him.

"Have you had a talk with our pastor?" said the peasant.

"Yes," said the King. "I have."

"Then of course you have our answer?" said the peasant. "We asked you to go in and talk with our parson, that he might give you an answer from us."

"I have the answer," said the King.

Meaning

1. Why did the parson not tell the king who he was?
2. What evils did the silver mine bring to the village?
3. How did the pastor persuade the people not to use the mine?
4. What was the effect of the decision not to use the mine?
5. What is the theme of the story?

Method

1. A *frame story* is a story inside another story. For some reason explained in the outer story, there is occasion to narrate the inner story, which is usually the more important of the two.

    Point out the boundaries of the inner story in "The Silver Mine."
2. How does the author prepare you at the beginning of the story for the King's final decision?
3. Why did the author have the mine discovered by persons with such varied occupations?
4. Think of the once-upon-a-time stories you heard in your childhood. What folktale qualities does this story have?

Language: Synonyms

The English word *synonym* comes from the Greek prefix *syn-,* meaning together, associated with, or like, and *onyma,* the Greek word for name. Synonyms are words similar in meaning.

In "The Silver Mine," the author refers to the storyteller as a *parson,* a *curate,* a *pastor,* and a *clergyman.* If you were to consult a thesaurus (thu·sôr′əs), a book or "treasury" of words, especially of synonyms and antonyms, you would find these four words listed under the same entry. Along with these four synonyms, you would find such other synonyms as *ecclesiastic, churchman, cleric, minister,* and *the Reverend.*

Although there is a relationship among synonyms, each word is still highly individual and brings its own force to the context. For example, look up the origin and meaning of *curate* and *pastor* and compare the shades of meaning each word has.

The following sentences, taken from the story, describe the parson or his actions. Consult a thesaurus to find synonyms for the italicized words. Could you substitute any of the synonyms for these words and still keep the present meaning?

1. " 'There are some, no doubt, who say the parson wants to be the only one to *counsel* and rule in the parish,' he continued."
2. "(He was) *distressed* over what he had heard."
3. "The parson staggered back a step. He stood there *dumb* and could not answer."
4. ". . . a man who has *renounced* his sweetheart. . . ."
5. ". . . a crimson flush leaped into his *roughhewn* face."

Discussion and Composition

1. Write a character sketch about the King, the parson, or the general nature of the villagers. Begin by describing in detail his, or their, particular characteristics. Illustrate your description by referring to what the character(s) say and do.

As part of your sketch, tell which episode in the story shows you the most about the subject you choose. Be sure to explain the specific qualities illustrated by the passage you select.

2. Do you agree that sudden riches corrupt people? Give reasons for your answer.

BORDEN DEAL
(born 1922)

Like T. J., the boy hero of his short story "Antaeus," Borden Deal knew the joys and difficulties of farm life. He was born in Pontotoc, Mississippi, to a family of cotton farmers. In his youth, growing up in the lean years of the 1930s Depression, he worked at various jobs around the country—for a circus, the Civilian Conservation Corps, and the Labor Department in Washington, D.C.

After serving in the Navy during World War II, he attended the University of Alabama, graduating in 1949. He published his first short story, "Exodus," in 1948, while he was still in college. Since then, he has written more than a hundred short stories and several novels. *Walk Through The Valley* (1956), *Dunbar's Cove* (1957), *The Insolent Breed* (1959), and *The Least One* (1962) are regional novels about farm communities. Deal now lives in Sarasota, Florida.

---

*ANTAEUS**

This was during the wartime, when lots of people were coming North for jobs in factories and war industries, when people moved around a lot more than they do now, and sometimes kids were thrown into new groups and new lives that were completely different from anything they had ever known before. I remember this one kid, T. J. his name was, from somewhere down South, whose family moved into our building during that time. They'd come North with everything they owned piled into the back seat of an old-model sedan that you wouldn't expect could make the trip, with T. J. and his three younger sisters riding shakily on top of the load of junk.

---

* **Antaeus** (ăn·tē′əs): in Greek mythology, a giant who challenged his enemies to wrestling matches, with the odds always in his favor because each fall to earth renewed his tremendous strength and led to his victory. Antaeus was killed by Hercules, who held him aloft, detached from mother Earth, and strangled him.

Our building was just like all the others there, with families crowded into a few rooms, and I guess there were twenty-five or thirty kids about my age in that one building. Of course, there were a few of us who formed a gang and ran together all the time after school, and I was the one who brought T. J. in and started the whole thing.

The building right next door to us was a factory where they made walking dolls. It was a low building with a flat, tarred roof that had a parapet[1] all around it about head-high, and we'd found out a long time before that no one, not even the watchman, paid any attention to the roof because it was higher than any of the other buildings around. So my gang used the roof as a headquarters. We could get up there by crossing over to the fire escape from our own roof on a plank and then going on up. It was a secret place for us, where nobody else could go without our permission.

I remember the day I first took T. J. up there to meet the gang. He was a stocky, robust kid with a shock[2] of white hair, nothing sissy about him except his voice; he talked in this slow, gentle voice like you never heard before. He talked different from any of us and you noticed it right away. But I liked him anyway, so I told him to come on up.

We climbed up over the parapet and dropped down on the roof. The rest of the gang were already there.

"Hi," I said. I jerked my thumb at T. J. "He just moved into the building yesterday."

He just stood there, not scared or anything, just looking, like the first time you see somebody you're not sure you're going to like.

"Hi," Blackie said. "Where are you from?"

"Marion County," T. J. said.

We laughed. "Marion County?" I said. "Where's that?"

He looked at me for a moment like I was a stranger, too. "It's in Alabama," he said, like I ought to know where it was.

"What's your name?" Charley said.

"T. J.," he said, looking back at him. He had pale blue eyes that looked washed-out, but he looked directly at Charley, waiting for his reaction. He'll be all right, I thought. No sissy in him, except that voice. Who ever talked like that?

1. **parapet** (păr′ə·pĭt): a low wall or protecting railing on the edge of a platform, roof, or bridge.
2. **shock:** a thick bushy mass.

"T. J.," Blackie said. "That's just initials. What's your real name? Nobody in the world has just initials."

"I do," he said. "And they're T. J. That's all the name I got."

His voice was resolute with the knowledge of his rightness, and for a moment no one had anything to say. T. J. looked around at the rooftop and down at the black tar under his feet. "Down yonder where I come from," he said, "we played out in the woods. Don't you-all have no woods around here?"

"Naw," Blackie said. "There's the park a few blocks over, but it's full of kids and cops and old women. You can't do a thing."

T. J. kept looking at the tar under his feet. "You mean you ain't got no fields to raise nothing in?—no watermelons or nothing?"

"Naw," I said scornfully. "What do you want to grow something for? The folks can buy everything they need at the store."

He looked at me again with that strange, unknowing look. "In Marion County," he said, "I had my own acre of cotton and my own acre of corn. It was mine to plant and make ever' year."

He sounded like it was something to be proud of, and in some obscure way it made the rest of us angry. Blackie said, "Who'd want to have their own acre of cotton and corn? That's just work. What can you do with an acre of cotton and corn?"

T. J. looked at him. "Well, you get part of the bale offen your acre," he said seriously. "And I fed my acre of corn to my calf."

We didn't really know what he was talking about, so we were more puzzled than angry; otherwise, I guess we'd have chased him off the roof and wouldn't let him be part of our gang. But he was strange and different, and we were all attracted by his stolid³ sense of rightness and belonging, maybe by the strange softness of his voice contrasting our own tones of speech into harshness.

He moved his foot against the black tar. "We could make our own field right here," he said softly, thoughtfully. "Come spring we could raise us what we want to—watermelons and garden truck and no telling what all."

"You'd have to be a good farmer to make these tar roofs grow any watermelons," I said. We all laughed.

But T. J. looked serious. "We could haul us some dirt up

---

3. **stolid** (stŏl'ĭd): unemotional; calm.

here," he said. "And spread it out even and water it, and before you know it, we'd have us a crop in here." He looked at us intently. "Wouldn't that be fun?"

"They wouldn't let us," Blackie said quickly.

"I thought you said this was you-all's roof," T. J. said to me. "That you-all could do anything you wanted to up here."

"They've never bothered us," I said. I felt the idea beginning to catch fire in me. It was a big idea, and it took a while for it to sink in; but the more I thought about it, the better I liked it. "Say," I said to the gang. "He might have something there. Just make us a regular roof garden, with flowers and grass and trees and everything. And all ours, too," I said. "We wouldn't let anybody up here except the ones we wanted to."

"It'd take a while to grow trees," T. J. said quickly, but we weren't paying any attention to him. They were all talking about it suddenly, all excited with the idea after I'd put it in a way they could catch hold of it. Only rich people had roof gardens, we knew, and the idea of our own private domain excited them.

"We could bring it up in sacks and boxes," Blackie said. "We'd have to do it while the folks weren't paying any attention to us, for we'd have to come up to the roof of our building and then cross over with it."

"Where could we get the dirt?" somebody said worriedly.

"Out of those vacant lots over close to school," Blackie said. "Nobody'd notice if we scraped it up."

I slapped T. J. on the shoulder. "Man, you had a wonderful idea," I said, and everybody grinned at him, remembering that he had started it. "Our own private roof garden."

He grinned back. "It'll be ourn," he said. "All ourn." Then he looked thoughtful again. "Maybe I can lay my hands on some cotton seed, too. You think we could raise us some cotton?"

We'd started big projects before at one time or another, like any gang of kids, but they'd always petered out for lack of organization and direction. But this one didn't; somehow or other T. J. kept it going all through the winter months. He kept talking about the watermelons and the cotton we'd raise, come spring, and when even that wouldn't work, he'd switch around to my idea of flowers and grass and trees, though he was always honest enough to add that it'd take a while to get any trees started. He always had it on his mind and he'd mention it in school, getting them lined up

to carry dirt that afternoon, saying in a casual way that he reck-
oned a few more weeks ought to see the job through.

Our little area of private earth grew slowly. T. J. was smart
enough to start in one corner of the building, heaping up the
carried earth two or three feet thick so that we had an immediate
result to look at, to comtemplate with awe. Some of the evenings
T. J. alone was carrying earth up to the building, the rest of the
gang distracted by other enterprises or interests, but T. J. kept
plugging along on his own, and eventually we'd all come back to
him again and then our own little acre would grow more rapidly.

He was careful about the kind of dirt he'd let us carry up
there, and more than once he dumped a sandy load over the
parapet into the areaway below because it wasn't good enough. He
found out the kinds of earth in all the vacant lots for blocks
around. He'd pick it up and feel it and smell it, frozen though it
was sometimes, and then he'd say it was good growing soil or it
wasn't worth anything, and we'd have to go on somewhere else.

Thinking about it now, I don't see how he kept us at it. It was
hard work, lugging paper sacks and boxes of dirt all the way up
the stairs of our own building, keeping out of the way of the
grownups so they wouldn't catch on to what we were doing. They
probably wouldn't have cared, for they didn't pay much attention
to us, but we wanted to keep it secret anyway. Then we had to go
through the trap door to our roof, teeter over a plank to the fire
escape, then climb two or three stories to the parapet and drop
down onto the roof. All that for a small pile of earth that sometimes didn't seem worth the effort. But T. J. kept the vision bright
within us, his words shrewd and calculated toward the fulfillment
of his dream; and he worked harder than any of us. He seemed
driven toward a goal that we couldn't see, a particular point in
time that would be definitely marked by signs and wonders that
only he could see.

The laborious earth just lay there during the cold months,
inert and lifeless, the clods lumpy and cold under our feet when
we walked over it. But one day it rained, and afterward there was
a softness in the air, and the earth was live and giving again with
moisture and warmth.

That evening T. J. smelled the air, his nostrils dilating with
the odor of the earth under his feet. "It's spring," he said, and
there was a gladness rising in his voice that filled us all with the

same feeling. "It's mighty late for it, but it's spring. I'd just about decided it wasn't never gonna get here at all."

We were all sniffing at the air, too, trying to smell it the way that T. J. did, and I can still remember the sweet odor of the earth under our feet. It was the first time in my life that spring and spring earth had meant anything to me. I looked at T. J. then, knowing in a faint way the hunger within him through the toilsome winter months, knowing the dream that lay behind his plan. He was a new Antaeus, preparing his own bed of strength.

"Planting time," he said. "We'll have to find us some seed."

"What do we do?" Blackie said. "How do we do it?"

"First we'll have to break up the clods," T. J. said. "That won't be hard to do. Then we plant the seeds, and after a while they come up. Then you got you a crop." He frowned. "But you ain't got it raised yet. You got to tend it and hoe it and take care of it, and all the time it's growing and growing, while you're awake and while you're asleep. Then you lay it by when it's growed and let it ripen, and then you got you a crop."

"There's those wholesale seed houses over on Sixth," I said. "We could probably swipe some grass seed over there."

T. J. looked at the earth. "You-all seem mighty set on raising some grass," he said. "I ain't never put no effort into that. I spent all my life trying not to raise grass."

"But it's pretty," Blackie said. "We could play on it and take sunbaths on it. Like having our own lawn. Lots of people got lawns."

"Well," T. J. said. He looked at the rest of us, hesitant for the first time. He kept on looking at us for a moment. "I did have it in mind to raise some corn and vegetables. But we'll plant grass."

He was smart. He knew where to give in. And I don't suppose it made any difference to him, really. He just wanted to grow something, even if it was grass.

"Of course," he said, "I do think we ought to plant a row of watermelons. They'd be mighty nice to eat while we was a-laying on that grass."

We all laughed. "All right," I said. "We'll plant us a row of watermelons."

Things went very quickly then. Perhaps half the roof was covered with the earth, the half that wasn't broken by ventilators, and we swiped pocketfuls of grass seed from the open bins in the wholesale seed house, mingling among the buyers on Saturdays and during the school lunch hour. T. J. showed us how to prepare the earth, breaking up the clods and smoothing it and sowing the grass seed. It looked rich and black now with moisture, receiving of the seed, and it seemed that the grass sprang up overnight, pale green in the early spring.

We couldn't keep from looking at it, unable to believe that we had created this delicate growth. We looked at T. J. with understanding now, knowing the fulfillment of the plan he had carried along within his mind. We had worked without full understanding of the task, but he had known all the time.

We found that we couldn't walk or play on the delicate blades, as we had expected to, but we didn't mind. It was enough just to look at it, to realize that it was the work of our own hands, and each evening the whole gang was there, trying to measure the growth that had been achieved that day.

One time a foot was placed on the plot of ground, one time only, Blackie stepping onto it with sudden bravado.[4] Then he looked at the crushed blades and there was shame in his face. He did not do it again. This was his grass, too, and not to be desecrated.[5] No one said anything, for it was not necessary.

T. J. had reserved a small section for watermelons, and he was still trying to find some seed for it. The wholesale house didn't have any watermelon seeds, and we didn't know where we could lay our hands on them. T. J. shaped the earth into mounds, ready to receive them, three mounds lying in a straight line along the edge of the grass plot.

We had just about decided that we'd have to buy the seeds if we were to get them. It was a violation of our principles, but we were anxious to get the watermelons started. Somewhere or other, T. J. got his hands on a seed catalog and brought it one evening to our roof garden.

"We can order them now," he said, showing us the catalog. "Look!"

We all crowded around, looking at the fat, green watermelons pictured in full color on the pages. Some of them were split open, showing the red, tempting meat, making our mouths water.

---

4. **bravado** (brə·vä'dō): pretense of bravery.
5. **desecrated** (dĕs'ə·krāt·ĕd): treated irreverently.

"Now we got to scrape up some seed money," T. J. said, looking at us. "I got a quarter. How much you-all got?"

We made up a couple of dollars among us and T. J. nodded his head. "That'll be more than enough. Now we got to decide what kind to get. I think them Kleckley Sweets. What do you-all think?"

He was going into esoteric[6] matters beyond our reach. We hadn't even known there were different kinds of melons. So we just nodded our heads and agreed that yes, we thought the Kleckley Sweets too.

"I'll order them tonight," T. J. said. "We ought to have them in a few days."

"What are you boys doing up here?" an adult voice said behind us.

It startled us, for no one had ever come up here before in all the time we had been using the roof of the factory. We jerked around and saw three men standing near the trap door at the other end of the roof. They weren't policemen or night watchmen, but three men in plump business suits, looking at us. They walked toward us.

"What are you boys doing up here?" the one in the middle said again.

We stood still, guilt heavy among us, levied[7] by the tone of voice, and looked at the three strangers.

The men stared at the grass flourishing behind us. "What's this?" the man said. "How did this get up here?"

"Sure is growing good, ain't it?" T. J. said conversationally. "We planted it."

The men kept looking at the grass as if they didn't believe it. It was a thick carpet over the earth now, a patch of deep greenness startling in the sterile industrial surroundings.

'Yes, sir," T. J. said proudly. "We toted that earth up here and planted that grass." He fluttered the seed catalog. "And we're just fixing to plant us some watermelon."

The man looked at him then, his eyes strange and faraway. "What do you mean, putting this on the roof of my building?" he said. "Do you want to go to jail?"

6. esoteric (ĕs'ə·tĕr'ĭk): mysterious; understood only by a small group possessing special knowledge.

7. levied (lĕv'ēd): To levy is to impose or collect a tax or a fine by authority or force; here, guilt is established or levied by the man's tone of voice.

T. J. looked shaken. The rest of us were silent, frightened by the authority of his voice. We had grown up aware of adult authority, of policemen and night watchmen and teachers, and this man sounded like all the others. But it was a new thing to T. J.

"Well, you wasn't using the roof," T. J. said. He paused a moment and added shrewdly, "So we just thought to pretty it up a little bit."

"And sag it so I'd have to rebuild it," the man said sharply. He started turning away, saying to another man beside him, "See that all that junk is shoveled off by tomorrow."

"Yes, sir," the man said.

T. J. started forward. "You can't do that," he said. "We toted it up here, and it's our earth. We planted it and raised it and toted it up here."

The man stared at him coldly. "But it's my building," he said. "It's to be shoveled off tomorrow."

"It's our earth," T. J. said desperately. "You ain't got no right!"

The men walked on without listening and descended clumsily through the trapdoor. T. J. stood looking after them, his body tense with anger, until they had disappeared. They wouldn't even argue with him, wouldn't let him defend his earth-rights.

He turned to us. "We won't let 'em do it," he said fiercely. "We'll stay up here all day tomorrow and the day after that, and we won't let 'em do it."

We just looked at him. We knew there was no stopping it.

He saw it in our faces, and his face wavered for a moment before he gripped it into determination. "They ain't got no right," he said. "It's our earth. It's our land. Can't nobody touch a man's own land."

We kept looking at him, listening to the words but knowing that it was no use. The adult world had descended on us even in our richest dream, and we knew there was no calculating the adult world, no fighting it, no winning against it.

We started moving slowly toward the parapet and the fire escape, avoiding a last look at the green beauty of the earth that T. J. had planted for us, had planted deeply in our minds as well as in our experience. We filed slowly over the edge and down the steps to the plank, T. J. coming last, and all of us could feel the weight of his grief behind us.

"Wait a minute," he said suddenly, his voice harsh with the effort of calling.

We stopped and turned, held by the tone of his voice, and looked at him standing above us on the fire escape.

"We can't stop them?" he said, looking down at us, his face strange in the dusky light. "There ain't no way to stop em?"

"No," Blackie said with finality. "They own the building."

We stood still for a moment, looking up at T. J., caught into inaction by the decision working in his face. He stared back at us, and his face was pale and mean in the poor light, with a bald nakedness in his skin like cripples have sometimes.

"They ain't gonna touch my earth," he said fiercely. "They ain't gonna lay a hand on it! Come on."

He turned around and started up the fire escape again, almost running against the effort of climbing. We followed more slowly, not knowing what he intended. By the time we reached him, he had seized a board and thrust it into the soil, scooping it up and flinging it over the parapet into the areaway below. He straightened and looked at us.

"They can't touch it," he said. "I won't let 'em lay a dirty hand on it!"

We saw it then. He stooped to his labor again and we followed, the gusts of his anger moving in frenzied labor among us as we scattered along the edge of earth, scooping it and throwing it over the parapet, destroying with anger the growth we had nurtured with such tender care. The soil carried so laboriously upward to the light and the sun cascaded swiftly into the dark areaway, the green blades of grass crumpled and twisted in the falling.

It took less time than you would think; the task of destruction is infinitely easier than that of creation. We stopped at the end, leaving only a scattering of loose soil, and when it was finally over, a stillness stood among the group and over the factory building. We looked down at the bare sterility of black tar, felt the harsh texture of it under the soles of our shoes, and the anger had gone out of us, leaving only a sore aching in our minds like overstretched muscles.

T. J. stood for a moment, his breathing slowing from anger and effort, caught into the same contemplation of destruction as all of us. He stooped slowly, finally, and picked up a lonely blade of grass left trampled under our feet and put it between his teeth, tasting it, sucking the greenness out of it into his mouth. Then he started walking toward the fire escape, moving before any of us were ready to move, and disappeared over the edge.

We followed him, but he was already halfway down to the ground, going on past the board where we crossed over, climbing down into the areaway. We saw the last section swing down with his weight, and then he stood on the concrete below us, looking at the small pile of anonymous earth scattered by our throwing. Then he walked across the place where we could see him and disappeared toward the street without glancing back, without looking up to see us watching him.

They did not find him for two weeks.

Then the Nashville police caught him just outside the Nashville freight yards. He was walking along the railroad track, still heading south, still heading home.

As for us, who had no remembered home to call us, none of us ever again climbed the escapeway to the roof.

Meaning

1. The city children wanted to plant grass, flowers, and trees, whereas T. J. wanted cotton and watermelon. How do these preferences reflect their lives up to this point?
2. To the narrator, the garden represents a new concept of spring. For T. J., the garden is a "bed of strength." Explain the difference in light of what you know of T. J.'s background and the myth of Antaeus, who needed contact with the earth in order to survive.
3. Only a person with leadership ability could accomplish the seemingly impossible task of creating a garden on a tar roof. List what you think are the qualities of an ideal leader, and show how T. J. measures up to them.
4. What two reactions to the adult world are shown by T. J. and by the other boys when they are ordered off the roof?
5. What is the theme of this story?

Method

1. Why does the author have a city boy narrate the story?
2. One of the most dramatic scenes in the story takes place when

T. J. confronts the three men. How does the author make this a tense encounter?

3. Until the three men appear, there is little conflict in this story. What do you think was the author's purpose in introducing the conflict at that point?

4. What do you think of the author's conclusion? Give reasons for your answer.

Language: Antonyms

The antonym (from Greek *anti,* against, and *onyma,* name) of a word is a word with the opposite meaning. For example, *dark* is an antonym for *light.* However, note that *light* can also be an antonym for *heavy.* Some antonyms are formed by using a prefix, as in *active-inactive,* or *natural-unnatural.* For what word is each of the following an antonym?

1. delicate
2. different
3. started
4. gentle
5. unknowing
6. gladness

Discussion and Composition

1. The country-born T. J. finds it hard to believe that the "gang" has no woods to play in. Imagine the reverse situation in which a city-born child moves to the country. Write an essay explaining the difficulties he or she might encounter in adjusting to country life.

2. If you were T. J., how would you answer someone who asked you, "What do you want to grow something for? The folks can buy everything they need at the store." Give some good reasons to support your position. Skim through the story to get a basis for your ideas.

GINA BERRIAULT
(born 1926)

Born to immigrant parents, Gina Berriault had no formal education beyond high school. While she trained herself to be a writer, she worked at various times as a waitress, store clerk, news reporter, and librarian. In 1963, she received a fellowship from *Centro Mexicano do Escritores* in Mexico City. In 1966, she was appointed a scholar to the Radcliffe Institute for Independent Study in Cambridge, Massachusetts. Her stories have been awarded two *Paris Review* fiction prizes, and have appeared in major collections.

The setting for most of Gina Berriault's stories is northern California, where she now lives. Her writing deals primarily with isolated people whose loneliness she portrays with vividly realistic details.

THE STONE BOY

Arnold drew his overalls and raveling gray sweater over his naked body. In the other narrow bed his brother Eugene went on sleeping, undisturbed by the alarm clock's rusty ring. Arnold, watching his brother sleeping, felt a peculiar dismay; he was nine, six years younger than Eugie, and in their waking hours it was he who was subordinate. To dispel emphatically his uneasy advantage over his sleeping brother, he threw himself on the hump of Eugie's body.

"Get up! Get up!" he cried.

Arnold felt his brother twist away and saw the blankets lifted in a great wing, and, all in an instant, he was lying on his back under the covers with only his face showing like a baby, and Eugie was sprawled on top of him.

"Whassa matter with you?" asked Eugie in sleepy anger, his face hanging close.

"Get up," Arnold repeated. "You said you'd pick peas with me."

Stupidly, Eugie gazed around the room as if to see if morning had come into it yet. Arnold began to laugh derisively, making soft, snorting noises, and was thrown off the bed. He got up from the floor and went down the stairs, the laughter continuing, like hiccups, against his will. but when he opened the staircase door and entered the parlor, he hunched up his shoulders and was quiet because his parents slept in the bedroom downstairs.

Arnold lifted his .22-caliber rifle from the rack on the kitchen wall. It was an old lever-action Winchester that his father had given him because nobody else used it any more. On their way down to the garden he and Eugie would go by the lake, and if there were any ducks on it he'd take a shot at them. Standing on the stool before the cupboard, he searched on the top shelf in the confusion of medicines and ointments for man and beast and found a small yellow box of .22 cartridges. Then he sat down on the stool and began to load his gun.

It was cold in the kitchen so early, but later in the day, when his mother canned the peas, the heat from the wood stove would be almost unbearable. Yesterday she had finished preserving the huckleberries that the family had picked along the mountain, and before that she had canned all the cherries his father had brought from the warehouse in Corinth. Sometimes, on these summer days, Arnold would deliberately come out from the shade where he was playing and make himself as uncomfortable as his mother was in the kitchen by standing in the sun until the sweat ran down his body.

Eugie came clomping down the stairs and into the kitchen, his head drooping with sleepiness. From his perch on the stool Arnold watched Eugie slip on his green knit cap. Eugie didn't really need a cap; he hadn't had a haircut in a long time and his brown curls grew thick and matted, close around his ears and down his neck, tapering there to a small whorl.[1] Eugie passed his left hand through his hair before he set his cap down with his right. The very way he slipped his cap on was an announcement of his status; almost everything he did was a reminder that he was eldest—first he, then Nora, then Arnold—and called attention to how tall he was (almost as tall as his father), how long his legs were, and how small he was in the hips, and what a neat dip above his buttocks his thick-soled logger's boots gave him. Arnold never

---

1. **whorl** (hwèrl or hwôrl): spiral or curl.

tired of watching Eugie offer silent praise unto himself. He wondered, as he sat enthralled, if when he got to be Eugie's age he would still be undersized and his hair still straight.

Eugie eyed the gun. "Don't you know this ain't duck season?" he asked gruffly, as if he were the sheriff.

"No, I don't know," Arnold said with a snigger.

Eugie picked up the tin washtub for the peas, unbolted the door with his free hand and kicked it open. Then, lifting the tub to his head, he went clomping down the back steps. Arnold followed, closing the door behind him.

The sky was faintly gray, almost white. The mountains behind the farm made the sun climb a long way to show itself. Several miles to the south, where the range opened up, hung an orange mist, but the valley in which the farm lay was still cold and colorless.

Eugie opened the gate to the yard and the boys passed between the barn and the row of chicken houses, their feet stirring up the carpet of brown feathers dropped by the molting chickens. They paused before going down the slope to the lake. A fluky morning wind ran among the shocks of wheat that covered the slope. It sent a shimmer northward across the lake, gently moving the rushes that formed an island in the center. Killdeer,[2] their white markings flashing, skimmed the water, crying their shrill, sweet cry. And there at the south end of the lake were four wild ducks, swimming out from the willows into open water.

Arnold followed Eugie down the slope, stealing, as his brother did, from one shock of wheat to another. Eugie paused before climbing through the wire fence that divided the wheatfield from the marshy pasture around the lake. They were screened from the ducks by the willows along the lake's edge.

"If you hit your duck, you want me to go in after it?" Eugie said.

"If you want," Arnold said.

Eugie lowered his eyelids, leaving slits of mocking blue. "You'd drown 'fore you got to it, them legs of yours are so puny," he said.

He shoved the tub under the fence and, pressing down the center wire, climbed through into the pasture.

Arnold pressed down the bottom wire, thrust a leg through

2. **killdeer:** a bird that lives in shore areas.

and leaned forward to bring the other leg after. His rifle caught on the wire and he jerked at it. The air was rocked by the sound of the shot. Feeling foolish, he lifted his face, baring it to an expected shower of derision from his brother. But Eugie did not turn around. Instead, from his crouching position, he fell to his knees and then pitched forward onto his face. The ducks rose up crying from the lake, cleared the mountain background and beat away northward across the pale sky.

Arnold squatted beside his brother. Eugie seemed to be climbing the earth, as if the earth ran up and down, and when he found he couldn't scale it he lay still.

"Eugie?"

Then Arnold saw it, under the tendril of hair at the nape of the neck—a slow rising of bright blood. It had an obnoxious movement, like that of a parasite.

"Hey, Eugie," he said again. He was feeling the same discomfort he had felt when he had watched Eugie sleeping; his brother didn't know that he was lying face down in the pasture.

Again he said, "Hey, Eugie," an anxious nudge in his voice. But Eugie was as still as the morning about them.

Arnold set his rifle on the ground and stood up. He picked up the tub and, dragging it behind him, walking along by the willows to the garden fence and climbed through. He went down on his knees among the tangled vines. The pods were cold with the night, but his hands were strange to him, and not until some time had passed did he realize that the pods were numbing his fingers. He picked from the top vine first, then lifted the vine to look underneath for pods and then moved on to the next.

It was a warmth on his back, like a large hand laid firmly there, that made him raise his head. Way up on the slope the gray farmhouse was struck by the sun. While his head had been bent the land had grown bright around him.

When he got up his legs were so stiff that he had to go down on his knees again to ease the pain. Then, walking sideways, he dragged the tub, half full of peas, up the slope.

The kitchen was warm now; a fire was roaring in the stove with a closed-up, rushing sound. His mother was spooning eggs from a pot of boiling water and putting them into a bowl. Her short brown hair was uncombed and fell forward across her eyes as she bent her head. Nora was lifting a frying pan full of trout from the stove, holding the handle with a dish towel. His father had just come in from bringing the cows from the north pasture to the barn, and was sitting on the stool, unbuttoning his red plaid Mackinaw.[3]

"Did you boys fill the tub?" his mother asked.

"They ought of by now," his father said. "They went out of the house an hour ago. Eugie woke me up comin' downstairs. I heard you shootin'—did you get a duck?"

"No," Arnold said. They would want to know why Eugie wasn't coming in for breakfast, he thought. "Eugie's dead," he told them.

They stared at him. The pitch crackled in the stove.

"You kids playin' a joke?" his father asked.

"Where's Eugene?" his mother asked scoldingly. She wanted, Arnold knew, to see his eyes, and when he glanced at her she put the bowl and spoon down on the stove and walked past him. His father stood up and went out the door after her. Nora followed them with little skipping steps, as if afraid to be left alone.

Arnold went into the barn, down along the foddering passage past the cows waiting to be milked, and climbed into the loft. After a few minutes he heard a terrifying sound coming toward the house. His parents and Nora were returning from the willows, and sounds sharp as knives were rising from his mother's breast and carrying over the sloping fields. In a short while he heard his father go down the back steps, slam the car door and drive away.

Arnold lay still as a fugitive, listening to the cows eating close by. If his parents never called him, he thought, he would stay up in the loft forever, out of the way. In the night he would sneak down for a drink of water from the faucet over the trough and for whatever food they left for him by the barn.

The rattle of his father's car as it turned down the lane recalled him to the present. He heard voices from his Uncle Andy and Aunt Alice as they and his father went past the barn to the lake. He could feel the morning growing heavier with sun. Someone, probably Nora, had let the chickens out of their coops and they were cackling in the yard.

3. **Mackinaw** (măk′ə·nô): a heavy woolen jacket, usually in a plaid design. The name comes from Mackinac, an island in Michigan which is the site of an Indian burial ground called *Michilemackinac* (which means green turtle). At one time, supplies such as Mackinaws were distributed to the Indians at Mackinac.

After a while another car turned down the road off the highway. The car drew to a stop and he heard the voices of strange men. The men also went past the barn and down to the lake. The undertakers, whom his father must have phoned from Uncle Andy's house, had arrived from Corinth. Then he heard everybody come back and heard the car turn around and leave.

"Arnold!" It was his father calling from the yard.

He climbed down the ladder and went out into the sun, picking wisps of hay from his overalls.

Corinth, nine miles away, was the county seat. Arnold sat in the front seat of the old Ford between his father, who was driving, and Uncle Andy; no one spoke. Uncle Andy was his mother's brother, and he had been fond of Eugie because Eugie had resembled him. Andy had taken Eugie hunting and had given him a knife and a lot of things, and now Andy, his eyes narrowed, sat tall and stiff beside Arnold.

Arnold's father parked the car before the courthouse. It was a two-story brick building with a lamp on each side of the bottom step. They went up the wide stone steps, Arnold and his father going first, and entered the darkly paneled hallway. The shirt-sleeved man in the sheriff's office said that the sheriff was at Carlson's Parlor examining the Curwing boy.

Andy went off to get the sheriff while Arnold and his father waited on a bench in the corridor. Arnold felt his father watching him, and he lifted his eyes with painful casualness to the announcement, on the opposite wall, of the Corinth County Annual Rodeo, and then to the clock with its loudly clucking pendulum. After he had come down from the loft his father and Uncle Andy had stood in the yard with him and asked him to tell them everything, and he had explained to them how the gun had caught on the wire. But when they had asked him why he hadn't run back to the house to tell his parents, he had had no answer—all he could say was that he had gone down into the garden to pick the peas. His father had stared at him in a pale, puzzled way, and it was then that he had felt his father and the others set their cold, turbulent silence against him. Arnold shifted on the bench, his only feeling a small one of compunction[4] imposed by his father's eyes.

At a quarter past nine Andy and the sheriff came in. They all

---

4. compunction (kəm·pŭngk′shən): uneasiness or regret coming from a sense of guilt.

went into the sheriff's private office, and Arnold was sent forward to sit in the chair by the sheriff's desk; his father and Andy sat down on the bench against the wall.

The sheriff lumped down into his swivel chair and swung toward Arnold. He was an old man with white hair like wheat stubble. His restless green eyes made him seem not to be in his office but to be hurrying and bobbing around somewhere else.

"What did you say your name was?" the sheriff asked.

"Arnold," he replied, but he could not remember telling the sheriff his name before.

"Curwing?"

"Yes."

"What were you doing with a .22, Arnold?"

"It's mine," he said.

"Okay. What were you going to shoot?"

"Some ducks," he replied.

"Out of season?"

He nodded.

"That's bad," said the sheriff. "Were you and your brother good friends?"

What did he mean—good friends? Eugie was his brother. That was different from a friend, Arnold thought. A best friend was your own age, but Eugie was almost a man. Eugie had had a way of looking at him, slyly and mockingly and yet confidentially, that had summed up how they both felt about being brothers. Arnold had wanted to be with Eugie more than with anybody else but he couldn't say they had been good friends.

"Did they ever quarrel?" the sheriff asked his father.

"Not that I know," his father replied. "It seemed to me that Arnold cared a lot for Eugie."

"Did you?" the sheriff asked Arnold.

If it seemed so to his father, then it was so. Arnold nodded.

"Were you mad at him this morning?"

"No."

"How did you happen to shoot him?"

"We was crawlin' through the fence."

"Yes?"

"An' the gun got caught on the wire."

"Seems the hammer must of caught," his father put in.

"All right, that's what happened," said the sheriff. "But what I want you to tell me is this. Why didn't you go back to the house and tell your father right away? Why did you go pick peas for an hour?"

Arnold gazed over his shoulder at his father, expecting his father to have an answer for this also. But his father's eyes, larger and ever lighter blue than usual, were fixed upon him curiously. Arnold picked at a callus in his right palm. It semed odd now that he had not run back to the house and wakened his father, but he could not remember why he had not. They were all waiting for him to answer.

"I come down to pick peas," he said.

"Didn't you think," asked the sheriff, stepping carefully from word to word, "that it was more important for you to go tell your parents what had happened?"

"The sun was gonna come up," Arnold said.

"What's that got to do with it?"

"It's better to pick peas while they're cool."

The sheriff swung away from him, laid both hands flat on his desk. "Well, all I can say is," he said across to Arnold's father and Uncle Andy, "he's either a moron or he's so reasonable that he's way ahead of us." He gave a challenging snort. "It's come to my notice that the most reasonable guys are mean ones. They don't feel nothing."

For a moment the three men sat still. Then the sheriff lifted his hand like a man taking an oath. "Take him home," he said.

Andy uncrossed his legs. "You don't want him?"

"Not now," replied the sheriff. "Maybe in a few years."

Arnold's father stood up. He held his hat against his chest. "The gun ain't his no more," he said wanly.

Arnold went first through the hallway, hearing behind him the heels of his father and Uncle Andy striking the floor boards. He went down the steps ahead of them and climbed into the back seat of the car. Andy paused as he was getting into the front seat and gazed back at Arnold, and Arnold saw that his uncle's eyes had absorbed the knowingness from the sheriff's eyes. Andy and his father and the sheriff had discovered what made him go down into the garden. It was because he was cruel, the sheriff had said, and didn't care about his brother. Was that the reason? Arnold lowered his eyelids meekly against his uncle's stare.

The rest of the day he did his tasks around the farm, keeping apart from the family. At evening, when he saw his father stomp tiredly into the house, Arnold did not put down his hammer and leave the chicken coop he was repairing. He was afraid that they did not want him to eat supper with them. But in a few minutes another fear that they would go to the trouble of calling him and that he would be made conspicuous by his tardiness made him follow his father into the house. As he went through the kitchen he saw the jars of peas standing in rows on the workbench, a reproach to him.

No one spoke at supper, and his mother, who sat next to him, leaned her head in her hand all through the meal, curving her fingers over her eyes so as not to see him. They were finishing their small, silent supper when the visitors began to arrive, knocking hard on the back door. The men were coming from their farms now that it was growing dark and they could not work any more.

Old Man Matthews, gray and stocky, came first, with his two sons, Orion, the elder, and Clint, who was Eugie's age. As the callers entered the parlor, where the family ate, Arnold sat down in a rocking chair. Even as he had been undecided before supper whether to remain outside or take his place at the table, he now thought that he should go upstairs, and yet he stayed to avoid being conspicuous by his absence. If he stayed, he thought, as he always stayed and listened when visitors came, they would see that he was only Arnold and not the person the sheriff thought he was. He sat with his arms crossed and his hands tucked into his armpits and did not lift his eyes.

The Matthews men had hardly settled down around the table, after Arnold's mother and Nora had cleared away the dishes, when another car rattled down the road and someone else rapped on the back door. This time it was Sullivan, a spare and sandy man, so nimble of gesture and expression that Arnold had never been able to catch more than a few of his meanings. Sullivan, in dusty jeans, sat down in the other rocker, shot out his skinny legs and began to talk in his fast way, recalling everything that Eugene had ever said to him. The other men interrupted to tell of occasions they remembered, and after a time Clint's young voice, hoarse like Eugene's had been, broke in to tell about the time Eugene had beat him in a wrestling match.

Out in the kitchen the voices of Orion's wife and of Mrs. Sullivan mingled with Nora's voice but not, Arnold noticed, his mother's. Then dry little Mr. Cram came, leaving large Mrs. Cram in the kitchen, and there was no chair left for Mr. Cram to sit in. No one asked Arnold to get up and he was unable to rise. He knew that the story had got around to them during the day about how he had gone and picked peas after he had shot his brother, and he knew that although they were talking only about Eugie they were thinking about him and if he got up, if he moved even his foot, they would all be alerted. Then Uncle Andy arrived and leaned his tall, lanky body against the doorjamb and there were two men standing.

Presently Arnold was aware that the talk had stopped. He knew without looking up that the men were watching him.

"Not a tear in his eye," said Andy, and Arnold knew that it was his uncle who had gestured the men to attention.

"He don't give a hoot, is that how it goes?" asked Sullivan, trippingly.

"He's a reasonable fellow," Andy explained. "That's what the sheriff said. It's us who ain't reasonable. If we'd of shot our brother, we'd of come runnin' back to the house, cryin' like a baby. Well, we'd of been unreasonable. What would of been the use of actin' like that? If your brother is shot dead, he's shot dead. What's the use of gettin' emotional about it? The thing to do is go down to the garden and pick peas. Am I right?"

The men around the room shifted their heavy, satisfying weight of unreasonableness.

Matthews' son Orion said: "If I'd of done what he done, Pa would've hung my pelt by the side of that big coyote's in the barn."

Arnold sat in the rocker until the last man had filed out. While his family was out in the kitchen bidding the callers good night and the cars were driving away down the dirt lane to the highway, he picked up one of the kerosene lamps and slipped quickly up the stairs. In his room he undressed by lamplight, although he and Eugie had always undressed in the dark, and not until he was lying in his bed did he blow out the flame. He felt nothing, not any grief. There was only the same immense silence and crawling inside of him; it was the way the house and fields felt under a merciless sun.

He awoke suddenly. He knew that his father was out in the yard, closing the doors of the chicken houses so that the chickens could not roam out too early and fall prey to the coyotes that came down from the mountains at daybreak. The sound that had wakened him was the step of his father as he got up from the rocker and went down the back steps. And he knew that his mother was awake in her bed.

Throwing off the covers, he rose swiftly, went down the stairs and across the dark parlor to his parents' room. He rapped on the door.

"Mother?"

From the closed room her voice rose to him, a seeking and retreating voice. "Yes?"

"Mother?" he asked insistently. He had expected her to realize that he wanted to go down on his knees by her bed and tell her that Eugie was dead. She did not know it yet, nobody knew it, and yet she was sitting up in bed, waiting to be told, waiting for him to confirm her dread. He had expected her to tell him to come in, to allow him to dig his head into her blankets and tell her about the terror he had felt when he had knelt beside Eugie. He had come to clasp her in his arms and, in his terror, to pommel[5] her breasts with his head. He put his hand upon the knob.

"Go back to bed, Arnold," she called sharply.

But he waited.

"Go back! Is night when you get afraid?"

At first he did not understand. Then, silently, he left the door and for a stricken moment stood by the rocker. Outside everything was still. The fences, the shocks of wheat seen through the window before him were so still it was as if they moved and breathed in the daytime and had fallen silent with the lateness of the hour. It was a silence that seemed to observe his father, a figure moving alone around the yard, his lantern casting a circle of light by his feet. In a few minutes his father would enter the dark house, the lantern still lighting his way.

Arnold was suddenly aware that he was naked. He had thrown off his blankets and come down the stairs to tell his mother how he felt about Eugie, but she had refused to listen to him and his nakedness had become upardonable. At once he went back up the stairs, fleeing from his father's lantern.

At breakfast he kept his eyelids lowered as if to deny the humiliating night. Nora, sitting at his left, did not pass the pitcher of milk to him and he did not ask for it. He would never again, he vowed, ask them for anything, and he ate his fried eggs and pota-

---

5. **pommel:** beat

toes only because everybody ate meals—the cattle ate, and the cats; it was customary for everybody to eat.

"Nora, you gonna keep that pitcher for yourself?" his father asked.

Nora lowered her head unsurely.

"Pass it on to Arnold," his father said.

Nora put her hands in her lap.

His father picked up the metal pitcher and set it down at Arnold's plate.

Arnold, pretending to be deaf to the discord, did not glance up, but relief rained over his shoulders at the thought that his parents recognized him again. They must have lain awake after his father had come in from the yard: had they realized together why he had come down the stairs and knocked at their door?

"Bessie's missin' this morning," his father called out to his mother, who had gone into the kitchen. "She went up the mountain last night and had her calf, most likely. Somebody's got to go up and find her 'fore the coyotes get the calf."

That had been Eugie's job, Arnold thought. Eugie would climb the cattle trails in search of a newborn calf and come down the mountain carrying the calf across his back, with the cow running down along behind him, mooing in alarm.

Arnold ate the few more forkfuls of his breakfast, put his hands on the edge of the table and pushed back his chair. If he went for the calf he'd be away from the farm all morning. He could switch the cow down the mountain slowly, and the calf would run along at its mother's side.

When he passed through the kitchen his mother was setting a kettle of water on the stove. "Where you going?" she asked awkwardly.

"Up to get the calf," he replied, averting his face.

"Arnold?"

At the door he paused reluctantly, his back to her, knowing that she was seeking him out, as his father was doing, and he called upon his pride to protect him from them.

"Was you knocking at my door last night?"

He looked over his shoulder at her, his eyes narrow and dry.

"What'd you want?" she asked humbly.

"I didn't want nothing," he said flatly.

Then he went out the door and down the back steps, his legs trembling from the fright his answer gave him.

Meaning

1. Describe the relationship between Arnold and his mother. How had their relationship changed at the end of the story?
2. How did the accident happen? What foreshadowing is given in the first paragraph of the story?
3. Why did Arnold pick peas instead of telling his family immediately about the tragedy? Do you think that his reaction was realistic? Why or why not?
4. Explain the significance of the title, "The Stone Boy."

Method

1. What purpose does the first paragraph of the story serve? What do you find out about the family, and especially about the relationship between the two brothers?
2. What is the climax of the story?
3. When do you find out how Arnold really felt about Eugene's death?
4. Arnold's father and mother both forgive Arnold and recognize that they have made a mistake. What is the evidence of their change of heart?
5. Why do you think the author has been called a pessimistic writer?
6. Is this a commercial or quality story? Why?

Language: Personification

You have learned that *simile* and *metaphor* are figures of speech used to compare two unlike objects. A *simile* is a comparison that includes the words *like* or *as*. For example, "It had an obnoxious movement like that of a parasite." A metaphor is an implied comparison. It does not use like or as. For example, ". . . the blankets lifted in a great wing. . . ." *Personification* is a figure of speech that gives human characteristics, such as human powers and feelings, to nonhuman or even lifeless ideas or objects. Identify which of these figures of speech is used in each of the following examples from "The Stone Boy."

1. ". . . feet stirring up the carpet of brown feathers. . . ."
2. "It was a warmth on his back, like a large hand laid firmly there. . . ."

3. "Arnold lay still as a fugitive. . . ."
4. "He could feel the morning growing heavier with sun."
5. ". . . the clock with its loudly clucking pendulum."
6. ". . . white hair like wheat stubble."

Discussion and Composition

1. In a paragraph or two, explain the difference between Arnold's feeling for his brother and the feeling he might have for a close friend.

2. The neighbors who come to the farmhouse after Eugie's death are characterized by a few telling details. Write a brief character sketch of some of your friends or neighbors.

JESSAMYN WEST
(born 1907)

Born in Indiana, Jessamyn West moved with her family to Yorba Linda, California, when she was a child. Most of her writing is set in rural Indiana and California. She attended Whittier College and married shortly after graduation. She taught in a one-room schoolhouse for several years, and was studying for a doctorate in English literature at the University of California when she fell ill with tuberculosis. She tells of her mother's battle to save her daughter's life in *The Woman Said Yes* (1976).

A long recovery period from her illness gave Jessamyn West the opportunity to begin writing. As her mother nursed her back to health, she told Jessamyn about her ancestors and of their pioneer life. Working in a reclining position because she was too weak to sit at a desk, Jessamyn West wrote fictional stories based on her Quaker heritage. *The Friendly Persuasion* (1945) her first book, which was later made into a movie, is a collection of these stories.

Jessamyn West has written novels, short stories, autobiographical books, and essays. She has written for *The New York Times Book Review* and other critical media. She is a much sought-after lecturer and teacher in the literary community and has been awarded five honorary doctorates in humane letters and literature. This story is from *Cress Delahanty* (1953), a collection of stories that originally appeared in the *New Yorker, The Ladies Home Journal, Harper's Magazine, Colliers, Woman's Day, The New Mexico Quarterly* and *The Colorado Quarterly*.

THEN HE GOES FREE

While her mother and father awaited the arrival of Mr. and Mrs. Kibbler who had called asking to speak to them "about Cress and Edwin Jr.," Mr. Delahanty reminded his wife how wrong she had been about Cress.

"Not two months ago," he said, "in this very room you told me you were worried because Cress wasn't as interested in the boys as a girl her age should be. In this very room. And now look what's happened."

Mrs. Delahanty, worried now by Mrs. Kibbler's message, spoke more sharply than she had intended. "Don't keep repeating, 'in this very room,'" she said, "as if it would have been different if I'd said it in the back porch or out of doors. Besides, what has happened?"

Mr. Delahanty took off his hat, which he'd had on when Mrs. Kibbler phoned, and sailed it out of the living room toward the hall table, which he missed. "Don't ask me what's happened," he said, "I'm not the girl's mother."

Mrs. Delahanty took off her own hat and jabbed the hat pins back into it. "What do you mean, you're not the girl's mother? Of course you're not. No one ever said you were."

Mr. Delahanty picked up his fallen hat, put it on the chair beside the hall table and came back into the living room. "A girl confides in her mother." he told his wife.

"A girl confides in her mother!" Mrs. Delahanty was very scornful. "Who tells you these things, John Delahanty? Not *your* mother. She didn't have any daughter. Not me. Cress doesn't confide in anyone. How do you know these things, anyway, about mothers and daughters?"

John Delahanty seated himself upon the sofa, legs extended, head back, as straight and unrelaxed as a plank.

"Don't catch me up that way, Gertrude." he said. "You know I don't know them." Without giving his wife any opportunity to crow over this victory he went on quickly. "What I'd like to know is why did the Kibblers have to pick a Saturday night for this call? Didn't they know we'd be going into town?"

Like most ranchers, John Delahanty stopped work early on Saturdays so that, after a quick clean-up and supper, he and his wife could drive into town. There they did nothing very important: bought groceries, saw a show, browsed around in hardware stores, visited friends. But after a week of seeing only themselves—the Delahanty ranch was off the main highway—it was pleasant simply to saunter along the sidewalks looking at the cars, the merchandise, the people in their town clothes. This Saturday trip to town was a jaunt they both looked forward to during the week, and tonight's trip, because of February's warmer air and suddenly, it seemed, longer twilight, would have been particularly pleasant.

"Five minutes more," said Mr. Delahanty, "and we'd have been on our way."

"Why didn't you tell Mrs. Kibbler we were just leaving?"

"I did. And she said for anything less important she wouldn't think of keeping us."

Mrs. Delahanty came over to the sofa and stood looking anxiously down at her husband. "John, exactly what did Mrs. Kibbler say?"

"The gist of it," said Mr. Delahanty, "was that . . ."

"I don't care about the gist of it. That's just what you think she said. I want to know what she really said."

Mr. Delahanty let his head fall forward, though he still kept his legs stiffly extended. "What she really said was, 'Is this Mr. John Delahanty?' And I said, 'Yes.' Then she said, 'This is Mrs. Edwin Kibbler, I guess you remember me.'"

"Remember her?" Mrs. Delahanty exclaimed. "I didn't know you even knew her."

"I don't," said Mr. Delahanty, "but I remember her all right. She came before the school board about a month ago to tell us we ought to take those two ollas[1] off the school grounds. She said it was old-fashioned to cool water that way, that the ollas looked messy and were unhygienic."

"Did you take them off?" Mrs. Delahanty asked, without thinking. As a private person John Delahanty was reasonable and untalkative. As clerk of the school board he inclined toward dogmatism[2] and long-windedness. Now he began a defense of the ollas and the school board's action in retaining them.

"Look, John," said Mrs. Delahanty, "I'm not interested in the school board or its water coolers. What I want to know is, what did Mrs. Kibbler say about Cress?"

"Well, she said she wanted to have a little talk with us about Cress—and Edwin Jr."

"I know that." Impatience made Mrs. Delahanty's voice sharp. "But what about them?"

Mr. Delahanty drew his feet up toward the sofa, then bent down and retied a shoelace. "About what Cress did to him— Edwin Jr."

---

1. **ollas** (ŏl′əs): wide-mouthed water jars.
2. **dogmatism** (dôg′mə·tĭz·əm): positive, authoritative statements of opinion.

"*Did* to him!" said Mrs. Delahanty aghast.

"That's what his mother said."

Mrs. Delahanty sat down on the hassock at her husband's feet. "Did to him," she repeated again. "Why, what could Cress do to him? He's two or three years older than Cress, fifteen or sixteen anyway. What could she do to him?"

Mr. Delahanty straightened up. "She could hit him, I guess." he ventured.

"Hit him? What would she want to hit him for?"

"I don't know," said Mr. Delahanty. "I don't know that she did hit him. Maybe she kicked him. Anyway, his mother seems to think the boy's been damaged in some way."

"Damaged," repeated Mrs. Delahanty angrily. "Damaged! Why, Cress is too tender-hearted to hurt a fly. She shoos them outside instead of killing them. And you sit there talking of hitting and kicking."

"Well," said Mr. Delahanty mildly, "Edwin's got teeth out. I don't know how else she could get them out, do you?"

"I'm going to call Cress," said Mrs. Delahanty, "and ask her about this. I don't believe it for a minute."

"I don't think calling her will do any good. She left while I was talking to Mrs. Kibbler."

"What do you mean, left?"

"Went for a walk, she said."

"Well, teeth out," repeated Mrs. Delahanty unbelievingly. "Teeth out! I didn't know you could get teeth out except with pliers or a chisel."

"Maybe Edwin's teeth are weak."

"Don't joke about this, John Delahanty. It isn't any joking matter. And I don't believe it. I don't believe Cress did it or that that boy's teeth are out. Anyway I'd have to see them to believe it."

"You're going to," Mr. Delahanty said. "Mrs. Kibbler's bringing Edwin especially so you can."

Mrs. Delahanty sat for some time without saying anything at all. Then she got up and walked back and forth in front of her husband, turning her hat, which she still held, round and round on one finger. "Well, what does Mrs. Kibbler expect us to do now?" she asked. "If they really are out, that is?"

"For one thing," replied Mr. Delahanty, "she expects us to

pay for some new ones. And for another . . ." Mr. Delahanty paused to listen. Faintly, in the distance a car could be heard. "Here she is now," he said.

Mrs. Delahanty stopped her pacing. "Do you think I should make some cocoa for them, John? And maybe some marguerites?"

"No, I don't," said Mr. Delahanty. "I don't think Mrs. Kibbler considers this a social visit."

As the car turned into the long driveway which led between the orange grove on one side and the lemon grove on the other to the Delahanty house, Mrs. Delahanty said, "I still don't see why you think this proves I'm wrong."

Mr. Delahanty had forgotten about his wife's wrongness. "How do you mean wrong?" he asked.

"About Cress's not being interested in the boys."

"Oh," he said. "Well, you've got to be pretty interested in a person—one way or another—before you hit him."

"That's a perfectly silly notion," began Mrs. Delahanty, but before she could finish, the Kibblers had arrived.

Mr. Delahanty went to the door while Mrs. Delahanty stood in the back of the room by the fireplace unwilling to take one step toward meeting her visitors.

Mrs. Kibbler was a small woman with a large, determined nose, prominent blue eyes and almost no chin. Her naturally curly hair—she didn't wear a hat—sprang away from her head in a great cage-shaped pompadour[3] which dwarfed her face.

Behind Mrs. Kibbler was Mr. Kibbler, short, dusty, soft-looking, bald, except for a fringe of hair about his ears so thick that the top of his head, by contrast, seemed more naked than mere lack of hair could make it.

Behind Mr. Kibbler was Edwin Jr. He was as thin as his mother, as mild and soft-looking as his father; and to these qualities he added an unhappiness all of his own. He gave one quick look at the room and the Delahantys through his thick-lensed spectacles, after which he kept his eyes on the floor.

Mr. Delahanty closed the door behind the callers, then introduced his wife to Mrs. Kibbler. Mrs. Kibbler in turn introduced her family to the Delahantys. While the Kibblers were seating

---

3. **pompadour** (p̌om′pə·dôr): hairstyle in which the hair is combed up and back from the forehead, often over a roll.

themselves—Mrs. Kibbler and Edwin Jr. on the sofa, Mr. Kibbler on a straight-backed chair in the room's darkest corner—Mrs. Delahanty, out of nervousness, bent and lit the fire, which was laid in the fireplace, though the evening was not cold enough for it. Then she and Mr. Delahanty seated themselves in the chairs on each side of the fireplace.

Mrs. Kibbler looked at the fire with some surprise. "Do you find it cold this evening, Mrs. Delahanty?" she asked.

"No," said Mrs. Delahanty, "I don't. I don't know why I lit the fire."

To this Mrs. Kibbler made no reply. Instead, without preliminaries, she turned to her son. "Edwin," she said, "show the Delahantys what their daughter did to your teeth."

Mrs. Delahanty wanted to close her eyes, look into the fire, or find, as Edwin Jr. had done, a spot of her own on the floor to examine. There was an almost imperceptible[4] ripple along the length of the boy's face as if he had tried to open his mouth but found he lacked the strength. He momentarily lifted his eyes from the floor to dart a glance into the dark corner where his father sat. But Mr. Kibbler continued to sit in expressionless silence.

"Edwin," said Mrs. Kibbler, "speak to your son."

"Do what your mother says, son," said Mr. Kibbler.

Very slowly, as if it hurt him, Edwin opened his mouth.

His teeth were white, and in his thin face they seemed very large, as well. The two middle teeth, above, had been broken across in a slanting line. The lower incisor[5] appeared to be missing entirely.

"Wider, Edwin," Mrs. Kibbler urged. "I want the Delahantys to see exactly what their daughter is responsible for."

But before Edwin could make any further effort Mrs. Delahanty cried, "No, that's enough."

"I didn't want you to take our word for anything," Mrs. Kibbler said reasonably. "I wanted you to see."

"Oh, we see, all right," said Mrs. Delahanty earnestly.

Mr. Delahanty leaned forward and spoke to Mrs. Kibbler. "While we see the teeth, Mrs. Kibbler, it just isn't a thing we think Crescent would do. Or in fact how she *could* do it. We think Edwin must be mistaken."

---

4. **imperceptible** (ĭm'pər·sĕp'·tə·bəl): unseen.
5. **incisor** (ĭn sī'zər): a cutting tooth at the front of the jaw.

"You mean lying?" asked Mrs. Kibbler flatly.

"Mistaken," repeated Mr. Delahanty.

"Tell them, Edwin," said Mrs. Kibbler.

"She knocked me down," said Edwin, very low.

Mrs. Delahanty, although she was already uncomfortably warm, held her hands nearer the fire, even rubbed them together a time or two.

"I simply can't believe that," she said.

"You mean hit you with her fist and knocked you down?" asked Mr. Delahanty.

"No," said Edwin even lower than before. "Ran into me."

"But not on purpose," said Mrs. Delahanty.

Edwin nodded. "Yes," he said. "On purpose."

"But why?" asked Mr. Delahanty. "Why? Cress wouldn't do such a thing, I know—without some cause. Why?"

"Tell them why, Edwin," said his mother.

Edwin's head went even nearer the floor—as if the spot he was watching had diminished or retreated.

"For fun," he said.

It was impossible not to believe the boy as he sat there hunched, head bent, one eyelid visibly twitching. "But Cress would never do such a thing," said Mrs. Delahanty.

Mrs. Kibbler disregarded this. "It would not have been so bad, Mr. Delahanty, except that Edwin was standing by one of those ollas. When your daughter shoved Edwin over she shoved the olla over, too. That's probably what broke his teeth. Heavy as cement and falling down on top of him and breaking up in a thousand pieces. To say nothing of his being doused with water on a cold day. And Providence[6] alone can explain why his glasses weren't broken."

"What had you done, Edwin?" asked Mrs. Delahanty again.

"Nothing," whispered Edwin.

"All we want," said Mrs. Kibbler, "is what's perfectly fair. Pay the dentist's bill. And have that girl of yours apologize to Edwin."

Mrs. Delahanty got up suddenly and walked over to Edwin. She put one hand on his thin shoulder and felt him twitch under her touch like a frightened colt.

6. Providence (prŏv′ ə dəns): the care and help of a supernatural being or force.

"Go on, Edwin," she said. "Tell me the truth. Tell me why."

Edwin slowly lifted his head. "Go on, Edwin," Mrs. Delahanty encouraged him.

"He told you once," said Mrs. Kibbler. "Fun. That girl of yours is a big, boisterous thing from all I hear. She owes my boy an apology."

Edwin's face continued to lift until he was looking directly at Mrs. Delahanty.

He started to speak—but had said only three words, "Nobody ever wants," when Cress walked in from the hall. She had evidently been there for some time, for she went directly to Edwin.

"I apologize for hurting you, Edwin," she said.

Then she turned to Mrs. Kibbler. "I've got twelve seventy-five saved for a bicycle. That can go to help pay for his teeth."

After the Kibblers left, the three Delahantys sat for some time without saying a word. The fire had about died down and outside an owl, hunting finished, flew back toward the hills, softly hooting.

"I guess if we hurried we could just about catch the second show," Mr. Delahanty said.

"I won't be going to shows for a while," said Cress.

The room was very quiet. Mrs. Delahanty traced the outline of one of the bricks in the fireplace.

"I can save twenty-five cents a week that way. Toward his teeth," she explained.

Mrs. Delahanty took the poker and stirred the coals so that for a second there was an upward drift of sparks; but the fire was too far gone to blaze. Because it had not yet been completely dark when the Kibblers came, only one lamp had been turned on. Now that night had arrived the room was only partially lighted; but no one seemed to care. Mr. Delahanty, in Mr. Kibbler's dark corner, was almost invisible. Mrs. Delahanty stood by the fireplace. Cress sat where Edwin had sat, looking downward, perhaps at the same spot at which he had looked.

"One day at school," she said, "Edwin went out in the fields at noon and gathered wild flower bouquets for everyone. A lupine, a poppy, two barley heads, four yellow violets. He tied them together with blades of grass. They were sweet little bouquets. He went without his lunch to get them fixed, and when we came back from eating there was a bouquet on every desk in the study hall. It looked like a flower field when we came in and Edwin did it to surprise us."

After a while Mr. Delahanty asked, "Did the kids like that?"

"Yes, they liked it. They tore their bouquets apart," said Cress, "and used the barley beards to tickle each other. Miss Ingols made Edwin gather up every single flower and throw it in the wastepaper basket."

After a while Cress said, "Edwin has a collection of bird feathers. The biggest is from a buzzard, the littlest from a hummingbird. They're all different colors. The brightest is from a woodpecker."

"Does he kill birds," Mr. Delahanty asked, "just to get a feather?"

"Oh, no!" said Cress. "He just keeps his eyes open to where a bird might drop a feather. It would spoil his collection to get a feather he didn't find that way."

Mr. Delahanty sighed and stirred in his wooden chair so that it creaked a little.

"Edwin would like to be a missionary to China," said Cress. Some particle in the fireplace as yet unburned, blazed up in a sudden spurt of blue flame. "Not a preaching missionary," she explained.

"A medical missionary?" asked Mr. Delahanty.

"Oh, no! Edwin says he's had to take too much medicine to ever be willing to make other people take it."

There was another long silence in the room. Mrs. Delahanty sat down in the chair her husband had vacated and once more held a hand toward the fire. There was just enough life left in the coals to make the tips of her fingers rosy. She didn't turn toward Cress at all or ask a single question. Back in the dusk Cress's voice went on.

"He would like to teach them how to play baseball."

Mr. Delahanty's voice was matter-of-fact. "Edwin doesn't look to me like he would be much of a baseball player."

"Oh he isn't," Cress agreed. "He isn't even any of a baseball player. But he could be a baseball authority. Know everything and teach by diagram. That's what he'd have to do. And learn from them how they paint. He says some of their pictures look like they had been painted with one kind of bird feather and some with another. He knows they don't really paint with bird feathers," she explained. "That's just a fancy of his."

The night wind moving in off the Pacific began to stir the eucalyptus[7] trees in the windbreak.[8] Whether the wind blew off sea or desert, didn't matter, the long eucalyptus leaves always lifted and fell with the same watery, surflike sound.

"I'm sorry Edwin happened to be standing by that olla," said Mr. Delahanty. "That's what did the damage, I suppose."

"Oh, he had to stand there," said Cress. "He didn't have any choice. That's the mush pot."

"Mush pot," repeated Mr. Delahanty.

"It's a circle round the box the olla stands on," said Crescent. "Edwin spends about his whole time there. While we're waiting for the bus anyway."

"Crescent," asked Mr. Delahanty, "what is this mush pot?"

"It's prison," said Cress, surprise in her voice. "It's where the prisoners are kept. Only at school we always call it the mush pot."

"Is this a game?" asked Mr. Delahanty.

"It's a dare base," said Crescent. "Didn't you ever play it? You choose up sides. You draw two lines and one side stands in the middle and tries to catch the other side as they run by. Nobody ever chooses Edwin. The last captain to choose just gets him. Because he can't help himself. They call him the handicap. He gets caught first thing and spends the whole game in the mush pot because nobody will waste any time trying to rescue him. He'd just get caught again, they say, and the whole game would be nothing but rescue Edwin."

"How do you rescue anyone, Cress?" asked her father.

"Run from home base to the mush pot without being caught. Then take the prisoner's hand. Then he goes free."

"Were you trying to rescue Edwin, Cress?"

Cress didn't answer her father at once. Finally she said, "It was my duty. I chose him for our side. I chose him first of all and didn't wait just to get him. So it was my duty to rescue him. Only I ran too hard and couldn't stop. And the olla fell down on top of him and knocked his teeth out. And humiliated him. But he was free," she said. "I got there without being caught."

---

7. **eucalyptus** (yo͞o′kə lĭp′təs): a tall tree native to Australia.
8. **windbreak:** fence row of trees that protects from the wind.

Mrs. Delahanty spoke with a great surge of warmth and anger. "Humiliated him! When you were only trying to help him. Trying to rescue him. And you were black and blue for days yourself! What gratitude."

Cress said, "But he didn't want to be rescued, Mother. Not by me anyway. He said he liked being in the mush pot. He said . . . he got there on purpose . . . to observe. He gave me back the feathers I'd found for him. One was a road-runner feather. The only one he had."

"Well, you can start a feather collection of your own," said Mr. Delahanty with energy. "I often see feathers when I'm walking through the orchard. After this I'll save them for you."

"I'm not interested in feathers," said Cress. Then she added, "I can get two bits an hour any time suckering[9] trees for Mr. Hudson or cleaning blackboards at school. That would be two fifty a week at least. Plus the twelve seventy-five. How much do you suppose his teeth will be?"

"Cress," said her father, "you surely aren't going to let the Kibblers go on thinking you knocked their son down on purpose are you? Do you want Edwin to think that?"

"Edwin doesn't really think that," Cress said. "He knows I was rescuing him. But now I've apologized—and if we pay for the new teeth and everything, maybe after a while he'll believe it."

She stood up and walked to the hall doorway. "I'm awfully tired," she said. "I guess I'll go to bed."

"But Cress," asked Mrs. Delahanty, "why do you want him to believe it? When it isn't true?"

Cress was already through the door, but she turned back to explain. "You don't knock people down you are sorry for," she said.

After Cress had gone upstairs Mrs. Delahanty said, "Well, John, you were right, of course."

"Right?" asked Mr. Delahanty, again forgetful.

"About Cress's being interested in the boys."

"Yes," said Mr. Delahanty. "Yes, I'm afraid I was."

---

9. suckering: removing shoots, pruning.

Meaning

1. Who seems to understand Cress better in this story—her mother or her father? Give reasons for your answer.
2. Contrast Mr. and Mrs. Kibbler with Mr. and Mrs. Delahanty. How do their relationships differ: husband to wife; parents to child?
3. What do you think Edwin started to say just before Cress walked in from the hall? Why do you think she came in at that moment?
4. How did Cress feel about Edwin before she knocked him down? Had her feelings changed at the end of the story? How do you know?

Method

1. The author reveals to you gradually why the Kibblers are coming over to visit the Delahantys. Why do you think she does not tell you at the beginning of the story?
2. How does the Kibblers' outward appearance and manner provide clues to their character and personality?
3. The main character, Cress, does not appear until the story is half over. Before you actually meet her in the story, how has the author prepared you to accept the kind of person she is?
4. What is the mood of the story? Is the mood the same at the end of the story? If not, how and why has it changed?

Language: Abstract and Concrete Words

An *abstract* word represents a generality, quality, or characteristic that may be difficult to define. An abstract word is a word such as *beauty* or *truth*—an idea that cannot be perceived by the senses.

A *concrete* word, on the other hand, stands for something that can be perceived by the senses, a word such as *chair* or *table*. Concrete words can be more or less specific. The word *rocker,* for example, is more specific than *chair,* but *chair* is more specific than *furniture.*

The following words have been taken from the story. Decide which words are abstract and which are concrete. Look again at each of the concrete words and decide which are the most specific.

1. victory	7. teeth	13. violets
2. birds	8. incisors	14. stores
3. hummingbird	9. flowers	15. bicycle
4. fun	10. notion	16. minutes
5. apology	11. plank	17. circle
6. Providence	12. impatience	18. handicap

Discussion and Composition

1. Reread the explanation of dare base. Explain how to make or do something useful around the house. Use transitional expressions such as *first, when, next, in the meantime, after a while,* and *finally.*

2. Each of the Kibblers is described vividly in two or three sentences. Describe someone you know or an imaginary character in fifty words or less. Be sure that all of your details convey a single main impression of the person you are describing.

RICHARD WILBUR
(born 1921)

Known primarily as a poet, Richard Wilbur has also written stories and plays, and he is well-known as a translator. He was born in New York City, the son of a portrait painter, but he has spent most of his adult life in small towns in New England. One of these seems to be the locale of "A Game of Catch."

He went to Amherst College and Harvard University and has been a college teacher since his graduation, first at Wellesley and then at Wesleyan University, Middletown, Connecticut.

His poetry, drama, and translations have won him almost every critical award available, including a Pulitzer Prize and a National Book Award. He collaborated with Leonard Bernstein and others on the Broadway musical *Candide*. He is known for his gentle wit, which is particularly evident in his verse translations of the great French playwright, Molière.*

A GAME OF CATCH

Monk and Glennie were playing catch on the side lawn of the firehouse when Scho caught sight of them. They were good at it, for seventh-graders, as anyone could see right away. Monk, wearing a catcher's mitt, would lean easily sidewise and back, with one leg lifted and his throwing hand almost down to the grass, and then lob the white ball straight up into the sunlight. Glennie would shield his eyes with his left hand and, just as the ball fell past him, snag it with a little dart of his glove. Then he would burn the ball straight toward Monk, and it would spank into the round mitt and sit, like a still-life apple on a plate, until Monk flipped it over into his right hand and, with a negligent flick of his hanging arm, gave Glennie a fast grounder.

They were going on and on like that, in a kind of slow,

* **Molière** (Mōl·yâr).

mannered,[1] luxurious dance in the sun, their faces perfectly blank and entranced, when Glennie noticed Scho dawdling along the other side of the street and called hello to him. Scho crossed over and stood at the front edge of the lawn, near an apple tree, watching.

"Got your glove?" asked Glennie after a time. Scho obviously hadn't.

"You could give me some easy grounders," said Scho. "But don't burn'em."

"All right," Glennie said. He moved off a little, so the three of them formed a triangle, and they passed the ball around for about five minutes, Monk tossing easy grounders to Scho, Scho throwing to Glennie, and Glennie burning them in to Monk. After a while, Monk began to throw them back to Glennie once or twice before he let Scho have his grounder, and finally Monk gave Scho a fast, bumpy grounder that hopped over his shoulder and went into the brake[2] on the other side of the street.

"Not so hard," called Scho as he ran across to get it.

"You should've had it," Monk shouted.

It took Scho a little while to find the ball among the ferns and dead leaves, and when he saw it, he grabbed it up and threw it toward Glennie. It struck the trunk of the apple tree, bounced back at an angle, and rolled steadily and stupidly onto the cement apron in front of the firehouse, where one of the trucks was parked. Scho ran hard and stopped it just before it rolled under the truck, and this time he carried it back to his former position on the lawn and threw it carefully to Glennie.

"I got an idea," said Glennie. "Why don't Monk and I catch for five minutes more, and then you can borrow one of our gloves?"

"That's all right with me," said Monk. He socked his fist into his mitt, and Glennie burned one in.

"All right," Scho said, and went over and sat under the tree. There in the shade he watched them resume their skillful play. They threw lazily fast or lazily slow—high, low, or wide—and always handsomely, their expressions serene, changeless, and forgetful. When Monk missed a low backhand catch, he walked indolently after the ball and, hardly even looking, flung it sidearm

1. **mannered:** affecting a particular stance and attitude.
2. **brake:** rough undergrowth.

274   *Richard Wilbur*

for an imaginary put-out. After a good while of this, Scho said, "Isn't it five minutes yet?"

"One minute to go," said Monk, with a fraction of a grin.

Scho stood up and watched the ball slap back and forth for several minutes more, and then he turned and pulled himself up into the crotch of the tree.

"Where you going?" Monk asked.

"Just up the tree," Scho said.

"I guess he doesn't want to catch," said Monk.

Scho went up and up through the fat light-gray branches until they grew slender and bright and gave under him. He found a place where several supple branches were knit to make a dangerous chair, and sat there with his head coming out of the leaves into the sunlight. He could see the two other boys down below, the ball going back and forth between them as if they were bowling on the grass, and Glennie's crew-cut head looking like a sea urchin.

"I found a wonderful seat up here," Scho said loudly. "If I don't fall out." Monk and Glennie didn't look up or comment, and so he began jouncing gently in his chair of branches and singing "Yo-ho, heave ho" in an exaggerated way.

"Do you know what, Monk?" he announced in a few moments. "I can make you two guys do anything I want. Catch that ball, Monk! Now you catch it, Glennie!"

"I was going to catch it anyway," Monk suddenly said. "You're not making anybody do anything when they're already going to do it anyway."

"I made you say what you said," Scho replied joyfully.

"No, you didn't," said Monk, still throwing and catching but now less serenely absorbed in the game.

"That's what I wanted you to say," Scho said.

The ball bounded off the rim of Monk's mitt and plowed into a gladiolus bed beside the firehouse, and Monk ran to get it while Scho jounced in his treetop and sang, "I wanted you to miss that. Anything you do is what I wanted you to do."

"Let's quit for a minute," Glennie suggested.

"We might as well, until the peanut gallery[3] shuts up," Monk said.

They went over and sat crosslegged in the shade of the tree. Scho looked down between his legs and saw them on the dim, spotty

---

3. **peanut gallery:** upper balcony of a theater and the people who sit there.

ground, saying nothing to one another. Glennie soon began abstractedly spinning his glove between his palms; Monk pulled his nose and stared out across the lawn.

"I want you to mess around with your nose, Monk," said Scho, giggling. Monk withdrew his hand from his face.

"Do that with your glove, Glennie," Scho persisted. "Monk, I want you to pull up hunks of grass and chew on it."

Glennie looked up and saw a self-delighted, intense face staring down at him through the leaves. "Stop being a dope and come down and we'll catch for a few minutes," he said.

Scho hesitated, and then said, in a tentatively mocking voice, "That's what I wanted you to say."

"All right, then, nuts to you," said Glennie.

"Why don't you keep quiet and stop bothering people?" Monk asked.

"I made you say that," Scho replied, softly.

"Shut up," Monk said.

"I made you say that, and I want you to be standing there looking sore. And I want you to climb up the tree. I'm making you do it!"

Monk was scrambling up through the branches, awkward in his haste, and getting snagged on twigs. His face was furious and foolish, and he kept telling Scho to shut up, shut up, shut up, while the other's exuberant and panicky voice poured down upon his head.

"*Now* you shut up or you'll be sorry," Monk said, breathing hard as he reached up and threatened to shake the cradle of slight branches in which Scho was sitting.

"I *want*—" Scho screamed as he fell. Two lower branches broke his rustling, crackling fall, but he landed on his back with a deep thud and lay still, with a strangled look on his face and his eyes clenched. Glennie knelt down and asked breathlessly, "Are you O.K., Scho? Are you O.K?," while Monk swung down through the leaves crying that honestly he hadn't even touched him, the crazy guy just let go. Scho doubled up and turned over on his right side, and now both the other boys knelt beside him, pawing at his shoulder and begging to know how he was.

Then Scho rolled away from them and sat partly up, still struggling to get his wind but forcing a species of smile onto his face.

"I'm sorry, Scho," Monk said. "I didn't mean to make you fall."

Scho's voice came out weak and gravelly, in gasps. "I meant—you to do it. You—had to. You can't do—anything—unless I want—you to."

Glennie and Monk looked helplessly at him as he sat there, breathing a bit more easily and smiling fixedly, with tears in his eyes. Then they picked up their gloves and the ball, walked over to the street, and went slowly away down the sidewalk, Monk punching his fist into the mitt, Glennie juggling the ball between glove and hand.

From under the apple tree, Scho, still bent over a little for lack of breath, croaked after them in triumph and misery, "I want you to do whatever you're going to do for the whole rest of your life!"

Meaning

1. How can you tell that Monk and Glennie resent the interruption in their game? Do you think Scho is as good a player as Monk and Glennie are? What are your reasons?
2. What effect does Scho's tree top "game" have on the game of catch on the ground below?
3. What does Scho do to attract attention to himself? Why does Scho pretend not to be hurt after his fall?

Method

1. The narrator in this story reports what he sees but does not interpret events. He says that Monk's "face was furious and foolish," but does not say that Monk was furious and foolish. Find other sentences and phrases that use this same indirect mention of emotions or feelings. How does the author alter this technique in the last sentence?
2. What effect does this disinterested, observing narration have on the reader? How do we know what motivates the characters to do what they do? Try to state the motivations of one of the three characters.

Language: Jargon

In describing the game of catch, the narrator uses a number of special terms drawn from baseball and a number of action verbs to describe the game. Try to define the words listed below. Some, like *lob*, will be defined in a dictionary. Others like *burn* may not be. Try to find the definition that is closest to its use in the story. Which words can be defined by the context in which they appear?

lob	dart	spank	flick
snag	burn	flip	grounder

Composition

1. Using the opening paragraph of this story as a model, write a paragraph describing a figure in action. You might choose a dancer, a tightrope walker, a person on a swing, or a player in any action game.

2. The final sentence of this story invites the reader to wonder about the future relationship the boys will have. In a short narrative, tell what you think will happen.

RAY BRADBURY
(born 1920)

Although he has written three novels, among them *Something Wicked This Way Comes* and *Fahrenheit 451,* Ray Bradbury is known mainly for his short stories. Most of these are what is called science-fiction, but they are not mere escape reading. There is a firm moral point of view behind all of his stories. Implicit in all of them is a rigorous social criticism. Bradbury neither praises nor condemns modern technology; rather he observes it with a critical eye and calls upon the reader to be equally critical—to see its uses and its abuses.

Bradbury was born in Waukegan, Illinois, but was educated in Los Angeles, where he now lives. He has been a full-time author since he was twenty-three years old. He is a great admirer of Edgar Allan Poe, and one can see in his stories the single unified effect and the same sense of horror that Poe achieves in his stories.

Bradbury has also written many plays and film scripts. He has written a dramatic version of "The Pedestrian." Like "The Pedestrian," all of his writing stresses the supremacy of the individual and the need for and power of the human imagination.

THE PEDESTRIAN

To enter out into that silence that was the city at eight o'clock of a misty evening in November, to put your feet upon that buckling concrete walk, to step over grassy seams and make your way, hands in pockets, through the silences, that was what Mr. Leonard Mead most dearly loved to do. He would stand upon the corner of an intersection and peer down long moonlit avenues of sidewalk in four directions, deciding which way to go, but it really made no difference; he was alone in this world of A.D. 2131, or as good as alone, and with a final decision made, a path selected, he would stride off sending patterns of frosty air before him like the smoke of a cigar.

Sometimes he would walk for hours and miles and return

only at midnight to his house. And on his way he would see the cottages and homes with their dark windows, and it was not unequal to walking through a graveyard, because only the faintest glimmers of firefly light appeared in flickers behind the windows. Sudden gray phantoms seemed to manifest[1] themselves upon inner room walls where a curtain was still undrawn against the night, or there were whisperings and murmurs where a window in a tomblike building was still open.

Mr. Leonard Mead would pause, cock his head, listen, look, and march on, his feet making no noise on the lumpy walk. For a long while now the sidewalks had been vanishing under flowers and grass. In ten years of walking by night or day, for thousands of miles, he had never met another person walking, not one in all that time.

He now wore sneakers when strolling at night, because the dogs in intermittent[2] squads would parallel his journey with barkings if he wore hard heels, and lights might click on and faces appear, and an entire street be startled by the passing of a lone figure, himself, in the early November evening.

On this particular evening he began his journey in a westerly direction, toward the hidden sea. There was a good crystal frost in the air; it cut the nose going in and made the lungs blaze like a Christmas tree inside; you could feel the cold light going on and off, all the branches filled with invisible snow. He listened to the faint push of his soft shoes through autumn leaves with satisfaction, and whistled a cold quiet whistle between his teeth, occasionally picking up a leaf as he passed, examining its skeletal pattern in the infrequent lamplights as he went on, smelling its rusty smell.

"Hello, in there," he whispered to every house on every side as he moved. "What's up tonight on Channel 4, Channel 7, Channel 9? Where are the cowboys rushing, and do I see the United States Cavalry over the next hill to the rescue?"

The street was silent and long and empty, with only his shadow moving like the shadow of a hawk in mid-country. If he closed his eyes and stood very still, frozen, he imagined himself upon the center of a plain, a wintry windless Arizona country with no house in a thousand miles, and only dry riverbeds, the streets, for company.

---

1. **manifest:** reveal.
2. **intermittent:** stopping and starting at intervals.

"What is it now?" he asked the houses, noticing his wrist watch. "Eight-thirty P.M. Time for a dozen assorted murders? A quiz? A revue? A comedian falling off the stage?"

Was that a murmur of laughter from within a moon-white house? He hesitated, but went on when nothing more happened. He stumbled over a particularly uneven section of walk as he came to a cloverleaf intersection which stood silent where two main highways crossed the town. During the day it was a thunderous surge of cars, the gas stations open, a great insect rustling and ceaseless jockeying for position[3] as the scarab beetles, a faint incense puttering from their exhausts, skimmed homeward to the far horizons. But now these highways too were like streams in a dry season, all stone and bed and moon radiance.

He turned back on a side street, circling around toward his home. He was within a block of his destination when the lone car turned a corner quite suddenly and flashed a fierce white cone of light upon him. He stood entranced, not unlike a night moth, stunned by the illumination and then drawn toward it.

A metallic voice called to him:

"Stand still. Stay where you are! Don't move!"

He halted.

"Put up your hands."

"But—" he said.

"Your hands up! Or we'll shoot!"

The police, of course, but what a rare, incredible thing; in a city of three million, there was only one police car left. Ever since a year ago, 2130, the election year, the force had been cut down from three cars to one. Crime was ebbing; there was no need now for the police, save for this one lone car wandering and wandering the empty streets.

"Your name?" said the police car in a metallic whisper. He couldn't see the men in it for the bright light in his eyes.

"Leonard Mead," he said.

"Speak up!"

"Leonard Mead!"

"Business or profession?"

"I guess you'd call me a writer."

"No profession," said the police car, as if talking to itself. The

---

3. jockeying for position: to maneuver for advantage; here, cars trying to get ahead of other cars, either on the highway or at the gas pumps.

light held him fixed like a museum specimen, needle thrust through chest.

"You might say that," said Mr. Mead. He hadn't written in years. Magazines and books didn't sell any more. Everything went on in the tomblike houses at night now, he thought, continuing his fancy. The tombs, ill-lit by television light, where the people sat like the dead, the gray or multi-colored lights touching their expressionless faces but never really touching *them*.

"No profession," said the phonograph voice, hissing. "What are you doing out?"

"Walking," said Leonard Mead.

"Walking!"

"Just walking," he said, simply, but his face felt cold.

"Walking, just walking, walking?"

"Yes, sir."

"Walking where? For what?"

"Walking for air. Walking to *see*."

"Your address!"

"Eleven South St. James Street."

"And there is air *in* your house, you have an air-*conditioner*, Mr. Mead?"

"Yes."

"And you have a viewing screen in your house to see with?"

"No."

"No?" There was a crackling quiet that in itself was an accusation.

"Are you married, Mr. Mead?"

"No."

"Not married," said the police voice behind the fiery beam. The moon was high and clear among the stars and the houses were gray and silent.

"Nobody wanted me," said Leonard Mead, with a smile.

"Don't speak unless you're spoken to!"

Leonard Mead waited in the cold night.

"Just walking, Mr. Mead?"

"Yes."

"But you haven't explained for what purpose."

"I explained: for air and to see, and just to walk."

"Have you done this often?"

"Every night for years."

The police car sat in the center of the street with its radio throat faintly humming.

"Well, Mr. Mead," it said.

"Is that all?" he asked politely.

"Yes," said the voice. "Here." There was a sigh, a pop. The back door of the police car sprang wide. "Get in."

"Wait a minute, I haven't done anything!"

"Get in."

"I protest!"

"Mr. Mead."

He walked like a man suddenly drunk. As he passed the front window of the car he looked in. As he had expected, there was no one in the front seat, no one in the car at all.

"Get in."

He put his hand to the door and peered into the back seat, which was a little *cell,* a little black jail with bars. It smelled of riveted steel. It smelled of harsh antiseptic; it smelled too clean and hard and metallic. There was nothing soft there.

"Now if you had a wife to give you an alibi," said the iron voice. "But—"

"Where are you taking me?"

The car hesitated, or rather gave a faint whirring click, as if information, somewhere, was dropping card by punch-slotted card under electric eyes. "To the Psychiatric Center for Research on Regressive Tendencies."

He got in. The door shut with a soft thud. The police car rolled through the night avenues, flashing its dim lights ahead.

They passed one house on one street a moment later, one house in an entire city of houses that were dark, but this one particular house had all its electric lights brightly lit, every window a loud yellow illumination, square and warm in the cool darkness."

"That's *my* house," said Leonard Mead.

No one answered him.

The car moved down the empty river bed streets and off away, leaving the empty streets with the empty sidewalks, and no sound and no motion all the rest of the chill November night.

Meaning and Method

1. What evidence is there that Leonard Mead is a nonconformist? Why does his habit of taking walks at night seem odd? What comment does his behavior make on the rest of the population?
2. Almost half of "The Pedestrian" is told by means of dialogue. How do the two speakers and their speeches differ? What is the effect of the repetition in the dialogue?
3. A symbol is something that has meaning in itself and also suggests something further, such as an attitude or value. How is Leonard Mead's house on St. James Street a symbol? What does it symbolize?

Composition

The Psychiatric Center for Research on Regressive Tendencies sounds forbidding. What do you think will happen to Leonard Mead at the Center? Will they succeed in making him conform to the norms of society? Will he be strong enough to resist? In a short sequel, tell what you think might happen to him. Try to give your readers reasons for your opinions about Leonard Mead's future.

A GLOSSARY OF LITERARY TERMS

Abstract and Concrete Terms: *abstract terms* are words and phrases that refer to intangible qualities, ideas, or general classes; abstractions have no specific physical reality that is readily apparent to any of the senses. Examples of abstract terms are *justice, peace,* and *hope. Concrete terms* stand for objects that can be perceived by the senses. *Brick, box,* and *typewriter* are examples of concrete terms.

Allegory: a narrative in verse or prose in which objects, characters, or actions stand for abstract ideas or moral qualities. An allegory has both literal, or real, and symbolic levels of meaning.

Alliteration: the repetition of the same consonant sound, usually at the beginnings of words. Alliteration may sometimes be used in prose, though it is mainly a poetic device. For example:

> ". . . the white town drowsing in the sunshine of a summer's morning; . . . the great Mississippi, the majestic, the magnificent Mississippi, rolling its mile-wide tide along, shining in the sun; . . ."

Allusion: a reference to person, place, event, or artistic work that the author expects the reader to recognize. An allusion may be drawn from literature, history, geography, scripture, or mythology. A statement is enriched by an allusion because in a few words an author can evoke a particular atmosphere, story, or historical place.

Ambiguity: double meaning. In literature, an author may deliberately use ambiguity to produce subtle or multiple variations in meaning.

Analogy: a form of comparison which points out the likenesses between two dissimilar objects; it attempts to use a familiar object or idea to illustrate or to introduce a subject that is unfamiliar or complex.

Anecdote: a brief account, sometimes biographical, or an interesting or entertaining incident. In writing an essay, a writer may use an anecdote to introduce or illustrate a topic.

Antagonist: the force or character opposing the main character or Protagonist.

Antonym: a word opposite in meaning to another word. For the word *happy,* for example, the following nouns are antonyms: *sad, depressed,* and *melancholy.*

Argumentation: a type of writing that attempts to convince the reader of the logic and the merits of a particular viewpoint (especially by giving specific reasons and examples), or that attempts to persuade the reader to accept a particular belief or opinion.

Atmosphere: the prevailing mental and emotional climate of a story; something the reader senses or feels. Setting and Mood help to create and heighten atmosphere. Edgar Allan Poe is noted for creating stories of atmosphere. In "The Masque of the Red Death" for example, an atmosphere of terror prevails.

Autobiography and Biography: both types of literature attempt to present an account of a person's life, usually in chronological order, using whatever facets, events, and other evidence are available. The *autobiography* is an account written by persons about themselves; the *biography* is written by another person.

Character: a person (sometimes a group of people, an animal, or a physical force) invented by an author.

Character foil: a character who serves by contrast to emphasize the qualities of another character. For example, the appearance of a particularly lazy, shiftless, and unenterprising character will strengthen the reader's impression of an active, ambitious, and aggressive character.

Characterization: the techniques an author uses to develop the personality of fictional characters so that they seem believable, act consistently, and speak naturally. These methods include characterization through:

    a. direct analysis by the author of a character's thoughts, feelings, and actions;

    b. physical description of a character's appearance;

    c. description of a character's surroundings, such as the room in which he or she lives or works;

    d. the speech or conversations of a character;

    e. the behavior or actions of a character;

    f. a character's reactions to events, situations, and other people;

    g. the responses or reactions of other people in the story to a character's behavior, and in some cases, their remarks and conversations about the character;

    h. the presentation of a character's thoughts through a stream of consciousness; that is, the author attempts to produce the uninterrupted flow (stream) of thoughts, feelings, associations, and memories that might take place in a character's mind (consciousness) at any given moment;

    i. a combination of two or more of these methods.

Cliché: any trite or commonplace expression that is no longer fresh or effective because it has been used too often. *Fair and square, the finish-*

ing touch, fit for a king, bundle of nerves, and *clear as a bell* are examples of worn-out expressions.

Climax: the high point or turning point of a story. The author builds up to the climax through a series of increasingly more complex incidents.

Coherence: the logical and clear relationship of one sentence to another within a paragraph and of one paragraph to another within a composition. Coherence is the quality in writing that links and binds the related parts of the composition into a unified whole. It is achieved through the use of transitional words and phrases (*accordingly, on the contrary, first, finally, however, nevertheless*); linking expressions (*this, these, they, it, that, he or she*), the repetition of key terms, and synonyms. **Unity** and **Emphasis** are also necessary for effective writing.

Commercial or Craft Story: a "formula" story written according to a set pattern. The plot is contrived, filled with coincidence, and has strong suspense. The characters are *stereotyped* and the theme is usually a conventional one (see **Theme**). Such stories often have an overflow of emotion and a romantic tone. There is little originality of character or theme, in contrast to the *quality* or *literary* story.

Comparison and Contrast: in writing, a method used to clarify and illustrate a subject. *Comparison* shows the similarities between two things, and *contrast* details the differences between things. They are often used together, but can be used separately. (See **Contrast**.)

Complication: rising action of incidents in a plot, building to the climax of a story or play.

Concrete Terms: (see **Abstract and Concrete Terms**.)

Conflict: the clash between opposing forces, people, or ideas in a story or play.

Connotation: the associated or suggested meaning(s) of a word, in addition to its literal meaning (see **Denotation**). The word *snowstorm*, for example, implies additional meanings beyond its literal meaning as "a storm with a fall of snow."

Context: for a word, the other words and phrases so closely surrounding it that they affect its meaning or use. Context often determines a word's meaning, as in the case of "rich" in the following examples:

> "The customer refused to buy the table because the edges were too *rough*."
> "The students felt that the last two questions were too *rough*."

For an event or incident, *context* includes the situation and circumstances that surround the event; we often speak of a specific event in its historical context.

Contrast: a striking difference between two things. In literature, to heighten or clarify a situation, an author may contrast ideas, personalities, or images. (See also **Comparison and Contrast**.)

Denotation: the literal or "dictionary" meaning of a word. (See also **Connotation**.)

Dénouement (dā ˈnoo ˈmän′): that part of the plot where the outcome or solution (permanent or temporary) of the main character's major problem is made known.

Description: the purpose of description is to make the reader share as intensely as possible in the sensory experiences of the writer; that is, the writer wants his or her audience to see, hear, smell, taste, or touch, in imagination, those things which the writer describes.

Dialect: the speech that is characteristic of a particular group or of the inhabitants of a specific geographical region. In literature, dialect may be used as part of a characterization.

Dialogue: the conversation carried on by two or more characters in a story

Diction: An author's choice, arrangement, and use of words.

Dramatic Monologue: speech or narrative by a person who reveals his or her own character while speaking or telling a story.

Emphasis: in writing, stressing what is important in the right places. It is achieved through the effective arrangement of words, sentences, paragraphs, and sections of a composition. **Unity** (sticking to the topic) and **Coherence** (logically relating all parts of a composition) are also essential for effective writing. (See entries for each.)

Epiphany: insight into life, or a moment of self-discovery, usually during a time of emotional or mental crisis.

Episode: one of a progressive series of occurrences or significant events in the plot of a story.

Exposition: in fiction, that part of a story or play where the author provides background material about the past life of characters and about events that have taken place before the story opens. The reader must know this information in order to understand the problem to be solved, and to believe in the main action of the story.

As a form of discourse, exposition is writing intended to give information, explain something, or develop an idea.

Fable: a brief narrative in prose or verse intended to teach a moral lesson. Many fables, such as those of the Greek writer Aesop, are beast fables, in which animals speak and act as if they were human.

Fantasy: a work that deliberately employs unrealistic, highly imaginative, unbelievable elements; or a departure from reality. A fantasy might take place in a dreamlike world, present unreal characters, or project scientific principles into the future (as in science–fiction stories such as Ray Bradbury's "The Pedestrian"). A fantasy can be a whimsical form of entertainment, or can offer a serious comment on reality. It usually has more than one level of meaning.

Figurative Language: language that gives new shape or form to the standard or literal manner of expression by means of imaginative comparisons called *figures of speech.* **Simile, metaphor,** and **personification** are among the most common figures of speech (see entries for each).

Flashback: a device by which an author interrupts the logical time sequence of a story or play to relate an episode that occurred prior to the opening situation.

Foreshadowing: hints or clues; a shadow of things to come. The use of foreshadowing stimulates interest and suspense and helps prepare the reader for the outcome.

Form and Content: in literature, *form* is the structure, pattern, or organization of a work of art that gives it a particular appearance or aspect. The short story is one form of fiction; the sonnet is one form of poetry. *Content* refers to the subject matter, ideas, or impressions shaped or governed by the form of the work.

For purposes of discussion, content (what is said) may be distinguished from form (how it is said), but the overall meaning and effect of a work of art stems from the successful fusion of both form and content.

Frame story: a story which is placed within the framework of another story; a story within a story. The outer story embodies the reason for the inner story, which is usually the more significant of the two.

Homonym: a word that is distinct from, but has the same spelling and pronunciation as, another word. *Hail* meaning "to call loudly" and *hail* meaning "small lumps of ice" are true homonyms. They are the same in spelling and pronunciation, but different in meaning, function, and origin. *Hail* and *hale,* however, are not true homonyms. They are homophones, being alike only in pronunciation.

Hyperbole (Hī·pûr'bə·lē): a deliberate exagerration for the purpose of emphasis or humor; overstatement. "I'm dying to hear what happened," is an example of hyperbole.

Idiom: an expression that could not be understood if analyzed logically word by word, but is nevertheless used naturally. *To turn the corner, to carry out,* and *seldom if ever* are examples of idioms. When the term is used in reference to an overall manner of expression, it denotes language natural to native speakers of a language.

Imagery: the *images,* or pictures and impressions, made in the reader's mind by the author's words. Although most imagery creates visual pictures, some appeals to the senses of touch, taste, smell, and hearing as well. Imagery results from the use of figurative language and vivid description.

Immediacy: the quality in writing which makes the reader feel directly involved in the action of a story, not just reading about it. Immediacy is closely related to atmosphere and setting. For example, the reader will be more able to sense fear and danger that a heroine faces when the author places her in a dark, dingy, locked room.

Irony: a way of speaking or writing in which the author's words mean the opposite of what they seem to say. For example, a writer might say of a character who has just taken several clumsy falls on the ice, "What a fine skater he turned out to be!"

It is not necessary for irony to be in a story but it is usually present to some degree. Setting, for example, may be used to establish irony. A beautiful spring day may be the background for a story of disappointment and unhappiness. A situation may be ironic when an event takes place that turns out to be the opposite of what the reader expected.

Jargon: (sometimes called argot, parlance, shoptalk, and vernacular) the special vocabulary of an identifiable group, occupation, art, science, trade, sect, or sport, such as *football* jargon. *Jargon* can also refer to language full of long words and circumlocutions serving little purpose other than to impress and bewilder the average person.

Legend: a story about a national hero, folk hero, saint, tribe, people, or historical event that has been handed down from the past, usually by word of mouth. Although they are popularly regarded as historical, legends contain facts that have been exaggerated or changed to suit each storyteller's purpose. King Arthur and his Knights are legendary heroes of England. In America, facts about such historical figures as Dan'l Webster and Abe Lincoln have been the basis for romantic and imaginary tales.

Local Color: details of dress, speech, locale, customs, and traditions which give an impression of the local "atmosphere" of a particular place.

Stories of "local color" flourished in American literature in the years following the War Between the States. Authors wrote about specific regions of the United States, as Bret Harte, the West; Mark Twain, California and the Mississippi region; and Sarah Orne Jewett, the Maine coast. An attempt was made to copy local dialects and to depict the characteristic appearance, mannerisms, and customs of the people and the period.

Melodrama: (from Greek *melos*, "song," plus *drama*, "drama") any play or drama with **a.** a sensational plot, **b.** characters who make extravagant displays of deep emotion, and **c.** an atmosphere of heavy sentimentality.

Metaphor: a likeness expressed in figurative language in which one thing is compared to another without using *like* or *as*. For example:

"Language is the dress of thought."

"Hope springs external in the human breast."

Mood: the predominating emotional atmosphere or feeling created in a literary work by its tone or tones. (See also **Atmosphere, Setting, and Tone.**)

Motif: an image or phrase that recurs, and thus provides a pattern within a work of literature.

Motivation: the force which drives a character to some action. Outside events and environmental influences may cause a character to act, or action may stem from a need, an inclination, a goal, or an inner fear.

Myth: a tale or story, related to *legend,* usually focusing on the deeds of gods or superhuman heroes. Myths played an important role in ancient cultures by helping to explain or justify the mysteries of nature and the universe. Bulfinch's *Mythology* is a well-known collection of the myths of ancient Greece and Rome. As a loose term, *myth* can denote any invented or grossly exaggerated story.

Narrative: the telling of an event or series of incidents that together make up a meaningful action; a story.

Narrator: one who narrates, or tells a true or fictional story. The narrator may be a major or minor participant in the action of the narrative or simply an observer of the action.

Novella: an extended short story that goes beyond the average short story length of two to three thousand words. A long short story is also sometimes called a *novelette.*

Objectivity: the quality in writing that is free from the expression of the author's personal sentiments and opinions.

Onomatopoeia: (on′ə·mat′ə·pē′ə): the use of words that imitate the sound, action, or idea they represent. Sometimes a single word sounds like the thing it describes, as *cuckoo* or *twitter.* Sometimes several words are grouped together to imitate a sound, as "murmuring of innumerable bees."

Paragraph Development, Methods of: there are several ways of developing a paragraph after introducing the main subject or idea in a topic sentence. The methods include **a.** giving many details and particulars, **b.** giving specific examples and illustration, **c.** telling an incident or anecdote, **d.** offering reasons, and **e.** using comparison and/or contrast.

Paraphrase: the restatement of a line, passage, or entire work, giving the meaning in another form, usually to clarify or amplify the original.

Pathos: the quality in writing that prompts the reader's feelings of sympathy or pity for a character. The term is from the Greek *pathein,* "to suffer."

Personification: a figure of speech in which a nonhuman or inanimate object, quality, or idea is given human characteristics or powers. For example:

". . . the clock with its loudly clucking pendulum."

Plot: the arrangement of incidents, details, and elements of conflict in a story. Plot is usually divided in the following stages:

  a. the *situation,* or problem, in which a narrative begins;
  b. the *complications,* or entanglements, produced by new or complex events and involvements;
  c. the *rising action,* or advancing movement, toward an event or moment when something decisive has to happen;
  d. the *climax,* or most intense moment or event, usually occurring near a narrative's major *turning point,* or crisis, the moment when the main character turns toward a (good or bad) solution of the problem;
  e. the *denouement,* unraveling, or ending of the problem with which the story began.

Point of View: the outlook from which the story is told. Each viewpoint allows the author a particular range or scope. There are two basic points of view:

  a. first-person narrator (author participant). The narrative is told by a major or minor character in his or her own words. The author, through this "I" narrator, is limited to his or her scope of knowledge, degree of involvement, and powers of observation and expression. Prudincis de Pireda's "Conquistador" is an example of first-person narration.
  b. third-person narrator (author omniscient). The author serves as an unrestricted, all-knowing observer who describes and comments upon the characters and action in a narrative. The omniscient author knows everything there is to know about the characters—their thoughts, motives, actions, and reactions.

To maintain more of an illusion of reality, many modern short-story writers adopt a *limited omniscient point of view.* An author using this device tells the inner thoughts and feelings of one character only, usually the main character. We are never told what other characters are thinking; we must infer this from their external acts. Toni Cade Bambara uses the limited omniscient point of view in "Blues Ain't No Mockin Bird."

Sometimes an author narrating in the third person attempts to keep his or her personal feelings *objective,* or impartial and detached. In contrast, when the author's opinions about the characters or events in the story are obvious, the writing is called *subjective.*

Protagonist: the main character, hero or heroine, in a story or drama. (The word, which comes from the Greek *protos* meaning "first" and *agónistés* meaning "contestant, actor," was originally used to designate the actor who played the chief role in a Greek drama.) See also **Antagonist.**

Quality or Literary Story: a story that reveals the author's originality and imagination in creating natural and interesting characters, realistic situations, and meaningful, often unconventional themes. It is usually written for those who appreciate "serious" literature. There is no set formula to be followed in writing the quality story as there is for the **commercial or craft** story.

Realism: the attempt to present life as it actually is without distortion or idealization. Realism often depicts the everyday life and speech of ordinary people.

A literary movement called realism began in America in the late nineteenth century with the works of the American critic and novelist William Dean Howells. The movement reflected the increased interest in the methods of science and registered a protest against the extravagance of feeling and emotion found in romanticism.

Repetition: the use of the same word, phrase, sentence, idea (or some slight variation of these) to achieve emphasis. Some repetition is found in prose, but it is most often used in poetry.

Rhythm: in poetry, the regular rise and fall of strong and weak syllables. (As the accent becomes more fixed and systematized, it approaches *meter.*) In prose, although rhythm is often present, it is irregular and approximate; prose rhythm is the effective and pleasing arrangement of meaningful sounds in a sentence.

Rising Action: that part of the plot where the action moves or rises toward a climactic event or moment where something is going to happen that will affect the fortunes (good or bad) of the main character.

Romanticism: the attempt to present life as the writer would like it to be; it pictures life in a picturesque, fanciful, exotic, emotional, or imaginative manner, and often reflects the writer's strong interest in nature and love of the strange and the supernatural. It is the opposite of realism, which deals with the ordinary events of everyday life in an unsentimental and factual manner.

A literary movement called romanticism flourished in English literature in the early nineteenth century with the works of such writers as Wordsworth, Coleridge, Byron, Shelley, and Keats, and in American literature in the mid-nineteenth century with the works of such authors as Longfellow, Hawthorne, and Melville.

Satire: the use of ridicule, sarcasm, wit, or irony in order to expose, set right, or destroy a vice, folly, breach of good taste, or social evil. Satire may range from gentle ridicule to bitter attack.

Science fiction: a type of *fantasy* that combines real knowledge of scientific facts and principles with imaginative speculations as to what life will be like in the future, or on another planet.

Sentiment and Sentimentality: *sentiment* is honest emotion. *Sentimentality* means having more sentiment or feeling than the situation calls for; artificial emotion.

Setting: the time and place of the events in a story; the physical background. The importance of setting as a story element depends on the extent of its contribution to characterization, plot, theme, and atmosphere. For example, a landscape that is uninviting, dull, and barren may be the backdrop for a story of loneliness and despair.

Setting is most often stressed in stories of *local color* where the author wishes to recreate the flavor and characteristics of a particular region or community. It also plays an important role in *science-fiction* stories where the author must have readers believe in the world of the future. In some cases, setting can play a central role. (See **Atmosphere**.)

Simile: a stated comparison or likeness expressed in figurative language and introduced by terms such as *like, as, so, as if,* and *as though*. For example:

"My love is like a red, red rose."

Sketch: a short, simply constructed work, usually about a single character, place, or incident. A *character sketch,* for example, may be a brief study of a person's characteristics and personality. As in art, a sketch may also be a "rough" or preliminary draft for a longer, more complex work.

Soliloquy: in drama, a speech delivered by a character alone on the stage or apart from the other characters. As a literary device, it is used to reveal character or give information to the reader or the audience.

Stereotype (Stock Character): an artificially conventional type of fictional character rather than an authentic human being. A stock character either possesses traits supposed to be characteristic of a particular class, or reminds the reader of characters often read about or seen on TV. Examples are the heavy-drinking newspaper reporter who always types with two fingers, and the gangster with a rough exterior and a heart of gold. Such characters always act the same way and reveal the same traits of character. Authors who wish to have the reader believe in a character do not use such oversimplified people in their stories. (See **Characterization**.)

Stream of Consciousness: in fiction, a literary technique by which characters and actions are presented through the flow of inner thoughts, feelings, reflections, memories, and mental images of one or more characters.

Style: a writer's distinctive or characteristic form of expression. Style is determined by the choice and arrangement of words, sentence structure, the use of figurative language, rhythm, and tone.

Subjectivity: the quality of writing in which the author's opinions, sympathies, personal beliefs, or tastes are obvious and sometimes even dominate the work. An autobiography, for example, is usually subjective. The author of a biography, however, generally strives for *objectivity*.

Surprise Ending: in fiction, an unexpected twist of plot at the conclusion of a story; a trick ending. It should be carefully foreshadowed to produce its striking effect. O. Henry often wrote stories with surprise endings.

Suspense: the uncertainty, expectancy, or tension that builds up as the climax of a narrative approaches; curiosity regarding the outcome of a narrative.

Symbol: a person, place, event, or object that is real in itself and also represents or suggests a relationship or association. For example, a heart symbolizes affection and love; a horseshoe, good luck; a lily, purity; a skull, mortality; and a torch, immortality. In fiction, some symbols have *universal* meaning, such as the association of spring with youth and winter with old age.

Some symbols are *personal,* that is, they have a special meaning within the context of a story. A character's name, for instance, may suggest her personality. "Candide" may be a name associated with a frank, outspoken, and "candid" character. The action of a story may also be symbolic. A long sea voyage might, during the course of a story, come to signify a person's journey through life.

The first time we read a story we might take the character's name, the objects that surround him or her, the setting, or the plot *literally*. On a second reading we may realize that one (or more) of these elements has a significance or meaning beyond itself.

Synonym: a word having the same meaning or meanings as another word or words in the same language, or having the same approximate meaning as another word. Most synonyms are interchangeable but at the same time vary widely in connotation. A standard dictionary of synonyms is Roget's *Thesaurus.* For the word *quarrel,* for example, Roget's lists the following nouns as synonyms: dispute, controversy, altercation, fight, squabble, contention, strife, set–to [colloquial], run–in [slang, U.S.], bicker, *démêlé* [French], feud, and vendetta.

Theme: the main idea of a literary work: the general truth behind the story of a particular individual in a particular situation. The theme of most short stories is usually implied rather than stated.

A *conventional* or traditional theme is one that conforms to our established moral standards and codes of behavior. Some familiar themes are that love conquers all, crime doesn't pay, or good triumphs over evil. Such oversimplified views of life are most often found in the commercial or craft story.

An *unconventional* theme is often critical of fashionable and established customs and ideas. The story of a young man who is unable to rise above the poverty into which he is born unless he resorts to dishonest dealings may suggest the theme that it is impossible to achieve success and remain honest. Another story may show that in some cases self-sacrifice can create more unhappiness than happiness. Such themes are usually found in a literary or quality story.

You should be able to state the theme of a story in one or two sentences. It is not a summary or an account of the plot. It is simply a general statement of the concept about life that the author had in mind, and embodied in the story.

Theme Statement (Statement of Theme): in an essay, the theme is the main idea, point, or topic to be discussed. A statement of theme usually appears near the beginning of a discussion. It is often accompanied by a statement of the author's purpose.

Tone: the attitude of the writer toward his or her subject, characters, and readers. An author may be sympathetic and sorrowful, may wish to provoke, shock, or anger, or may write in a humorous way and intend simply to entertain. To misjudge the tone of a work is to miss its full meaning.

Topic Sentence: A clear, brief statement of what will be discussed in the paragraph; it is usually placed at the beginning of the paragraph. (See also **Paragraph Development, Methods of**.)

Understatement: the representation of something as less than it really is for the purpose of emphasis or humor. For example, in agreeing with a friend's praise of a new sports car, the owner might say, "It is rather nice, isn't it."

Unity: in writing, the organizing principle that links together all the parts of a work. In essay writing, this means the singleness of purpose, theme, or topic (or all three) that links all the subordinate parts of a composition into a whole. See also **Coherence** and **Emphasis**. In fiction writing, unity means that all the elements of a narrative relate to a single controlling idea.

The very nature of the short story gives to it a greater unity than that found in other fictional forms, such as the *novel*. A short story is usually limited to one main conflict, focuses on one significant episode, presents one main theme, is told from one point of view, and attempts to create a single, unified effect. A novel, on the other hand, may become long and involved, relate numerous key events in the life of its main characters, and analyze several aspects of personality. It is not concentrated or confined. The short story, because it must give exactly enough information to create its desired effect, is more intense.

Vignette: a brief, yet significant sketch of a person or event. The meaning of a vignette is usually subtly implied rather than stated. It often forms part of a longer work.

THE LANGUAGE ARTS PROGRAM
LIST OF SKILLS

Throughout the text, language arts have been integrated with the presentation of literature. The majority of language arts activities appear in the end-of-selection questions and assignments under the headings **Meaning, Method, Language, Composition,** and **Composition and Discussion.** Others are introduced and discussed in the general introductions, and still others, especially those concerning word origins and derivations, are covered in text footnotes.

The following indexes are intended to serve as guidelines to specific aspects of the language-arts program in *A Book of Short Stories 1.*

Point of view (narrator), 4, 78, 94, 132, 142, 150, 193, 217, 277

Protagonist, 3, 71

Satire, 207

Science fiction, 279

Sentiment and sentimentality, 168

Setting, 5, 10, 51, 70, 79

Stereotype (characters and/or situations), 79

Stock character, 79

Style, 125, 150, 168, 178, 277

Surprise ending, 217

Suspense, 14, 193

Symbol, 5, 25, 142, 161, 217

Theme, 6, 124, 167, 177, 192, 217, 232, 244

Titles, (significance), 124, 132, 141, 150, 161, 258

Tone, 5, 133, 142, 150, 168, 198

VOCABULARY DEVELOPMENT

Language activities (in order of appearance in text): finding exact meaning, 71; meaning from context, 51; onomatopoeia, a word from a sound, 80; colloquial usage, 94; nonstandard English, and dialect, 142; Latin roots for English words, 151; figures of speech, 162; denotation and connotation, 168; the use of adjectives, 178; repetition for effect, 178; 207; prefixes and suffixes, 193; forming adjectives and adverbs, 217; synonyms, 233; antonyms, 245; abstract and concrete words, 271; jargon, 278

Word origins, 64fn., 75fn., 87fn., 93fn., 173fn., 200fn., 232, 245, 250

COMPOSITION:

Narration:

Inventing a plot, 72

Writing a short story about a day-dream, 81

Making up an interview, 133

Writing an ending, 151

Writing about a turning point in someone's life, 199

Writing dialogue, 199, 218

Extending a story, 278, 284

Description:

Writing a character sketch, 53, 125, 143, 233, 259, 272

Describing a place, 168

Describing a mood, 179

Describing an action, 278

Exposition:

Explaining the meaning of similes and metaphors in a story, 52

Comparing and contrasting conflicts of two characters, 72

Developing one or two topic sentences by using examples from reading, 95, 143

Writing the first paragraph of a newspaper story, 133

Explaining procedures for interviewing, 134

Comparing and contrasting stories, 126